SECRETS IN SHADOW AND BLOOD

The Secrets in Shadow and Blood

A Fae Guardians Novel

LP

Lana Pecherczyk

The Secrets in Shadow and Blood

ASIN: B08TT8G99P
ISBN: 978-0-6450884-3-4

www.lanapecherczyk.com

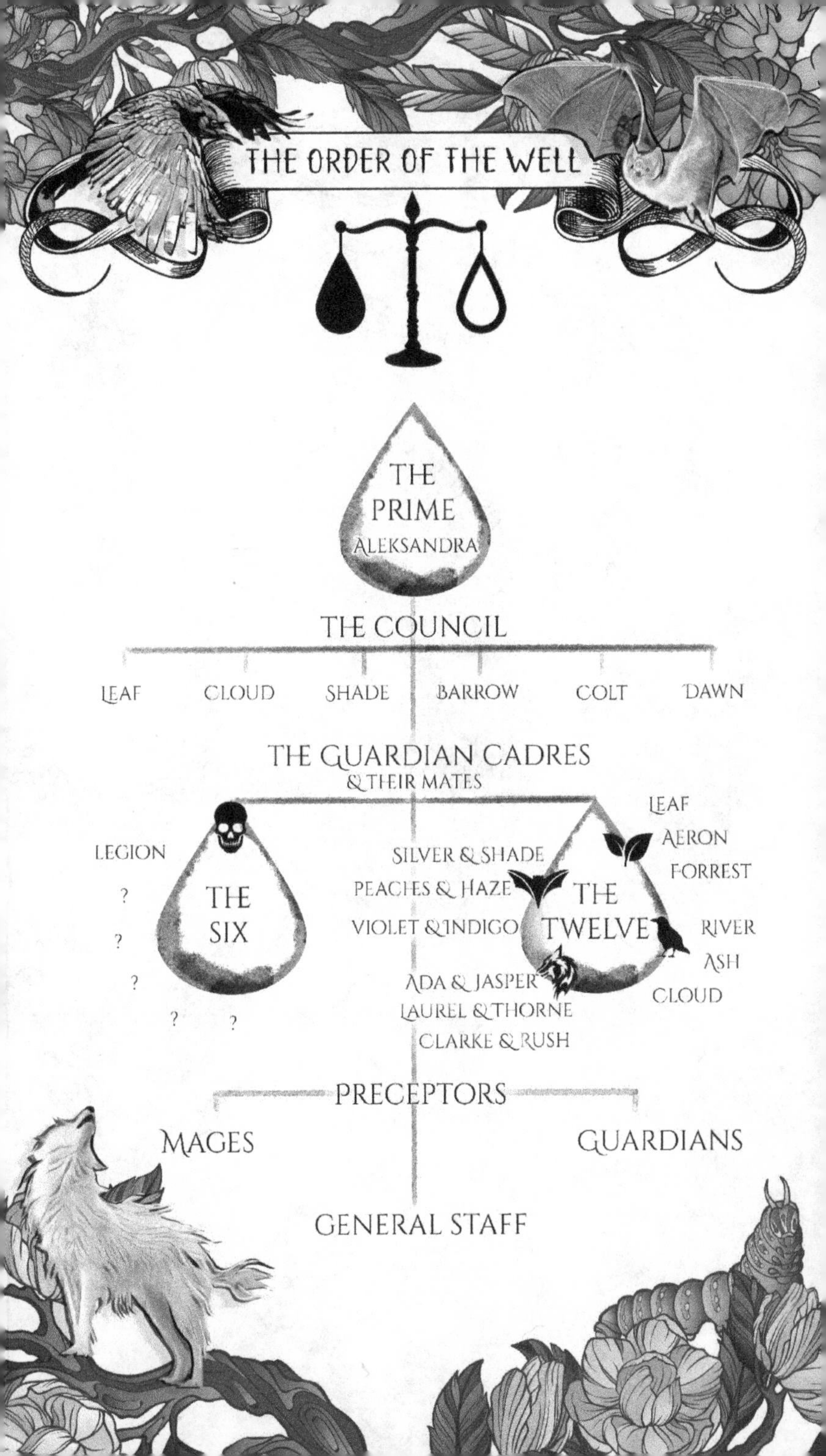
THE ORDER OF THE WELL
THE PRIME
ALEKSANDRA
THE COUNCIL
LEAF
CLOUD
SHADE
BARROW
COLT
DAWN
THE GUARDIAN CADRES
& THEIR MATES
THE SIX
LEGION
?
?
?
?
?
SILVER & SHADE
PEACHES & HAZE
VIOLET & INDIGO
ADA & JASPER
LAUREL & THORNE
CLARKE & RUSH
THE TWELVE
LEAF
AERON
FORREST
RIVER
ASH
CLOUD
PRECEPTORS
MAGES
GUARDIANS
GENERAL STAFF

EL
WINTER COUR
ACONITE CITY
ICE WITCH
ACONITE SEA
THE ICE FOREST
HUMAN TERRITORY
UNSEELIE KINGDOM
SEELIE KINGDOM
CRYSTAL
CITY
RUSH'S
CABIN
MEANDERI
WOODS
WHISPERING
WOODS
CRESCENT
HOLLOW

NE
OBSIDIAN MINE
OBSCENDIA
CLAW
BASIN
ORDER
POST
AUTUMN COURT
RUBRUM CITY
CORNUCOPIA
TRADE CITY
FENRYSFIELD
THE CEREMONIAL
LAKE
THE ORDER
OF THE WELL
DELPHINIUM CITY
SPRING COURT
HELIANTHUS CITY
SUMMER COURT

BLURB

In the shadows, vision can turn blurry. Truths can become lies. Enemies can become lovers.

When Violet inexplicably wakes thousands of years after a nuclear holocaust, she finds the world very different. Fae exist now. They're vicious, animalistic monsters who pervert magic and can morph into any shape—including vampires. They hoard the bounty of the new world, and keep humans banished to the wasteland. At least, that's what the humans of today have told her. Determined to make up for an unforgivable mistake in her past, she becomes a covert assassin and seeks revenge for her human brethren. And she's good at it. But when the thing she hunts saves her life, injuring himself in the process... her crystal clarity suddenly becomes blurry.

Vampires are meant to be monsters, not protectors... not charismatic, annoyingly handsome and loyal and... *everything*.

CHAPTER ONE

There is power in a name. It conjures imagery. It reminds. It condemns. For Vivienne Masters, she always thought her name meant she could master anything she set her mind to. Class valedictorian. Above average GPA. MIT graduate. Nuclear Physicist.

It all seemed to be working. She *was* the master of her life. She'd proven to her father that a woman could succeed just as well as a man. She had people working for her. She had power. Or so she'd thought.

In one single moment, it was all ripped away. Worse. It was flipped upside down. She'd gone from being at the top of her castle, to being the one who made it all crash down. She'd gone from sleeping in her bed to waking in a field, vomiting. Then running. Fleeing.

Last night, all she'd thought about was how to keep herself warm in the Vegas apartment ill-equipped for the nuclear winter, and then...

I'm in hell.

This is my punishment. This is my fate.

Under the watchful gaze of the full moon, Vivienne wiped black puke from her mouth and stumbled over rocky terrain, pushing past pain in her bare feet. A few hours ago, she'd awoken to thunder—an earthquake—and then found herself in the middle of a waterlogged rocky field. No grass. No trees. No Vegas. Just endless rocks. Black sludge kept coming out of her mouth as though someone had pumped her lungs full of tar while she'd slept. Nothing made sense.

Arctic air whipped like razor blades cutting through her oversized sleep T-shirt. The shirt came to her thighs and for some reason was frayed at the edges and threadbare. She'd only bought it a few years back. Definitely not long enough to fall apart like this.

There were more things that didn't add up in her addled mind. Before her, beyond the rocky terrain, was a lush forest where nocturnal wildlife hooted and whooped.

The news networks said forests were dying. Animals were going extinct. But this was the epitome of life and definitely *not* suffering from a nuclear winter, like the one she'd seen outside her window before going to sleep.

A flapping sound had her whirling around and searching the starry sky. Clouds crossed the moon. No. Not clouds. Dark, winged shapes coalescing like a brewing storm. Vivienne squinted and gauged the distance—a few hundred feet away and gaining. They flew out of formation, almost drunk and not like birds. But why would birds be flying about this late? Maybe bats? The shapes grew closer, bigger, and Vivienne picked out something that made her stomach roll... a cage dangled between two humanoid shapes, wobbling as they flew.

Flew.

As in, moved through the sky with great big leathery wings sprouting from their backs.

Too long she stared in wonder at the image from *The Wizard of Oz*. There had to be at least eight of them. Shadowed faces searched the rugged field beneath them, getting closer by the second. Hunting.

She jolted.

Hunting her?

She glanced at the forest a few hundred feet away and then back to them. One thought blocked out all others in her mind. *Get to the forest.* Get to cover. Hide.

She ran as fast as she could. Pain lashed her feet, making her wince. Her tattered night shirt caught on twigs and weeds, ripping it further. This wasn't a dream. This was real. Painful and terrifying.

So if not hell, then where in damnation was she? Why were flying men chasing her?

Flapping turned to thunder. Yips of excitement. A war cry of bloodthirsty hunters as they found their prey.

Flee!

Just get to the forest. Get to shelter.

She ran over the rocks, dried grass and sand. But with every step, they flew closer and hope slipped away.

This is insane.

The words hammered in her head with every step, as though she could shift reality by thinking it. *Insane. A dream. Wake up.*

Thunder crashed ahead, shaking the ground. Sand blasted and sprayed before her. *A bomb?* She skidded to a halt, her mind reeled as the vision came into focus under the night sky.

One of them stood between her and the forest. He scratched a short, dark beard as he assessed her with a twinkle in his eyes. A leather baldric crossed the front of his lushly embroidered black tunic. The hilt of a sword peeked over his shoulder. Long dark hair had come loose from a bun during his flight. Pointed ears stuck out at the sides of his head. Leathery wings stretched out in a show of dominance. A dagger made of something glossy and ivory wobbled on his hip as he stepped closer.

Not human.

Then the sky rained black bullets. One, two, three winged figures landed next to the first. More behind her. The ground thundered. It shook. Something rattled and thudded as more landed.

A woman screamed.

Another shouted obscenities. Prisoners, Vivienne realized with dread. Those voices belonged to prisoners in the cage. She daren't turn away from the demon in front of her.

"Oh, human." The first winged man crooned, flashing razor sharp fangs. "You think you can outrun us?"

If Vivienne was human, then what did that make him? Maybe she'd been right. He was a demon. And this was hell. Acceptance dropped into her stomach. She'd built the nuclear weapon that destroyed the world. It was time to pay for her sin.

She collapsed onto her hands and knees, crying out as jagged rocks dug into her skin. Her head hung in shame. Ropes of dirty hair dangled around her face. Everything inside her crumbled. She was tired. So damn tired.

"Fight!" A woman's raspy voice. "Don't let those bastards win."

"Get up!" A second woman. "Help us."

Vivienne lifted her chin, eyes darting over her shoulder to locate the cage. Two dirty and bite-riddled women were huddled inside, their fists curled around the bars, their faces squeezed between the gaps. An older female with silver hair, and a smaller Asian woman. They looked at her with hope—as though Vivienne could save them. Another woman was on the cage floor, possibly dead, her body at an odd angle and covered in wounds.

Desperation.

Pain.

Suffering.

It bled from their every pore. They were Vivienne's fate. These women knew it, yet the hundreds of bite marks oozing blood did not stop their will to survive.

"You can't win," the first winged man said with a cruel laugh, his speech a little slurred. "Despite what the females say."

His derisiveness only spurred the women on. They

shouted more encouragement to Vivienne, more curses to the winged men.

"Don't let the bastards win."

"Fight back!"

Fury shone in the prisoners' eyes.

Don't let the bastards win.

It was something her mother said when Vivienne had come in crying from a scraped knee, doing her best to beat her domineering and relentless brothers. Vivienne had laughed. Cussing was naughty, but it was their little secret.

Defiance bubbled in Vivienne's body. It pushed into her extremities, rippling goosebumps across her skin. She lifted her head and gazed into the eyes of her attacker.

"You can't save them," he taunted as he strode toward her. "You belong to us. To the Unseelie High Queen." He shook his head incredulously. "We own you."

His male companions chuckled. Such a human trait coming out of these demons. Vivienne's gaze dropped to the emblem on his embroidered tunic. A crown of antlers, thorns and roses.

Violet didn't care who, or what, they were. She wasn't owned by anyone.

"They drank our blood!" a woman shouted.

"They're vampires!" said the other.

"Shut them up." The leader jerked his head toward the cage, his eyes turning an odd shade of red.

"Yes, Gastnor. I mean, Captain." A thud. A crash. "Shut it, filthy Untouched bitch."

The sound of air being forced from a throat.

Vivienne glanced in time to see a soldier yank silver hair. The woman's head hit the bars, but she still had the courage to shout, "Our blood makes them drunk. They're dr—"

Another yank on her hair. Another hit. Vivienne turned away.

"Yeah, that's right. You shut up." The soldier's voice filtered back to her.

The sickening dull thud that followed sent rage vibrating through Vivienne. One hand gathered dirt. The other found a rock.

Gastnor. A name demystified the beast. It made him weak. Blood and flesh, not shadow and nightmares.

His boots stopped at Vivienne's knees. She slowly stood and met his red stare, almost at eye level. In it, she glimpsed doom, imagining the screams of helpless victims.

Gastnor.

She threw dirt in his eyes and then swung the rock. But before she landed any hits, her legs lifted as another pulled her back. *So fast.* They'd moved so fast. She thrashed about, kicking and screaming.

No use.

They had her pinned.

A solid wall at her back. Men on either side, laughing like a bully poking a fish in a barrel. Gastnor swiped dust from his red eyes, his smile turning wicked. Those fangs glinted in the moonlight.

They descended on her, finding any piece of flesh they could sink into. Stings, burns, and white hot scalding pain pierced her all over. She bucked. She scratched. She thrashed.

They took her to the dirt.

Tongues licked, mouths latched and fangs pierced. On her legs, calves, neck, wrists. Baring her teeth, she growled like a she-devil. If this was her end, she would go down fighting.

With a blow to her face, sparks dashed before her eyes. As the blood drained from her, she felt a lightness. A floating sensation. A sea of black clad shoulders and wings undulated as they drank from her. Between them she snatched glimpses of clouds in the night sky. Unnatural sleepiness washed over her. Then her head lolled to the side where a set of milky eyes became her world. The third woman in the cage. Dead.

Vivienne's entire life had been proving the men in her life wrong. And here were more of them... sealing her fate. Her mother would be sad.

Don't give up.

The vampires thought she had. Whatever was in her blood made them lose their wits. She could see it, a physical response coming over them. They turned lax. Weak. Drugged. Heavy. Their hold slipped.

The woman with silver hair mouthed something through her dry and cracked lips. *Don't let the bastards win.*

Vivienne tugged on her wrist, crying out as fangs ripped through her flesh. The pain cleared some of the fog in her mind. Her nails raked a face so hard she gouged flesh. A male roar of pain gave her fuel to kick. A vampire popped off her inner thigh. She writhed, hissing like a wild cat. Another hit to her face. A dizzying blow.

More stars.

More light.

More... *defiance.*

Don't let the bastards win. It was Vivienne's little secret. This fighting against the patriarchy, this silent war she and her mother had waged. They'd been tired of coming in second place. And while her mother had given up, she'd placed all of her hopes in Vivienne.

She was in control of her fate. Not them. And she would not go down gently. Ever. She screamed until the sun burst from her skin. Night turned to day. Weight lifted from her body and she felt like she was floating, only for a second. She became the stars in the sky, the moon, and she watched down from above. Then the hissing of vampires grounded her.

Night returned.

Darkness.

Vivienne blinked, not sure what had just happened, but after her eyes adjusted, she found the vampires—all of them—rubbing their eyes and stumbling, either stunned or blind.

Did the sun shine only for a moment?

"Get the sword," the silver-haired woman shouted. "Anything."

Vivienne commanded her ravaged, bite-riddled body to move and scrambled to her feet.

A vampire behind her lay on the ground, staring

blindly at the sky, not even trying to blink, rapture in his expression.

"So good," he mumbled, writhing and touching himself as though every press sparked pleasure. "So good."

"At his hip!" the woman reminded.

Vivienne tugged his dagger from its sheath and then relentlessly forced it deep into the vampire's chest, surprised at the resistance, the wet crunch, and then the warm blood gushing over her fingertips. She froze. They weren't dead like in the myths. These vampires were alive. Animal. Feral. And the knife in her hand was made from something slippery and cream colored, not a wooden stake. Not even metal. When the hilt pushed into his sternum, she let go and the vampire took his last breath.

She'd just killed someone. Nausea rolled in her gut. She gagged.

"Hurry!"

Inhaling deeply to force her revolting stomach to stay put, she summoned the feisty spirit of her youth, the same one her mother had coaxed into her, and wrenched the dagger out. She moved methodically from vampire to vampire, shoving the dagger into each chest. With each vampire killed, she became numb.

And then she made it to Gastnor.

She found him, cursing, still half-blind from the strange burst of light, and trying to staunch the bleeding from his face. Her scratch had run deep scores from his eye to his jaw. His flesh was still caught beneath her broken nails. A moment passed between them—a weighing of each other. He understood his limitations. He was drunk and half blind. She wasn't. He glanced at the cage, at her, and then took to the sky, his enormous wings beating like receding death drums.

In the resounding silence that followed, a sob burst from Vivienne's lips. She'd survived?

"The key," came the croaking voice of the silver-haired woman. "It's on that one's belt."

Vivienne scoured the dead bodies until she found it. Her fingers trembled and her knees wobbled as she plugged the key into the padlock on the cage.

"I'm Vivienne," she panted, gulping air.

"Anika," the silver haired woman said. "That's Suzy."

Suzy waved, then caught sight of the blood on her hand and cleaned it on her peach patterned blouse.

Anika wasn't gray and old, like Vivienne had initially thought, but young with her hair bleached and dyed. It looked like spun moonlight against her brown skin. Suzy was petite, pale, and frightened. Wide-eyed like a porcelain doll. She looked like she would break like one too.

The barrel unlocked, the padlock clicked open, and the cage door swung out. Vivienne stepped back, allowing the women to exit.

Anika checked a vampire for signs of life. Suzy kicked one for good measure. Then something strange happened, and Vivienne had no way of rationalizing it, only to know it happened, because the other two women saw it too.

Little balls of light floated out of the corpses like fireflies. They swam around as drunk as the vampires had been, then slowly lifted to join the stars in the sky. All three women watched, stunned, frozen to the spot at the sight of something so magical borne from such violence.

Then, when the last ball of light faded, as if they were all struck by the same thought, they turned to the cage. To the third woman who hadn't made it.

"She's dead," Vivienne intoned, stating the obvious.

"She's not like us," Suzy whispered, hugging herself. "And not like them."

"What do you mean?"

Suzy replied, "She didn't have those lights coming out of her body."

"And she's from this time, not ours." Anika pointed at Vivienne's night shirt. "Led Zeppelin. It gives you away."

"I still don't understand."

"It's been two thousand years since we went to sleep. Or rather, were frozen."

"Come again?"

"Frozen," Anika repeated, and then continued. "I know it's hard to take in, but something happened to the world while we were out. Life evolved—mutated. I think to survive the harsh post-nuclear climate, animal and human DNA merged and mutated. These new beings—fae, they call themselves—are in control of this green land. The humans of today have been banished to a wasteland."

"Are they all this vicious? The fae?"

Anika shook her head. "I don't think so. Maybe."

They all stared at the dead woman. She looked the

same as Vivienne, but apparently, their birthdays were millennia apart. Could it be true?

Well, this wasn't a dream. It wasn't hell, either. And it certainly wasn't Vegas City. So... they'd been frozen?

Suzy's shoulders slumped. "Her name was Margaret. Sounds so normal, right?"

Vivienne nodded. She could see what Suzy meant. A normal sounding name for an irregular situation just didn't seem right.

Anika frowned and inspected an old gash on her arm. "Apparently humans are tastier than fae—no matter what time they're from. Except, for some reason, Margaret's blood didn't make them drunk and her wounds aren't closing as fast as ours. They drained her dry."

Vivienne looked at Suzy and Anika. Their wounds had scabbed over.

"Mine are still oozing blood," she stated.

Anika took a fallen vampire's cape and pressed it against Vivienne's worst wounds. "Suzy and I were in the cage for about a week or so. We heard a lot of things, like, their saliva has an anticoagulant in it to combat the natural fast healing of fae. If you're like us, which I suspect you are because your blood made them drunk, your wounds will heal faster than normal after the anticoagulant runs its course. The histamines will also wear off faster for you."

"Why does our blood make them drunk, but not hers?" Vivienne glanced at Margaret. "And *why* do we heal faster, but not her?"

Anika shrugged. “I think it has something to do with us being from the past. When I saw your shirt, I screamed out to let you know. I’d hoped...”

“It worked. Your words spurred me on. They reminded me of something my mother used to say. Thank you.” Her chest constricted at the realization that her mother was probably dead. She winced at the sting in her neck as she irritated a bite and used some of the cape to press there. “How do we get to the human city?”

“That’s just it,” Anika added, eyes locking with Suzy. “I don’t think we should.”

Suzy shut down. She crouched and hugged herself, hiding her face between her knees. Vivienne crouched beside her and reached out. Sometimes when there were no words, a touch was enough.

“Margaret was a scout,” Anika explained. “Apparently she was tasked with hunting us down to bring us to the humans.”

“Us? You mean, me too?” Vivienne spluttered. “Specifically? B-but, how would she even know about us?”

“She said they’ve been waiting for us for a long time. As were these fucktards.” She spat on a corpse.

“But that’s good, right? That the humans were looking for us?”

Relief flooded Vivienne. She wasn’t alone. There was hope.

A guilty look flashed over Anika’s expression. “I... I don’t know how to say this, but in my old life, I was a welder. I worked for the military. And Suzy there was a geologist. It was her job to source uranium. And you..." Anika squared her shoulders as she met Vivienne's horrified gaze. "You're a nuclear physicist."

"How did... How did you know?" Vivienne couldn't breathe.

"The human knew. The vampires knew." Anika shrugged. "I don't know how to explain it, but they've all been waiting for us to thaw out."

"Are you inferring what I think you're inferring?"

"That they want to use us? Yes, I am. I think whether it's this queen, or the humans, they want to use us for what's in our heads."

"This is just so unbelievable." Vivienne's hope went crashing to the ground.

"Not just the queen. The humans. They're at war with the fae. Whoever captures us captures power."

"We can't be together. Ever."

"Agreed."

They looked at each other. Suzy hugged herself tighter.

"So what now?" Vivienne asked.

Anika scanned the vampires and started tugging clothing from their bodies. "To occupy my mind while we were in that cage, I thought about this exact question. What would I do if we ever got free? We can't go to the humans—history has told us what humans do with a nuclear bomb. No offense. The Unseelie High Queen is also after us, and it won't be fun if we're caught. So we split up. We change our names. We assimilate. We become fae. We live out our lives. Alone. That way no one can use what's in our heads and make history repeat."

"How?" Vivienne gaped. "I know nothing about this world."

"We were in the cage for a long time, and we listened. We asked Margaret a million questions. We can tell you what we know. Let's get moving out of here first. I saw a river not far from here. It will probably lead us to a town." She glanced at Suzy, still sitting on the ground. "I don't know about you, but I'm not ready to split up. Not yet."

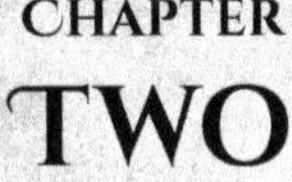

CHAPTER TWO

"First off," Anika said, as she spooned a heap of stew into her mouth. "We have to change our names. They're too..." She glanced around the empty inn and lowered her voice. "Human."

They'd found this inn—The Entitled Stag—and a small town a few miles along their river trek. It looked like something out of the Middle Ages. There were no power lines. No tall buildings. No asphalt roads. No cars. Not in this town, anyway. When Vivienne had queried it, Anika told her certain substances like metal and plastic were outlawed. She didn't know why.

Hidden beneath their capes, no one recognized them as human. All three women had covered their ears with their long hair, and remained as subdued as they could, trying not to draw attention.

The sun had risen an hour ago. The place was virtually empty, probably too early for most. When they'd arrived in blood crusted clothing, the custodian—a small wrinkled old man-type fae with tufts coming out of his ears—cared more about their coin than anything else.

They were in Unseelie territory. When Vivienne had questioned the name Unseelie, Anika guessed this new world culture was derivative from old myths about fairies and Celtic legends. Unseelie fae were rather vicious when slighted. Seelie fae were a little more benevolent. Apparently.

There was sense in finding ritual or religion to latch onto when the world was unstable. If the people in Vivienne's time had started evolving into something else, they would have reached for something familiar to combat their fear of the unknown.

"Okay," Vivienne said, keeping her voice low. "So, what is a fae name?"

"Something more natural," Anika mused. "Like Rose or Smoke."

She threw a worried glance to Suzy, who huddled beneath her cape and toyed with her food. Her peach patterned blouse stuck up through the collar, so Anika poked it back down. Suzy gave her a grateful glance.

"Peaches," Vivienne murmured. "Like that?"

"Exactly like that." Anika studied Vivienne. "And you... you were pretty violent back there. Perhaps Violet is a good name for you. It's close enough to violent."

Vivienne shrugged. "I suppose I can get a little... aggressive sometimes."

She blamed her beefcake brothers for that. They never

let her win at any game. Once, while playing in the backyard when she was around ten, she'd gotten so fed up with them striking her out that she swung the bat and hit the catcher in the mask. Then she threw the bat at the pitcher, breaking his nose.

A sharp pang hit between her ribs. Unless her family had thawed out, she'd never see them again. They were hard to be around, sometimes cruel and egotistical, but they were the only family she knew. She would miss her mother the most. The quiet woman had always been happy to sit in the shadows, but this was where she'd conducted her symphony—directing Vivienne to be better, to grow taller, and to succeed so she didn't have to marry a man for money as she had.

A scraping sound behind the bar had them all jumping, but it was just the old wrinkled custodian setting out his condiments for the morning.

"You should be Silver." Vivienne gestured at Anika's head. "For the hair."

"Peaches, Violet and Silver," said Anika. "I like it. Let's start now."

Vivienne—now Violet—nodded.

"Are we really going to separate?" Peaches blurted, eyes wide and alert. "I'm not like you guys. I'm not a fighter. I don't want to be alone."

Silver bit her lip, the struggle all over her face. None of them wanted to split, but they also knew what could happen if they were all caught together.

"One night," Silver conceded, and Violet nodded. "One night and then we go our separate ways."

AFTER VISITING the local market and stocking up on supplies, the three women collapsed onto a bed in the single room they'd hired at the inn. They'd bolted the door, closed the curtains, and put out the candles. Only a small fire smoldered in the fireplace, crackling and spitting.

Huddled under the single blanket, they all should have passed out exhausted but couldn't sleep. Now that the quiet had replaced the noise, all Violet could think about were those vampires she'd killed and how it had felt to drive the dagger through their chests. Every moment had been a surprise, from the reality of the force needed to get the dagger through, to the warm gush of blood, to the glowing balls of light that had risen from the corpses. Had they come from *all* the bodies? Did she check? Violet felt both Peaches and Silver twitch, their movements shaking the thin mattress.

"Should one of us take watch?" Violet asked, sitting. "Just in case."

Peaches raised her head, her pale face stark in the low firelight. "You think they're still after us?"

"No," Silver clipped. "They're all dead, and that last one flew away injured. We're fine."

"Are you sure?" Peaches asked.

Doubt prickled Violet. "Did you check all of them? Their vitals, I mean."

Silver paused, too long to allay their fears.

"I'll take the first watch," Violet offered. She tossed the covers back and collected the soldier's dagger from their bags. It was bone, she'd realized. Carved like ivory.

"Get the one we bought from the market," Silver suggested. "No one will know you're using it in here."

Violet slid her gaze Silver's way. The dagger they'd bought at a secret backdoor stall was metal, but supposedly extra deadly to fae. If they were caught with it, they'd be imprisoned by the Order of the Well. They were all willing to take that risk for the peace of mind it gave them. Violet discarded the bone dagger and found the metal one. Then she sat by the fire, with her back to a wall, and stared at the door and the single window, despite them being two stories high.

When the two women fell asleep, and she heard their even breaths, Violet started to relax. They were safe. They'd survived. Every instinct in her wanted to stay with these women, but out of them, she was the one with dangerous knowledge in her head. If Violet was captured, their enemy might be able to find another way to source uranium, or they might have blacksmiths or other metal workers in this time for which to build the bomb casings and lab equipment.

If Violet left, then the two women could stay together at least. She toyed with the possibility of leaving in the middle of the night, but it turned out that staying awake wasn't possible for her either. The past twenty-four hours caught up, and Violet fell asleep.

A scream woke her.

Blinking through the darkness and her frayed nerves, Violet saw a dark figure hunched over the bed, wrestling with the two women. The window was open. Broken glass on the floor.

"Stupid humans," the intruder hissed. "Your scent is stronger when you're all together. I tracked you all the way here."

Violet leaped to her feet and shoved the dagger straight into the dark shape, this time remembering to exert extra force, to push through the resistance of bone. Silver rolled out from beneath him and plunged her own dagger in. Peaches found a bowl and cracked it over his head.

The intruder crumpled to the floor. But Violet wasn't going to risk him healing and waking again. She stabbed him, over and over. She kept going until her face was covered in a warm, sticky mess.

Don't let the bastards win.

Seconds later, Silver's hand wrapped around Violet's wrist, halting her next stab.

"Vi..." she cried out. "He's gone. Look."

Those little balls of light popped out of the body.

"I had to make sure."

Peaches watched with uncertain eyes. Silver struck a match and lit a candle, shining the light toward them.

"Are you okay?" Violet asked Peaches.

She nodded, clutching her neck. “I think he got me... just a little bit.”

“But you fought back,” Violet said. “You did good, Peaches.”

Silver checked her wound. “Not deep. Violet got to him just in time.”

Him.

Violet rolled the heavy figure over to see his face, so normal looking except for his ears, fangs and wings. “It’s definitely one of the soldiers.”

Silver’s eyes watered. “I’m so sorry, I mustn’t have checked them all. You were right.”

“Don’t be hard on yourself,” Violet said. “We were all so confused. And it wasn’t like we checked them. And... I fell asleep on my watch. It’s me who should apologize.”

They all stared at the dead vampire, quietly pondering what this meant.

“They’re going to eventually find us.” Violet wiped the dagger on the vampire’s cloak. “We can’t stay here.”

“He said our scent was stronger together,” Silver noted grimly.

Peaches sobbed. Silver squeezed her shoulder.

“Maybe you two can stick together. It’s just me who needs to leave,” Violet said. “I mean... I’m the one who knows how to build the...”

“No.” Silver’s hard gaze met Violet’s. “You heard him. They can track us by our scent, and it’s stronger together. It pains me to say, but at least if there are three of us in three different locations, then it's harder for them to build another bomb."

Violet's shoulders drooped. She had a point. "We can't ever be in the same place."

"I'd rather stick together as well, but you both know this is the right choice, dammit."

Violet nodded, her eyes burning. She was a grown-arsed woman, damn it. She never cried, so she lifted her chin and swallowed her fear.

"Before we part ways," Silver said, gently taking the dagger from Violet. "I think we should exchange something. To prove this was real. To prove we are real. That we survived, together."

"Silver from Silver," she said, and cut a lock of her hair to hand to Violet, and then did the same for Peaches.

Violet found her old Led Zeppelin shirt and cut two scraps from it. Peaches did the same to her blouse. They threw the remnants of their old garments into the fire and watched their history burn.

Peaches tucked away her talismans into a little coin bag, looking stronger than Violet felt. "I'll keep them on me always," she promised. "I'll think of you all and—" she choked up. "I'll pray that you're doing well."

Violet had but one thought on her mind as she walked out of town that night. She would do anything to master her new fate, her second chance. This time, she wouldn't be bullied into a profession she never wanted. She wouldn't succumb to family pressure. She would do things her way.

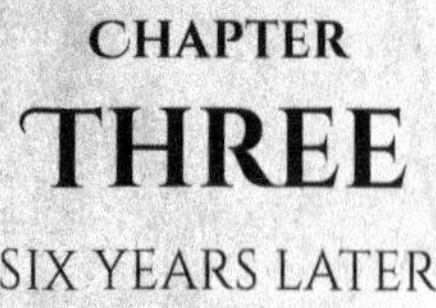

CHAPTER THREE

SIX YEARS LATER

Dim light shone through the cave entrance and into the sweltering obsidian mine. Violet paused raking and straightened to watch the dance of fluffy snowflakes as they twirled inside, unaware of what waited within. Blistering heat robbed them of innocence until they ended on the floor, dying in a murky puddle. Nothing much flourished in here, but it was a job all the same. Violet could turn up, do her work, and go home. No questions asked. Only the occasional whipping if she fell behind, but it was tolerable.

Nerves crept up her spine as she realized the light had dimmed more than usual. Night was coming. A walk home in the dark would not only be freezing, but put her at risk to the unsavory nocturnal fae prowling.

"You know," a high feminine voice squeaked from behind her. "I heard they put a human on the Seelie throne. How disgusting is that?"

Violet glanced over her shoulder at Mitzie, then studiously ignored the pink-haired pixie and went back to work.

"Makes you glad you're not Seelie, am I right?" Mitzie snorted, then mumbled under her breath: "Humans on fae thrones. What's Elphyne coming to..."

Violet swept the broken rock piles like they were her world. Sweat dribbled down her neck to roll between her breasts, making her shirt stick to her skin. Damn it. If she didn't dry off for the walk home, it would all turn to ice.

Something out of the ordinary glinted in the black refuse, and when Violet bent down to inspect it, she found a small palm-sized piece of metal. She pocketed the outlawed shard before anyone caught her.

"Hey, Vi. Violetta. Viola-face. *Vanilla Bean.*"

Before answering, Violet checked to see if the foreman watched, but the bulbous nosed hobgoblin only had eyes for the sands falling in the hourglass as he leaned against the rocky wall. Violet had always thought goblins would be short. But this guy was at least six feet tall. His barbed whip lay flaccid in his hand, just waiting for an excuse to be used. Violet turned the full force of her glare toward Mitzie.

"Shut up," she hissed through her teeth, channeling her best Unseelie temper.

The pixie's prismatic dragonfly wings flitted in vexation, stirring black dust. "No need to get your *lesser* panties in a twist. I was just telling you about the human queen. That's all."

Calling someone Lesser Fae was an insult, but at least Mitzie believed Violet was fae.

You could blow Mitzie's tiny frame over with a breath, but she had the attitude of a giant. Her four-foot-ten was a veritable dwarf compared to Violet, but looks were deceiving in this harsh version of Violet's old world. Whether giant or pixie, friend or foe, she never knew who would stab her in the back. Everyone deserved her suspicion, and in this Unseelie nation, everyone deserved to look out for themselves. Don't ask for help. Don't expect it.

For the past six years, it had suited her fine.

"It's none of our business whether a human is queen, or not," Violet said, then lowered her voice and spoke through her teeth. "To be honest, it's probably all a lie. No fae in their right mind would elevate a *manaless* being. No fae would revere one of the filthy Untouched."

"Yeah but... it's true. Chami told me last night at the tavern. Aren't you the least bit curious? I mean, how did this filthy Untouched catch King Darkfoot's eye?" Mitzie kicked the obsidian chunks closest to her in the direction of her pile, then picked one up and stared at it dreamily. "I'd add the Seelie King to my harem for sure." She gasped with an idea. "Do you suppose the human has a magic woo-hoo? More magic than mine?"

Violet snorted. "No one has more magic in their woo-hoos than pixies."

Mitzie tossed her hair. "I know, right? So what makes this woman so special? They say she's filled with mana. Did you hear? Like, more than even *the Guardians*."

Violet sighed heavily and leaned on her rake. She leveled her gaze at her colleague. “No. It’s not possible. In all the years I’ve lived here, I’ve never seen such a thing. Humans don’t have mana.”

“You’re right. She probably used some kind of poison.” Mitzie’s eyes widened. “Is it a new weapon? Will there be another war?”

“Mitzie,” Violet warned. “I just want to get home before dark. Not all of us have a harem of male protection to escort us. Can we just go back to work?”

The pixie rolled her eyes. “Don’t hate me because I’m mated.”

“Shut up and do your work.” Tempest arrived wheeling a barrow of mined obsidian from deeper within the system. The female orc’s bulging biceps took on a dark green hue in the dim cave light, and like most of the miners, she was covered in black dust.

Mitzie bared her piranha teeth and hissed.

Tempest lowered the wheelbarrow and snarled except, with her under bite, it looked rather comical. If only Violet could summon a smile. Instead, she sighed and crouched to sweep refuse into the wooden pan before unloading it into her own wheelbarrow. Her job was to collect the bits that fell out of barrows, so that’s all she did.

The scientist in Violet wanted to stop and listen to Mitzie, to work out exactly how a human, like her, could end up on the Seelie throne. The urge to dissect information and work out how things ticked would always intrigue her, but from the moment she became Violet, she'd buried that part of herself and put her inquiring mind to work as a fae. Humans didn't factor into it.

Cold air bit her face as she wheeled her barrow out of the cave system. The snow had stopped, but the miserable atmosphere turned her wet shirt into an icy straight jacket. She forced her arms to work, her thighs to push, and her aching muscles to move her up the hill to the dump site. Other dirty workers measured her load, marked it down, and then let her empty. Wiping the cold sweat from her brow, she nodded at the supervisor and took her wheelbarrow back for the night shift miners. Then, with a sniffling nose, she collected her fur-lined cape from the staff room—a simple wooden shack built next to the mountainside—clocked out and went home.

Five minutes into her walk, she'd discovered a new definition of torture: trudging the two-mile path with wind lashing her face. Her boots crunched on the thin layer of fresh snow, freezing her toes through the leather. Her snot froze. It hurt to breathe. And she swore her black-stained sweat was turning to ice on her chest. Dammit. She'd forgotten to dry off before leaving the mine, and she'd forgotten her second favorite headscarf.

She wished she had wings.

Shivering, she hugged her cape and made her way down the final leg of the winding path into Obscendia, the small mountainside village she currently called home.

On either side of the street, the houses were barely visible beneath the dying sun, and it stank like sewage. Nocturnal fae children had ventured out of their homes and played in the snow, but upon seeing her, they snarled and hissed before running inside. She may have been awake in Elphyne for six years, but she'd only been in Obscendia for a few months. Newcomers were shunned. Mitzie was the exception.

Bad attitudes, shit-smelling streets and lice ridden mattresses were what someone like she deserved. But it was home. For now.

Obscendia was nestled between Redvein Forest and a rocky mountain range, a few miles east from the Unseelie capitol, Aconite City. Like much of the Unseelie realm, some houses were swallowed by the mountainside, and some were deep underground. Violet's place was two streets down, to the left, and backed onto the edge of the forest. The rent had been cheap because the creatures in the woods were known to venture close to the village.

It was all she could afford.

The last ray of sun disappeared behind the tiled rooftops, jolting her with alarm. *Damn it.* Violet was not in the mood for trouble tonight. She increased her pace, eager to get home, but still wasn't fast enough. A shadow peeled away from a high garden wall.

She ducked her head and kept walking, but the shadow stepped before her, blocking her way. Forcing her body language to project confidence, she lifted her chin and looked the vampire directly in the eyes.

Dark brown, not red.

Good.

That meant he wasn't in a blood frenzy.

The rest of him did nothing to allay her fears. His clothes were in tatters. His frame was thin. His facial features were gaunt and hollow. Starving, possibly desperate.

Trouble.

Generally, vampires came in two types. Those who scavenged and fed upon sleeping animals, and those who could mesmerize their prey into volunteering. But Violet knew there was a third kind—*Fangs descending, red eyes, snarls*—she blinked her memory away. This was not the time to allow panic to reign.

"Well, well," the vampire crooned, giving her an appraising once over before settling on her scarred ears. "What have we here?" He glanced over Violet's shoulder. "What do you think? What kind of meal is she?"

"I'm warning you," she said. "Move, or you make my hit list."

The moment they tasted her blood, her cover was blown.

A feather light touch explored the scarred, rough shell of her curved ears. Violet flinched away and whipped around with a scowl, preferring to show her back to the one vampire, not the two behind her.

"I reckon she's just a little lesser fae," one of them said. His own pointed vamp ears were chipped and notched as though something had taken a bite out of them. "Maybe she's an elf. Maybe someone done her harm."

Another touch on her ear. "Coz she ain't got no mana to fight them off."

Snickers.

Violet growled and shuffled to the side so she could see them all at once.

"Go float yourself," she snapped.

More laughing.

"I might not have mana, but I have weapons." She patted her cape as though she held daggers beneath, but the truth was, her only dagger right now lay within her boot. She probably shouldn't have confirmed her lack of mana, either.

"But we're hungry," the third vamp whined.

"Go to a feeding house, then." Violet continued walking. "Or hunt in the woods."

All three jogged to keep up with her, agape that she had the gall to turn her back on them.

"What if we asked nicely?" one of them said. Maybe the first one. Violet wasn't looking. And she wasn't replying. Who knew what words might be perceived as an invitation to them. "Looks like you already fed plenty of our kind."

After a few more steps, they stopped.

"Fine," one shouted after her. "We have your scent."

"You smell tasty... almost like... human."

Violet stopped. She tensed. Her fingers curled into fists. Then she walked away, their cackling laughter a twisted symphony at her back.

"We'll see you tonight!"

By the time she arrived at her small, one room unit, her mouth was dry and her heart thudded erratically. With trembling fingers, she unlocked the heavy wooden door, bolted it behind her, and went straight to check the latching on the single window.

But these damn wooden locks were easily breakable.

Despite the cold tiredness seeping into her bones, Violet refused to use the fireplace and instead lit the room by a single oil lamp. She didn't deserve the comfort of heat so she shivered and scrubbed the obsidian powder from her body with icy water. She kept waiting for pneumonia to come for her, but strangely, she hadn't been sick for the six years she'd been awake in this time. There had to be an explanation, but all she could come up with was that the germs were different in this time. No fae really got sick, not like the humans used to.

She fed herself with stale bread and old cheese, washing it down with a treasured cup of hot spiced milk that may have gone a little sour but she ignored it. To warm up, she went to the wooden man she'd fashioned out of old planks of wood. It was one thick beam with smaller beams sticking out of it. She wrapped her fists in rags and set to work, hitting the wooden man, imagining he was a vampire.

Head. Her fist whipped out and hit the center of the beam.

Heart. Her second jab went to the chest.

Dead. She roundhouse kicked it. The wood wobbled and she steadied it, her gaze wandering to the wall behind where she'd pinned research on vampires. Her eyes hardened on it. Then she stood back and repeated her workout. First taking out the eyes, like she had with the vampire mob. Since the bright lights never came back, she had to use her fists. Heart with a stake. Then drive it in and make sure he's dead. The process had served her well. When she was hot, sticky, and full of leg trembling wobbles, she crawled onto the pallet she called a bed and lay staring at the thatched ceiling, listening to the sounds of the forest above her easing breath.

The howl of a wolf.

The hushed whispers of the wind.

The distant piercing shriek of a wild creature.

The howl cut off mid note, as though something had taken it down.

In Elphyne, there was no top of the food chain. Humans could be meat. Fae could be sustenance. Monsters could be fodder. Perhaps, if there was one species at the top, it would be the High Fae. The royals and the Guardians of the Order of the Well—those with abundant mana.

Another haunting cry in the distance.

Her stomach rumbled.

What she wouldn't give for a cheeseburger. Or a Coke. She'd even take a stick of broccoli. Not once had she seen the vegetable in this time. There were strange frost-hardy berries, and plenty of brussel sprouts or beets... but no little trees. Tears burned her eyes and she dashed them away with a sniff. There were just some things that would never come back.

Stop thinking about all the things that are now extinct.

Because of her.

She checked the window, confirmed the latch was

closed, and then went back to staring at the ceiling until her lids drifted. She forced them open, fighting the sleep. When that didn't work, she rolled to her stomach and placed her hand under her lumpy straw pillow to clutch a smooth, long rod and sighed as relief stole over her frame.

In all the ways the world had changed, this had stayed the same. Elements. Fire was hot. Metal was hard. If she had her old lab, so many things would still be the same. The laws of physics never changed.

Violet wondered if Peaches and Silver were alive. And if they were, had they taken the same route as Violet? Had they decided to become what she'd become? Had they done everything to protect themselves, or worse, flipped it and become the hunter? Did they let what happened to them define them?

Instantly, her mind went to Peaches. The fragile woman had looked on the brink of collapse. An ache in Violet's chest surged. Her throat clogged. She shifted her hand from the metal rod and dug her hand beneath her mattress to where a small metal tin laid. Inside were two scraps—one piece of Peaches' colorful printed blouse, one lock of Silver's amazing hair.

Staring at the scraps, Violet couldn't help feeling they needed her, just as she needed them. Her one woman vendetta against vampires hadn't filled the gap in her heart as she'd hoped it would. With a sniff, she tucked the box back away and rested her weary head.

Violet's eyes popped open. The room was black. The lamp had burned out. She must have fallen asleep. Shit. Sleep usually came in short fits, but when she knew she'd been marked by a vampire, she stayed awake all night.

She listened. Why was she awake? Was it more than her paranoia? Without moving, she pushed her senses out and listened through the pounding of her heart. With her ears, with her nose, with the little hairs on her arms—she *listened.*

A shuffling sound near the window. She tensed. Glass cracked. Then came a puff of wind gusting against her face, lifting hair at her temple.

A snicker.

They're here.

She still lay on her stomach, her hand still shoved beneath her pillow. Aching muscles had almost atrophied from lactic acid build up. She feared she wouldn't be able to move when the time came.

And then it did.

A shifting in the atmosphere heralded their journey through the window. They were so silent, she almost missed them. Her fingers clenched around the cold, metal rod beneath the pillow. She held her breath and waited, urging herself to be patient.

When vampires stole into a room in the middle of the night, they never expected their victim to be awake. Their highly tuned senses could pick out the sound of breathing from hundreds of feet away.

They must think Violet's steady breathing and pulse meant there would be no contest.

They were wrong.

The instant she felt the telltale prickle along her neck, she twisted and plunged her iron stake into the chest of the closest vampire. He never saw her coming. Rolling to the side, she caught the next one—the vamp with the notched ears. The stake missed his heart, but lodged into his side.

He swiped with taloned fingers and gnashed with fangs. Violet ducked, collected a second dagger from beneath her pallet and shoved it straight into the third vampire as he reached down to take her. She had to get metal into all of them, or they'd be able to shift into a bat or into angel form or use their mana—if they had enough—to harm her. Eyes wide and full of shock were the last thing she saw before she finally allowed herself to take in a deep gulp of air.

All three vampires crowded the floor of her tiny one-room apartment. Blood pooled, a glossy black varnish glistening in the moonlight.

Violet allowed herself a moment to finish gathering her breath, and then she assessed. The first one was dead. The third, too. The stake was still in the side of the notched-eared one as he bled out.

"*Floater* bitch," he slurred, blood coating his teeth.

Blood on his teeth?

Violet slapped her neck, right over the old bite scar and felt wetness. Not even a sting. My God, he'd somehow managed to sink his teeth into her. He was that fast.

"Nimble fucking creatures," she cursed, shaking her head, and then kicked him.

She'd thought the first vamp she'd killed was the one who had been closest to her, but it had been this guy. If she'd not been used to waking at the slightest sound, the histamines in his saliva could have kept her asleep. She might have slept through the entire feeding. Most vampires preferred to return to the same food source nightly, but with her... they might not be able to stop themselves. She might never have woken.

"Goddammit." She found a cloth and applied pressure to the bite. She might dribble blood for at least ten minutes, despite her faster than normal healing. If he'd finished feeding, he'd have produced a counteractive enzyme to help her heal. It made little biological sense for them to kill their food supply.

Unless they entered a bloodlust state like the ones who'd fed on her six years ago.

Violet yanked the dagger out of the third dead vamp, just as manabeeze started easing from his body. The glowing light moved, casting haunting reflections on her prey. She stabbed into the notch-eared vampire. Not a kill shot in the heart, but in the stomach. He cried out in pain.

Crouching down, she cocked her head. "Not so scary once access to your mana is taken away, are you?" She dug the dagger in and wiggled it around, then bit her lip to restrain her temper. "You can't shift. Can't cast spells. Can't even mesmerize me."

Eyes blazing with black fire glared at her. He surprised

her by showing fortitude she'd not expected in a bloodsucker. He gripped the stake in his side and yanked it out, holding her gaze the entire time. She jumped on top of him and pushed the remaining dagger deeper, this time keeping hold of it as she peered into his dirty, clammy face.

"Where is your roost?" she asked calmly. He might have told others about her. She couldn't risk her cover being blown... and she never passed up the chance to rid the world of more of the bloodsucking scum.

"Screw you."

Her eyes narrowed at his slightly slurred words. She glanced down at his wounds, disbelieving they were the cause. No... it was more likely the drop of her blood he'd tasted.

"Last chance," she said. "Tell me where your roost is, and I'll let you go."

His eyes widened. He'd forgotten humans can lie.

The little bastards liked to congregate in packs. Their large family roosts were often run by the females, and unless it was rutting season, the males were kicked out to wander the streets, thereby creating havoc to all other fae, animal, and the poor unfortunate human who was brave enough to venture out of their fortress at Crystal City.

Disgusting species.

He licked his sharp teeth and his eyes lost focus. "You taste... like something else. Something more... what... what are you?"

"Someone you clearly underestimated."

But he was already gone, falling under the spell of her

unique blood. His eyes rolled, and he actually smiled as though he were about to enter Nirvana, not Hell. He must have taken more than a drop. She wouldn't get any sense out of him tonight. What a shame.

With a twitch of the dagger handle, she pushed the blade into his chest cavity and relished when she hit his heart. The metal did its job, swiftly cutting the vampire's life. Manabeeze popped out of his body and floated to the ceiling, buzzing about until they found the open window and escaping into the night. When it was done, she sat back, resting against the wall. Her room was a mess.

She had a long night disposing of bodies ahead of her, but she didn't complain. She got on with it.

This was her penance. And Violet the Violent was becoming its master.

CHAPTER FOUR

Indigo stood on top of the tiled outpost roof and scowled at the miserable winter sea surrounding the island. The snow-covered shore glowed under the full moon. Wind buffeted the outpost stone and wood building, rushing up four levels to greet him. He pulled his wings around his body. At this height, he could almost see around the island. A lush forest was on one side, and the sea everywhere else.

The moon was so bright tonight—a sign the moon goddess was strong. He raised his face and bathed in her glow.

A shadow to his right announced his fellow Guardian's arrival. Shade, one of the only two other vampires in the Cadre of Twelve, landed on the tiles with deft skill, barely making a sound. To the untrained eye, they'd see nothing. Perhaps, at most, a dark blur. But Indigo was a shadow master. He could see through the darkness to the truths beneath.

"No luck?" Shade queried.

"What do *you* think?"

"Tetchy."

"Thirsty."

"So drink. The woods are well stocked with game." Shade's tone was smooth and cultured. Everything sounded easy when it came from his mouth.

"I tried. Their blood tastes like cardboard."

Shade took Indigo's jaw between his thumb and forefinger and searched his face. For a moment, all Indigo could see was the perfectly chiseled features of his superior. "Your eyes are dull. Your skin is sallow." He let go. "Even if it tastes like shit, drink it. Eventually your senses will come back."

"You don't know what it's like," Indigo mumbled, glancing back at the moon, wishing the goddess would come down and fix him.

"I get it. I've scented it too."

"But you never tasted it."

Ire slithered within Indigo, disturbing his inner peace. It was as though the shadow snake coiled around his torso had woken, ready to carry out vicious retribution. He inhaled the night deeply and then forced himself to calm, to try and imagine taking blood from a mundane fae or animal, but all his body wanted was Well-blessed human. His mouth watered for the flavor. Hungered for it. Every cell in his body was in a frenzy for it.

He got hard just thinking about it.

Three months ago, he'd had his first and only taste of that alluring blood. From the moment the sweet liquid had entered his mouth, it was like experiencing the stars at midnight. The moon itself. He'd craved more. It wasn't only the flavor or the drugging properties, but what he'd found within the blood—her thoughts, desires, and her secrets. Her love.

He'd never felt closer to another being in his entire life, and it had taken all his self-control to avoid seeking her out for another hit.

Thinking about it made him squirm. Electricity thrummed along his skin in anticipation, coaxing desire from his system, as though the mere thought of that day conjured the possibility of feeding from her again. Feeding, pinning her down, driving his cock in deep until he couldn't tell where she started and he ended. Until he didn't want to.

But that human belonged to the Seelie High King, Jasper Darkfoot. He was a powerful wolf shifter, ex-Guardian, and mated to Ada—the woman Indigo had tasted. The woman who held enough mana within her that she could power the sun.

She wasn't the only one. Two other humans had awoken from days long since past in this world. They were strong and blessed by the Well. And all of them were mated to wolf shifters. *Well-blessed* mated, which meant they could share mana and emotions. They had a union more revered than any other in this realm.

He would find no relief there. Only his death. Jasper would rip his throat out. Indigo wouldn't stand a chance against him, not unless he had his own Well-blessed mate's mana to tap into.

It was rare for a vampire to commit to one person. Indigo's parents had been one of the few monogamous couplings in their home town, and that had come at a cost. But while vampires were often polyamorous, wolf shifters were not.

Besides, he was never in love with Ada. Perhaps enthralled. Entranced. Seduced. It wasn't real.

So it made no sense why Indigo had been waking in cold sweats with a raging cockstand and the echo of dreams of the woman he'd fed from. One that reminded him of the moon.

She was human. She was sustenance. He shouldn't want her the way he did. Part of him knew it was purely the blood talking, but part of him wondered... what if it wasn't? What would he do with a mate like her? For starters, he would only need to feed once or twice every month. He'd be able to feed from the same person. He'd be able to share more than blood.

"Stop thinking about it," Shade muttered.

"I can't."

"How goes the search for the weapon maker?"

"It doesn't. I've searched all over Elphyne. She has to be beyond the wasteland and in the human city. That's the only reason I can think I haven't scented or sensed her.

There must be forbidden metal or plastic blocking her location from the Well, and me."

Theoretically, this human should have a similar scent as Ada. There were minute changes in note to her fragrance, ones that only someone such as he could pick up. Someone who'd tasted the special blood. He was both cautiously thrilled to meet another with the honeyed blood and terrified. What if she never let him feed from her? What if she did?

"But *have* you searched everywhere?" Shade's voice purred through the darkness.

Indigo snapped his attention to his colleague, seeing him clearer than he did during the day. Smooth dark hair styled effortlessly on his head, despite his flight in. Dark eyes the females called soulful. Sometimes Indigo wanted to hate the fae. Shade never had to try. He never failed. He'd probably never had to take sustenance from sleeping prey. All he did was crook his finger at a pretty female, and she offered her vein and warm comfort between her thighs. Shade would probably taste this magical human blood and be able to walk away.

But the older vampire had strict rules he lived by, rules that shaped his behavior, and rules were never Indigo's thing.

The expression on Indigo's face must have told Shade everything he needed to know. He nodded his head, satisfied, and then added, "You have to go home, Indigo. It's time. Think of it as a grand adventure."

Indigo rolled his eyes but smiled. It was true. He loved a challenge. The only reason he had entered the ceremonial lake was because he thought it sounded like fun. He'd never once believed he would be discarded and float. Of course, he never thought he'd take the life of an innocent during a spate of bloodlust.

"You're right," he conceded. "I need to feed."

"And then head into Obscendia. Haze will meet you there."

"What's Haze doing there?"

"Working with your brother to investigate mana-warped corpses that have cropped up in Unseelie lands."

"Why am I only hearing of this now?"

"You've been busy. The Prime said not to bother you until you found the human in Clarke's premonition."

Indigo frowned. Clarke was the first Well-blessed human to wake and mate with one of the Guardians, Rush. She also had powerful psychic abilities they'd learned to trust without question, but it irked Indigo that he wasn't being kept in the loop with the involvement of his brother Demeter. "If Queen Maebh finds out my brother is working with a Guardian, she'll throw him in the dungeon. Or worse."

"She won't find out. You know Haze is the best of us at hiding. But you should go. He said he found something, and I have things to do here."

Indigo raised his brow. "We still don't know who the traitor is?"

Shade's jaw clenched and he scowled at the sea. A few months earlier, they'd discovered humans had been portaled into Elphyne to raid villages for metal. The only way metal would travel through a portal was if a Guardian had carried it.

So a Guardian was working with the humans of Crystal City, and they had no clue.

"You're wasting time," Shade grumbled.

Indigo saluted.

"Fucking do that again and I'll smother you with shadow."

Indigo smirked and then stepped closer to the roof's edge, staring in the direction of his hometown, just a few miles across the sea and snow. He took a deep breath and prayed to the goddess in the moon for strength—he would need it when he saw his family.

"Okay. I'm going," he said. But didn't move.

Shade planted his palm between Indigo's wings and shoved him over the edge.

Indigo's curse echoed against the outpost's walls. He tumbled in the air, snapped his wings out, and then caught a stream of wind. Shade was lucky Indigo had already been in angel form. A fall from a height for a wingless vampire could be as deadly as it was for another. Righting himself, he turned back to the smirking vampire on the roof, and made a rude gesture.

But Shade's wide-lipped grin only stretched further because he knew he was right. Indigo couldn't hide from his family forever. In fact, he should probably visit them first. Eat the morning frog, as his old preceptor at the Order used to say. Do the worst thing first. Then the rest was a breeze.

Eating frogs... *disgusting*.

CHAPTER FIVE

Violet stood outside a simple rubble stone building cut into the side of a mountain. She kept to the shadows between porch columns and peered through a window to where a family of vampires interacted inside. Her layers of woolen clothing were starting to wear thin. Her boots were sodden, her toes were borderline frostbitten, and she couldn't feel her nose.

She should be home, warming up after dragging the vampire bodies into Redvein Forest and leaving them for the night creatures to eat, but she'd found something inside the notch-eared vampire's pocket. A card from one of the taverns in the center of town. If it wasn't for the fact she'd found the exact same card in the pockets of the other two vampires, she might have dismissed it. But there had to be a link.

Perhaps it was the local drinking hole for an entire colony of vampires, not just a family roost. Perhaps it was an underground feeding house where they mesmerized unwilling donors against their will. She wouldn't be surprised if vamps went in there and paid coin for live blood shows. Vampire kink. She shuddered. Gross.

But her curiosity had won over her self-preservation instincts. The more information she was armed with, the better to survive. And if she killed a few vampires along the way, all the better for it. And now Violet was here. Not investigating the drinking hole, but across the road at the house where she'd seen a group of well-dressed vampires enter. Purely by chance she had seen them leave the tavern, well fed, and in high spirits. So now she had two targets.

A feeding place on one side of the street, and a potential roost on the other.

She would come back during the day when it was safe to investigate more. Over the past six years, she'd discovered vampires were nocturnal, but not allergic to the sun like in the lore from her time. The only similarities these creatures had to Dracula were their wings, sanguineous diet, and the ability to shift into a bat. They weren't even dead, but alive and warm-blooded like any other animal—it made sense since all fae were somehow descendants of a mutated animal and human hybrid. Oh, and they could use mana—*magic*—to move fast, manipulate shadow, and mesmerize their prey. Apart from garlic making vampires vomit because it was actually food, it had no ill effects. Neither did a crucifix. These fae didn't even know who God was. Violet's Italian Nonna would be turning in her grave.

One constant remained true. A stake through the heart killed them. Metal, not wood.

Beneath her cape, her gloved fingers closed around the iron stake attached to her belt. She'd come across the metal rebar in the mines and had shaved it down to a point.

Violet paused upon sighting a tall, leather clad figure strolling into the room. He stopped by a regal looking female vamp by the fireplace. He had olive skin and the kind of face that made you look twice. There was an air of mischief about him—a twinkle in his dark eyes, an almost permanent curve to his sensuous lips. The breadth of his shoulders exuded strength. With all his weapons and leather, he looked like a trickster god straight out of some dark mythological hell world.

He'd kept his bat-like wings visible, which was unusual. Vampires often shifted them away while indoors... unless he wasn't staying long. Curious, Violet took in his striking frame. He had the body for sport and action. Short locks had been swept off his face as though he'd brushed them with his fingers. Shaved sides displayed pointed ears and accentuated a square jaw. A tiny blue light twinkled beneath his eye. A Guardian!

Violet stiffened and clutched her iron stake. *Stupid.* Of course he was a Guardian with all that battle gear. The stake would not save her from the likes of him. The permanent sparkling teardrop signaled he was one of the brutal, unforgiving warriors working for the Order of the Well. They were rumored to not give a shit about the plight of the general population, and it was often said they only came into town to kill Unseelie, who they decided were mana-warped monsters, and then tax the town for their "help" in getting rid of them.

See the flight of a kingfisher, and you're dead by morning.

That was the saying, or something like that, and now she knew why. The Guardian leather uniform had kingfisher blue piping accentuating the broad shoulders and tapering down to a narrow waist.

The Order of the Well was a fae organization that claimed to have the interests of Elphyne at heart, but Violet knew they were also taking the lead in squashing the resistance from humans, claiming this threat fell under their "Protect the Integrity of the Well" mission statement. Violet didn't trust them. She likened them to the church in the fourteenth century, persecuting anyone who stood against them as heretics. If it wasn't for them, humans and fae would have already come to an accord. Humans should be out of the wasteland and sharing in this bountiful land.

Humans weren't perfect. Sometimes they were selfish, just like the fae. But there was also a potential for good. For redemption. She had to believe that. This new world was painted in shades of gray, just as the old one had been.

Damn it. With the Guardian in town, she couldn't take down the roost during the day. While most vampires were nocturnal, Guardians had been conditioned to function in the sun. Well, that was what she'd heard. Mitzie had a tendency to waffle on. This was Violet's first encounter with a Guardian. If he scented her kills' blood on her, she'd be dead. Then again... because of the Order's selfish ways, claiming to only get involved if mana or forbidden metals were used, maybe the Guardian would ignore her completely.

It was rumored they could sniff out metal like bloodhounds.

The fear hit her with the force of a snowstorm. She froze, despite her heart pounding rapidly. He might even scent her now. Forcing her heart to calm, she kept her eyes on him as he spoke with the female vampire. From the tightness across his shoulders, and the tick in his clean-shaven jaw, he wasn't happy with the conversation. She strained to hear, but caught only the raised, terse cadence of the female. Then the Guardian completely stilled.

Another arrived. This one was huge. Shaved head, tattooed, and built like a linebacker. No, bigger. Good Lord, his thigh was thicker than Violet's waist. He whispered something in the first Guardian's ear. The two of them squared off, their eyes simmering, but then they smiled as though they were old friends. Violet relaxed a little until the first one's nose tipped into the air, and he stormed off... thankfully not in the direction of the exit but to the stairway leading deeper into the house.

The female at the fireplace clenched her jaw and shouted a name... it sounded something like Peter, although that was so human, so Violet didn't think it was the case.

"Whatcha looking at?"

Violet whirled around.

It was the first Guardian. The mischievous one. Next to her, he casually peered through the window.

A million thoughts traveled through her mind, colliding and competing for dominance. How did this Guardian get here so fast? Flown off the roof? Did he know?

Of course he did. He could scent out metal. Why else would he be next to her?

But did he *know?*

Up close, he was even more disarming. He looked down at her, eyes crinkling in humor. "You have no idea how long I've been searching for you."

He glanced down as though he could see right through the fur-lined cape to where her fingers hurt from clutching the stake. His eyes widened, but then a crease flashed in his right cheek and her stomach flipped. When he smiled in that boyish way, full of innocent charm and dangerous misconceptions, she almost forgot he was the enemy and she was his next meal.

He continued to stare at her like he knew things.

Secrets.

Hers.

Shit. He knew she was human. He knew she'd been killing vampires. He knew about the outlawed metal in her hand. The one that could mean a death sentence.

He stepped forward. She jerked back, wincing as the sudden movement tore open her neck wound. She knew the instant he scented her blood. His smile dropped. He became predatory still, brown eyes locked onto her neck.

"You're bleeding," he muttered, and then lifted a finger to swipe the blood. He stared at the red stain, shocked, as though he couldn't believe he'd done that. Then his pink, pointed vampire tongue darted out and gave his finger a slow lick. His eyes fluttered. "This is how I sensed you."

"Don't even think about it, bloodsucker."

Her words seemed to snap him out of his daze. Dark brows slammed down, and the boyish charm vanished. She had no doubt there was a lethal, ruthless warrior lurking beneath the shadow of his perfection. It was how tricksters worked, right? Loki probably smiled the entire time he killed Baldr.

"And you have old scars beneath the new one," he said, focusing on her neck, his frown deepening. A low growl emitted from the base of his throat. His next words came through clenched teeth. "Someone *fed* from you?"

"*Indigo*." A deep, angry male voice. The second Guardian. "You done?"

Indigo whirled with a snarl to face the large vampire. Strangely, Indigo also stepped before Violet, as though trying to block her from the newcomer. To protect her? Or to keep her?

"Haze," Indigo greeted through his teeth.

Violet didn't wait to hear more. She ran.

CHAPTER SIX

"We don't have time for this," Indigo said to Haze, with a nonchalant nod in the direction the human took off.

Haze's lip twitched. "Was it her?"

"Yes. I tasted her to be sure, but... she'd been fed on. Badly."

"No wonder she ran."

"She was packing metal, too."

"*Crimson.*" Haze scrubbed his face. "Your brother is on his way. We need to get his statement before the queen's spies catch up."

"You go. I'll get the girl."

"Give her a few minutes. Let her think she's escaped."

A slow smile stretched Indigo's lips. "Playing with the prey. Didn't think you had it in you. Sadistic bastard."

"You have no idea." The big vampire stared at Indigo. "She called you a bloodsucker."

"Of all the nerve." Indigo rolled his eyes, attempting to keep the conversation light. There were things in Haze's past he kept hidden—things that caused him to tattoo himself in power-enhancing runes, courting the attention of the inky side of the Well. The only other fae Indigo had seen with this much desire to become invincible was Cloud. And that crow-shifter was messed up.

Pressing Haze was not a good idea.

Haze snorted, then rolled his eyes as well. They chuckled.

The thing was, since they'd lost a place in their home roosts when joining the Order, they became their own. A roost of three—Indigo, Shade, and Haze. They were family. They kept each other fed, healthy, and they viciously protected their own.

"All right. I'm going in." Haze tipped his chin. "I'll meet you back at the outpost once you collect her."

The moment Haze left, Indigo's senses filled with the memory of hers. Every fiber in his body needed to chase. She was... his mind blanked at the memory of her pink tipped nose and her smooth pale skin. The dark slashes of eyebrows made the more striking in contrast. Clarke had been right, this woman's scent had drawn him outside, and when he'd found her spying, he was intrigued. Humored. Dare he think it, a little excited.

Who was this fragile woman who thought she could peer into the home of vampires?

He scanned the dark street and lifted his blood-smeared finger to his nose. Inhaling deeply, he let her essence infuse his lungs. Hunger raked its claws against his composure. The old scars on her neck flashed before his eyes and he frowned. The past six years hadn't been kind to her.

He caught her scent trail above the crisp snow, and now that he wasn't struck dumb by her allure, he noted something else—blood. Not hers. Lots of it.

He snarled.

And metal.

Taking to the sky, he tracked the human to a small room by the edge of town. A broken window gave him the perfect view to where the stench of stale blood was stronger. She wasn't there, but the evidence of her devastation was. Slick and viscous liquid pooled on the floor. Drag marks led to the door, and a depressed trail went straight through the snow to the woods.

A coldness crept up his spine. For the first time during his months long hunt, he wondered who this woman was. The scars. The metal. The spying. What was she capable of? Murder?

He lifted his nose and picked up her trail again.

Into the woods.

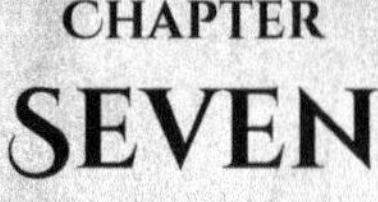

CHAPTER SEVEN

Violet ran as fast as her sodden boots would allow in the snow-covered forest. She figured it would be easier to lose him in here. She had the cover of trees if he flew. Beyond the forest was Aconite City, or further south, the sea. That was a better option. It was probably time she left Unseelie territory and head into Seelie lands. She'd only remained for so long because killing vampires, saving their prey, had made her feel something other than guilt.

Her cape billowed under the moonlight, flashing darker than the night. Trees and branches hit her face. Snow crunched underfoot. Boots slipped on ice. The only sounds in the forest were her steps, her rasping breath, and the wind.

She should be alone, but the tiny hairs on the back of her neck lifted as the sensation of being watched settled over her. There were things that lived here, things existing in nightmares. She couldn't allow fear to enter her mind. One slip, one hesitation, would mean capture by either the creatures that watched, or the vampire hunting her. The Guardian. Because she could hear him now, somewhere behind, his heavy boots thudding in the snow, an echo of hers.

Hot male breath panting. Boots crunching. Heart thudding.

Together, they were a symphony of sound.

Stomp. Gasp. Thud.

Crunch. Breathe. Beat.

Her scarf blew off, floating away. Her gloves ripped open on twigs and sharp thorny branches as she steadied herself. The burn of blood welled in her palms.

He was getting closer.

And she hurt. Her lungs, her eyes, her face. It all stung as wind bit her body, ravaging through woolen layers to bone. She would not go down like this. Not after everything.

Don't let the bastards win.

Violet could hear nothing through the roaring of blood in her ears. She stopped and listened. Silence. She strained her senses. The iron stake burned through her gloves as though it was a scalding brand. She turned, scouring the shadows. *Come on come on.* Where is he? Forcing her breathing to slow, and her heart to stop pounding, she listened.

A white blanket of snow covered the ground. On the horizon, a mix of tree types made uneven black shadows. Under the full moon, snow twinkled like diamonds, dusting branches and catching on evergreen leaves.

There was no movement except the cloud of her breath. No birds. No creatures. It was as though all had been frightened away by the pursuing Guardian, wherever he was. She had no doubt he watched her from some dark, hidden place, ready to pounce. Maybe even... dread settled with the awareness of being the mouse caught in the lion's trap.

The prickling at the back of her neck intensified. Slowly, she looked up, expecting to see him in the branches, but only found the stars twinkling eerily.

"Boo." Hot breath at her ear.

She whirled around, brandishing her stake. An almighty scream ripped from some primitive place in her throat. She stabbed on reflex, repeating her mantra in her head.

Head. Heart. Dead.

Blind them. Take away their ability to see. Then go straight for the heart, no hesitation, no second thoughts. No mercy.

Her strike went up, into his face. He dodged. She tried again. He stepped to the side, a lopsided grin on his lips, a lock of dark hair falling over his forehead. When she stabbed and missed again, he cocked his head in bewilderment and delight, as though he couldn't believe she fought back, and loved every minute.

Anger swarmed her body. Fae were so used to dominating humans, to using them like museum pieces, curating them in palaces and forcing them to perform. Yes, she'd heard the stories about humans being kidnapped if they dared venture outside the walls of Crystal City. She'd heard stories of how musicians were slaves in nightclubs, or how they performed privately for kings and queens, spelled to never stop, not even when their fingers bled.

How dare humans want a semblance of life? How dare they want to share the abundance of Elphyne? How dare they want to survive, to make amends for a single mistake?

She lunged. He stepped back and took her wrist before twisting, taking her with him until the stake fell from her fingers. A cry burst from her. Still rotating, he wrapped his wings to hug tight across the two of them.

Suddenly trapped in a vampire-made cocoon, she snarled and thrashed, hating that every cell of her heat starved body begged to sink into him. She whimpered at the unfairness of it. She would not die here tonight. She had things to make up for. Lives to save. To kill.

"Shh," he said. "Calm down, woman."

Calm down, woman.

Another voice, another time. Memories.

Calm down, woman. Go help your mother in the kitchen.

More memories bubbled up, like fizzing ferment. This time, the laughter was her father's. Her brother's. Laughing because her two left feet couldn't kick the football. Because her clumsy arms couldn't catch a baseball. Because she couldn't run as fast, jump as high, or punch as hard. Their indifference as she won first place ribbon at the science fair. Their confusion at her valedictorian speech, at the *snooty* words she'd used. Their damned faces... so hard to please... until she announced she was moving into nuclear physics... building weapons... being one of the boys. All so she could see that flicker of respect in their eyes.

Her first stupid, deadly mistake.

Be the master, not the mastered.

And like a trigger, her thoughts detonated into self-preservation. She heaved and thrashed and screamed. She would not go down. Her teeth gnashed. Strength came from somewhere deep in her reserves. But the asshole... he giggled! It was a warm, rich sound that melted her insides.

"That tickles," he murmured hotly against her ear.

She shoved her elbow back, satisfied at the *oof.*

He tightened his embrace, his arms and wings, until she couldn't breathe.

"While I thoroughly enjoy this *us* time, you need to calm the fuck down," he growled, mirth fading from his tone.

Liquid leaked from her eyes, only to freeze in the arctic air. Would she fight to her last breath? Would she need to?

Be smart. Think about this clearly.

Chest heaving, she reined in her thoughts. She clambered her way back to sanity and to *think.* If he wanted her dead, he'd have killed her by now. Twice he'd come across her. The first time, she'd fled. The second time, she'd attacked first. He'd not tried to mesmerize her—if he even could. Not all vampires had that skill. The danger might not be as dire as she imagined.

She relaxed, her arms going limp, her chest still heaving beneath the steel band of his arms. Male spice, sweat, and pine surrounded her. And warmth. Goddamned heat.

Squeezing her eyes shut, she ordered herself—surrender now, live to fight another day.

Together they breathed. They listened to the silent forest. Their hearts slowed as one.

It felt... annoyingly nice. His warm body against her colder one.

The intimacy of the moment was not lost on her, and the instant she lowered her guard, confusion roared to the surface, revolting against her body's instinct to succumb to his comforting embrace.

"What do you want?" she ground out.

"You don't really want to know that." His voice had turned gravelly, rough.

"That's a stupid answer." She squirmed.

"You also don't want to do that."

"Why, you'll smother me again?"

"No. I'll bite you. Maybe lick you. Maybe..." He nuzzled into her neck, inhaling deep. "*Crimson*, you smell so good."

"Bite me and I swear to God I'll rip your testicles clean off your body."

He burst out laughing. It was deep, it came from the belly, and it tickled Violet's neck, sending goosebumps rippling all the way to her nipples. His humor stole into her like an unwanted intruder, reaching into the dark crevices that hadn't felt joy in close to a decade.

"What's so funny?"

"You," he blurted. "You Well-blessed humans from the old world are all the same. Surprising. Funny. Cute."

He booped her nose.

She blinked, agape.

She was supposed to be angry, violent, scary. This was her childhood all over again. Unlike what her father had claimed, she could be all these things *and* be a woman. Damn him. Booping her nose. Jerk.

He loosened his grip, easing away, until his wings opened and the cold air whooshed in. She shivered and scowled.

He held something out to her. It was her scarf. Gingerly, she took it and wrapped it around her head, using the movement to disguise searching for her fallen stake. Even though Guardians could access their mana with metal in their hands, it would still wound him more than another substance. The stake was her best defense.

"It's gone," he clipped, showing real displeasure for the first time since she'd met him.

The realization squirmed in her gut, making her doubt herself even more. She had run from him. She had attacked *him.* And this was the first time he was angry—no. She shook her head. *Stop trying to humanize him.* He's the enemy. Fae. Vampire. Bloodsucker.

"What has gone?" She feigned ignorance.

"The metal weapon you're searching for."

Their gazes clashed. In his, she found no compassion, only wariness. It made her stupidly yearn for the amusement that had lit up his face earlier. She growled in chagrin.

"I would have thought a Well-blessed human such as you would understand the harm metal does. Although..." His voice trailed off as he searched her body, up and down. His gaze stuck on her gloved hands with disappointment, and to the skin showing above. "Perhaps you aren't Well-blessed after all. You have no blue markings." His brows winged up thoughtfully. "Although, that could just mean you're not mated."

"I don't know what you're talking about."

He stepped back and eyed her curiously. "You *do* know you can access mana, like the fae, right? I can smell it on you. It's like you've taken a bath in a power source. You reek of magic."

"That's impossible." She'd done no such thing.

His eyes narrowed. "How long have you been awake in this time, Weapon Maker? Don't you think you would have aged by now? Just a little bit?"

She stepped back. What was he talking about? Aged? She touched her face as the odd realization hit. She'd been in her early thirties when the nuclear winter had hit. Should she have a wrinkle or two? No. Her family had good genetics. Her eighty-year-old Nonna still looked like she was sixty.

That's all it was.

Something else he'd said registered. *Weapon Maker.* So

he wasn't after her because of the vampires... or the metal... but...

"H-how did you know?" she stuttered, licking her dry lips. She'd told no one except Peaches and Silver. Were they okay?

"That you build weapons?" he asked.

She nodded. Perhaps the vampire had reached into her mind somehow. She knew the skill wasn't unheard of in the more powerful fae. It went hand in hand with mesmerization.

He lifted a shoulder. "Our Seers told us."

Psychics. Like the ones who had sent Gastnor and the first vampires after her.

Violet pretended the intrusion of privacy didn't affect her. "I refuse to build weapons anymore, so if that's why you're after me, you can just leave. I've forgotten everything, and even if I hadn't, the equipment needed just doesn't exist anymore."

The crease in his cheek flashed. "I'm not leaving, and you're coming with me to the Order."

"Dream on," she muttered.

"You think you can outrun me?" He stared at the snowy landscape. "A storm is coming."

"I've killed more vampires than you can imagine." The boast blurted out before she could stop it.

Darkness flittered over his features and he hissed. Two razor sharp fangs taunted her.

Violet recoiled, using the movement to reach into her boot and draw out her backup dagger. She also had an aluminum shard, but that would be useless in a fight. She lifted the blade to his jaw.

"I wouldn't if I were you," he warned calmly, as though he couldn't care less about the steel so close to his jugular.

"Why not? I think I would enjoy slicing you open."

"Ooh." His eyes crinkled at the corners. "But didn't you hear? Blood turns vampires on."

"You know what turns me on?" She pressed in.

"Tell me." He took another step closer, too excited, too into it.

She ground her teeth, frustrated at his facetiousness. Her retort died in her throat as the dagger nicked skin, drawing a single drop of his crimson blood. It rolled down the thick column of his neck, down the Adam's apple, and onto his leather collar. He didn't seem to care.

"Hi," he said softly, eyes searching her face. "I'm Indigo. What's your name?"

"I'm not going with you," she said, a little disarmed at his words. Was he flirting?

He gripped her shoulder. "You need me, human. You won't survive the night out here in the snow. Especially not in this forest."

Violet hesitated.

"And you can't go back home," Indigo added, reading her expression. "I saw the blood on your floor. The town council will scent it. You made the mistake of killing in your own home."

"It was self-defense. They entered without consent."

"Perhaps. Perhaps they won't care when they find out

the reason you mutilated your ears was to look like fae only so you could kill us." His eyes narrowed on Violet. "You might even attract the attention of the Unseelie High Queen's enforcers."

She stared at him, weighing up the best answer. She could tell him she'd been hunting his kind for years. She could say it was self-defense, but that would be a lie, or at least only part of the truth. In the end, she settled for, "I could just kill you and run."

While she'd been concentrating on his hand on her shoulder, unyielding fingers locked around her wrist and squeezed until she let go of the dagger with a cry of pain. Infuriated, she kneed him in the gut and then pummeled his front, aiming for his throat. *Choke him.* Next were his eyes.

Head. Heart. Dead.

He covered her mouth with his hand and then drew her close, slamming her back against his front with such ease, she wondered if she ever stood a chance of besting him in a fight. He retreated behind a tree trunk. It took her a moment to realize his actions came from a different place than hers. He moved stealthily. Seriously. And in no way like he'd done in the past. It was as though—she froze as a twig snapped. *Someone is coming.* Slowly, almost imperceptibly, his wings closed partly around them and they melted further into the shadows behind a tree.

The crunch of multiple footsteps became audible.

Through the gap in Indigo's wings, Violet saw dark figures come into view down the snowy path, cursing at their load, dragging something behind them. Three figures dragging three bodies wrapped in canvas and rope.

Despite the warmth radiating down her back, ice cold fingers trailed down Violet's spine. Perhaps she wasn't the only one who used this forest to cover their dark deeds and swallow their secrets.

CHAPTER EIGHT

With his arms and wings locked around the woman, Indigo summoned his mana and activated the shadow snake coiled against his body. Usually it appeared like a dark tattoo, but now it slithered to life, slipping against his flesh until it unwound and oozed out of his jacket's collar. He willed its mass to spread and enshroud them both in shadow, forming a layer of protection against the interlopers. If they looked Indigo's way, they would see only shadow.

For now, they were invisible.

Just as well, he could scarcely contain his reaction when the identity of the three figures came into view, all dragging corpse-shaped bundles like sleds. The first was Gastnor, the vampire Captain of the Queen's Guard. The second, he failed to recognize, but the third sent fury radiating down his spine. It was Bones, the old world human who had worked for their human enemy, the leader in Crystal City. The Void.

Two different enemies working together. Joining forces?

Bones was supposed to be dead.

A few months ago, after the Order had taken Bones prisoner, they'd lent him to Queen Maebh to interrogate about the Void's plans. The Order's attempts had been unsuccessful. The queen had given them crumbs of information, claiming her luck no better than theirs, and then claimed Bones was dead—an unfortunate result of her efforts. Indigo cast his mind back to how the information of this death had come into the Order. Had a fae somehow lied? Or was it simple misdirection?

Perhaps Bones *had* died... and was now alive. Necromancy was not beneath the queen's growing skills. She'd been alive for millennia herself.

Indigo narrowed his eyes and opened his hearing.

"How far must we drag these bodies? My balls are turning to ice."

"This should be far enough. Unwrap the covers. We want the tachi to scent them."

A rush of air tickled Indigo's fingers as the woman's breath puffed in surprise. He tightened his grip. She squirmed, her soft bottom pressing into his crotch. His eyes fluttered closed at the contact.

She smelled like his own personal elixir, custom distilled for his enjoyment, and it took all the control he'd carved into his bones over the past few months to stop himself from burying his face into her neck, biting a vein, and sipping the nectar as it spilled out.

When Clarke had originally told him about this human, she'd alluded to the possibility she might be Indigo's mate—his *Well-blessed* mate. He frowned. If that were true, then they'd have matching blue mana-infused markings on their arms. Rush and Clarke had them. Laurel and Thorne had them. And now the Seelie High King and Queen had them.

But there were no marks. There was no bond. This human was not his.

A stone sank in his stomach. Was he... disappointed? Did he *want* to mate with this woman who had murdered his kind and had tried to murder him? She claimed to have no mana, but he could smell it on her. In the cocoon of his wings, he could also smell a trace of forbidden metal. Perhaps she'd been using the substance for so long, she'd surpassed her ability to access personal mana stores. Perhaps she was permanently blocked.

He must be mentally damaged to want her as his mate. Or maybe his parents had drilled the idea into his head so much as a child, that finding a soul mate was all he could think about. And she was the biggest challenge of them all. That excited him.

Her second gasp brought his attention back to the intruders. The canvas had been pried from the bodies, and what lay inside was a sight not fit for any female. Mangled, deformed faces. Flesh turned inside out. Bones on the outside of the body. And the stench—rotting meat. He tried to close his wings so she wouldn't see, but her determination proved impossible to resist. She wriggled and tugged on his wings, touching him in a place no other dared, insisting they watch the burial.

This violent woman was quite possibly as disturbed as him.

Quite possibly even more attractive.

Their struggles invited the stares of the three interlopers. He stilled, willing his breath to quiet, hoping she sensed the danger and did the same. Vampires could hear the intake of breath from hundreds of feet away, and Gastnor was one of the oldest. Indigo didn't fancy killing the Captain of the Queen's Guard tonight. It was better to stay hidden.

Pity his human didn't have the same thought. She made a hissing snarl, then wrenched free of his grip and ran forward.

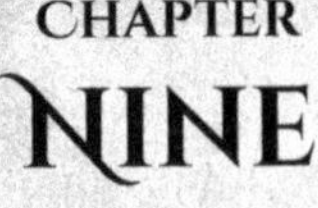

CHAPTER NINE

It took Violet a moment to recognize Gastnor through his wrinkled face and graying hair, but the mangy scar down his cheek gave him away. It had been Violet's own fingernails that had scored him, after all. The moment she made the connection, a blanket of red fury covered her vision.

All she could think of was to bury her dagger deep into Gastnor's heart. To feel the heat of his blood run over her fingers. It seemed fitting, considering he'd felt hers.

Violet wrenched away from Indigo and ran forward at breakneck speed. It took her five paces before she remembered the dagger was still on the ground somewhere behind her. All she had left was a tiny shard of aluminum.

Her snarl of vengeance died in her throat and she stumbled to a stop, just before the row of corpses. It was as though time stood still. The world slid on its axis. Reality shifted.

What have I done?

All three interlopers turned their heads, seeing her for the first time.

One of them was human, gaunt and harrowed with dark circles under his eyes. Shorn dark hair clumped in patches, as though someone had taken clumsy scissors to his head, or he'd pulled his own hair out.

Recognition sparked in his expression and then *he* ran toward *her*.

"Help me," he croaked, staggering closer with fear in his dark eyes.

The third fae's taloned hand snapped out and yanked the human back. The action dropped his hood from his head to reveal a dirty red beret. Violet's heart stopped.

He was a redcap goblin—so vulgar and murderous that they dipped their beret in the blood of their victims. Gnarled pointed ears, craggy faces, and talons as sharp as the dagger Violet had left behind.

"Who are you?" Gastnor bellowed.

The red lining of his cape flashed as his hand hovered over the hilt of a long bone sword discolored with old blood.

"Help," the prisoner hissed as he struggled against the stocky redcap. He pulled free and vaulted over the corpses to get to her.

Violet stepped back, slipped on ice beneath the snow and landed hard, staring at the dark branches slashed across the midnight sky. She expected the human to land on her, but there was nothing.

Blinking, she sat up.

An avenging demon stood beside her, his leathery wings splayed out in aggression, the wingspan twice as wide as she was tall. Indigo held the human suspended by the neck, but it was the fury mottling his expression that truly instilled fear. A shadow snake slithered around his leather clad body. It twined around his arm, and when it reached his wrist, Indigo threw his hand toward the redcap. The snake flung through the air and coiled around the goblin's neck, strangling him.

Indigo bared his fangs. "Gastnor, shame on you and your queen. She has kept a very important prisoner from us. The Prime will not be happy about this."

Gastnor ignored Indigo's threats and instead locked onto Violet, eyes widening with recognition.

"Filthy manaless floater." His face contorted with rage and he slid his sword free to point at her. "You cost me my youth. You almost cost me my life."

She swallowed. The only way to age a fae was to permanently suck their mana dry. The queen must have turned him old and cut his magic strength in half... all for losing the three humans he'd been tasked with bringing to her.

Gastnor vaulted over the bodies. Violet shielded herself, flinching back, knowing there was no escape from this fate. Hell had caught up to her.

She waited for death.

And waited.

Nothing.

A gurgle.

She glanced up, shocked to see the tip of the bone sword protruding from between two wide bat-like wings. Indigo had stepped in front of her.

He'd saved her life.

He'd *protected* her.

This vampire. This fae. This enemy.

Indigo's shadow snake jumped from the goblin to Gastnor, coiling tight around his neck. Gastnor hissed and lashed out, but not at the Guardian—at Violet. He tried to claw his way around Indigo to get to her, determination on his scarred face.

"Filthy bitch," Gastnor spat and struck out. "I remember you now. I will make you suffer. I will keep you in my thrall until I drain you dry, and then I'll share you around, just like your friend."

Taloned fingers curved around Indigo and scraped her cape, tearing a hole through the wool. Still with the sword in his stomach, Indigo grasped Violet's flailing wrist, and then they were airborne.

A scream lodged in her throat. Too many snow-laden branches blocked their escape. She ducked as the lash of sharp twigs tried to take them down. They couldn't get through the trees to clear sky. Indigo changed their trajectory, heading forward instead of up. They ricocheted against trees like a ball in a pinball machine, hitting trunks, jumping and clawing over branches where they could.

The handle protruding from his stomach wobbled

every time they hit a tree. Blood dribbled onto the snow as they passed. Then they hit one too many branches and plummeted. The wounded Guardian rolled mid-air, cradled Violet against his chest, and became a shield against the ground.

They crashed into a snow drift, sinking deep and hitting frozen earth beneath. Violet jarred her shoulder, her hip. Something sharp dug into her thigh. But Indigo... the crash did too many things. It pushed the sword deeper into his abdomen. It crushed his wings. It spilled blood from his lips.

A pained groan escaped him. Glassy eyes locked onto her as she clambered to her feet, blinking her vision into focus through the dim light. Heaving in deep lungfuls of stinging air, numbness took over. Her mind wouldn't work. Her body wouldn't move.

He'd saved her. Every time.

And now this trickster angel lay broken in the snow, and she wasn't sure if she should save him.

This was her chance.

Escape.

The word screamed in her mind. Do it. Run. Survive.

But he'd acted the opposite of how her brothers had always acted. He was the opposite of the kind of man her mother warned her against. He'd put her first.

He must have seen her doubt because he gripped something around his neck—the shadow snake—and flung it at her. The dark slithering mass wrapped around her wrist, locking tight like twined rope. The other end wrapped around his wrist, forming a shadow cord between them. Pain pumped into her. *Agony.* In her stomach. In her head. In her back. She fell heavily to her knees.

"What have you done to me?" she gasped.

His smile became sick, dark, and twisted.

"I made sure you can't leave me," he gurgled, blood dribbling down his chin.

The whites of his eyes showed. He forced his gaze back to her with purpose.

"What I feel, you feel," he snarled. "What happens to me, happens to you." He craned his neck forward. Pain screamed down her spine as it must have done with his and he looked her in the eyes. "I die, *you die.*"

He flopped back into the snow, exhausted.

Violet could hardly breathe from his agony. "Are you mad? We'll both die."

"Not if I shift."

"Shift to what, a bat?" she joked, acid on her tongue. How would that help them?

"No. I can't protect you like that. At the very least, I need to shift my wings away," he replied. "It's not ideal, but it's—" He winced as he pulled the sword from his stomach, causing a new gush of blood.

A hot poker stabbed through her gut. She screamed in torture, doubling over, grasping at the phantom wound on her stomach. Nausea rolled. Her skin heated with prickles. And then it dulled.

Panting on her hands and knees in the snow, she waited until her mind gathered focus and looked up.

Indigo had lifted himself into a slumped position, resting his forearm on a propped knee.

"See?" He bared bloody fangs. "I'm fine."

His wings were gone. The archaic, bloody bone sword stuck out of the snow. The wound she glimpsed between torn leather had closed over. And a long line of shadow connected their wrists like manacles.

CHAPTER TEN

Indigo laughed when the human glared daggers at him, which only infuriated her further. It made her face screw up and her eyes twinkled like snow. The sharp twinge at his wound site was worth the laugh. This grumpy one's smile would be hard won, but he had an inkling he'd like to find it.

"What now?" she gritted out.

"Now I take you to the Order."

"So I am a prisoner."

"That remains to be seen."

"On what?"

"On your behavior."

"You expect me to believe you would just let someone like me go? I admitted I killed your kind."

"Fae don't lie."

"But you omit truths and tell misleading stories." Her

teeth chattered from the cold. "Exhibit A: You said my behavior dictates my prisoner status, but you haven't told me *how* I should behave. Exhibit B: You said, remains to be seen. That could mean anything. Exhibit C: You keep saying you're fine but I can feel your pain. Clearly there are degrees to lies."

Her voice trembled on the last words, betraying her emotions. Did this human care that he was mortally wounded, or was it fear for her own wellbeing?

Indigo's brows quirked. His humor died, and he busied himself with pushing to his feet and checking his wound. Indeed, she was right. He was not fine for extended motion. Purple puckered lines surrounded the sword entry point. The skin over the top was weak and thin. It ached like a motherfucker. If he moved suddenly, it would rupture.

Feeding would expedite the healing.

He glanced at the human. She glared back. No, he wouldn't feed from her. Not now. Not ever. Because in doing so, he would have to put his trust in her as much as she would have to in him. If her blood took away his senses, he would be vulnerable to slaughter. From the multiple bite marks on her neck, he suspected this was how she'd slayed so many vampires. She'd used herself as bait.

Anyone with that much self-disrespect was not a person to be trifled with.

The sooner they got to the outpost, the better. He'd never more regretted neglecting to take a portal stone with him. Usually vampires flew short distances, so the expensive stones were better left for the wingless.

That led him to another problem—he was almost empty of mana. Refilling from the Cosmic Well would take time spent in nature. The closest source of power was a natural spring at the outpost. Without it, refilling might take days to reach full capacity. Hours, perhaps, to have enough mana to fuel another shift.

He squinted into the distance. Nothing but snow flurries, trees and endless night. For now. But he'd leaked blood everywhere. Any vampire with a nose would scent him, even in this snow. Then there were the natives of the forest, among them monstrous fae named tachi.

Calling the tachi cannibals would be kind. They had been known to eat themselves on occasion. Gastnor had been wanting to take advantage of the tachi appetite to rid himself of incriminating evidence, just as the human probably had with her victims.

With deliberate intention, Indigo shucked off the apprehension riding his system. This was an adventure, just like Shade had teased. He had a grumpy little human to protect, creatures to avoid, and a growing snow storm to survive.

"We'll head south." He pointed ahead.

Without waiting for her blessing, he walked. The shadow snake snapped taut and dragged her behind him. He quietly smiled at her bumbling curses while she tried to keep up, but his mirth swiftly dissipated when his wound ached to the point of pulsing pain. Hunger hit him as his body craved for the sustenance to heal. A gust of biting wind caused him to slip on ice and fall to a knee where he stayed a moment to catch his breath, his cheeks heating.

Crunching footsteps drew closer behind him.

"You're unwell," the woman noted grimly, the cloud of her breath visible over his shoulder.

"I'm fine." He took another moment before standing and testing his face for the telltale tachi harbinger signs. If one stalked them, he'd have bloodless wounds. He found nothing but skin stubbled with day old scruff. "We have to keep moving."

If he submitted to his hunger now, they would both be in danger. The snow might be driving the forest fae to ground, but the moment Indigo became complacent, they would return. Unseelie fae thrived on weakness and the only thing keeping them hidden and at bay was the metal stashed on his body—a brass knuckleduster, the dual-swords on his back, and a dagger in his boot.

"I won't die out here because of your stubbornness."

"I said I'm fine," he snarled.

She stilled, eyes wide and watchful.

Irritated, he plowed onward, leading the way south. Without wings to wrap around himself, the cold air drilled through his leather until his skeleton turned to ice. He supposed he could save himself some pain and use his last scrap of mana to cast an insulation spell, but his shadow snake required a sliver of mana to remain active. The moment he emptied his personal reserves, he risked the human's escape.

So he trudged on, head down, arms folded, realizing that perhaps he was as stubborn as her.

Even when he was young, he'd been stubborn. He remembered a time his elder brother Demeter had played a joke on Indigo. He'd taken advantage of Indigo's fascination for the vampire goddess in the moon and wrote a secret message on parchment. He told Indigo it was from her and to view it, he had to take it to the lake and read its reflection. When Indigo did, he found a message that told him to fly to the moon and meet his true love. Part of Indigo knew it was too far, that it must be a joke, but he'd tried none the less. He flew so high the air thinned and he lost consciousness. He was lucky the lake was beneath him. And he was lucky to have survived.

Come to think of it, he never really got on with Demeter. His brother used to love playing so-called practical jokes on him, whether it was a dagger accidentally dropped on the foot, or shoving him off a roof as a child. Indigo always put it down to Demeter being the older brother and resenting having to take care of Indigo while their parents worked. Maybe he still held onto that grudge.

Long minutes passed. The quiet solitude of their journey left him with nothing but tumultuous thoughts and the trickle of hunger creeping in, despite his best efforts to focus on the cold. His recent cardboard feed at the outpost was not enough to gratify. Not with the luxury meal walking next to him, taunting him with the possibility of knowing he could feed once from her and last weeks before feeding again. His tastebuds watered at her closeness. Each gust of biting wind pushed her alluring scent into his nostrils, sending his urges into a tailspin.

No one will track and covet her as you will. It has to be you. That's what Clarke had said to him months ago.

This grumpy woman wasn't like the others who'd awoken from the old world. She was violent and vicious. She would stab him the moment he turned his back.

And he loved it. It turned him on. Having a female defy him at every turn was another challenge to set his heart racing. So maybe she wasn't his mate, but vampires rarely settled down, anyway. His parents were an exception, and even though they'd always hoped their children would follow in their footsteps, Indigo was used to disappointing them. Maybe not anymore.

She made little grunting sounds as they trudged. The idea of chipping away at her hard exterior made his stomach zing. He imagined what it would be like to feed from her... to make love to her. It wouldn't be gentle. It would be a battle every time. Surprising. Gratifying. Feeling those dainty but deadly fingers on his skin, wondering if she would bite or brush him. Stab or stroke him. Pleasure or pain. He tugged at his collar and cleared his throat.

Her sidelong glance reminded him that she felt his bodily sensations as her own. And just like that, his mind went to dark, filthy places. He'd not fucked another with this shadow bond active, but suddenly he wanted to use it in many delicious and indecent ways. He could make her come purely by arriving at completion himself.

Stop thinking about it. She was his mission, not his lover. Instead, think of—

Old wrinkled trolls.

Dead bodies.

Disgusting lumpy food shoveled into laughing mouths with bits of flesh stuck between teeth.

That did it. He silently gagged but continued to fill his mind with things he hated until his ill-timed lust abated, only to be replaced with a different kind of lust. Goddess save him. His body knew he needed sustenance and demanded he take it from the closest source. His legs turned to lead. His mind fogged. Flashes of red hit behind his eyelids and suddenly, he wasn't in the white snow, he was sitting in a pool of liquid blood, waking from a blood-lust fugue, agape at the pieces of raw flesh in his hands, realizing they'd come from the body he'd ripped apart.

Regret surged and the memory forced him to his knees.

I'm fine.

But the heat of the coming sun already made him lethargic.

The sky had lightened to purple. They should be safe from pursuing vampires now, perhaps even the nocturnal tachi, but they needed to keep going. No matter how much the sun caused his muscles to atrophy or his mind to mist. He'd trained for this.

A warm weight landed on his shoulders and then small, steady hands slotted under his arms to wrap around his waist, hauling him up.

Her act of kindness sparked an ache between his ribs,

both in defiance and in yearning for more of her touch, so much that when she ducked beneath her cape to share the warmth, he pulled her close.

"You die, I die," she muttered, shivering against him.

He glanced down at the shadow snake coiling between them and scowled. He could have sworn it disapproved.

They stood as temporary allies against the snow and listened to the rushing wind until she murmured, "Six years."

Her sharp bone structure somehow looked wrong, as though her true form was meant to be softer, curvier, and more forgiving. *Too skinny.* Lines bracketed her lips. Pain haunted her eyes. None of it was from aging. He wondered how old she'd been when she built the weapons that destroyed the old world. How old was she now? What had happened between?

She had been surprised he knew her secret. She'd been surprised anyone knew. That meant only one thing, she'd done everything in her power to keep her true identity hidden. She was either ashamed or afraid. Perhaps both. But a woman who believed she was manaless had trained herself to kill fae.

She wasn't afraid.

"Six years?" he repeated.

"You asked a while back how long I'd been in this time."

Her eyes snapped to his. Anger hardened her features and then she looked away, clearly grappling with hidden frustrations.

"What's your name?" he asked quietly.

From the clench of her stubborn jaw, he thought she might refuse him.

"Violet," she replied. "Well, that's my name now. The only one that matters."

"Tell me what you want, Violet." Perhaps if he gave it to her, she'd trust him, and this would all run smoother.

"It's none of your business."

"I beg to differ. I'm the only one who doesn't want to use what's inside your pretty little head. I may be the only one you can trust."

She snorted. "Flattery will get you nowhere."

"Are you sure? Because I could go all day. All night too."

"Besides, you're wrong. You're not the only one. Humans don't want to use me."

Her eyes turned distant, and he wondered if she conjured a particular person in her mind. Maybe there was another grumpy human she went home to every night. A male. The thought made him tense and his talons ache to release from his fingertips.

He added dryly, "Yet here you are, killing for the humans. Again, might I add."

"I don't kill for them."

"But you did kill vampires... for what? To protect your kind from being fed on? Or are you lying, and this is some sort of sideways strategy from the humans—send in alluring assassins such as yourself to ensorcell and entrap us."

She winced.

He pressed on. "Were you not building the old world weapons for someone else? Did this person not take advantage of you?"

She paused, thinking, then groused, "None of your business."

"Did I hit a nerve?"

"I make my own choices now."

"Did you not before?"

"Shut up. Just... shut up."

Another scowl animated her face, and this time, he realized why he liked seeing it so much. Like a smile might, her bad mood brought life to her otherwise dead eyes. It was the difference between a full and a waning moon. He'd rather the ire than nothing. It meant passion still existed deep within her soul. A goddess. One spark would kindle a roaring inferno.

Not that he should care. She was the enemy.

He sighed. Every time he told himself that, the excuse felt weaker. If he was being honest with himself, he'd secretly wanted her to be like the other humans who'd mated with the wolf-shifters in the Cadre of Twelve. He'd hoped she'd be an ally, a companion, someone he could go back to, time and time again. A partnership like his parents'. And then there was her blood...

Another hit of biting, snow-filled wind struck them.

"We can't stand here all night. A storm is coming," she grumbled.

He frowned at new marks along her cheek. He touched them gently, pressing. Little tiny slices of skin. No blood.

"What?" she blurted, somehow sensing his unease.

"Do I have bloodless wounds on my face?"

She squinted, inspecting him. He thought maybe he'd overreacted, but then she lifted her fingers to the cut of his cheekbone and pressed. "Yeah, right here, beneath your blue teardrop. That's all I can see, anyway."

He spat a string of curses before saying, "Tachi. We won't make it out of here before sunup unless we find shelter." He scoured the snow clumped woodland and dragged her along until he found a broad conifer and pointed. "That will do."

He pushed through the low hanging evergreen boughs and started scooping out the snow beneath, then thought better of it.

"Get in," he ordered, holding back some branches.

"But what's a tachi?" she asked, falling into the shelter as he tugged on the shadow bond.

He put his finger to his lips. After waiting a breath to see if the wind followed, he directed her to scoop out snow and then pulled branches and needles down from the inner trunk to line the floor. Sensing the urgency, she pressed her lips closed but did as she was told.

He left the shelter to find more boughs from alternate trees. As he collected, she cursed in vexation as he went too far, dragging her half out of the shelter, and then the tension on the shadow bond would relax as she shuffled closer. The small entertainment was enough to take his mind off the blood oozing down his front, creating a warm path that quickly turned cold.

After the last of the boughs were placed against the conifer's outer branches, creating a teepee like enclosure for them, he rubbed some drier needles in pine resin before setting it alight with a burst of mana. With a whoosh of heat, flames sprung to life in their own little campfire. He might have needed that scrap of mana for the coming battle, but he needed Violet not to freeze to death more.

Indigo withdrew Bloodletter and Bloodbane, his twin swords, and held them ready over his thighs as he sat on the side opposite to the fire, centering himself.

Neither of them spoke, but Violet's eyes were wide and skittish.

She should be worried. He already watched her like a starved beast and, until now, until he shared this tiny enclosed space with her, he'd believed he was in control of his urges.

Exhaustion and pain closed his eyes.

He didn't have time for this. Not with an hour left before dawn and a tachi preying on them. Not with him perilously close to being empty of mana. Lighting the fire in the shelter had depleted him. All that was left was the amount fueling the shadow bond.

She shuffled closer and he tensed. After a few more moments, she closed the gap between them and draped her cape over his shoulders.

"Bite me and you die," she mumbled. "But we'll stay warmer like this."

His fingers tightened around the hilts of his swords.

For long moments they sat in silence, his senses

straining for the sound of unnatural wind, moaning, or the crunching of feet in the snow.

"Indigo?" she asked quietly.

"Shh."

"What exactly is a tachi? What are these cuts?" She touched the side of her face, tracing over the tiny slices.

He opened his eyes and debated whether to tell her. Having her frightened would do no good. But then again, everything he'd learned about her told him she was not a woman to balk at creatures such as these. She would probably see them as a challenge. An adventure.

A small smile lifted the corner of his lips.

The fire crackled strongly and dawn knocked at the door. The odds were they'd successfully avoided the creature, but he wanted her respect, and testing her reaction could reveal her character. Truth was more evident through behavior than words.

"A tachi is the cousin of a djinn. Do you know what that is?"

Her brows puckered. "I know what it was in the mythology from my time. A creature that granted wishes and lived in a lamp."

He snorted. "Your old myths were watered-down versions of the truth. Many of these creatures existed once. Before the humans of your time stamped the Well out with your industrial revolution."

"I suppose that makes sense. All the metal and plastic."

"Both these creatures work with a maelstrom wind. A djinn uses mana to power his tempest, but a tachi... that's something else." She clamped her lips shut. He continued, "A tachi works with a parasitic sentient wind that hunts ahead and then brings back a sample of its prey to its host. This is why no blood was present in our wounds."

"Parasitic wind? Probably more like parasitic microbes or bacteria." Violet shook her head at her words. "God, it's been years and I still try to inject logic and science into this world. Stupid."

"I don't think so," he murmured, evaluating her. "I think it's smart. Clever. Beyond what we have in this time. Others would think so too."

"That's not necessarily a good thing." She cleared her throat. "So it's a vampire?"

"Worse. A cannibal that does not discriminate. It's been known to eat itself on occasion." At her hitched breath, he cocked his head. "Did you not wonder what kind of creature you were feeding your corpses to?"

Because he'd smelled the old evidence near the entrance to the forest behind her place. Old bones. Old death. He suspected she'd been slaying vampires for the entire time she'd lived in Obscendia. Perhaps longer in other towns.

I've killed more of your kind than you'll ever know. He should despise her. Many of his kind would. Perhaps even Haze. Possibly Shade. But Indigo had never worried about his family. They weren't the sort to feed without consent, and it seemed like she had a code to her hunting. She'd only hunted vampires who thought they were entitled to feed from anyone... which was a lot. He slid his gaze her way and smiled at the disgruntled pout on her plush lips. How could he be angry at her for killing when he'd also killed his kind and other fae? It was his job.

She hugged herself. "It didn't matter what I did with them as long as they were gone."

And there was the truth.

The woman had a death wish. Feeding unscrupulous creatures was as much of a danger to oneself as it was to anyone else.

"So what now?" she asked.

"If we're lucky, the fire and shelter of the tree will keep the tachi away until the sun comes up. And then we travel."

"And if we're unlucky?"

"Then we have to get through the parasitic wind to attack the tachi. It will die the same way all fae can die."

"Metal through the heart."

He gave a grim nod just as a deep, guttural moan filtered through the branches. A sudden lull in sound softened the atmosphere. It was as though the forest held its breath. And then the tree shook. Pine needles and pitch fell on their faces. Indigo went stone cold. He pushed Violet down into the dugout.

"Stay down," he grunted, covering her with his body.

"I can fight." She pushed against him.

"Perhaps if you had not denied the Well, you could. But six years of carrying metal has made you useless. Perhaps even mortal. Stay. Down."

Defiance flared in her eyes, and if he wasn't preparing for the fight of his life, he'd grin.

Fuck it. This might be his last chance. He kissed her quickly, hotly, and passionately before flashing a grin and torpedoing through the branches, swords first.

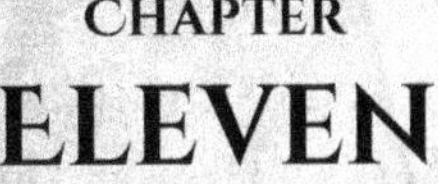

CHAPTER ELEVEN

Violet lay stunned. Her lips tingled from the heat of Indigo's kiss as she stared into the kaleidoscope of branches and twigs flickering in the firelight.

He'd *kissed* her. Then he'd smiled and ran headlong into certain death.

That damned vampire was going to get himself killed. Get them *both* killed.

But somehow more adrenaline pumped through her veins now than before.

Feral growls and snarls shook the ground as Indigo battled something big, heavy, and vicious. With her heart kicking, she knew she couldn't stay in there for long. He'd forgotten they were linked by the shadow bond. It plucked and tugged as he fought, moving through the conifer as though it didn't exist. But she did. Soon she would be torn asunder, or at the very least, yanked through the tree, stabbing herself in the process.

The enormity of the situation hit her hard.

Violet was a scientist at heart. She liked risk, but she liked having a plan going into it. Cause and effect. Hypotheses, theories, preparation. This was...

A parasitic, biting wind?

How could she battle that?

She needed time to study it. Would it burrow into her body and then she would become its host? Would she become something else? Terror filled her mind and she began to think that maybe the humans of Crystal City were foolhardy to want to leave the safety of their barren land. Would they ever truly be ready to live among the wild things that preyed out here?

Violet's wrist yanked outward and she skidded closer to the branches shielding her from the fight. An overwhelming sense of helplessness flowed over her and she squeezed her eyes shut to gather her resolve. She was so out of her depth.

Working in the obsidian mines and dealing with vampires had been a cakewalk compared to this. She'd studied them and worked out their weaknesses before jumping into attack. Risks had been mitigated. She gritted her teeth and considered Indigo's words.

Perhaps if you had not denied the Well, you could. But six years of carrying metal has made you useless.

Useless.

She swallowed over the lump in her throat.

Had she been wrong?

Could she dare to hope she had the ability to wield mana innately like the fae? That somehow, this cosmic entity of power had looked past her devastating mistakes and granted her something special? Three other humans like her could. Or was it all lies?

She dug into her pocket to touch the last remaining piece of metal she owned. The scrap from the mine.

Metal has made you useless.

White light had blinded Gastnor and his vampire soldiers as they'd fed on her. Maybe the light hadn't been a dream. Maybe it had come from inside her. It had felt weird. Hot. Pure. Safe. Maybe carrying metal for six years *had* blocked her from accessing and harnessing that power.

One thing was for sure, she would never know if she didn't test the theory out.

Violet gripped the small shard of aluminum. Even if Indigo was wrong, and ridding herself of it did nothing, she couldn't very well use the tiny thing to shove into the tachi's heart. So she buried it deep beneath snow. Then she found a dry branch and shoved it into the small campfire, making sure to roll it about the pine sap bubbling on the kindling. When she was certain enough sap stuck to her branch, keeping it flammable, she used the shadow bond as a guide, found the gap in the tree, and dove into the fight.

She was not prepared for what she found.

Indigo's short hair lifted straight into the air, and he

squinted against a mini tornado surrounding him. A monster stood a few feet away.

Scraps of clothing hung from the tachi's humanoid limbs. It stared down at Indigo with glowing yellow eyes. Iridescent liquid leaked from its eye sockets, ears and nose like some kind of biohazardous pus. The substance rolled over saggy jowls before falling and hissing on the ground. Long, straggly hair clumped on its head, leaving patches of bald scalp. Random flaps of flesh on limbs moved over holes and wounds, as though it had indeed nibbled at itself. Two pointed and furred ears twitched in vexation. It almost looked... like a cross between a human and a fox. An eight-foot human. Perhaps it had been once.

Indigo struggled to make headway toward the tachi, using his short swords like lances. And it seemed to work. The metal sliced through the wind like Moses parting the Red Sea. Until it didn't. Until both the tachi and Indigo noticed her, right there, right within reaching distance.

Indigo flashed fangs with a snarl. His assault became frantic as the tachi reached out to Violet with a drool-laced gurgle. He took one thundering step closer, exploding snow with his weight. The wind became her world, lifting her hair. Razors bit her face. She shoved the torch forward, hoping to scare it away, but the flames instantly suffocated. Stunned, she lowered the stick. How could she be so stupid to think fire would be a good weapon against wind?

The tachi howled its hunger. Indigo stabbed through the hurricane. His sword hit monster flesh, pierced, but the wind had thrown his trajectory off course. He only glanced its thigh and then one of his swords was knocked from his hand. The wind picked up in ferocity, roaring about them.

The two battled before her, now a blur of limbs and teeth as they moved too fast for her human eyes to track. Through the whirlwind, she glimpsed fangs, blood, and glowing eyes. Indigo's fight pulled her into the fray by the shadow bond, she stumbled and tried to yank her arm back. Pain stung her all over and she had no idea if it was his or hers.

This was the creature she'd fed the vampire corpses to? This impossible monster that was perhaps once human? Were there more?

This had to be some kind of magic fueled wind. It defied logic.

Six years of carrying metal has made you useless...

Albert Einstein once said only two things are infinite. The universe, and human stupidity. And he wasn't sure about the former.

Was there any coming back from this?

She'd spent the past six years focusing on revenge when she should have been listening to the world around her. She'd done the very thing the fae accused humans of doing—destroying the world through ignorance. Violet shut her eyes and prayed, murmuring against the wind. She prayed to whoever listened. The Well... God...

"I swear to you, now, here, if there is any truth to what Indigo told me, and I truly have this ability to harness mana... please... give it back to me..."

Agony ripped through Violet, bulging her eyes. It

started at her feet and fired up her legs as though someone had injected napalm into her veins. Pressure built beneath her skin until something ripped out of every pore. The sun burst in the night, breaking dawn.

Not the sun.

Her.

And then it was gone. The heat in her veins. The pressure. The power. Gone. She was cold again, shivering beneath her cape. Without a tachi to direct it, the wind had no focus. It felt more of a lazy breeze than a hostile energy. Both Indigo and the monster had recoiled from the light. Both were creatures of the night, and she'd blinded them.

Indigo's ears perked up. He clicked his tongue a few times before stumbling to the stunned creature. The tachi walked in circles, moaning to himself. Indigo blinked wildly as he used both his failing eyesight and what Violet realized was echolocation to fumble about until he found the sword. He circled the creature as it walked in circles. Violet watched, stunned and awed as Indigo moved like a panther in the shadows, at one with his darkness.

Then he drove the sword through the tachi's heart.

There was no howl. No death scream. Just a dying of the wind. A silence descending. And a beast that may have been human once falling to the ground. Snowflakes swarmed around manabeeze rising from the body to join the dawn light peeking through the trees. For a moment, it was magical. Ethereal. The balls of glowing life-force floated up. The snowflakes went down, gathering thickly in clumps until the tachi started to look like one of the trees surrounding them. They daren't remove the metal sword from its heart. Not yet. Not until the last little buzzing ball of mana left its body.

Her stomach hurt. Looking down, she found no wound. It must be—

Indigo collapsed to his knees, then face first into the snow. Deep red splats against the white glowed as the manabeeze drifted nearby. She rushed over, rolling Indigo's dead weight to see his face.

"Hey."

No response.

She checked down his leather front and opened the rip in his jacket to reveal a hot, sticky mess inside. She covered her mouth. It was worse than before, almost like the tachi had dug his fist inside and removed a chunk of flesh.

"Indigo?" she croaked.

Silence.

"Hey." She patted his cold jaw and remarked the difference in temperature between her own face.

Too much blood loss. He was going into shock. *"Jesus Christ."*

Panic triggered her pulse.

"Indigo." She shook him. "Wake up."

He grumbled something about sleeping.

"You're bleeding pretty bad."

"... fine by the morning. Safer if I sleep."

"It is morning!"

"Huh." Long lashes fluttered, coming more out of his daze. "Then why can't I see?"

"That's my fault. This light came out of me. Maybe you were right about the mana thing. I don't know. I... What do you mean, fine by the morning? Will your mana replenish? Will you shift?"

His nod looked more like a loll. More blood oozed over her fingers as she tried to staunch the wound.

"*Jesus*. Oh, God. Look at all the blood." She patted his cheek again. This is why she never went into medicine. It was okay when she didn't care if the person lived, but this was too messy. Too sticky. Too... "Hey. Wake up. Do you want me to die, too?"

He shoved her away with a sudden surge of energy. She tumbled back and landed ass first into the snow.

She scrambled back to him, and he tried it again, this time hissing at her like a wild, ravenous beast. His eyes were no longer dark liquid pools but burning orbs of lava. Recognizing the vampire affliction, she held her palms up in surrender, careful not to startle the injured animal. Another layer to their shared pain brought everything into focus. He was hungry. Starving. Craving.

Her.

"You need to feed." The realization settled on her with dread. If he hit a full bloodlust state, he might not be able to stop, and she would be powerless to protect herself. Even if her blood made him drunk, he might rip into her arteries first.

He flung his hand. "Go. Away."

"But... the shadow snake." It still connected them.

He fell backward, his head landing hard on the snow,

all energy spent.

"Go," he muttered. "Head south. Haze will find you. He's a sucker for a damsel. Just don't call him a bloodsucker."

"But—"

"Before I eat you and rip you limb from limb." He snarled. At least, he tried to snarl. The life was draining from him. He was losing all sense, his mind succumbing to the cold.

She swallowed.

"The tachi's blood," she suggested. "I'll bring it to you."

"No!"

She stopped.

"Poison," he gritted out.

Violet checked his wound again. The bleeding seemed to have stopped.

"I'll be fine," he whispered. "Heal fast."

"Not fast enough," she grumbled. She should find him food, but with the way the snow and wind was picking up, it was unlikely she'd catch anything until morning.

After a few more wasted seconds of inaction, she decided to collect his swords.

A quick tug and she'd yanked one from the dead monster, and found the other half buried in the snow. The blood was poison, so she washed the blade in the snow before coming back to stand over him.

Through it all, he'd kept a watchful eye on her, his chest heaving with labored breaths.

"Kill me then," he said.

Violet laughed bitterly. Killing Indigo would be the easy option. They'd both die. End of story.

She'd end her eternity spent in damnation, and he'd end his eternal hunger. No more worries.

But... no more penance. How would she make up for all the suffering she'd caused?

And then there was the little, tiny, insignificant fact that in the few hours she'd spent with him, her world view had shifted dramatically. She'd *prayed* to the Well, and it had *answered*. Hadn't it?

It had forgiven her.

Had it?

Or was this her grasping at connections in a tumultuous time?

Was she finding sense where there was only coincidence? She never was a believer in the chaos theory. Whatever the case, they needed to get to shelter or they would both die. And as stupid as it seemed, if the Well had forgiven her then maybe... maybe she had a right to live.

The threat of a pointy sword wasn't enough to motivate Indigo into moving. He only closed his eyes. While she stared at him, thinking about what to do next, snow and wind came in hard and fast, numbing her face. This wasn't the fluffy, fun snow. This was unforgiving, heavy, suffocating kind. For a girl who grew up in the desert, she wasn't sure if she'd ever get used to it.

Violet tossed the swords into the tree dugout and then set about dragging Indigo's heavy body inside. With him dipping in and out of consciousness, it took multiple tries.

Once inside the dugout, she checked his wound and packed it with her headscarf. The bleeding had completely stopped, but it was better safe than sorry. Once satisfied the bandage would keep, she braved the elements and continued to secure their shelter for the coming blizzard. The fight with the tachi had dislodged many boughs resting against one side of the conifer. With her cape wrapped tightly, she reset what she could, but in the process her body temperature lowered to a new extreme.

Numb feet, fingers, and nose. Sluggish brain. Possibly frostbite.

Unavoidable hypothermia was setting in. The only directive her mind grasped was to follow the shadow link —follow the dark, almost-not-there cord to safety. Except when she tried to grasp it as a guide, her fingers went right through it like a mirage. But she already knew that. Stupid. It was only tangible around her wrist.

Within the tree teepee, the small fire was on one side of the trunk and Indigo on the other. The air had less bite in here, but it wasn't warm. If the small fire went out while he was unconscious and unable to light it again with his mana, they'd freeze to death. Again, her stupidity for the past six years drilled into her. She could have been learning to harness her power, instead of denying it. She could be powerful. Strong. Invincible.

Instead of drinking from the Holy Grail, she'd ditched the wine and kept the damned empty brass chalice.

She forced her frozen body into action and stripped twigs and pine needles from the inner boughs before setting them by the fire to dry out as much as possible. It wouldn't be enough.

She shivered. She was colder than she'd ever been. And Indigo was worse.

His brows pinched in the middle as he huddled over himself, lying on his side. She crouched and reached for him, but he flinched back. At least he was shivering. If his body temperature lowered too much to shiver, he would be in trouble. He didn't speak for a long time and then, as though coming out of a haze, he mumbled something.

"What?" She crouched lower by his head, but his face had gone lax. "No." She slapped him hard on the cheek. "You can't sleep yet. Not until we've warmed up."

Two chocolate colored eyes flipped open with a scowl. Violet rolled him onto his back and opened his jacket. It was soaked. Both blood and snow-logged. So were her clothes.

Fuck.

She jammed the heels of her palms into her eye sockets and shook her head.

"I can't believe I'm going to suggest this," she intoned, "but we need to strip and hug."

Something like panic crossed his expression.

"I get it. I smell," she ground out. "I'm a filthy, floater human. I'm your prisoner. You don't trust me. Whatever. But we need to warm up. Unless you've got mana to spare, this is how it's going to be. Now hold the scarf to your wound while I remove your clothes."

He either had no energy to argue or he knew she was right because, when she started to remove his clothing, he let her without preamble. She had the sense that no one would force a warrior this size to disrobe if he didn't want to. He was too big, too lithe, too dangerous. Too full of surprises.

He'd saved her from Gastnor.

At the thought of the Captain of the Queen's Guard, a simmering pool of hatred flared to life in her gut. Gastnor was probably still alive. *Bastard.* Violet imagined all the ways she could kill him as she removed Indigo's outer layers. First his pants, then the jacket. Then his torn undershirt. The more she revealed of his body, the more she confirmed how much power he'd hidden beneath that leather battle uniform.

She'd never met a vampire like him. And she imagined the other Guardian—the big one—he'd be even more impressive. Either of them could crush her throat with a single fist. Snap her head right off. And that was without his talons.

Violet quickly shed her own clothing, shivering painfully the entire time but grateful that the campfire was starting to work. Again, the items had moved through the shadow snake as though it was a mirage, but by this stage, her inquiring scientist mind had all but collapsed in on itself. She wasn't even affected by Indigo's nudity.

Well, almost.

How could she not think about the carved perfection? Hewn from rock that was rough but had somehow ended up smooth. While she inspected him, he roused enough to trail his own lingering gaze down her front as she sat on her haunches. His attention stopped at her chest and his eyes turned smokey. He ground his teeth and then suddenly rolled away from her, hunching over himself and the scarf at his stomach wound. Every tendon and muscle defined with tension. His nude, taut buttocks flexed.

For a moment, Violet's mind blanked.

No wings.

No scars except what remained from his recent sword wound.

Nothing between his shoulder blades but defined musculature.

Unbidden, her palm landed on the flat of his back. Smooth, velvety skin. She stroked idly, mesmerized. When he shuddered, she realized what she was doing and snatched her hand back.

Stupid. Touching a monster like that. Her mind must be

truly numb. Every moment spent with him was dangerous. He was someone she could never fall asleep next to.

She needed a weapon to protect herself. If he decided she was as good as a midnight snack, then she had no defense except the drugging properties of her blood. His swords were in front of him, along with the weapons attached to his battle gear. If she went for those, he'd notice. She blew on her hands and then gathered her cape.

The aluminum shard.

She'd buried it in the snow here somewhere. It might not be much of a defense, but it was something. There hadn't been a night that she didn't have something metal in her hands as she went to sleep. Slowly, quietly, so as not to alert Indigo while his back was turned, Violet moved to the side where she buried the shard. It was still beneath the snow. A bone deep sense of shame and guilt tried to drag her down as she collected it.

Indigo may have saved her life—twice—but he was still a vampire. And he was starving, injured, and looking at her weirdly. He might not be able to control himself.

Shuffling beside him, she laid down lengthwise and draped her cape over them like a blanket. Indigo flinched when she brought her body flush against his. And when she slipped her arm around his abdomen, avoiding his wound, the echo of his agony bordered on desperation. She clutched that metal shard tighter and held it between them.

Violet tried to keep her eyes open for as long as she could. The sharing of body heat would work better if she was the little spoon, but she liked it this way. She felt more in control.

Better for her to do the stabbing in the back than the other way around.

The moment the thought hit, she realized that, perhaps, this was why Indigo had rolled over. To make her feel safer. But did vampires have a conscience? Did they care?

She fidgeted.

Indigo captured her twitching hand against his chest. He held it firm against his growing warmth until she stilled, and then they simply laid there.

That tiny movement and her world shifted again.

CHAPTER

THIRTEEN

Indigo woke with lead in his bones and surrounded by heat.

Sun must still be up.

And that smell—something so pure and needed. *Want it.* He nuzzled into it, rooting around with his nose to stir the scent beneath the dirt and blood. He inhaled satisfaction. Light, musky, feminine. It was there. And it begged to be savored.

Feminine?

His eyes popped open and everything came crashing back. The mission. The tachi. The human sleeping in his arms. Violet. Her grump. Her sass. Her beautiful brain —*Crimson save him*—her breasts had been glued to the wet fabric of her underwear. The image was burned into his mind. And now she dozed in the shelter of his arms.

Alive.

Violet had kept him alive. She'd dragged him into the

tree, undressed him, and kept him warm through the blizzard. Taking his mind back further, he remembered more. The way Gastnor had tried to assassinate her. The warped corpses they were trying to bury. Bones.

High Queen Maebh had somehow lied to the Prime of the Order of the Well when she'd said Bones had perished during her interrogation. She'd kept him alive, and for some reason he was assisting Gastnor in the disposing of carcasses—or he was being forced into helping. He had tried to flee, after all.

Two dangerous factions working together did not bode well, even if one party was coercing the other.

Haze had been in Obscendia to gather information about rumors the Unseelie Queen was conducting unnatural experiments with mana. Demeter had not yet arrived when Indigo had left to chase down Violet. The chances that these experiments had something to do with the corpses in Redvein Forest were likely.

The sooner Indigo returned to the outpost and apprised Haze of their find, the better.

Then there was the matter of Violet.

In his arms.

She clearly held mana within her. Light had exploded from her body at such intensity it had rendered him temporarily blind. She needed training. He'd seen the possibilities flicker in her eyes as she'd threatened the point of the sword at him.

He tensed and gathered his bearings. First, he closed his eyes and concentrated on his own body, meditating on the sensations that worked through his system. Warm. Content. A little sore at the middle. Not enough mana replenished as he'd hoped—hardly at all. Definitely not enough to shift his wings out. He frowned. Perhaps they hadn't slept as long as he'd hoped, or...

The warmth.

He cast his gaze around the tiny dugout. They were snowed in. Sunlight glowed against the snow casing surrounding their tree teepee. The fire was out. He was naked. She, almost. But they were warm.

He must have cast an insulation spell during the night. Perhaps that was why his personal well had not replenished. That and the shadow snake still binding him to the woman sleeping in the crook of his body.

His heart galloped in his chest at the awareness of their position, at her soft curves in repose, at the desire unfurling low in his belly. When he'd gone to sleep, it had been Violet at his back, not the other way around. That's the way he'd intended.

His arm was draped over her front, only a thin layer of fabric separating his hand from her breast. His brows raised. He'd cupped her during sleep?

He didn't dare move an inch.

Violet gave a sleepy moan and arched into him. He muttered some kind of curse as parts of him tingled that shouldn't. *Well preserve him.*

"Jesus. I fell asleep?" she mumbled, wriggling, unaware of the effect she had on him. She fumbled around for something. He'd be curious, except he couldn't focus on more than the hardness growing between his legs.

She stilled. "Um..."

Her hair tickled his face. More of that feminine scent drove into him, embedding deep, sparking something he'd never thought he'd feel. Mating instincts.

There was a reason vampires rarely mated. Males became protective, possessive, and passionate. To a point that defied logic. Even wolf shifters could not compare against a vampire in the throes of his mating hormones, or a female vampire in heat. Some called them rabid. Some called them insatiable. All Indigo knew was that if he gave in to the feelings bubbling inside him, bloodlust would be the least of his worries.

He'd never let her go.

She wasn't a vampire, she'd never understand, and since they weren't in a Well-blessed union, there would be no sense in submitting to these irrational desires. He had to cut it off now before it got worse.

"Indigo, if that's what I think it is, I swear to God..." she grumbled with a pointed wiggle of her bottom.

He let out a burst of air that turned into a haggard growl of warning. She had no idea the game she played at, or the caged monster she poked. His mother still talked about the day she first mated with his father and how she'd almost died—quite literally—from the intensity. Hours and hours they spent locked in a room. Days. She wasn't allowed to feed, or to even come up for air. Vampires failed to retain sustenance feeding from each other. So his mother and father had almost starved themselves, both lost in their haze of mutual passion and obsessiveness.

Violet wasn't a vampire.

She'd been damaged by them.

He swallowed.

Violet would never forgive him. She didn't even like him. She feared his kind. Hated them to the point of murder.

"Indigo?"

"Please don't move," he begged, squeezing his eyes shut. "Don't talk. Just give me a moment."

He wanted to invade her in every possible way. Every vampire mating urge was blending with the craving for her blood. He wanted to sink his teeth, his cock, and his soul in. He wanted to roll around in her blood and take everything she had to give. To drown in it. In her.

And more.

She recoiled in shock.

Must sense his desire, his urges.

He withdrew, wincing at the ache in his gut, but grabbed his battle leathers and then broke through the ice wall that had formed around the tree during the blizzard. The cold splash tempered his turmoil, but it didn't last long. He kept the insulation ward up, despite the cost to his mana stores. It was senseless to take it down when he didn't have enough mana to shift and fly.

With stiff and painful movements, he half-dressed then stood as sentry, face to the midday sun, welcoming the lethargy it placed on his cells, hoping to slow his cravings. He winced at the light. A fresh blanket of velvety snow sparkled, adding to the glare. The wound at his stomach had healed enough to carry on with their journey.

A rustle behind alerted him to her arrival. She shuffled over, nostrils flaring, and jutted her chin. The obstinate square of her shoulders was at odds with her dirty face. He had the feeling he could throw this woman naked into the Ring at Cornucopia, before thousands of unruly cheering fae, and she'd lift her head like a queen... no, like a goddess.

Her messy nest of dark hair triggered something primal in him. Was it messy because of the tachi battle, or had it gone awry from their co-sleeping, quite possibly from when he'd hunted with his nose? Every cell in his body rejoiced at the memory, begging for another inhale, wanting to go back to that fleeting moment when nothing else mattered but capturing her scent.

She belonged to him.

"What the hell is going on?" she demanded.

His eyes narrowed. "What do you mean?"

"You're acting cagey. I don't like it."

A smile tugged at his lips.

She jabbed her finger at him. "If you make fun of me for keeping us warm, I swear I'll cut off your—" Her eyes dipped to his crotch, to where his pants were partly open at the front placket. His jacket was unbuttoned, giving her a clear view of his naked torso. He certainly wasn't as perfect as Shade, or as bulky as Haze, but Indigo knew his aerial prowess gave him sculptured muscles that most envied. She clamped her mouth shut, a blush staining her cheeks. She averted her gaze but couldn't hide the wash of desire he'd felt down their bond. Irrefutable attraction.

He raised a brow. "You'll cut off what... my dick?"

"You're a *dick*head. And I hate you."

"No, you don't."

"Yes, I fucking do."

"No. You. Don't." He closed the gap, a step with every deepening syllable. "I know this, Violet, because that flash of light last night—it was your gift manifesting. You have mana pouring into you from every fiber around us. It's the life force that ties the world together." His finger trailed down her shoulder. "I can smell it on you. I can smell other more feminine parts of you, too. And when that scent flourishes along with the sensation of your desire down this bond, there's no point lying about it."

She stared at him.

He held her gaze for a moment, then deliberately let his attention trail down the length of her body, knowing what she looked like beneath the layers of clothes, imagining what she would feel like again... Imagining what it would be like to sleep next to her every single day. Or night. Or—

A cold, hard splash hit his face. He blinked rapidly as white snow fell from his lashes. She'd slapped him with a snowball. In the face.

"You just declared war, human." He pointed at her with a grin.

She backed up, expression stern, already packing another, and then ditched the ball at his head. He dodged.

"I will never submit to you, vampire. So you can just fuck—*oof.*"

Violet landed face first in the snow as he tugged on the shadow snake. He threw his head back and roared with laughter as she lay there, stunned and spluttering.

Indigo put his hand to his ear. "What was that? I can't understand you with your face in the snow."

She lifted her head, spat snow, and scowled. It looked like vitriol would spew from her mouth but she held it back with thinly veiled restraint. It was times like these he wished the shadow snake revealed more than bodily sensations. Lust and hate walked hand in hand, and he knew which one he wanted to cultivate more. But did she?

He kissed the air in her direction, which infuriated her further. Before she could add to the drama, he finished getting dressed and strapped on his baldric and swords. When he was done, he found her muttering to herself.

"Violet the Violent," he teased. "What's next, a tickle war?"

Her gaze snapped to his. "A thank you for saving your life would be nice."

A snort escaped him, but then he sobered at the thought. She had saved his life. It was likely true.

He touched his fingers to his lips and then pushed his hand down and out toward her in the hand sign for gratitude. "Your turn."

She scoffed and clenched her jaw, but hastily repeated the hand sign to him.

"So I saved your life, but I'm still your prisoner." She tugged on the shadow link.

"Mark my words, human." His tone lowered for effect. "You will remain linked to me until I deem you trustworthy, and saving my life because you would also die, is not an act of valiance. It's an act of selfishness. Until I see no more secrets in your eyes, we will forever remain attached."

Perhaps longer.

CHAPTER FOURTEEN

Violet hated the journey through Redvein Forest. Indigo claimed he hadn't replenished enough mana to shift his wings out because he'd sacrificed it to keep their insulation ward running, but she sensed he withheld details. There was more he wasn't telling her, but she couldn't really complain considering it felt like she walked through a cozy spring day instead of the icy cold forest.

The trek would take another couple of days at this rate.

After only an hour of walking, the intensity of Indigo's hunger pangs grew down the shadow link.

Violet gripped the aluminum in her pocket more times than not. The more she walked, the more guilt weighed heavy on her soul. Logically, she knew Indigo wouldn't kill her. Everything he'd done so far had been to keep her safe, or at the very least, deliver her safely to the Order. But that was the thing about anxiety... it didn't conform to logic. It itched and scampered beneath the surface, finding ways to break through until even the smallest possibility of her worst fears coming true was amplified.

If anyone tasted her blood, they'd know her secrets. If anyone found out her secrets, they'd find a way to force her to do things she didn't want to do. If she used her gift, she'd succumb to the lure or power like she did last time.

And people would die.

But this was why she became a slayer—to master her fear, to turn it upside down, and to own it. She'd told herself the pain was good. The pain and threat of imminent death from vampires was what she deserved. It kept her sane. It kept her alive. It kept her accountable.

She was just about to unclench from the aluminum when Indigo stopped. For a moment, she thought he'd caught the sound of the enemy, but he only looked at her grimly, squinting in the glaring sunlight. Perspiration dotted his forehead.

"I need to feed," he confessed.

Here we go.

Violet gripped the shard tighter. She waited. Ready. It wasn't a big piece of metal and would have been useless against the tachi, but maybe if she lodged it deep enough into Indigo, it would stay inside and cause him harm. Maybe.

He faced her, hunger in his eyes. But they weren't red. Not yet.

Indigo cocked his head, lifted his chin and scented the air in a way that was wholly inhuman. His brows knitted and then his gaze whipped to hers. He stalked closer, prowling with the grace of a predator. She backed up, stumbling over willow twigs and roots. The snow was thinner here. The trees were thicker, and the ground cover consisted more of woodland underbrush that had escaped much of the storm.

When her back hit a trunk, warmth trickled down her fingers. She'd cut herself on the metal. Tendrils of darkness spread from the shadow snake, growing to turn the small sheltered patch of woods into something more sinister.

Her heart forgot to beat.

It was stupid of her to believe he was cut from a different cloth than the vampires she'd hunted. He was coming for her, which meant he didn't care about consent. Any second now, and he'd take her blood, just like they all did.

She was starving as much as he was. No one had a right to—

His hand whipped out to her side and retrieved something from inside a hole in the tree trunk. White, furry, fluffy. A rabbit kicked its thumper feet like a jackhammer. Indigo met Violet's wide-eyed stare with steady consideration.

He said, "You should do something about that cut on your hand."

Then he proceeded to stroke the rabbit to calm it. Long, elegant fingers ran over the white fur from head to tail, then back again. He repeated this until the kicking stopped, and then he used his nose to run along fur as though seeking something. A vein, she realized.

Was that what he'd been doing in her hair when they'd awoken?

She flinched and looked away. She couldn't watch.

Indigo completely turned his back on Violet and walked away, his broad shoulders hunched over the tiny animal. When he returned, not five minutes later, the rabbit was still alive and the hunger she sensed down their link had lessened. Not diminished, but lessened from ravenous to bearable.

He held the fluffy thing between them. Its little feet dangled and thumped.

"You didn't kill it," she noted rather dumbly.

"Why would I? You're the one that needs to eat its flesh." He shuddered and dangled it from side to side, trying to entice her. "If you're hungry, take it."

He knew she was.

She glowered.

It was written all over his lying face. This was a challenge. A test of some sort. If only she knew what the correct answer was.

"Take it," Indigo repeated.

The rabbit blinked at her, its big eyes glistening.

"No," she replied. "I'll wait."

Faster than her eyes could track, Indigo was upon her, yanking her empty hand out of her pocket and holding it before his eyes ablaze with fury.

The rabbit hopped away, free.

Outraged, Indigo slowly brought her clenched fist to his face. He trailed his nose along the top of her hand, bumping over the knuckles.

Blood trickled down from her fist to her forearm to her elbow. But he paid it no attention. He kept his gaze locked firmly on hers. Some kind of recognition clicked behind his eyes.

"You've been very naughty, Violet." He flung her hand down and her heart raced. Wildness flashed in his eyes like lightning before the thunderstorm.

"Fuck you."

Her words were the button on his restraint. He came at her, all darkness and fright, pinning her arms to her sides. The smell of leather and male sweat invaded her senses. The snake snapped around her body, coiling tightly like a rope from her thighs to her neck. In an instant, she couldn't move. Completely at his mercy.

He reached beneath her cape and trailed a warm hand over her stomach, her hip pocket. He slipped those long fingers inside and scooped the aluminum out.

His brow arched, eyes full of disappointment.

She squeezed her eyes shut to hold the tears back. It was the guilt that did it to her, not the fact she'd been caught out. Guilt over fearing him when he'd saved her life. Twice. Guilt over knowing her gift was there and using metal to stifle it. Was there anything left of her conscience?

She clenched her jaw. This was a battle she had to fight. He didn't get to pass judgment. He, who was powerful. He, who made the shadows bend to his whim. He, who had never felt out of control in his life. He, who never had to prove anything or fear anything.

He stepped back and roared his frustration, trembling with emotion until the tendons in his neck popped with red rage. Shaking his head, he crunched the aluminum in his hand before setting it alight with some kind of blue fire. When the flames died down, he flicked molten metal from his hand into the snow, heedless of the pain in his hand.

"You lied. Again," he ground out.

"You have no idea what it's like for me." She pointed at him. "You don't get to judge me."

"Judge you?"

"You have all this power and no one thinks you're their next meal. You're the predator, not the rabbit. I'm the rabbit!"

He stepped closer, his nostrils flaring. "But you don't have to be. Don't you see?"

She choked up. "See what?"

"The metal stopped me refilling from the Well while we slept. The entire area was blocked, simply because you held the metal. No mana wanted to be near you, and since I had to sleep and walk next to you, I was blocked too. My free pass only works with my own weapons. The Well somehow knows what's mine. It always knows. You're single-handedly making this harder for yourself. For us." He hit his chest with his fist.

She frowned at what he'd said. Metal actively repelled mana, not just stopped it in its tracks? So she wasn't just harming herself, but others around her?

Indigo's voice softened. "Violet, I can teach you how to protect yourself."

"You're the problem!" she shouted. "You!"

He raised his voice to match hers. "I'm the solution. It's you humans who believe you're above the rules the Well has set, but you're not. If your past mistake has taught you anything, let it be that."

All fire in her system extinguished. She shut down. He just went there. Her next words tumbled quietly out.

"I get it. I can't have power if I hold metal, but it's my choice, isn't it? Maybe I don't want the gift. You fae from the Order all think you're so much better than everyone else. You Guardians think you're chosen or something. But you're not. You're just the lucky ones who survived the initiation ritual." She paused to take a deep breath. "I'm just the lucky one who survived. I'm not special."

I don't deserve a gift. I'll mess it up.

Nearby birds squawked and took to the sky. When the beating of their feathers died down, silence descended, and the look Indigo gave cut right to her heart. The snake uncoiled from her body and resumed its connection between their wrists.

"Do not attempt to hold metal again while you're in my presence," he said curtly. "Or the next time, I won't be so forgiving."

CHAPTER FIFTEEN

Within minutes of destroying Violet's hidden metal, Indigo felt his mana replenish at a noticeable rate. It was as though it had been waiting on the other side of the divide, pooling in preparation for release. But keeping him from replenishing wasn't what outraged him. It was her self-deprecating words.

For long minutes, they continued to trudge through the snow in silence, all the while his mind hurled questions at the omniscient Well, as though it could hear him and answer. Was this woman meant for him? Why else would he react so strongly around her? Why else would her blood taste like honeyed nectar? Why give her this power, this gift, only for her to throw it back?

Sometimes when he prayed, he imagined the Well as a sentient being—a presence reacting to his own emotions—a mythological goddess in the moon. Vampires believed the moon held power over water, over the tides, over the Well. So they often paid homage to it, to her. But his prayers were never answered. At best, it was like shouting into a ravine and hearing an echo.

Violet's outburst hadn't just been a victim lashing out at her captor, her words had cut cruelly to the core of his beliefs.

Every Guardian's initiation was different. They'd all entered the ceremonial lake and were dragged down by the Well Worms. They'd all had their souls stripped from them and judged. But none of them talked about what they saw during the moments they were judged. All Indigo knew was that they had different experiences.

He'd joined the Order because he thought it would be fun. He'd submitted to the Guardian initiation because he was reckless. He'd survived the ritual. The other six applicants had not.

He supposed it had made him cocky and maybe a little self-involved. The Well had picked him. He had to believe that because if it hadn't, then he wasn't special. He was just lucky.

He left his family because they'd been too focused on him finding a mate and changing the rules of vampire society. They'd wanted his support, and all he'd wanted was a purpose not of his parents choosing. If the Well didn't pick him, if he was just lucky, then he'd let down his parents for nothing.

By the time he'd harnessed enough mana to shift his wings out, he'd successfully stewed in his mind so much that he couldn't understand his thoughts. Another hour had passed, and he knew his stores had refilled abnormally fast, but he didn't want to focus on why.

He was tired. Mentally and physically.

The instant his wings snapped out, he gathered Violet into his arms and took to the sky. He didn't even smile when she jolted and clasped her hands around his neck with a squeal. Couldn't raise the humor at her discomfort, or her joy. She glanced up at him every so often while they flew, but all he managed to do was beat his wings and stare straight ahead.

She feared him.

Still.

That had been the purpose of her keeping the metal. What would she do if she ever found out he'd lost control once and killed because he couldn't stop feeding? He'd pulled his victim apart with his bare hands because he wanted to get to the deeper arteries.

Flying this way meant all he could smell was her. All he wanted was her. But she hated him. Feared him. She might never stop.

He wanted her; he realized. The way a male wants a female. The way a lost soul wants to be found. From the moment he'd seen her glittering eyes peeking over the windowsill at his parents' house, his blood sang with yearning. She needed to believe in him. To believe in the life Elphyne offered. And for that to happen, he had to prove to her that she was safe, that she was special, and that she was valued. Or he had to find a way to make her fight for it.

The sun was setting when he landed them in the yard of the outpost. Every muscle in his body ached. The snow here had thinned, but a crisp note still clung to the air as though it would be back tomorrow.

No stone wall surrounded the outpost, not like at the Order compound. Here the walls were the ocean and the forest. The island. The population was about fifty and the buildings consisted of a keep with a lookout tower, and a few smaller outbuildings scattered about, one of which belonged to the Cadre of Twelve should they have business in the north. Or the nightmarish Sluagh that made up the Six, but Indigo had never seen them there. Their purpose in the Order still remained a mystery to him, and everyone else as far as he was aware.

A Guardian sentry at the tower gestured in greeting to Indigo as he strode past the keep, Violet in tow. He took them straight to the small outhouse building the cadre occupied further into the estate.

Indigo burst through the front wooden door and halted in his tracks. Violet slammed into his back with an *oof*. He tensed as his senses picked up something. An intruder in the quaint four-bedroom home. In the living room.

Blood. Just a small amount. Someone was feeding.

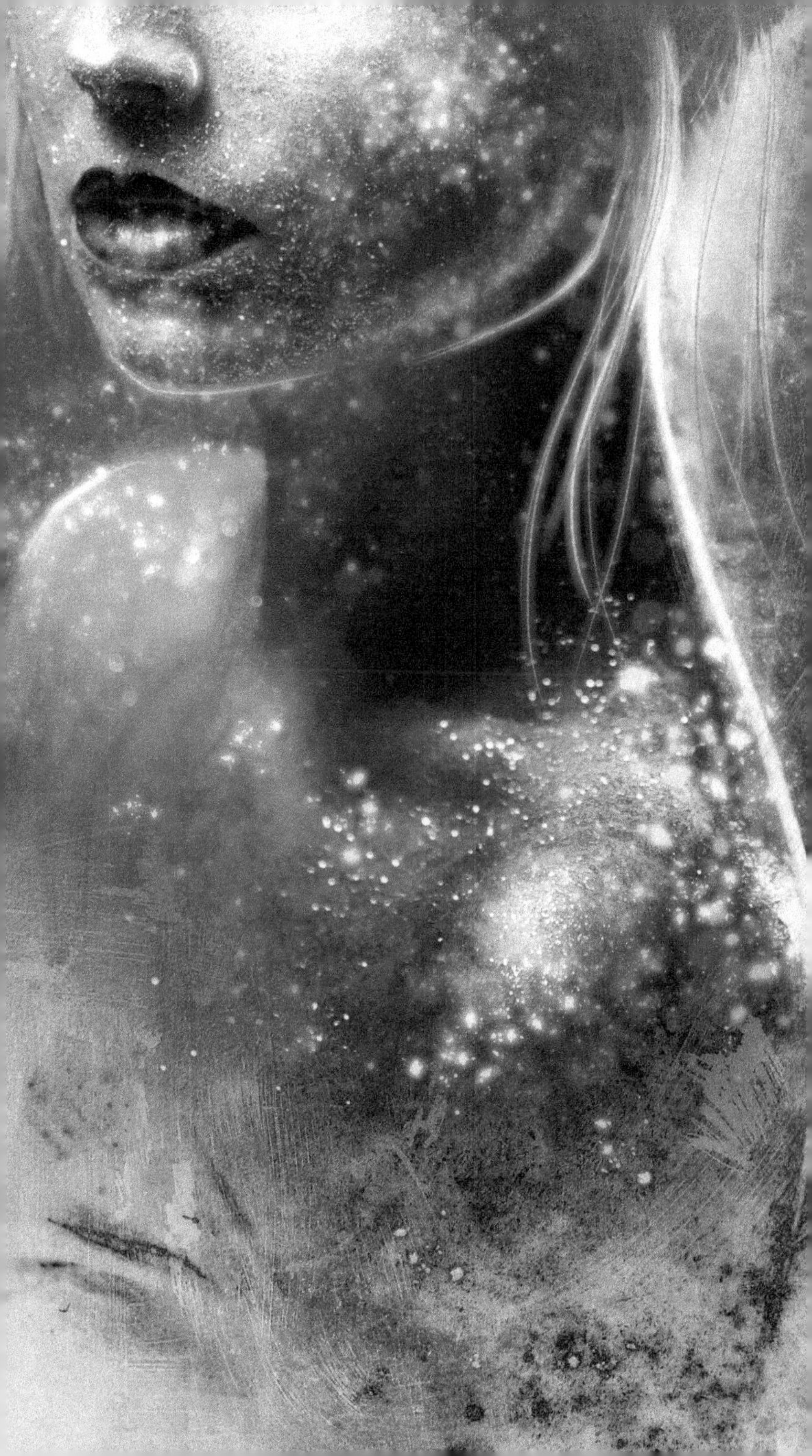

CHAPTER SIXTEEN

Some kind of wildness took over Indigo. It bled down their bond and coursed into Violet's veins, urging her own senses into alarm. It oozed from her every pore. She tried to stand back, but Indigo shoved her behind him and shielded her with his wings, backing them up until she hit a side wall of the foyer, almost knocking over a small table carrying various pieces of leather armor. Before shadow and darkness swallowed her whole, she glimpsed talons distending from Indigo's fingertips.

"Indi?" A deep, cultured voice came from somewhere nearby.

Indigo's low growl reverberated down his back.

Why would he behave like this... in his own home?

A feminine giggle floated into the room, and then a whine of protest as though she hated being interrupted. A low male grumble of regret. An order to stay put. Footsteps drew closer. Indigo's growling increased in decibel and rattle. Like him, Violet's hackles were up. She prepared to fight, anyway she could. Her eyes darted to the dagger clipped to Indigo's belt and she weighed her chances.

He said he'd not go easy on her next time she held contraband. She regretted the words she'd shot at him earlier, but the essence of them was true. She shouldn't have a gift from the Well. She'd proven power in her hands was destructible. The first chance she got, she should see to it that her gift never manifested. If that meant squirreling away metal on her person, then so be it.

"I'm in the middle of breakfast," the deep voice said, closer this time. His next words were laden with disapproval. "Indi, you clearly haven't been feeding yourself. Join me. There's plenty of Mage to go around."

Another vampire. She held her breath, eyes dipping to Indigo's dagger again.

"I'm fine," Indigo clipped.

"You don't look fine."

Violet couldn't help the snort escaping from her nose. So Indigo was like that with everyone.

"I..."

A scuffle. Violet's heart pounded. She itched to reach for Indigo's dagger, but instead, her hand did something strange. The turmoil she sensed from Indigo plucked at her heart. With a surge of compassion, she placed her palm between the vampire's wings, right on the rolling muscles locked hard and hot.

He shuddered. Tension visibly released from his posture.

Pity her own body didn't get the memo.

A soft light started to glow from beneath her skin, from her fingertips to her face. It started small, like budding fireflies, reflecting on Indigo's back. But the luminous flux swiftly grew to a glare that made her squint. Bright tendrils peeled off her skin and battled with Indigo's shadow. It was as though Violet could see into the fabric of life, to the threads of the weave itself. Her glow was a full body, every pore, light leak. And she was powerless to stop it. With every heartbeat, every hurried breath, it grew brighter, and brighter until—

Shadow surrounding Violet grew inexplicably darker, swallowing her light, dominating. Tendrils of black swarmed until a face and then the body of the most disgustingly handsome vampire Violet had ever laid eyes on appeared next to her, fitting between the shelter of Indigo's wings and the wall. Sensuous lips grinned knowingly at Violet, flashing a perfect set of teeth with two razor sharp fangs.

"Well, well," he purred, raking his hot gaze up and down her body. "Has our little Indi caught himself a glow toy? A night-light?" He squinted. "Maybe a glow bug."

In an explosion of movement, Indigo's wings contracted and disappeared altogether. His taloned fingers curled around the intruder's throat, fangs bared and hissing. He shoved the handsome Guardian against the wall.

A feminine squeak drew Violet's attention to a woman

standing at a doorway, hastily untying long wavy auburn hair and trying to cover the tiny puncture marks at her throat. Her Kingfisher-blue Mage's robe gaped open at the front, and her underdress was in disarray, the ties half undone.

Violet narrowed her eyes at the Mage. She didn't appear to be mesmerized against her will. She looked... flushed with excitement. Disheveled, but eager for more. The sight went against everything Violet believed about feeding. The Mage *must* have been mesmerized. Surely. Why else would she stay and not run?

"Shade?" the Mage said to the vampire pinned beneath Indigo's hand, a frown pinching her brow. A blue fireball sprung to life at her fingertips, ready for deployment. Her wide-eyed stare bounced between Violet's glowing skin and Indigo.

In her six years roving the Unseelie realm, it wasn't often Violet met a Mage. As far as she knew, most of them stayed cloistered at the Order, studying the effects of mana and the Well. Sometimes they ventured out to heal those rare fae that needed it and every time they did, Violet had been curious. Was this the closest fae vocation to her old profession? Would studying mana be similar to studying nuclear physics? She'd spent most of her days working, and her nights hunting. So she'd never had a chance to ask.

Maybe one day soon she would.

Violet shifted her gaze back to Shade. From the blue twinkling teardrop beneath his eye, he was definitely a Guardian. Except, where Indigo was playful and roguish, this one was sophisticated with a side of unabashed sex. Both were equal in body frame—broad shouldered, well-muscled, and tall. They seemed matched in every physical way, but from the unworried lazy stare of Shade, Violet believed he was the one with the power.

"It's all right, Sweetheart," Shade answered the Mage. "Indigo is overreacting."

"Oh. Okay then. As long as you have things under control."

Shade clicked his tongue. "Darling, you know I've always got things under control."

The Mage powered down her fireball and gestured to her throat. "I have to get back to work. If you're not done, perhaps it's wise if we take this to another room."

Shade then arched his brow at Indigo. "This is getting rather tiresome, Indi."

Indigo leaned closer until their noses almost touched. "Come near her again and I'll—"

"Are you threatening me?" Death entered the room on Shade's breath.

This was getting out of control. They were both Guardians. Weren't they on the same side? Violet put her palm on Indigo's arm, hoping it would have the same effect as before. He tore his gaze from Shade and met Violet's stare. An instant later, Indigo returned to himself. The savagery left his eyes. He let go of Shade and stepped back, taking Violet with him to a safe distance. Ten feet away, near another doorway.

Shade smoothed himself with precision until his

clothing and hair returned to rumple free. He gave Violet a look filled with humor and knowledge of things to come.

"You must be the Well-blessed human," Shade noted, eyes dipping to Violet's hand. "This makes sense now."

I'm so confused. None of this made sense. Instead of letting the vampires kill each other, she'd stepped in to... to what... save Indigo? Talk him down? Empathize with him?

Violet glanced down at the hand Shade had indicated, and her heart jumped into her throat. With her inner light dimmed, a new light had been born. Blue contour lines swirled and curved over her skin. They glittered like the ocean on a summer's day.

"What the hell is this?" She held up her hand. "Indigo?"

But his dark, wide eyes were locked on his own hand, glowing with identical matching markings, a small tilt to his lips.

Shade's deep, velvety laugh filled the room. Even the Mage smiled quietly.

"This isn't funny." Violet's brows slammed down. "What is this?"

Shade leveled serious eyes on Violet. "I suggest you feed him before he loses control. A vampire under the influence of mating hormones *and* starving at the same time isn't a pretty picture." A short, derisive snort burst out. "And you haven't even consummated the union. Good luck with that." Before he left to follow the Mage, he tossed a glance over his shoulder and met Indigo's stare. "The moment Haze gets back, I expect a full debrief."

"He's not back?" Indigo frowned.

Shade stopped. "You look surprised."

Indigo placed a hand on Violet's sternum. "He should be here."

She scowled at him.

"When you two are done sorting out that"—he gestured between Violet and Indigo—"and I'm finished with breakfast, we will discuss Haze."

Indigo refused to remove his hand from Violet's front for a full thirty seconds after Shade and his smiling Mage had left.

"What's he talking about, Indigo?" The mating? The feeding? And how on earth did Shade know they hadn't consummated their—whatever they were. Prisoner and captor! There would be no mating happening. None.

He had the decency to look contrite before cursing softly under his breath and rubbing his temples. "I didn't think it would be like this. Feeling each other's emotions." He glowered at his mating markings and then the shadow snake connecting them. "Both of them are amplifying each other."

"Vampires don't mate," she insisted.

Vampires *never* mated. She knew this because she'd been studying them for half a decade. They went through a rutting season for two months out of every year. The males hop promiscuously from bed to bed. Then once they beget a female with child, they were often kicked out of the roost so the females could raise their children in a colony together, hence why she found so many nomadic male vampires wandering the streets at night. Many of them ended in the royal service or shacked up in some kind of bachelor roost because they didn't know what to do with themselves.

But then again… Violet also believed vampires either fed by mesmerizing live prey, attacking them against their will, or feeding while they slept. None of that included consent, and dare she think it, enjoyment. She'd just seen a gorgeous, seemingly smart Mage willingly invite a vampire to drink more from her.

Violet chewed on her nails and then spat when she realized they were so dirty.

"Let's get you some food," Indigo grumbled.

CHAPTER SEVENTEEN

The kitchen was small and well stocked. No meat, but plenty of vegetables, herbs and grain. Four stone walls, a larder, a stove, and a wooden table laden with utensils.

Violet watched Indigo go to a basket of onions and pick one. "I don't know, is this good?"

Tension and confusion burst out of Violet in a sharp bark that one might construe as a laugh. Feeling ridiculous, she sighed and leaned her elbows on the wooden table, holding her face in her hands.

"What is my life now?" She shook her head and stared at the blue marks on her hand. Lines glittered just beneath her skin but, unlike the glow from before, she felt no heat from these. They were like a tattoo, or a map. "First I make the goddamned bomb that destroys life as we know it. Then I wake up thousands of years later, mauled and attacked by Wizard of Oz demon monkeys that turn out to be vampires. In hell. This is still it. It must be. I thought I was already doing penance. But I don't know anything, really. Maybe hell isn't real after all. Big, bat demonic vampires are just part of life now. And I'm mated to one. Apparently."

She laughed again, but this time, it was a crazed hiccup sort of laugh. As a scientist, she'd never believed in religion. She'd wanted facts. But her entire waking life in this time had moved beyond old beliefs. Fed by hunger, exhaustion, and the feeling that she spiraled out of control, hysteria set root and expanded in her body. Her laughter became hot, silent tears running tracks down her cheeks to drop darkly on the wooden tabletop. Great wracking sobs took over her body.

Her toes hurt.

It could be frostbite.

That made her cry more.

She couldn't remember the last time she'd cried this hard. Or was she still laughing? No, crying. Definitely crying now. She hadn't cried this hard when she'd learned the outcome of her old vocation. Not when multiple sets of fangs tore into her. Not when the damned goblin supervisor whipped her on the first day for spilling a wheelbarrow of debris on his feet. Not when the very thing she'd lived to hate had saved her life and captured her.

But now?

Why now?

She was still his prisoner. Worse. She was at the mercy of some kind of mating union—a special blue-marked mating that everyone seemed to accept at face value. They didn't care who she was, or what crimes she'd committed in the past. Apparently because the Well accepted her, they would. Shade didn't care that she was a human and Indigo was a vampire.

Another breath gushed from her lungs, releasing more tension, and she eased back to stare between her arms at the slate floor. The sudden exhale slammed a realization into her. Why on earth would she drop her guard like this? Crying in front of a vampire, for heaven's sake. A distant part of her brain screamed at her to be wary—to watch the predator who seemed to be taking over more parts of her life every minute of the day.

But a louder part of her brain, the one linked to her heart, had begun to... to... be okay with it. It was part of that shifting of the horizon. Just when she thought it would stop, the ground moved again.

Then again, maybe this crying was something altogether different. Maybe it was because she was, dare she think it, finally safe. Tears welled anew at the thought. Indigo was willing to attack his own kind, his brother in arms, to protect her. He would never feed from her if he knew it caused her pain. She knew this with absolute certainty because the new mating bond linked them emotionally. He would hurt himself if he hurt her. Even without that rationality, there was something indescribable building in her gut. Trust.

Maybe she could finally sleep.

The notion paralyzed her.

Six years.

It had been six long years since she'd slept soundly. Did she dare to hope there was a chance things would be different? That she'd have her very own monster to protect her from others? To help her make things right?

An onion rolled on the slate floor and hit her dirty, threadbare boot.

"Don't like the stinky things?" Indigo's voice pierced her fractured mind. "That's cool."

She glanced up through puffy eyes and caught his completely beguiled and bewildered expression. His left cheek popped as his lips squished to the side in thought. She tried to hold it in, but the look of earnest coupled with confusion had her bursting into another fit of laughter. This time, it was real mirth that warmed her from top to toe. When his pointed ears twitched in chagrin, she doubled over, clutching her middle.

He muttered darkly, "I had thought seeing you smile would, I don't know, make my day. But now I'm not so sure I like being the butt of your joke."

Violet wiped her nose with the back of her dirty sleeve. Unable to form words, she moved her fist in a circular motion over her heart, hand-signing her apology. Something she never thought she'd do to a vampire, but this was a week for firsts. And the action somehow soothed her enough to say, "It's just, I'm tired. This is all... so unexpected. And confusing."

"What about this?" He held up something that looked like a zucchini.

She smiled gently and took it from him. "Perfect."

Bolstered, he went around the room opening boxes and drawers, pulling out random vegetables and sacks of grain.

"What about this?" Something round and small.

Violet squinted at it. "A potato?"

"If you say so."

"We have to cook it."

He shuddered in disgust and then tossed it to her. "You can do that."

She laughed again. Why was this funny? Why was seeing the domestic habits of a creature she'd once hunted so funny? He kept moving about the room, pulling out items of food to garner her reaction, as though, despite his words to the contrary, he chased her smile. She *felt* it—an echo of his eagerness to please her filtered down their new bond.

Did he do it because he hated sensing her sadness, or did he hate sharing her hunger? Maybe. But her intuition said his reality was shifting just as much as hers was. He probably never expected to be paired with a human from the old world. This vampire. Her enemy.

Somehow, they managed to source enough food to make a vegetable soup. While it bubbled away on the stovetop, Violet sat down on a stool beside the kitchen counter and waited. And watched the shadow snake clinging to the both of them. The head part was wrapped around her wrist. It smirked at her.

"So... mated," she eventually said. "What does that actually mean?" He raised an incredulous brow, so she quickly added, "I don't need the mechanics of physical mating explained, but I'm talking about this marking. This blue bond. How is it different to the snake and what does this mean for me? Am I still a prisoner?"

Indigo poured the steaming soup into a bowl and pushed it before her. Then he stood back and met her eyes, studiously staring until she picked up the spoon.

"I suppose we don't need the shadow link anymore." He glanced down at the snake dangling between them. It sprung to life and slithered back to him, wrapping around his torso before disappearing beneath his jacket collar and settling on his skin like a tattoo, peeking at her from his neck. "It's not like you can leave this island."

She watched him warily.

"Don't look so surprised," he said. "Even if you somehow managed to get beyond the sea surrounding us, our bond connects our souls. I can sense you like a moon-beam in the dark."

Violet contemplated her soup. What would she do anyway if she escaped? Go back to hunting vampires? It had left her decidedly hollow and unfulfilled. Maybe she could search for Peaches or Silver. She blew on a spoonful before sipping the surprisingly flavorsome liquid. Her stomach clenched in knots, rejoicing at being fed. She stopped eating after halfway and placed her spoon down.

"All of it," Indigo demanded.

"What?"

"Eat all of it."

"I'm not hungry."

"Bullshit."

"Excuse you! Your shadow snake isn't linking us. You don't know what my stomach feels."

He placed his palms on the table and leaned closer, staring through long dark lashes. "Unlike the shadow snake which connected our physical sensations, the Well-blessed bond shares our mana and emotions. I can tell you feel guilty about something. Eat. Or there will be consequences."

Fury simmered beneath her skin, but a little thrill skipped in her blood at the idea of what his consequences would entail. And when she realized her mind had almost taken a dirty dip, she finished the soup as per his watchful gaze.

"What about you?" she asked, pushing the empty bowl away.

"I'm fine."

"You should hunt. Or at the very least go and find that pretty Mage. She seemed willing."

She hadn't forgotten Shade's warning, or that he'd suggested Violet be the one to feed Indigo. She always thought she'd be disgusted if it came to that, but Indigo didn't feel like all her other experiences. He was warm. He worried about her hunger. She hadn't balked at Indigo's face nuzzling into her hair while they'd slept. She hadn't flinched at his embrace. And she hadn't run screaming for the hills when she felt his arousal pressing into her rear.

No... she'd felt—

With effort, Violet forced her mind to blank and

wrenched it back to reason. Indigo needed to feed. Having him turn into some sort of blood-hungry beast that could sense everything she felt was not an option. Heat flushed her face and she reached for an errant potato to toy with.

"I'll feed soon," he grumbled. The flex of his stubbled jaw gave away nothing but stubborn pride as he casually tossed the bowl into a porcelain sink for cleaning. "But first we need to get cleaned up and start teaching you how to manage your gift. Then I can debrief with Shade. We need to figure out what the hell happened to Haze."

Her gaze snapped up. "Who's Haze?"

"He is one of the Twelve, and along with Shade, he is closer than a brother to me. You saw him at Obscendia."

"Why did you say *we* need to figure it out?"

"Violet." His voice deepened, his expression turning serious. "From here on out, it's always going to be we."

Her fingers clenched around the potato, then eased.

He grimaced at a wet cleaning cloth and dropped it, muttering something about disgusting habits of foodies.

"Come on. Let's train," he said.

"For what?"

"Can't very well have my mate blinding everyone when she gets afraid." His lips curved suggestively. "Or blinding me when she's excited."

Violet threw the potato at his head.

CHAPTER EIGHTEEN

Indigo took Violet to the only source of power on the island—a small hot spring nestled between the forest and a rocky snow dusted outcrop. It was the kind of landscape he thought may have been a volcano once, but the surrounding mountain had flattened and all that was left of the hills and valleys were the springs and shiny rock. During the day, the water was crystal clear turquoise. At night, it glowed with the bioluminescent life synonymous with the Well.

Violet's outburst in the kitchen concerned him. A lot had happened to her in a short period of time, and the woman may keep returning to the brave face she wore like a mask, but with the new Well-blessed bond linking their emotions, he knew her scars ran deeper than the bite marks on her skin.

He stopped at the edge of the spring and dropped the towels in his arms before unclipping his bloodstained baldric. The two swords clattered as they met the ground. Then he removed his belt. Next were the small weapons cached around his fighting leathers. The knuckleduster. A dagger.

She eyed him with suspicion from beneath the cowl of her dirty cape.

"I know I apparently have zero choice about this blue-marked mating, but I'm not bathing with you. So just forget about it."

Next was his jacket. With nothing beneath, the frosty air nipped at his skin, causing him to suck in his abdominals, but he plowed onward. He toed off his boots, and then hooked his thumbs in the belt loop, regarding her coolly. While she made valiant efforts to keep her eyes on his face, he could feel her uncertainty, her curiosity and, yes, cautious attraction. And when he gathered his shadow around himself, essentially rendering him invisible, he felt her surprise.

The pants came off, and he stepped naked into the water, hissing at the heat. He waded to thigh high and then swam until he reached a chest high depth a few feet in. When he turned back to the shore, she stood with her arms folded, glaring at the ripples he'd left behind.

Well-blessed mate or not, she was not ready to be left alone. She still had the look about her of a stunned deer right before it bolted.

"The water is warm," he called out. "Come in."

"So you can see me, but I can't see you. That's hardly fair."

"Don't like it? Use your gift to chase the shadows away."

She stuck out her chin and folded her arms.

So he peeled off a piece of shadow and sent it slithering toward her over the water. Disbelieving eyes watched the darkness move, carving a path through the liquid, disturbing the heat-loving aquatic life. When the shadow reached her feet, he said, "Last chance. Summon your gift and get in."

He would have accepted at least an attempt to undress, but she remained stoically stubborn. So the shadow snake lashed out, connecting with her ankle. He swam backward, just a little. The tension pulled taut. She stumbled, the hood of her cape fell back, revealing dark tangles of hair and a dirt-streaked face. A warrior princess, cut from stone but weathered by tears. To Indigo, she was the perfect choice for him. Unbending. Resilient. The kind of female who would join him wherever life would take them. The kind who would take him places too. The moment the Well-blessed bond had hit, he'd stared at his blue marks with a profound sense of rightness. The Well hadn't failed him. His instincts had run true. And he wouldn't make the mistake of doubting them again.

He tugged the shadow snake.

"You bastard," she bit out, resisting the pull, eyes searching blindly for his hidden form, but he made no other movement in the water. "You're going to drag me in whether I'm undressed or not."

"Your gift is a mirror image of mine, Violet. I use

shadow to conceal. You can use light to misdirect. Either blast your light like you did before and chase the shadows away, or direct your glow to conceal your body."

"I told you I don't want this." She lifted her blue twinkling hand.

He tugged. She stumbled another step, her boots hitting the shore with a splash.

"Whether you want it or not doesn't matter. You have it. And you have a responsibility to use it wisely."

"I'm choosing nothing. Just leave me alone."

The panic hammering him down their bond caused alarm, but he kept pushing. She couldn't run from this.

"The queen won't leave you alone. The human leader won't leave you alone. Gastnor won't leave you alone." He moved closer to the bank and flicked his fingers in the water, splashing her. "If the families of the vampires you murdered ever find you, they won't leave you alone."

Eyes glittering with defiance glared back at him.

"There she is," he said, lips curving. "Don't hide her away. Use her. She's magnificent."

The stubborn woman folded her arms and inspected the blue marks on her hand. Thinking hard, her brows puckered in the middle. She glanced over at him—or in the direction he'd splashed from—and sighed. Her capitulation eased into him like the smooth flow of water around them, and when her fingers went to untie the loops at the neck of her cape, he dipped beneath the surface to gather his composure.

This was a training exercise.

But it was also an exercise in restraint. His. He'd been given what he'd wanted. A mate more beautiful and clever than he'd ever dreamed of, but she was also the most alluring thing since the invention of blood. When he resurfaced, she stood on the shore in her undergarments, hesitating and hugging herself.

The moonlight turned the bite marks on her flesh to slivers of silver. They went from her neck, to her arms, to thighs and then feet. Only her torso remained smooth and wound free. The more Indigo inspected the scars, the more he thought, perhaps, his earlier assumption had been wrong. The bites weren't from her using herself as bait. They were old. Years old. Had they happened all at once?

The image of Gastnor's furious attack on her caused his chest to constrict.

He dropped his shadow concealment and her eyes immediately met his.

"Why does the Captain of the Queen's Guard want you dead?" He listened to her reaction down both their bonds.

Fury. Hatred. Disgust. Fear.

"What's next for the training?" she asked.

"You're changing the subject. Answer my question, Violet."

"Is there any way we can reverse this mating thing?"

So stubborn.

"Why are you so against this bond?" His voice lowered to almost inaudible as his eyes dipped to the scars on her body. "Against me?"

He thought she'd finally reveal where her hatred for his

kind came from, but she only took a deep breath and exhaled, then sat on the shore, dipping her toes into the warm water. Shivering from the cold air, she stared at her feet and answered in a way he never expected.

"I'm not a good person, Indi. I devoted my old life to building weapons of mass destruction. Do you understand what that is? I suppose you can call it magic so big and strong, it wipes out the realm in a single hit. But then, by some sheer strike of luck, I survived. I came here and do you think I did something good? No. I spent my time killing every vampire I could get my hands on.

"I'm not stupid. I know I've discriminated against your race and I know how wrong that is. I don't deserve this. I don't deserve you." She punched the silt at her side. "I don't understand how the Well chose me. It defies logic."

Indigo considered her words and swam a little closer. He needed to understand more about where she was coming from. "What was your world like? I mean, why did you feel the need to invent these weapons?"

"My world was so much bigger than this." Tears brimmed in her eyes. "It was beautiful. Chaotic. Not magic, but so full of life. It's why this is even more incomprehensible. I don't think there are more than a million humans or fae left in this world, but in my time, there were *seven thousand* times that amount. We had millions more hectares of land and ocean. I guess I got into nuclear physics mainly because we were all trying to outdo each other. Everyone was trying to be bigger and better."

"And who were you trying to be better than?"

"My dumb brothers and father. The government was just throwing money at this industry, and only the biggest and brightest people succeeded in it. I thought that's what I had to do to get my father's respect, but as it turned out... I wasn't the only one trying to shine brighter. Everyone—every man, woman, and child—we all competed against each other. We were all fighting for space, fighting to be heard among the noise on our big, giant planet." She picked at her underclothes, frowned, and then hugged her knees, shivering. "But I think we all ended up screaming into the darkness. No one heard because we weren't listening to each other."

"It seems to me you understand the toll of your actions like no one else can."

"That's because I'm part of the cause!"

"And you sound like exactly the kind of person the Well should pick."

She stared at him. Blinked. "No, I'm not."

"You're someone who understands the loss, and will do anything to prevent it from happening again. Am I wrong?"

She frowned and looked away, studying the glowing reeds alight with natural mana as they swayed in the night breeze. A little water sprite slid down the reed, dancing and twirling about, curiously watching until it plopped in the water and disappeared.

"I've killed, Indigo," she muttered sadly.

"So have I."

"Not at this level."

"That depends on who you're talking to."

"Being Well-blessed means I've been *gifted.* Rewarded. I just... I can't accept it."

"Why?"

"Because then—" She choked up. "I get away with it. I messed up then. I messed up now. I make bad choices, so why should I receive something this important? It's not right."

He yanked on the shadow snake until she tumbled into the water, under clothes and all. He kept pulling as she spluttered, trying to catch her breath and adjust to the sudden heat of the springs. When she made it to him, submerged to the shoulders, she hit him. Small fists glanced off his wet chest.

Seeing how ineffectual her attack was outraged her, and she tried it again. This time, with an elbow to the nose. Blinding pain burst in his face, but he captured her wrists and held them hovering in the air between them. Staring deeply into her eyes, he projected calm down their bond until the heaving of her breath slowed. Her calming became a visible thing. The pain in her eyes turned soft. The tension in her shoulders eased. The sight was probably as rare as catching sight of the mythical Elfant. And he wanted to see more.

Uncurling her fist, he brought her fingertips to his cheek and traced them along the glittering blue Guardian marking. The twinkle reflected in her eyes.

"Do you know what this symbolizes?" he asked.

She shook her head.

"Me neither."

A sharp laugh shot out of her and she slapped him playfully with her other hand. He grinned, loving this side of her, but kept her fingers to his face.

"None of us truly know," he said. "But we've made assumptions. Some at the Order believe this symbol is a tear the Well sheds for the lives Guardians must take in order to keep the peace and protect its integrity. But there are some of us, mainly the Guardians ourselves, who believe it's a reminder that there is pain in the world. That there is suffering. That without it, we wouldn't know joy. Do you understand?"

"It sounds like hippy mumbo jumbo."

"I don't know what that is, but I do know you didn't kill those vampires because of some sick warmongering desire." He trailed his fingers down her scar riddled neck. Hesitant at first, but when she didn't stop him, he took his time exploring, learning the texture of her skin. "Nor did you kill them out of revenge."

"You don't know anything about me."

"Ah, but that's where you're wrong." His blue-marked hand clasped hers. "I've been listening from the moment this connected. There is a sadness about you, Violet. And a defiance. You don't think you're worthy, but you're trying to be. My bet is you slayed because you believed you were saving lives. Maybe you even thought it was to save your human brethren... or some close friends."

She pulled her hand away.

"You've been chosen, Violet, because you have suffered, and you have caused it. You know how precious life is. You've looked death in the face and it changed you."

"I don't know if it's that simple."

"Maybe not. Maybe you're just some person that was in the right place at the right time. But the question remains the same."

"What's that?"

"What will you do with your power now? Will you shout into the darkness, or will you listen?"

She bit her lip, anguished. He wanted to reach for her again but held back. What he had to say next wouldn't be welcomed.

"There is more to the story of your world's death than you know. You may have built your bomb, but another set it off. Violet, this man who destroyed your world is alive today. He wants you for himself. Clarke has *seen* it. She's also seen that Maebh is after you, and—"

"Stop. Just stop."

His jaw clicked shut.

"I've never met this woman, Clarke. How am I supposed to believe you?"

"You know it's the truth in your heart. I can't lie to you."

They shared another silent stare, both swimming in and out of their emotions, trying to clear the murkiness. Violet was the first to look away, and when she did, she lowered herself into the water and lifted her gaze to the starry sky.

"He's here too... the man who dropped the bombs. How can that be fair?"

"It's not. But it makes more sense why you've been brought back too."

She snorted, still refusing to look at him. "It just means we're both lucky."

"No. It means he cheated. And the Well wants your help to make it right."

More silence. It looked like she floated in stars, the reflection was so clear. She glowed softly without even realizing it. Like the moon.

Indigo's chest constricted and he found it hard to breathe. This woman. This goddess. His.

"Let's say I believe you," Violet said. "Let's say I want to help stop this mad man. How do I listen?"

His eyes crinkled. "You've already started."

"How?" She stretched her arms out and trailed them over the water, swirling the stars.

"You gave up metal and you were rewarded with power. Is that not telling you something? Is that not a conversation worthy of your ears?"

"Yes, it is," she admitted. "But technically, you took the metal from me. And wanting power is what got me into this mess in the first place. My family was hard to impress. My father was into sports, and my two brothers were stars. I couldn't compete. All I was good at was science, and the only way to grab their attention was to do something I thought was, I don't know, macho or something. It's stupid now that I look back at it, but back then, I didn't care. I just wanted to be better than them. To beat the bastards. To join them. I wanted to fit in."

"How about we start small? With a little more glow."

She swam to meet him. "Okay."

"Okay?"

She met his eyes and nodded.

"Then there's only one thing left to do." He looked pointedly at her glistening skin, specifically the undergarments she'd failed to remove, and clicked his tongue with disapproval. She was too stubborn to learn to glow without the right motivation. "That needs to come off."

CHAPTER NINETEEN

Violet almost laughed in Indigo's face. And the simple fact that she did meant she'd made the right choice in trusting him. In joining him. She could joke around with this vampire. This enemy. This... mate of hers. It hadn't escaped her notice that she should be feeling furious about it all, or at the very least averse to the idea she was now irrevocably linked to a fanged fae.

But spending time with him felt good, like dusting off cobwebs from a favorite rocking chair. Familiar. Easy. As warm as the waters they soaked in. How could this be wrong?

With each passing second, Violet realized Indigo wasn't smiling. He was deadly serious as he floated half submerged, his chin dipping low in the water, watching her. He reminded her of a crocodile. Sharp teeth just waiting to snap and drag her under.

Instead of fear, nervous excitement tickled her veins.

She cleared her throat. "And exactly how does being nude help with my training?"

He answered as though he'd been waiting for it. "Motivation."

She snorted, putting the pieces together. "So let me get this straight. You think that if I'm nude, I'll be so embarrassed for you to see me, that I'll summon my gift. Just like that. Training done."

Instead of answering her question, he stared some more. It felt as though nothing separated them. He emerged enough to talk.

"Do you know how vampires learn to fly?" he asked.

She shook her head.

"When I was two, my mother took my brother and me onto the roof of our roost. Back then we didn't have the resources of an entire colony the way most vampire families do. We were an unconventional family unit because our parents were mated, and so were ostracized by much of the community. We struggled to make ends meet without colony support and my parents had little time to teach us the ways of life, so mother took us to the roof and left me with Demeter to finish my training. The moment she left, he pushed me off. The first time I broke ten bones in my body."

"You were two!"

"The second time, I broke six."

"Indigo."

"The third time, I flew. And I learned to fly faster than anyone else in our town. I can still fly rings around any winged fae in the Order."

"So you want to push me off a roof?"

He bit his smile. "I want instinct to guide you, as it did with the tachi. If you're concerned about me seeing you without your clothing, then naturally you'll shield yourself."

The water parted for her as she pushed toward him and then stopped, inches away. "Seems logical... except for one thing."

"Which is?"

"You're assuming I *don't* want you to see me naked."

Her words hung suspended. The air grew thicker by the second as his arrogance dissipated like the swirling steam coming off the water. Despite the night, bioluminescent glow illuminated their faces enough for her to catch indecision in his eyes. The questions... the hope. The uncertainty. Or was that what she sensed down the bond?

His hair collected icicles as he'd not dipped beneath the water for some time. The same frost gathered on the tips of his pointed ears and his facial scruff. He needed a shave, but she... liked it. It made him messier. Disheveled. More like her.

Violet's gaze dipped to Indigo's wet lips as they curved into a smug, sensual smile. He was too clever to fall for her misdirection.

"Glow, Violet."

She splashed him. "Make me."

Another exciting dip in her stomach.

What was she doing? Flirting?

His movement was quick, deft, displacing mist the only sign. A strong hand wrapped around her neck. A thumb pressed against her throat. Water dripped from his arm, swirling more mist into eerie patterns.

"This could be your last breath," he warned as he studied her. "*Glow*."

Violet's heart rate remained steady, and it surprised her as much as him. "You won't hurt me."

She glimpsed fangs as he watched where his thumb swiped against her pulse point. "I could bite you right here. Then lap at your blood as it spills into the water."

His touch was a hot brand against her skin. It set her on fire. Every inch of her body became hyperaware, hypersensitive, and aching for more... of him. Warm water caressed her naked skin. One step closer and they'd be touching down the length of their bodies.

"But you won't," she repeated with an unavoidable shiver.

He applied a small amount of pressure, blocking her airway. "I could drown you."

"Your scare tactics aren't working," she rasped. This should frighten her, but it didn't.

Her nipples peaked. Heaviness pulsed between her legs, and a small moan slipped from her lips. With a wingless naked vampire in this pool of water, surrounded by magical lights, she didn't feel so different. So alone. So on the wrong side.

"Why isn't this working?" he muttered, a slight frown marring his brow as his thumb pressed against her airway, teasing. "I thought you were afraid of me."

She pushed into him.

"Maybe I want you to hurt me," she rasped, shocked at her own words.

The night became so deathly silent, even the wind forgot to breathe. The stars forgot to pulse, and the moon disappeared altogether.

She couldn't understand it herself. Maybe it was punishment. Maybe it was the only way she knew how to be. Maybe it would be freeing.

Master the pain.

The pressure at her throat was suddenly gone. He'd moved again, too fast. Needles pierced her scalp as he clenched, roughly catching in her nest of hair. Her lips parted. Her eyes widened. And he tilted her head back, exposing her neck.

Yes.

This was what she needed. This chased the nightmares away. Something sensuous over the scars.

Would it hurt? Could she face the fear and turn it around?

A small guttural sound and he lunged inward, claiming her neck with his mouth. But there was no pain. No piercing of the flesh. Just hot, wet tongue probing and licking, rolling and suckling over every inch of exposed flesh.

From her collarbone, up the neck tendon, to where he devoured below her ear. Ravenous. Starved. Indigo pressed her lower back until their hips met and his arousal dug into her.

Her knees buckled and she clutched at him, nails scraping, wanting more. More.

Hot lips slid along her jaw, mumbling something, tickling. The deep rumbles made their tryst all the more elicit. Baritone vibrated to her core, shaking everything up. She gasped, arching into him, pulling him closer.

"Bite me," she blurted. "Make it hurt."

More mumbling against her flesh, and then... he pulled away, disoriented.

Violet tensed. Her words echoed in her mind. *Bite me bite me bite me.* And with each passing second of silence, of inaction, anxiety knotted her stomach. *Make it hurt.* Wind pushed against her skin, reminding her of how exposed she was. This was...

Her eyes darted about, landing on the glowing reeds, the rocks, the sky. Anywhere but him. She tried to push him away, to hide the heat burning her face.

She'd not taken a lover in this time. At first she'd thought it was the fear, the trauma of what had happened to her. But she'd tried to get into bed with a few male fae. She'd tried. No one had excited her enough. She'd ended up stopping things before it got too heated. It had all felt like dirt until now. Until this thrill, this dancing with the enemy who wasn't an enemy.

Violet pressed her palms against Indigo's chest, but he

held her steady. No words, just watching her, branding her lower back with strong, unyielding hands. She pushed him again. And again. Harder. Rougher. Water splashed. Icicles fell from his hair, from the tips of his pointed ears, but he remained steady. Unfazed. She thrashed and snarled, raking her nails down his skin.

"Do something!" she shouted. *To me. Do something to me.*

He dunked them beneath the water. Warmth surrounded her like an embrace. Everything quieted. The night. Her mind. Her soul. Glittering patterns of blue glanced off the hard planes of Indigo's face. His hair splayed and drifted about, his eyes echoing her anguish. Tiny ribbons of red curled from his cheeks—where she'd scratched him.

Her eyes burned, and she wasn't sure if it was the water, or something else.

She wanted to gasp, but couldn't. The water was a straightjacket.

But he kept her down until her heart finally slowed to a steady thud. He lifted them to break the surface. Air burst into her lungs. They stared at each other for a long time, the steam rising to kiss their skin. He cupped her face, angling in closer. He hesitated, only a second, and then he kissed her. Slow, sensuous, and something else. Something she wasn't prepared for. Gentle. Tender. A sweep of his tongue against her teeth. A slide into her mouth. An affectionate suck on her bottom lip.

A kiss worthy of someone who deserved it.

It hurt more than any physical pain. Her heart burst. Violet pulled away just before an amused, masculine voice slid into earshot.

“Oh, come on. Don’t stop on our account.”

CHAPTER TWENTY

Darkness exploded, enshrouding Violet.

It was as though a blanket had been dropped. Not a blanket. Leathery wings. Indigo's.

Someone was here at the springs—*someones*—and her vampire had protected her dignity.

Violet's heart thudded hard. The lust running through her veins turned to pure adrenaline. Indigo's wings had sprung into being and wrapped around them so fast, she'd had no time to see who the voice belonged to, but from the way every muscle in Indigo's body tensed and twitched with violence, he wasn't welcome.

Indigo looked down at her, the whites of his eyes showing, his lashes spiked, his top lip curled to bare fangs. The sheer panic bleeding from him incited her own.

"What are you doing here?" Indigo snarled, turning his attention back to the intruders.

"Making pancakes." A snort of derision.

The sound of something hitting the snowy ground made every hair on Violet's body stand on end. What was happening?

"Take another item off and it will be the last thing you do," Indigo threatened.

"Wait. You're kidding, right?" said another male. "We all use this power source."

"River's right. You don't own it."

"Fucking crows," came another deep grumbling voice. Footsteps crunched. This voice had a deep gravelly snarl to it. Animalistic. "Always need to start shit."

Another set of footsteps joined the first. A masculine, labored sigh. Violet could see none of it. She was plastered to the length of Indigo's warm, hard body while hidden within the cocoon of his wings. The scent of male sweat mixed with minerals became her world. No one could see her and all she could see was a solid, smooth chest glowing softly blue from the marks on her arm.

She pushed ineffectively against him, but he wrapped his arms around her tighter.

She pushed again, this time adding a twist in an attempt to face the gap between his wings as they crossed over her back. "Lemme see."

Indigo sank into the water and released the pressure on his wings, just a little, then spun her and wrapped them back up. At least she could see. They must look ridiculous. Two heads sticking out of a pod submerged in water.

But, strangely, the pressure made her feel safe. Like a weighted blanket.

On the shore were four Guardians in their black battle leathers. Two crow shifters perched on top of a rocky outcrop. One had glossy black wings, the other's were tipped in blue. Next to them stood a tall, tanned warrior with his hands on his hips. Shoulder length auburn hair revealed fur-free pointed ears where it was tied back. A furious silver-haired wolf shifter stood next to him with his arms folded.

Violet gasped as she noticed the blue Well-blessed mating marks glowing at the cuff of his leather jacket on one hand, and up near his neck. He stared at the most heavily tattooed crow shifter who, in turn, sneered at Indigo as though he had just riled a mouse, not a vampire. From the smug expression on his face, Violet guessed he was the one who'd spoken first.

The crow shifter with blue-tipped wings—must be River—continued to undo the bone studs down the middle of his jacket. He flexed his shoulders and the wings snapped shut before disappearing all together. A single feather floated into the water. River's jacket was halfway off before Violet realized he intended to join them in the springs.

The shadows grew inexplicably darker. A low rumble vibrated against Violet's back, coming from deep within Indigo.

"Thorne is right, River," the auburn-haired elf said,

glancing at Violet, then Indigo. He stepped back and lifted calloused palms. "We'll come back later."

River unbuckled his belt. "I'm not going anywhere. I just spent my stores wrangling a damned naga and my balls are freezing off. I need the springs."

His tattooed companion, still crouched on an outcrop of rock, remained sneering at Indigo, as though he was more interested in his reaction than anything else. Wind caught a lock of his medium-length loose curls, revealing eyes like sapphires.

None of the Guardians were afraid of the vampire at her back slowly drawing power from their surroundings. They should be. His fury and blind rage bubbled into her. It choked, wanting to take over. Gritting her teeth, she fought the urge to rip shreds through the intruders.

It's not me, she told herself. *It's not my emotions. It's his.*

"Cloud," the elf clipped a warning to the tattooed Guardian.

"*Forrest,*" Cloud mocked back.

River rolled his eyes.

Cloud turned his attention to the scowling wolf shifter and said, "I'm surprised your female let you off your leash."

"Don't push me, Cloud," Thorne growled. "And if Laurel ever catches you calling her my female, don't come crying to me."

"And you"—Cloud sneered at the elf—"where's your ball and chain?"

"Don't answer him," Thorne clipped. "He must have forgotten to take his meds."

Forrest frowned, confused. "Ball and chain? I'm not mated."

"He means Aeron, dumb-ass." River placed his thumbs through the belt loops of his breeches and stared obviously at the warrior elf.

To Violet, Forrest didn't seem like much of a threat at first. His bronzed, lightly freckled skin coupled with tarnished long hair reminded her of some southern farm boy, but when she looked closer, everything about him screamed deadly. From the blood stained battle armor, to the sharp sword at his hip, bow slung over his shoulder, and scar cutting from his jaw to his arched ear. The moment River's words sank in, Forrest's friendly face hardened into something dangerously close to savage. He flexed his fists, causing biceps to bulge, almost busting the seams on his leather.

This male would gut you in your sleep. Violet leaned back into Indigo.

"This party blows," Cloud announced, holding his unflinching gaze on Indigo. "Put your clothes back on, River."

River lifted his eyes to the sky and gave a frustrated groan, but flicked his jacket back on. He left it gaping open over a set of well defined abdominals sporting almost as many power-enhancing tattoos as his fellow crow, who had them up to his neck.

Violet was surprised crows were in the Order, let alone promoted to cadre level within the Twelve. From everything Mitzie had told her in her daily gossiping, crow shifters were notoriously cheeky, recalcitrant, and thieving nonconformists, but she supposed, on reflection, that made them good spies and assassins. The blue Guardian teardrop twinkled on both of their faces, proving that the Well did indeed have a sense of humor, or dark plans of its own.

Her mind went back to what Indigo said about the man who'd triggered the bomb being alive today. Maybe the Well recognized that to win control of this land, once and for all, sometimes you need a monster to kill a monster.

As if reading her mind, Cloud arched a brow at her. Neither crow made to leave. Clearly they weren't backing down, despite their words. No, from the smirks on the crow shifters' faces, it seemed like a game had begun.

And Indigo saw it as a sign of aggression. An act of War. Power rippled from them, vibrating across the water as though a boulder had been dropped. The waves of air hit them on the shore, rushed up their bodies and buffeted their hair. The same power crawled over Violet's skin like little insects coming alive.

Weren't these Indigo's friends? Co-workers... something?

Then she remembered how he'd behaved with Shade, someone Indigo called brother. Indigo had been possessive and reactive. It must be the mating bond.

In the space of a day, Violet had suddenly become the most important thing in Indigo's life.

She didn't know what to think about that.

"You idiots," Thorne growled and gave a pointed look at Indigo's and Violet's matching glowing marks. What was visible of them, anyway. "Look."

River's eyes widened marginally. Even Cloud slowly got to his feet. He withdrew a dagger from his boot at the same time. Thorne held his hand toward Indigo, as one would tame a wild beast. Funny, considering he was the most feral looking of them all.

"Forrest," Thorne ground out. "Get Shade. Now."

"I say let them deal with Indi. They asked for it." The bronzed warrior stood back and folded his arms.

"He's fine, aren't you, Indi?" Cloud said with a teasing smile that turned his cruel expression into something remarkable. If he wasn't sneering so much, he'd give Shade a run for his money with his looks.

The steel wall surrounding Violet twitched. Both crows burst into action. But they didn't attack. In a blur of dark feathers and leather, they took to the sky laughing, as though this was the most entertainment they'd had all day.

Something splashed to their right. Then something else on their left.

"Our clothes!" Violet gasped, spotting her cape.

"Crimson help us," Thorne mumbled, then let loose another string of curses. When he was done, he turned to Indigo and said in a placating sort of way, "We're going.

Clearly we should have stopped at the house first and spoken with Shade."

After they'd gone, Violet was left in the strong embrace of a vampire, realizing that she'd actually felt safe. Wanted. Needed. And she wanted to sink back into him. Where did that leave her shifting world view now?

CHAPTER TWENTY-ONE

"I know the room isn't much, but it's better than sleeping in the snow under a tree," Indigo stated as he entered one of the guest rooms at the cadre's house set apart from the main keep. Only four simply furnished bedrooms were available. This one consisted of a bed, rug, stone walls, fireplace, and window. It suited the Guardians fine for brief visits during an extended mission in the north.

Wrapped in a towel, Violet entered ahead of him and rotated, her expression blank. The life she'd shown at the springs had dimmed, and he worried it was the kiss. *Too soon.* She'd pulled away when he'd been tender and had only come to him when he'd been rough.

In two quick strides he went to the fireplace and crouched to stick his head below the chimney. A shrill whistle notified the resident fire sprites to come down from whatever nook or cranny they inhabited. When he straightened, he met his mate's eyes.

She frowned. "You're just going to leave me here? After everything?"

"You're safe, and you need time to process... us. I need time to deal with... whatever has brought everyone here."

"You don't get to decide what I need to process."

"Violet, twenty-four hours ago you wanted to kill me. What happened between us in the springs was very different."

He wanted her. But his motivations weren't the problem. For all he knew, she would try to escape again or do herself harm. All he should be offering her right now was stability. Unfortunately, his body didn't care about being decent. It just wanted to—he scrubbed his face, shutting down his train of thought before he ended in a place he shouldn't be.

The sprites dropped from the chimney like flaming bombs. There were two of them—one female and one male, as was common in permanent residences such as these. Rather than living in the wild, the sprites liked a steady home to start a family. He could see the appeal in that.

They hopped about the log in glee, coaxing the tinder to life, blowing air on their sparks catching fire. Violet held her pale hands before the burgeoning flames, and then she did something strange. It was as though the moment the heat started to infuse her icy skin, she backed off. She went to the window and shivered as she looked out at the night.

Make it hurt, she'd pleaded with him.

"Stand by the fire," he said.

She ignored him.

"Violet." He took a step, but she cut him a glare.

"So I'm not a prisoner?"

He wasn't sure how to respond to that. She'd agreed to help them with their mission to take down the Void—he hoped—but he didn't trust her. And if she tried to leave, he'd find her.

Fiery eyes speared into him and it took everything he had to keep his smile from showing on his face. There she was. Every time he caught the light in her eyes, it brought his own to the surface.

Feigning nonchalance in case her spark went out again, he went to an ornate wooden trunk at the foot of the bed and rifled through the contents for something to wear. Transient Guardians shared these guest rooms. Unlike the main Order campus, this outpost was run by whoever stayed. It was common to leave extra supplies where possible.

He found a pair of buckskin breeches and a simple black woolen sweater. Both a little big, but they would do. A long, linen tunic was at the bottom of the trunk. It smelled like mothballs but it was clean. He tossed it on the bed for Violet. When he was dressed, he sat heavily on the bed and ran his hand through his wet hair, flicking out excess moisture. The weight of Violet's attention followed him the entire time.

He wanted to smile. She was no shrinking violet, as her

name suggested. This woman was strong and trying to suppress it. The more time he spent with her, the more he wanted to know why. The more he needed to know, so he could protect her.

"Will you ever let me go?" she asked, eyes narrowed.

Her words cut him. He'd hoped after their conversation about the Void, that she'd not ask such questions. But she had. She might always ask them. He wanted to tell her it was the Prime's choice, but the truth was that with the Well-blessed union, and his vampire mating hormones churning, he'd never let her go. It wasn't a selfish act. It was just fact. He wasn't biologically programmed to leave her. If they were separated, or if one of them died first, the other wouldn't be far behind.

"Unlikely," he confessed.

She scoffed and rolled her eyes. "So that behavior down in the springs... what was that, you marking your territory?"

He leaned back on the bed and considered her. She clung to her towel. Messy hair had turned to silken strands plastered across her face and shoulders. The dark slashes of her brows stood out starkly against her pale, undernourished skin. But since lighting the fire, fresh blood bloomed in her cheeks.

Bite me.

She'd insisted.

Make it hurt.

Her eyes then had been fever bright. When a woman said things like that to a vampire, his blood heated. His fangs ached. Just the memory of it urged him to tug her towel away, reveal her skin, and take her to bed. He could bite her. He could lick all over her body and feast between her legs. But, unlike some of his vampire brethren, making it hurt wasn't really his thing. He'd rather have her squirming and squealing in a puddle of bliss.

There were others, like Shade, who lived and died by the code he set with his routine, both for feeding and in the bedroom. He had rules. And he had repercussions if his partners disobeyed them. It worked for him. Females around the realm lined up to be his donor.

But with Indigo, with his one fatal mistake and loss of self-control years ago, he wasn't sure if he could provide that stability for Violet. If pain truly was what she needed.

She stepped toward him. "What happened?"

There were too many answers to that question.

"To you," she elaborated. "Why did you feel the need to attack your friends down there?"

"They're not my friends," he stated and got to his feet. "Well, mostly. And don't ever make that mistake. Particularly with the crows. They'll stab you in the back the first chance they get."

"So explain it to me."

"You've been studying vampires a long time, and you've never seen what happens when one actually mates?"

She shook her head, narrowing her eyes.

He grasped the back of his neck. "My parents are mated. They live in Obscendia."

"I was only in that village for a few months. I, um, moved around a lot."

With the trail of dead vampires she left behind, he wasn't surprised.

"There's a reason for it. The mating behavior," he explained. It had to do with fighting against the promiscuity and establishing a new pattern. Suddenly, he didn't want to have this conversation. He strode for the door and opened it. Before leaving, he glanced over his shoulder. "Spend this time practicing. Call on your gift. Glow. Send it away. Repeat."

She didn't answer.

"I'm going to see why the others are here. I'll be back by dawn. And this goes without saying, but don't try to escape. Our new bond means I can track you anywhere, even without the shadow snake linking us."

"You said I'm not a prisoner."

"You're not. But you're mine."

She flipped up her middle finger. This time, he let his smile out to play.

"Oh, and Violet?" he said, hand on the doorknob. "If you ask me again, I *will* bite you, and I *will* make it hurt... but only if it's for the right reasons."

He would give her whatever she needed, even if it cost him.

"And if it's not?" she asked quietly.

"Then I'll make it feel good."

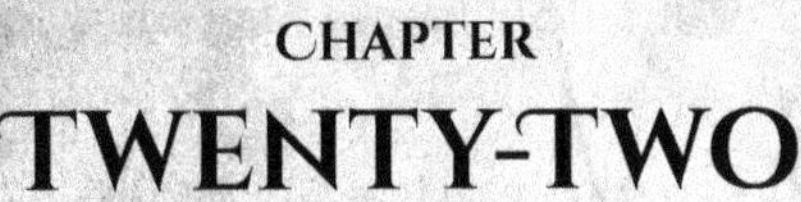

CHAPTER TWENTY-TWO

The moon was high when Indigo made his way down to the sunken fire pit outside the cadre cottage. A thin layer of snow gathered on the ground. Lower ranked Guardians patrolled, ensuring no fae had flown, swum, or portaled to their private island. Any Mages onsite stuck to the main outpost keep and left the cadre to do their business. Tonight, there were six of them in total. Seven, if Indigo included himself. Most wouldn't stay the night. Haze still wasn't there. A niggling feeling tugged in his gut. The vampire should have been back by now.

Ash, the third crow-shifter in the Twelve, had appeared from somewhere and stood by the fire on his own while everyone else sat on the granite benches. Perhaps he'd been there all along. The quiet Guardian often lurked nearby. Unlike his two shifter brethren, who hid nothing, this fae hid everything. He stood with his hands in his pockets, locks of shoulder length hair falling over his eyes as he intently watched the flickering flames. Ash was the first to note Indigo's arrival. It was a holding of the breath. A silence in the shadows.

These males were dangerous. All of them. Indigo's emotions eased, simply from knowing Violet was safely in the room, nowhere near these mostly unmated warriors. His reaction at the springs was only a taste of what would happen in the future if he felt his relationship with Violet was threatened. And he could potentially be heightened like this for months, depending on when, or if, he and Violet consummated their union.

When, he told himself. When. He just had to prove to her a few things first.

He went straight to the only fae who might have an idea of what he was going through—Thorne. But Shade's steady palm stopped him.

"Haze is in trouble," Shade murmured. "He has to be."

It was almost impossible to think the big fae was anything but invincible, but Haze never messed around with promises. If he said he was doing something, he'd do it. Indigo nodded grimly. "You may be right."

"What happened with your brother?"

"Demeter wasn't there when I left to track Violet. Haze was about to talk to him and planned to meet us here afterwards." Perhaps Demeter hadn't even turned up. Or perhaps he'd ambushed Haze on behalf of High Queen Maebh—he was in her royal guard, so it wasn't a far stretch to think he'd aligned with her. But even if he did, what was her motivation? She'd been quiet for decades. It had also been years since Indigo had been with his family. Anything could have changed.

A shrill whistle came from the fire pit as one of the Guardians became impatient. The sudden piercing sound startled the fire sprites into crackling and spitting.

Ash took his place beside the other two crows on a long slab of granite, the flames painting his features with golden hues. He ran his fingers through his hair and pulled it back to tie with a cord. All three crows stared intently at Indigo, the menace in their eyes dulled. While Indigo would never go so far as to say they were afraid of him, after the power he'd leaked at the springs, they were wary. They were clever. They'd tested him. They knew about the insatiable monster buried deep within his soul, just waiting to be unleashed. One snap, and he'd not stop coming at them until they were unrecognizable.

For now, it was enough to keep them at bay.

"If you have something to say, Cloud, say it," Indigo challenged.

Cloud's disheveled black curls softened otherwise hard features Indigo had only ever seen smile for wicked reasons. The indignant crow shifted unimpressed eyes to Indigo but said nothing.

"Just sit down," Shade said, coming up behind Indigo, before lowering himself to the bench. "We need to sort out a few things tonight."

"Like what?" River asked, folding his arms.

"Like the reason you lot are here."

"The Prime sent us."

"Yes, but she sent you for the reason she sent Indigo, Haze and I here—"

"The Queen is going mad," Cloud said.

A nod. A shrug. A raised eyebrow.

River raised his palms. "Let's not jump to conclusions. All we know at the moment is that mana-warped bodies are being dumped."

"It's true," Indigo confirmed. "I caught Gastnor dumping them."

Shade nodded grimly. "And he also witnessed Bones. Alive. Helping Gastnor."

Cloud stood swiftly, fists clenching at his side. "That floating scum of the Well. He's dead."

"I can assure you, he's not dead. He's very much alive and seemingly working with that craggy old vamp... or being used somehow." Indigo studied him. Whatever history Cloud had with Bones, it went deep and dark.

When Shade and Cloud had interrogated the mercenary human a few months ago, Shade had confessed quietly to Indigo that Cloud had almost taken it too far. Cloud was the Prime's favored assassin and thief, but he never killed gratuitously, or for revenge. Not that they knew of, anyway. Some sort of secret moral code drove Cloud's actions, and none of them knew what, only that the Well approved enough to grant him Guardian status.

"You have history with him, don't you?" Indigo said to

Cloud. "Was Bones somehow alive when you were in Crystal City?"

Cloud's eyes flashed, but he said nothing and sat.

Thorne glared at Cloud and rubbed his beard. "If Bones is alive then, you need to tell us, Cloud. For a mortal to remain alive for so long means he has been drinking mana like the Void. They could be madder than Queen Maebh by now."

Murmured agreements passed around the campfire.

Shade scrubbed his hair, something he only did when he was unsettled. "Whatever was in Bones' head must have been too valuable for the queen to dismiss. When we sent him there for her Sluagh to interrogate, they must have found something too good to share. Something to do with the reason she's dumping mana-warped corpses."

Indigo said, "We had word out of her court that she's been reclusive since Jasper killed Mithras and took the Seelie throne."

"Word from who?" Forrest asked, and took a sip of water from his cup.

"My brother Demeter is one of her guards."

"And this was the one who was meant to meet up with Haze?"

Shade stretched his long legs out. "Correct. Except neither have reported in."

"If he's blooded kin, can't Indigo communicate with him?" Forrest lifted the cup in his hand toward Indigo. "Contact him now. Let us all hear."

Indigo bristled at the insinuation he was only trustworthy if they all heard the conversation. He took the cup, glanced at Shade and received a nod, so cut his finger and let a drop enter the water of the cup. He used his blood connection to Demeter to track him through the network of mana in Elphyne water. Blood called to blood.

"This might not work," Indigo said. "He's in the guard. He could be in clear view of everyone when this call comes through. And there might not even be water nearby."

"They all know he's related to a Guardian, though, right?" Forrest asked.

Indigo shrugged. "My relationship with my family hasn't exactly been copasetic since I initiated."

They all nodded with understanding. None of them were close with their families. Joining the Order seemed to have that effect. Any familial expectations were cut dead in their tracks the moment one entered the ceremonial lake.

"I say do it anyway," Cloud said. "Maybe we'll catch some conversation we're not supposed to hear."

Indigo sat with the cup between his knees, staring at the contained water, waiting for the connection. The other Guardians came closer to watch but stayed out of view. If the connection worked, Indigo would be able to see whatever reflected into the water nearby Demeter at the time, and the same would be true in reverse.

No answer came, which wasn't too worrisome. A fae had to be near a body of water to receive a call. If they weren't, then there would be no answer.

"I'll keep trying." Indigo cut the spell and the blue glow died.

"Do you trust him?" Forrest asked.

"Before I joined the Order, my answer would have been yes." But even as he said the words, he remembered all the times his brother had teased him as a child. There was a mean streak in Demeter.

They all turned thoughtful. It was the same for all of them. The cadre had become their new family, as disturbed as they sometimes were. Despite Indigo's warning to Violet, and knowing he might not get along with all of them, they would protect each other with their lives.

"Someone needs to tell the Prime about Bones," Thorne grumbled.

"And we need to get eyes on Haze," Shade reminded them. "I suggest a few of us head into Aconite City. Indi, you go back to Obscendia and interview your family. Find out what really happened after you left."

"And what about your human?" Forrest asked.

Indigo tensed. "What about her?"

The fae darted uncertain eyes around the campfire. "Isn't she like the others? Shouldn't she be trained?"

Indigo relaxed. "Yes, she should."

It was Cloud who offered the next words. "The Mages here can help if she's not ready to head back to the Order."

"The Prime won't like that," Indigo replied.

"The Prime can suck it."

A snort from Shade. "Very well. Crows, you're with me. Between us, I think we can get an understanding of Haze's whereabouts. Forrest, you go with Indigo to Obscendia. Thorne deal with the Prime."

Thorne swore, but nodded.

"Let's refill before we go." Cloud stood, then shifted condescending eyes to Indigo. "Unless you and your mate have a problem with that."

"Fuck off."

Black feathered wings snapped out and he took to the sky. River joined him. When Indigo looked for Ash, he found him already gone. Sometimes Indigo wondered if Ash could manipulate shadow like a vampire, or if he was just that fast. Forrest was the only one left who had to walk, a fact he realized when Thorne announced he didn't need to refill. Grumbling, Forrest set off to the springs.

As Thorne made to leave, Indigo stopped him. "I'd like a word."

Thorne sat back down cautiously. "What is it?"

"It's about... Violet."

Shade raised his brow but didn't leave. The vampires kept nothing from each other, so he would find out, eventually.

"She's not accepting her gift." Indigo took a deep breath. "There are bite marks all over her body. When I found her, she'd just killed three rogue vampires in her home. Had even disposed of them by feeding their corpses to a tachi in the woods."

Thorne gaped. "How the fuck did she do that if she's refusing her gifts?"

Indigo shrugged. "Metal weapons."

All three shifted uncomfortably. Thorne frowned. “But the contraband is all gone now?”

“Yes.”

“That’s not so bad,” Thorne mused. “Clarke and Laurel both had contraband on them when they awoke. If we hadn’t been there to remove it, their gifts wouldn’t have manifested either. If Violet had no one to guide her, it’s logical she would have thought the metal was her best protection.”

“But it went further than protection,” Shade noted. “She used the metal to actively kill our kind.”

Thorne whistled slowly. “I don’t envy you, Indi, but I’m sure she’ll be worth it. I know Laurel is.”

For long moments, they stared at the crackling fire. Then Indigo blurted, “She doesn’t think she’s worthy of the gift.”

“Because of the slaying?” Thorne asked.

“Or the bite marks?” Shade added.

“Probably all of it. And... because she built the weapon that destroyed the old world.”

“Ah,” Shade said, as if that made everything make sense.

Indigo continued, “There’s more to it, and I intend to find out. But in the meantime, she... um...” He thought about her request at the springs. “She... um... wanted me to hurt her. While we were... you know.”

Shade slipped his hands into his pockets. “Sounds like she needs you to give her some boundaries. Take some of the weight of that guilt off her.”

Indigo leaned forward. "How?"

Thorne cleared his throat and stood swiftly. "You vampires might be used to sharing, but this is too personal for me. I'm going to leave. But before I go, I'll just say one thing, Indi. I tried to make decisions for Laurel, despite her telling me what she was ready for, and I almost lost her. Don't do that."

"He's not wrong," Shade said after Thorne had left. "Sometimes failing to set your own boundaries can be harmful. But if she needs the cathartics of what I think you're saying, having a trusted ally take on that burden can be very freeing." Meeting Indigo in the eye, Shade slowly got up. "Ask Sweetheart to train Violet while you're gone."

"You call her sweetheart all the time?"

"It's the name she's earned from me," he said, in all seriousness. "She'll be able to help if Violet has any questions about her... darker desires. If at all."

Indigo had a lot to think about. Shade left him sitting by the fire, contemplating.

Dawn was a few hours away still, and he'd said to Violet he would be back by then, but he needed a game plan before leaving for Obscendia, so stayed to think. Maybe he should take her with him. She was clearly in a fragile state and starting to trust him. This break could be two steps backward.

But she needed training. And she was safe here at the outpost. For whatever reason, Gastnor wanted her dead. It was better to face the anxiety of leaving her unattended around other males, than to worry about her being in the territory of an enemy. If Gastnor discovered Violet slayed those vampires, then Indigo would have a very different battle on his hand. The Unseelie would exact justice on her for her crimes. Indigo wouldn't let that happen. She may be confused about herself, but she had suffered enough.

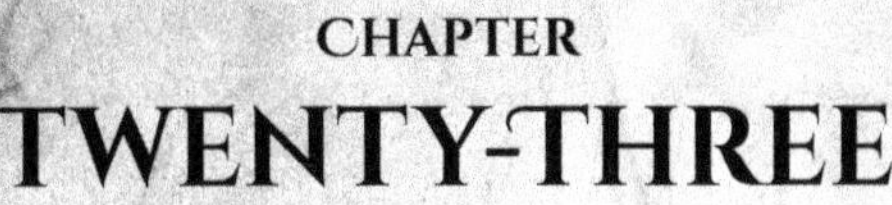

CHAPTER TWENTY-THREE

When Indigo returned to the bedroom, he half expected Violet to be asleep, but she sat at the edge of her bed, still wearing her towel and staring out at the darkness through the window.

The fire was nothing but a smolder. It wasn't the sprites' fault. They'd done what they could with the only log. The rest of the cut wood sat on the hearth, waiting to be added.

Indigo placed a bowl of soup he'd just cooked on the wooden trunk. It wasn't the best soup, but he copied what Violet had made earlier in the kitchen. Hopefully, it wouldn't poison her.

"I brought you some food."

"There's an owl out there," she muttered. "I can't figure out if it's a shifter, or just an owl."

Her eyelids blinked slowly. It looked as though she was exhausted but refusing to sleep.

"Some of the Mages here are owl shifters, like the Prime."

"Oh." A pause. "Must be nice to be able to fly away on a whim."

"It is." He picked up the tunic, still untouched where he'd left it. "Any time you want to fly, I'll take you."

She flinched as he tried to put the tunic over her head.

"Violet," he growled. "You need to eat. You need to dress and to keep warm. And you need to train. Your gift is how you will protect yourself."

Her jaw stubbornly clenched and he suddenly saw the truth in Shade's words. Her own boundaries were failing her. He had to step in. But he also didn't want to push her too far, or to lose her the way Thorne almost lost his mate. He'd only just found her. He took her jaw in his fingers and brought her reluctant gaze to his.

"Violet, tell me what happened when you woke in this time. Tell me about the scars." *Help me understand.*

Fear lit up their bond. She tried to pull away and shut down, but he applied a steady pressure on her jaw, the kind that said he was in control. Nothing bad would happen to her while he was here. This was a safe place.

Moments passed while he kept their gazes locked. Eventually, the fear passed. She was more fragile than he'd initially thought. Her shoulders dropped and she started speaking.

"There were at least eight of them, maybe more. It was hard to tell and I've blocked much of it out." She swallowed. "They all wore Maebh's black uniform. And they already had three human prisoners in a cage."

"Tell me about the cage."

"The women had been in there for weeks. One of them was dead."

Indigo bared his teeth. "Were all the women like you?"

She shook her head. "Only two. The ones who lived. The other was a spy from Crystal City."

Indigo cupped her nape, relishing the warmth. "And the bite marks?"

"They attacked me. They got drunk off my blood. The two in the cage warned me it would happen, so I watched for it... for that moment their senses were muddled and then... I managed to fight them off and—" Her eyes dimmed as she focused inwardly. "I drove their own weapons into their hearts. Then I freed the others."

That was why the bite marks had scarred. The vampires hadn't finished their feed, and the healing enzymes weren't released. No wonder Violet had a vendetta against his kind. They'd brutalized her. His touch softened on her nape.

"Gastnor was one of them, wasn't he?" Indigo asked.

Her nod was almost imperceptible, but he felt the dash of angst through their connection.

Feeling her suffering triggered so many emotions in Indigo, fury and rage chiefly among them. He had to squash it all. For her sake. Unlike some of the older fae who could master their emotions and mana, he was relatively young in comparison, and had no idea how to switch off the connection between them. He wasn't even a century old. Unlike Gastnor, who'd been the queen's captain for longer than Indigo had been alive. Gastnor knew better than to do what he did to Violet.

Gastnor's retaliation changed things. Indigo definitely had to burn Violet's apartment. He had to cover her tracks. If the queen had any valid reason to contest the Order for Violet's custody, then there might not be much he could do to protect her.

He also didn't want Violet to feel trapped. He wanted her to feel free. And cherished. And loved. The same way his parents were with each other. For now, he would have to settle for doing what he could.

He took the tunic and tugged it over her head. Begrudgingly, she let him, but when he brought the soup to her, she turned her head.

"I'm not hungry."

He put the bowl down with deliberate intent. "Violet. I heard what you said in the springs. I understand."

The air seemed to grow thicker. The sensation of their connection swelled. He felt it tingle all down his arm. She was listening, despite her eyes locked outside the window.

"You don't think you deserve this life."

"I killed them all, Indigo."

"No, you didn't. You made the bomb. You didn't set it off."

"What's the difference?" she snapped.

"Everything. And until you can see that, I'll take the burden of that guilt away from you." He put the bowl back in front of her. "You will eat. You will warm yourself. You will sleep. You will train. You will get strong. And when I get back, if I find out you haven't been doing these things, then there will be consequences. I don't know what these will be yet, but I know you can't make that decision by yourself. Am I wrong?"

Defiance flared in her expression, but down the bond he felt an easing of her worry. Just a sliver. A drop.

"Do you understand, Violet? Those are the rules."

Somehow, it wasn't quite working. He'd not hit the right button. And then he remembered what Shade had said about cathartics. Maybe she needed the pain. Maybe it was a safe place for her to release the pressure of her guilt. But as he thought about going through with it, his own instincts rebelled. He'd never been the kind of fae who could hurt without just cause. It was the reason he took it so hard after he'd killed during a spate of bloodlust.

After he'd made his mistake, he'd gone a bit wild. Drinking, partying, picking fights. He'd told himself he entered the ceremonial lake because it was an adventure. His parents had called him reckless. But maybe it had been more than that.

He'd always started with good intentions, but in the end he was unable to control himself. He'd never forgive himself if he took it too far with Violet.

Thorne's warning to listen to her blared loudly in his mind. Whatever Violet needed, for whatever reason, he would find a way to give it to her. He hadn't been wrong when he told her she needed time to process. They both did. This outpost was a safe place to do so.

The next words were difficult to say. "Tomorrow, I will be gone for a few days. Tell me if you want to remain here or go to the Order with Thorne."

"Where are you going? Why?"

"Guardian work," was all he said. "Around."

She stared darkly at him for a while, but she had to prove herself before he divulged too many details of their missions. She had to give a little something first—at least look after herself.

"Here, I suppose," she mumbled and rested her chin on her knees.

Good. That was something. "Then I'll send a Mage to train you. You might be surprised with what she has to share."

"What does that mean?"

"Sweetheart is experienced in the kind of... interaction you requested at the springs. If you're unsure, ask her anything. If I had to call any of the Guardians my friends, it would be Shade and Haze. Actually, they're more like family than my own. Shade trusts Sweetheart, and I trust him with my life."

More silence stretched and Indigo thought, perhaps, he'd said the wrong thing, but he couldn't let it show. Not even an iota of doubt. Because she needed to believe he was the unwavering one. She needed to believe that through all the uncertainty of her past few years, she now had a home. With him.

She'd doubted herself at the springs, and now she seemed to shrink into herself.

Without a word, Violet lifted the soup spoon to her lips. She ate a few spoonfuls and then rolled over and went to sleep. He sighed at the unfinished soup, but he couldn't expect her to change overnight.

CHAPTER
TWENTY-FOUR

Violet woke to the sun pouring through the window and Indigo gone. He'd waited for her to fall asleep, and then he'd gone to do whatever it was he had to do. True to his word, she wasn't a prisoner, but she assumed this "freedom" was some kind of test.

You need to process.

He wasn't wrong. She'd never in her wildest dreams imagined she'd be in this position. She studied the blue marks on her arm and remembered how respected the Well-blessed union was to others in Elphyne. It was a rare union. Until recently, only a handful of them had ever occurred. Indigo's face flashed in her mind. Then it was his body, glistening in the steam and water of the springs. His smile. Then the way he pushed her with wickedly arousing intent—his fingers wrapping around her throat, tangling in her hair, gentling on her face. The slow sweep of his nose across her wet cheek. The gentle, sensuous kiss. Her body tingled in all the right feminine places.

"Stupid," she mumbled to herself. "Acting like a teenager."

She threw her blanket back, intending to get out, but something clattered to the ground. Frowning, she picked it up and found an intricately carved bone dagger inset with rubies. The leather sheath was beautifully burned and scorched with floral patterns. When she pulled the dagger out, Elven runes glowed softly on the blade. She'd heard about these runes... they kept the bone from breaking during battle. They also kept the blade sharp.

There was a note.

You seem to be fond of hiding weapons on your person. I look forward to hunting for this one.

—Indi.

Biting her lip to stop a smile, she dressed in her dried clothes, and strapped the dagger to her belt. She considered hiding it somewhere on her person, purely to see if he would frisk her or pat her down, but decided on having it where she could easily access it. At least until she was comfortable walking around this new place.

No one stopped Violet as she explored the perimeter of the outpost. The guards took one look at her blue arm markings and then shifted their gaze away to brood out at the forest or sea. Three smaller stone and wood buildings surrounded the larger keep as part of the main settlement. There was one lookout, and a few smaller buildings including the stone cottage where she'd slept the previous night. There truly was nowhere to go unless she wanted to enter the woods and become a hermit. Even there, Indigo would find her eventually.

His presence softly sang through their bond wherever she walked. When she went in some directions, the sensation grew stronger. In others, it went weak. *Intriguing*. The moment she decided she wanted to know more, her old analytical instincts took over. All emotion drained from her mind and she became doggedly determined to understand how the bond worked. For an hour, she lost all sense of time and immersed in experimenting with the limits of the bond. It was like a homing beacon, she'd surmised by the end of her walk.

From here on out, it's always going to be we.

The thought didn't frighten her like it might have once done. Indigo knew the worst of her, her darkest desires and shames. He wanted to help. And he would find her. Anywhere and everywhere. She'd told him last night, but again, right here and now, she decided to stay. This was worth seeing through. All she knew for sure was that she wasn't a quitter. She was a survivor which meant her only option was to work through her messed up mind and find a way to live with what she'd done.

And to make sure she listened to what the world wanted, she needed training. These people were her best bet.

"There you are."

Violet turned and found the auburn-haired Mage who'd fed Shade yesterday. In the light of day, some of her features were more obvious. The tips of her hair looked like they had been dipped in white ink. The same went for her lashes, and even her eyebrows. Freckles dusted her nose. Her ears were round, like Violet's. Gorgeous tawny feathered wings slotted through the back of her blue Mage robe and draped down her back like a regal mantle.

Definitely an owl shifter. A majestic, stunning shifter.

"Hello." Violet forced a smile. "Sweetheart, is it? I'm Violet."

The Mage laughed. "Oh, I see you've been talking to Shade. Only he's allowed to call me Sweetheart. It's a pet name we have for... well, other times. Probably best you call me Skye."

"Okay... nice to meet you, Skye."

"So, Indi asked me to find you and assess your gift. I'm more than happy to help, but are you sure you don't want to go to the Order? They're more equipped there. I only have a few small stones that were chips taken from the original elemental obelisks."

"I'm not ready to go to the Order," Violet replied, a little too curtly, and then winced at herself.

"Let's head inside and get something to eat. I'm famished. I'll show you where everything is. The keep kitchen is better stocked than the cadre's cottage. Those males have no idea how to look after themselves or how to restock. Come on."

They passed two patrol Guardians. One was in the single tower, and one carefully surveyed the sea. Both wore reinforced leather helmets, and neither had wings. Despite being so far from the next village, they were always vigilant. None of the Guardians Violet had met the previous night were around. They must have all left along with Indigo.

A tiny sliver of worry unfurled in Violet's stomach before she realized what it was and stamped it out. Surely she wasn't concerned about Indigo's welfare. Preferring not to dwell on it, she hurried after Skye.

The kitchen looked much like the one in the cottage, except larger. Skye had set up a platter of cut fruit on a stone tray.

"Help yourself," she said, gesturing to the tray.

"Will you tattle to Indigo if I don't?" Violet was half joking, but part of her needed to know. Was he serious with his rules? Would there really be consequences if she didn't follow them?

"Doesn't bother me if you eat or don't." Skye looked confused, but then her eyes widened with a conspirator's wink. "Oh. I see. *Should* I be telling him? I mean, do you want me to?"

Violet blinked. "I don't know. Should you?"

"Wait." Skye took a cherry and popped it into her mouth. "Are we talking about the same thing?"

"You tell me." Violet just wanted to know whether Indigo would be angry if she decided she wasn't hungry—if food was too good for someone like her. She wasn't sure if she'd go that far, but sometimes she thought about it. The guilt weighed her down so much that nothing much else came through.

"Well," Skye said. "Shade won't feed from me if he finds out I break one of his rules while he's here."

Violet's brow squished. "If you don't eat enough, he won't eat from you? That's weird."

"Oh no." Skye giggled. "Different kinds of rules. Like..." She lowered her voice. "In the bedroom rules. Kinky rules."

"*Ooh.*" Now it was making sense. Violet didn't think that's what Indigo meant. But then... "Wait. You *want* Shade to feed from you?"

Skye almost choked on her fruit. "Obviously. Who wouldn't?"

Violet didn't know how to respond, so started eating. "Obviously."

After a long pause and a noticeable stare, Skye went to find her special stones. The fruit actually tasted good. Juicy. Sweet and tart at the same time. Some new varieties that had been born since the fallout, and some older fruits like apples and plums that had weathered the test of time. The best of both worlds.

When Skye returned, Violet put all thoughts of Indigo behind her and Skye launched straight into the assessment. She laid out six stones on the countertop.

Skye pointed to each as she spoke. "In a moment, you can hold each stone, and from the amount it glows, we'll ascertain your elemental affinity. It will help us understand your gift, and what spells you can access with training. Start with that one."

Something clicked inside Violet and a rush of endorphins hit. Learning. Investigating. This was her jam and for the first time in a long time, she felt like herself. Through studious research and experimentation, she could rule out the unexpected, or at least mitigate the risks. There would be fewer chances she'd mess up.

The first stone was dark and smooth. It didn't glow, but it warmed. When she told Skye this, she nodded and said, "That's chaos. Makes sense you don't have much of it considering what Indi said your gift is."

"He told you that too?"

Skye's white tipped lashes lifted. "Is it a problem that we've spoken about you?"

"No, it's just... No, it's not." She put the rock down. "What else did he say about me?"

"This one's next." Skye pointed to the jagged brown rock and waited for Violet to pick it up before speaking. "He said you needed guidance. That you were to be protected with our lives. And to trust you."

"And you all just do what he says?"

Skye shrugged. "He's one of the Twelve. Only the council sits above him in the Order ranks, and Shade sits on the council. He also told me you need to be cared for."

The rock did nothing in Violet's hand. She put it down. "That's all Indigo said?"

"He also said you might want to talk about a few things." Skye frowned at the jagged rock. "No earth affinity. That's a shame. We need more earthers. Okay, what about this one?"

This one was a crystal clear rock. It glowed and heated

so brightly that the light rays burst through Violet's fingers. "Whoa."

Skye smiled. "One guess for what that one is."

"Light?"

"Close. Spirit. Clarke almost broke our spirit obelisk. It's also linked with intuition and telling the future. Interesting." Skye cocked her head, considering Violet. "Spirit is the antithesis of Chaos—something Indi is strongly affiliated in."

"So we're opposites," Violet mumbled.

"That's a good thing. You balance each other out. That's better than being the same, believe me. It's the reason why Shade and I will never have more than our little arrangement. We're too similar. Haze, on the other hand, now if I could get him to feed from me..." She whistled long and low before refocusing on the stone. Her voice became more chipper. "Okay, this one."

"Wait." Violet held up her hand. "Have you ever fed Indigo?"

"That's probably not a question I should be answering right now." Skye tapped the next rock. "Come on. Keep going."

"No, I want to know."

Skye's tawny brows puckered. "Promise you won't get all possessive and attack? I mean, I'm just a simple Mage. A lover, not a—"

"I get it. And you have nothing to worry about. Indigo and I aren't... well, we've only just met."

"Oh, honey." The pity in Skye's voice matched her pout. "You're not still trying to fight this mating bond, are you?"

Heat exploded in Violet's cheeks and she glowered. "Did Indigo feed from you or not?"

Skye tossed her hair. "Of course. But he was always polite. Don't worry, it was nothing like my arrangement with Shade. Indigo and I never met between the sheets. Goodness. Now, you're making me blush. Moving on."

She tapped the rock with red stripes through the black. Begrudgingly, Violet picked it up, wondering why the hell she was so grumpy about the fact Indigo had fed from this female. The rock also glowed brightly, just like Skye's smile.

"What is this one?" Violet asked.

"Elemental Fire. Together with spirit, you have the power of the sun, moon and stars at your disposal. Very lucky." She gathered the last two and placed one in each of Violet's hands. Not much happened. "Water and Air. You have more air than I expected. There's energy in that." She tapped her lips. "You know, I've worked with Laurel a few times. She's Thorne's mate. Her affinities aren't too dissimilar to yours. It would be advantageous for your education if you sought her out at some point. Having a similar background to you, I'm sure she'd have a lot to say."

Stomach still churning from the news about Indigo feeding from her, Violet fiddled with the rocks for a moment and tried to force her mind away from him. Why was she thinking about him all the time? Did she... miss him? She put the rocks down.

"What are the other humans like?"

"I haven't met Queen Ada, but the other two are nice. For humans. I mean... you know what I mean."

Violet arched her brow. "I'm not sure I do."

"The point is, you should meet them."

Violet was uncertain how she felt about meeting others like her. At least Peaches and Silver already knew what Violet's vocation had been. An ache in her chest bloomed. She missed those women, more and more each day.

"So that's it?" Violet chewed on her fingernails.

"Well, as I mentioned, these rocks are too small to give us a good indication of the intensity of your gift, only what affinities you have, but considering the other humans that awoke from your time have deep reservoirs of mana, then it's safe to say you have too. They have so much they might never have to refill from a source of power. It's incredible, really. Some of us fae don't even have enough mana to light a candle." Skye collected the rocks and placed them in a pocket of her robe. "Let's head outside to the fire pit. We can begin your first tutorial there."

Violet made the "Thank you" hand sign to Skye. The female had taken time out of her schedule to help Violet. Skye blushed, bowed, and then gestured for Violet to follow. Violet almost did, but at the last minute went back to nab a few more slices of fruit. They tasted too good to leave behind.

CHAPTER TWENTY-FIVE

Gastnor had always been the queen's fae. He'd followed her into the first War against the humans. He'd bled for her. Given his body to feed her whims. His mana to her. But after he'd returned to her six years ago, without the precious Well-damned humans she'd tasked him to find, the queen had permanently removed part of his lifeforce, making him age and look like one of the cursed Untouched he often hunted.

When they'd discovered the three female humans had special blood, his guards had gorged themselves. They were owed this reward. He remembered thinking at the time, the queen wouldn't care. She would probably do it herself. Maybe they'd even feast together. He'd always planned on bringing them back alive, and that's all the queen needed. Their life. Their brains.

But that human.

The one at the end.

The one who'd scraped her nails down his cheek and hit bone.

She'd ruined everything. Because of her, his queen had permanently taken part of his soul. Because of her, his queen had stopped inviting him to her bed. Because of her, Gastnor had trouble feeding. No one wanted to donate to a wrinkled, old fae. They wanted beauty. They wanted perfection.

And since he'd caught her scent in Redvein Forest, he could think of nothing else. That's why he tracked down her living quarters in Obscendia. It was why he stood at the door now with a cold smile on his face.

Inside was evidence of the human's crimes. She'd killed his kind. She'd broken a sacred Unseelie law, and now she was as good as his.

CHAPTER TWENTY-SIX

Indigo went back to Obscendia with Forrest. The elf had used his gift with animals to call a kuturi to him and had flown on the winged beast beside Indigo. The journey had taken most of the night, and when they landed, Indigo could feel the burden of the rising sun.

The moment they'd landed, Forrest had swatted the wild kuturi on the rump, and Indigo headed straight for Violet's old apartment. They rounded the decrepit street. Black-coats milled about, swarming like flies on a rotting carcass. Indigo's shadow snake exploded, expanding to hide him. He grabbed Forrest's arm and tugged him into the shadow fold, rendering them both invisible.

Well versed in how shadow magic worked, Forrest allowed himself to be dragged to the darker side of the street. Invisibility worked better if there was more darkness to add to the shadow snake's mix. Indigo kept a firm hand on Forrest's arm and pressed them both to the wall, heart pounding wildly, watching the queen's guards pick apart Violet's home.

Queen's guards. Not regular Unseelie soldiers. These had red lining beneath their capes. And if the queen's guards were here, then the captain wouldn't be far behind. But the soldiers didn't stay long. Perhaps this was the tail end of their inspection. After the last soldier left, Indigo kept the shadow shield alive another few minutes, just to make sure no stragglers remained and noticed them. Then he let go of Forrest and called the snake back to him.

"You want to tell me what that's all about?" Forrest asked, hand casually moving to rest on the dagger at his hip.

"This is Violet's house."

Forrest's spine straightened. "Your mate?"

Indigo nodded.

"What would the queen's guard want with her?"

Elves' noses weren't as sharp as a vampire's. Forrest wouldn't be able to scent the traces of different types of blood in the home. Nor would he recognize what that meant. That Violet had slaughtered multiple fae.

Indigo wasn't stupid. He knew he should be furious that Violet had killed his kind, but vampires had violated her liberties. If he put himself in her shoes, if anyone had done that to him, he'd retaliate.

He also knew that if anyone tasted Violet's blood, she was in danger, not only from the secrets they could sell to Maebh, but from them draining her dry. And... it pained him to think, but if the vampires she'd attacked were sleep-feeders, the scum who fed on fae without consent, then perhaps they deserved punishment. Maybe not death. But something. Unseelie, of all fae, knew the dangers of offending another.

He'd done worse than kill a couple of sleep-feeders. Every Unseelie guard that had been scouring Violet's home had done worse. Crimson, even the sunny faced Forrest had done worse. It wasn't for Indigo to judge. That was the Well's job. And it had chosen Violet. It had kept her safe in the ice, then thawed her out and rewarded her with power. Whether it was because it saw potential, or she wasn't as bad as she claimed to be. Didn't matter. What mattered was keeping her safe.

"She slayed some vampires," Indigo confessed. "Plus, she knows how to build the old world weapon that destroyed everything. If the queen uses this crime as an excuse to bring Violet in—" Indigo shook his head at the implications.

Forrest held his hand out. An instant later, flames danced over his knuckles.

"Then we need to destroy the evidence," Forrest said.

Indigo grinned. "I was hoping you'd say that."

"No, you weren't. You would have done it anyway."

Between the two of them, and keeping themselves hidden by shadow, they had enough power to burn the apartment without spreading the incineration into the houses and woods beyond. When it was done, they swiftly made their way to Indigo's old family home.

Sunlight blazed, weighing down Indigo's arms as he

knocked on the door of the simple townhouse building. Half expecting to have to return at night, both Forrest and Indigo were surprised when the door opened to reveal Indigo's mother in a robe.

"Indi?" she frowned. "What, in the name of the Well, are you doing here at this time?"

He hand signed an apology over his heart. "I never got to speak with Demeter, and he's not answering my calls."

His mother was a proud vampire with a stiff back. No matter how poor they'd been, or how dirty they'd become, or how desperate, she'd always stood with her shoulders straight and her chin out. Probably because she'd nabbed the most promiscuous bachelor in town—his father. Or was it the other way around?

His mother cast her wary gaze at Forrest and raised her brow before returning to meet Indi's eyes. "Demeter isn't here. He never showed up."

"And where did Haze go?"

"Haze?"

"The other Guardian who was with me."

"He left when Demeter failed to show." She shrugged. "If you want to know more, you should speak with your sister. She's the one who speaks more frequently with your brother."

"We'll come back tonight."

"Indi." His mother took a single step out, then winced at the sunlight and went back. Her gaze softened on him. "Why don't you stay. For the night."

"Father won't like that."

"You'd be surprised at what he likes these days."

Indigo held up his palm. "I really don't want to know."

"Oh, pish tosh. I don't mean it like that, although, he's still got the pep in his step, if you know what I mean. As virile as he was at your age."

"Please don't."

"What I really meant was that he understands your decision to join the Guardians. You're just both too stubborn to get past it."

"He told me to never come back."

His mother waved her hand dismissively. "He's a grump. Come on. You can sleep in Demeter's old room. He's not used it since he joined the queen's guard." She looked Forrest up and down. "I suppose you'll be needing rest too."

Forrest, who was seventh in line to the Autumn Court throne, bowed deeply and honorably. "I would be eternally grateful for whatever scraps you could throw my way, m'lady."

She giggled. "You elves. Always so charming with words. Come on then. I'll find something for you too."

As she walked away, Indigo rolled his eyes at Forrest and murmured "Suck up" to which Forrest grinned and mouthed, "Always."

Since Forrest had been traveling all night, he gratefully took the couch and was asleep before his head hit the pillow.

Indigo took his brother's bed. It was a simple room, as were all of them. But the sheets were clean and the decor dust free. Indigo shifted his wings away, unbuckled his baldric, but left his battle uniform on in case he had to wake suddenly.

He laid down on the coverlet and stared at the ceiling, unable to stop thinking about Violet. His Violet. His mate.

His mother hadn't even noticed the blue Well-blessed markings glittering on the back of Indigo's hand. He smiled when he thought of what his father's face might look like when he finally learned about the mating. Part of the reason he'd been so angry about Indigo joining the Order was because they'd wanted their children to follow in their footsteps and mate a nice, normal vampire. They wanted to change the status quo, to push the boundaries that ostracized them from their own community.

His parents had suffered for their love, but they'd never given up.

To his father, joining the Order was as good as a death sentence. No one in their right mind would think it was a path to finding a mate. The mortality rate was high. Until Rush a few years ago, not a single Guardian had mated. Ever. Now there were four of them, and their unions were accepted purely because they were Well-blessed.

If Indigo had picked any female off the streets, the Prime wouldn't allow her to board at the Order. Not in the way she'd allowed Clarke and Laurel to.

Guilt peppered Indigo. He should probably take Violet to meet the Prime. She'd be waiting for an introduction, but Indigo wanted Violet to feel more secure first.

He wondered if she'd slept well. If she'd slept peacefully. He hoped she'd found the dagger he'd left her. He also hoped she would, indeed, try to hide it on her person. And he looked forward to a treasure hunt... He would start at her ankles, then pat up her legs. She would try to fight him off, but he'd know she liked the game because she'd hidden the dagger in the first place. So when his frisking took him to her shirt, he would slide his fingers inside, right up her bare flesh and... Indigo's body tightened. His cock hardened, pressing painfully against his leather breeches.

"Shit," he mumbled and tugged at his pants with a grimace. He couldn't wait to get back to her. To lie beside her. To wrap his arms and wings around her and feel her against every inch of his body. That soft rear end. Just like in the woods. How she'd arched into him.

"Shit," he ground out again. This time, he palmed his erection. He squeezed. It felt good. So good that his resolve melted and he undid his pants to spring his painfully hard length free with a long, guttural groan of relief. He could virtually smell Violet right now. That feminine musk. It thrilled him. It did more than that. He stroked himself, watching the twinkling blue of his Well-blessed markings, and dreamed she was thinking of him too.

"Hey."

Something wet hit Indigo's face. He swatted it away.

"Fangface."

Another wet splash.

Indigo sighed and opened his eyes. Night had arrived along with his youngest, most annoying sibling, Florence. She held a wet dish rag in her hand. Younger than him by a decade, she was the last of his family brood and had only been ten when he'd joined the Guardians. They hadn't really seen each other since.

"You're bigger than I imagined," she said, studying him. She could talk. She had to be at least thirty now and had the body to match. But she still looked as innocent as a teen in the face.

Brown hair, large brown eyes, and the same know-it-all-trait most of Indigo's family had. Looking back, that confidence had probably evolved as a defense mechanism against the rest of the community for being so different.

Indigo wiped his face. "That better have been water."

She flicked the wet rag again. "Why? Does it bother you?"

He narrowed his gaze and sat up. Immediately she stepped back, her eyes darting to the metal swords on the bed. He gathered his baldric and strapped it back on before standing up, towering over her.

"Florrie," he said. "You know I'm always here if you need me."

She snorted. "You're too busy saving the world."

He snorted back. At least the jibe wasn't as it used to be —something about being a coin-grubbing party pooper. Perhaps the public were finally seeing the Order wasn't their enemy. They were there to protect the realm, no matter which race. Even the humans, when he thought about it. They were too ignorant and stupid to know the harm they did to the land. Fae understood the magic they had access to could be ripped away in a heartbeat.

"If you need me," he repeated. "I'll be here."

She stared a moment, and then must have made some kind of internal decision to move on because her next words came out with extra verve.

"So who is the handsome elf you brought?" She waggled her brows. "Is he taken? And more importantly, will he feed me?"

"I don't know. Ask him yourself."

She flicked the rag at his face again. "Maybe I will."

"Good. But before you do, I need to know if you've spoken with Demeter lately."

Florence turned back to Indigo with shadows in her eyes.

His heart sank. Shit.

"What's happened?" he asked, already feeling an ominous weight on his shoulders.

"He's just..." Florence popped her head outside into the hallway and then checked for eavesdroppers. "He's different, that's all."

"How so?"

"He used to be fun, even after he joined the guard. I mean, with you, we get it. Being a Guardian doesn't give much room for home life, or settling down with a family, but Demeter?" She shook her head. "In the past six years, he's gone from absent to non-existent."

"Ma said he didn't turn up last night."

She bit her lip.

"Florrie?"

"He turned up. He just didn't stay long."

Alarm bells went off in Indigo's mind. "Did he say what he was doing here?"

Florence clutched Indigo's shoulder. "He's not in trouble is he?"

"Depends what he's done. Haze never showed at the outpost. Demeter was supposed to meet him."

"I'm sorry, Indi. There's not much else I can tell you. Only that he popped in. I saw him in his room, but when I came up to say something, he was already gone."

"Did he portal, or shadow walk?" Many vampires had various skills with shadow. Shade could travel between them, skip from one place to another. But he'd not known Demeter to have that skill. It took a lot of mana to maintain, and Demeter hadn't been that blessed with a large mana capacity.

Florence shrugged. "He was just there, and then not there."

Indigo sighed, and hand signed his thanks. "Anything else you can tell me?"

She shook her head and waited a few seconds before asking, "So... can you go and put in a good word for me with your elven friend now?"

He stifled an eye roll and followed her to the living area where Forrest had been sleeping on the couch. He wasn't there. Must have sensed waking in a hungry house of vampires wouldn't be a great place to be. His mother was in the kitchen, banging around, opening cupboards and setting cups out. She saw Indigo arrive and straightened.

"You're awake." She pointed to a bar stool at the counter. "Sit down. I'm just getting breakfast ready. Your father is due back from the markets with some fresh blood."

Florence sighed laboriously upon seeing Forrest had left and slunk into the seat next to Indigo just as a banging at the backdoor alerted them to his father's arrival. Indigo tensed as the tall vampire entered the room with a paper bag and clinking bottles. The male was classically handsome and still looked as slick as the day his age froze in his mid twenties. He put the bag down on the countertop and then nodded briefly to Indigo before taking his mate, Indigo's mother, in a searing kiss.

Florence rolled her eyes, but Indigo smiled. It was nice to know his parents still felt the same after a few centuries together. His mother broke away from their kiss with stars in her eyes, patted her mate on the chest, and then smiled at Indigo. His father took a moment to drag his eyes away from his mate.

"I brought your companion something foodies eat. It's in the bag," he said, and then handed Indigo a bottle of blood. "It's supposedly oxen, but you never know with these markets."

Indigo eyed the bottle warily, then slid his gaze to his father. He wasn't going to mention the fact he'd told Indigo to never come back? Everything was just forgotten?

Seeing their restlessness, Indigo's mother hurried and started pouring the contents of bottles into glasses.

Florence pouted as she sipped hers. "I would have preferred elf."

"Well, you get what you get," Indigo's father said, then picked up a cup and shoved it at Indigo. "Take it."

He reached out, but before he could grasp the cup, his father slammed it down and gripped his hand, shoving up Indigo's leather sleeve.

"What's this?" he barked, glaring at the mating marks. "Is this what I think it is?"

Both his mother and sister gasped and started making cooing sounds. Indigo gave a curt nod. His mother jumped up, rounded the counter, and pulled him into an embrace.

"Oh, my son," she crooned. "The first of our roost to be mated... and it's a Well-blessed mating at that. See, Drake? See what our son has done?"

Indigo's father gently let go of his wrist and smiled—the first genuine smile he'd sent Indigo's way in almost half a century.

"This will do wonders for our movement."

Indigo's brow arched. "It's a movement now?"

"Of course, honey," his mother said to him. "We'll forever keep trying to make it acceptable for vampires to choose lifemates. It's just not right otherwise. So who's the lucky vampire? When will we get to meet her?"

He cleared his throat and stood. "She's a Well-blessed human."

Silence.

He could have dropped a pin and heard it.

His mother spoke first. "What does that mean?"

"She's from the old world. She was frozen in time. The Well woke her up and filled her with mana."

"Like the Seelie Queen?" Florrie gasped. "You're mated to a queen?"

"No," he laughed. She was more like a goddess. He blushed. "Her name is Violet."

Florrie clasped her hands together and squealed. "I can't wait for the ceremony. Please tell me you'll have one. Other fae races have them."

"I don't know... is this what vampires are doing now?"

His father thumped his chest and squared his shoulders, as if what he was about to say was his pride and joy. "We—and the movement—are trying to instill regular fae traditions so that it's not so uncommon for vampires to mate. We're still working on a mating ceremony, but a dinner would be a nice start."

"Dinner?" he drawled. "We don't eat."

"She does. And if we invite—"

Indigo held his hand up. "No, we don't want others around. There'll be no ceremony."

His mother took his hand and looked at him with glistening eyes. "But just us? Will she meet us?"

Violet may not even accept their bond, but a little fluttering in his stomach wanted her to, and he wanted to formalize it, even if it was sitting down with his family.

"I'll see what I can do," he said. "She's still getting used to this world."

"Perfect." His mother clapped her hands together, and he could already see the wheels turning in her mind as she met his father's eyes.

He would have hoped his father had accepted his return without the surprise news, but he supposed he couldn't choose his family. He was lucky to have them at all. And if he was being honest with himself, the falling out had gone both ways. After he'd mistakenly killed a donor, he'd joined the Guardians to get away from their pity.

"So what does this mean for you now?" his father asked.

"I still have work to do. The dinner will have to wait awhile, but I'll talk to Violet. For now, I need to speak to Demeter. If anyone hears from him, or Haze, please contact me." His eyes went to Florrie. "You can contact me for anything, and I'll come. Now, did anyone see where Forrest went?"

His mother answered, "He mentioned something about a little bird telling him to check on a fire."

Indigo frowned. Forrest had gone back to Violet's house? If a little bird had indeed spoken to Forrest, it could either be one of the crows or an actual bird, considering he could communicate with the animals.

Every instinct wanted Indigo to return to Violet, but he had to see this through. He smiled at his mother and touched his fingers to his lips then pushed them down and out.

She blushed and thrust the cup at him. "Don't forget to

drink before you leave. Don't want to go out on an empty stomach."

INDIGO HEARD FORREST talking as he walked up the side alley to Violet's old charred door, but paused just at the threshold when he realized someone else was with him in the room. A female someone.

"All's I'm saying is that no one has seen Violet in two days, and I come here to check on her and you're sifting through her belongings. So either fess up, or I'll sic my harem onto you and you'll tell me, anyway. What have you done with her?"

Sic her harem?

Indigo pushed open the door and found Forrest leaning casually against the soot stained wall, his brows raised at a trio of pixies. Two males flanked the female. The first male was bigger than any pixie Indigo had seen. Broad shouldered and muscular, his leather garb and dark mo-hawk was the polar opposite of the second male—a blond, athletic type Indigo thought was probably more comfortable in sunny Helianthus City rather than this cold wintery town. The first had iridescent navy wings, the second had icy blue wings. But it was the pretty pink-haired female who stole the show. She bared piranha fangs at Indigo as he strode in.

"Where's Vanilla Bean?" she snarled.

"Vanilla?" Indigo frowned.

"Don't forget the bean," Forrest added with an all-knowing look.

The pixie stabbed a sharp bone spike through the air in their direction. "You know I mean Violet."

"Mitzie," the blond pixie said, putting a gentle palm on her shoulder. "Don't provoke the Guardians."

"I don't give a flying fuck who they are, Citron. If they've hurt my friend, I'll gut them until Moonsday."

The leather in Indigo's jacket creaked as he tapped his finger on his dagger. He and Forrest met eyes.

"How do you know Violet?" Indigo asked.

"How do *you* know her?" Mitzie narrowed her eyes.

"Let's go Mitz," said the dark-haired male, his voice a deep rumble. "These cunts ain't gonna give us anything, love."

"Wait." Indigo held his palm out.

Mitzie's eyes shot straight to the glittering blue marks and then widened. "You... no. It can't be." She thwacked the back of her palm on Citron's chest. "You see that? Violet's woo-hoo is more magical than mine!"

Forrest snorted, then relaxed and resumed his search of the charred apartment, lifting and sifting black debris. Mitzie rounded on Indigo.

"You mated with her?" she accused, her eyes glimmering. "Just tell me she's safe? Please?"

"She's safe." For now. The sooner he got back to the outpost, the better, and they still had to search Redvein Forest. "What do you know?"

Mitzie sheathed her bone spike into a slot at her belt. "I worked with her."

"You're her friend?"

She laughed, a high melodious tinkle that had her mates' gazes soften on her.

"I don't think anyone can call Violet a friend. But that's why I liked her. She was upfront, you know? For an elf, that's pretty hard to find." A deep inhale and then exhale. "She just disappeared so suddenly, and then that *warada-dick* from the queen's guard turned up asking questions. We came here to check out her place and found it torched."

At the mention of Gastnor, Forrest slid his eyes Indigo's way. Indigo clenched his jaw. He had to finish the rest of his business out here and then head back to Violet. The outpost was vastly out-manned now that the rest of the cadre had left. Indigo had thought Violet would be safe there, but if Gastnor was here, chasing her down in her workplace and home, then he had no time to waste.

"Found something," Forrest said, levering up the charcoal length of what looked like a pallet bed. Beneath it was a small tin box.

"Bring it," Indigo said. "We'll dispose of the metal when we get back."

Forrest tossed the box to Indigo, and he shoved the box in a jacket pocket.

"Is she happy?" Mitzie asked, her brow puckered.

Indigo met her eyes. "I don't know. But she will be. I'll make sure of it."

CHAPTER TWENTY-SEVEN

Indigo flew into the outpost island sometime around midnight. They'd spent the past two days scouring Redvein Forest for the corpses Gastnor had tried to feed to the tachi and any other evidence that might condemn the Queen. Other Guardians had helped, but the time couldn't have passed quick enough. His need to see his mate was an itch beneath his skin, ratcheting up his blood pressure.

The only thing keeping him sane was the constant, steady sense of her down their bond. He followed that bond and stormed into the cadre house where the sense of it was strongest. He burst through the bedroom door, not caring if she was asleep. In the corner, on the bed, Violet quickly covered herself with a blanket. He could have sworn he caught the flash of a bright light. A glow, as though she'd caught a firefly beneath the covers. With a daring lift of her chin, she challenged him with her gaze.

The silent dare prompted him to reassess his entrance. Had she been doing something wrong? He scanned the room. The fire still crackled. So, she'd refreshed the logs. Good. An empty plate sat on the trunk. She'd eaten. From the look of her damp hair, and tunic, she'd recently bathed. A lick of hot satisfaction traveled down his spine.

"Did you miss me?" he drawled with a tilt of his lips.

"You could have knocked first," she snapped.

Her sass only made his lips stretch wider. "Ah, but how would I know you're hiding something then, Petal."

"Petal?"

"How about Vanilla Bean?"

Her lips parted. "You saw Mitzie?"

He strode to the bed, stopping as his shins hit the frame. "First tell me what you're hiding."

"Nothing."

"Wicked humans with your lying mouths."

He wished he could say he was furious at her deceit, but he enjoyed these games between them. The day they stopped happening would be the day he died. If there was ever a time for her to fight back, to assert her protest, it was now. He all but begged for it. But instead of opening her sweet mouth and shooting some kind of retort, she clamped it stubbornly shut.

Indigo opened his senses to her emotions, to what her mouth failed to say. He held out his marked hand between them and focused, turning his fingers over, making a fist, studying their connection in a way that told her exactly what he was doing. She was nervous. Bashful. And something good... something... excited or lifting. It tingled him like bubbles underwater. Unfortunately, he needed more help to ascertain her lies. A bigger bond.

The shadow snake shimmered to life, coursing along his torso, uncoiling from its sleep until it slithered out of his collar. Violet's eyes widened as the darkness came her way.

"What are you doing?" she asked with a nervous laugh.

"Seeing if you're lying."

Her mouth opened and closed a few times before she answered. "Fine. I lied. Are you happy?"

The snake reared back, ready to strike and wrap around her wrist at the slightest provocation. Like him, the snake had a twinkle in its eye. He cocked his head and rested his knee on the bed, dipping the mattress.

"What did you lie about, Violet?"

She licked her lips, hesitated, but then drew her hands out from beneath the covers. They glowed softly with a pulsing light, as clear and pure as the moon. Triumph roared through him. She'd been practicing. The boundaries he'd set had worked.

"I can summon the light," she mumbled. "But I can't seem to turn it off."

"Show me."

She held out her glowing fingers. "And this..."

Light peeled away from her hand in ribbons. She twirled the light-ribbons around her finger. It was like watching electrically charged smoke. She made a fist and the smoke dissipated, but the glow remained.

"See? Stupid."

"It's not stupid. It's a step in the right direction. I'm so proud of you." He recalled the snake. "Violet, you've been following my rules. You deserve to be rewarded."

"Tell me about Mitzie."

He sat back on his haunches. "I was kind of hoping to give you a different kind of reward, but okay."

Her grin lit up her eyes, and he knew right then that he would forever give her what she wanted, even if it cost him. Seeing those lights made everything worth it, even the bad news he was about to give.

"We found Gastnor rummaging through your place," he revealed. "When he left, we set it ablaze, destroying any evidence he probably hoped to go back for. But"—he paused, not liking the next bit—"he already knows what you've done. Any vampire with a nose could have scented the old blood. All we hoped to do was make the task of proving your crime a little more difficult."

Violet clawed the blanket. "And Mitzie?"

"She came looking for you with two of her males." Indigo smirked. "They threatened us."

"Her heart's in the right place."

"She said Gastnor had been asking about you at the mines." His mood turned sour. "If he's gone that far to chase you down, I suggest we leave for the Order. You'll be safest there."

Her focus turned inward and guilt-ridden eyes swung his way. "I made a mistake, Indi. I shouldn't have killed them."

"Tell me about them. About your kills."

"There's nothing to tell. If someone attacked me, I defended myself. For those I hunted down, I researched their feeding habits first. I only killed the ones who fed without permission." She lifted her chin. "I warned every single one to stay away from me, but they came anyway."

"Well then—" He shrugged. "Every vampire knows if they feed without consent, the consequences could be dire."

"But sleep feeding—"

"Is an archaic practice that should be outlawed. But we're talking about the Unseelie Queen, here. She'll outlaw that when the Well freezes over. I'm more concerned Gastnor has you in his sights."

Another kind of fire lit up her eyes as she glared at the poor blanket, ripping it to shreds with her gaze. Fury. Hatred. Determination. It all hurtled down their bond like lava.

"Let him come," she spat. "I won't let the bastard win. I'll be waiting for him."

Indigo's hand enveloped hers. "Violet, believe me when I say, getting you to safety is the best option."

"I won't run from him." Her eyes snapped to his. "I won't."

She was so full of energy. So wild and tame at the same time. Sitting there, half neat and tidy with her brushed hair and pressed tunic, but with so much life glimmering in those dark eyes. She was a siren he would dash himself on the rocks for.

"Well-dammit, I missed you," he confessed in a rush of breath, his hand clenching to avoid reaching out. "I thought about you every minute I was away."

She bit her lip. His fangs ached, wanting to bite that plump flesh too.

"Did you miss me?" he asked. Hoped.

"No."

"Liar."

Contrary to her words, a flare of longing battered his own. Two waves crashing against each other. It stifled him. Stole his breath. Knowing she wanted him set his blood pumping. He stared as she wet her lips.

With painstaking awareness of her attention, he undid his baldric.

She watched every step of the way—the unbuckling of the clasp, the hauling over the shoulders, the clatter of weapons to the ground.

Violet made the first move. She grasped the segmented pauldrons on his jacket and dragged him closer. Their lips clashed hard, knocking teeth. *Blood.* Sweet, blissful, honey. Just a drop. Enough to sear through him, to trigger a taste of the bone deep satiation she'd bring, to light the fuse and send him into a frenzy of craving and want. If only he could have more. If only he didn't have to hold back. A strangled growl rumbled out of some deep, dark place in him. She moaned, kissing him hungrily, passionately, and perfectly. It was all he could do to hold her steady, two hands on her lower back as she ravished him.

She fumbled with the bone studs on his jacket until he

helped her, popping each one so it gaped open. And when her hands slid beneath his undershirt and hit skin with a strangled whimper of need, he fell in love with her. Completely and utterly. Firelight warmed her eyes as she pushed his shirt up higher and drank in the sight of him. With a single finger she traced the bunching of his abs, the line of a muscle angling toward his breeches, the dark trail of hair disappearing beneath. She stopped at the waistband and stared at his arousal pushing against the leather, yearning all over her face. Without waiting for permission, she went for his breeches, unraveling the cord and buttons with single-minded tenacity.

He speared her hair and cupped her head, feeling the curve of her skull in his palm.

"Violet." His warning came out hoarse, rough, and weak. Because he wanted her to touch him. He craved it, even if she wasn't ready, even if this could ruin everything.

She stroked his erection over his pants, tearing a curse from his lips. He wasn't ready for this. He wanted *her* first. To kiss and taste, to suck and lick. This would undo him—bring him perilously close to losing control of the monster locked away inside. But she pulled his heavy length free from the unforgiving leather and stared with hungry eyes. There was no doubt of her intentions. If he looked in the mirror, he imagined his expression would be the same. Want. Need. Lust. He dragged his thumb across her cheek and she lifted her gaze to him with a silent challenge.

Tell me to stop, she seemed to say.

Never.

A thrill skipped through him as he waited. He knew he walked on dangerous ground. Or maybe it was that single drop of her magic blood, working through his system, simmering a low heat, making his skin feel tight. And it was that sinful look that weakened him.

"I thought of you like this," he confessed. "While I was alone, when I slept."

She lowered to hover her lips over the tip of his cock, smiling as her hot breath teased him. He sucked in a breath at the anticipation, at the sensation that almost came.

"Did you touch yourself?" she whispered, lips butterfly kissing him. Pleasure shot up his spine. He flexed his hips, chasing more, but she pulled back. "Did you?"

"Yes."

"And you thought of me?" A squeeze along his shaft.

"*Well-damn*, yes," he burst out.

"Mmm." She licked over his crown and then took him in deep. All thoughts blanked from his mind. All sense narrowed down to that one point of contact. The pressure of her wet, wicked mouth.

He pulled her hair back to watch her face, the satisfaction, the smug delight in her expression, and it made him impossibly harder.

"Did you think of me too?" he rasped.

"Mm-hmm."

"Did you touch yourself?"

She bit him. Nipped him. He pulled tight in her hair, an action prompting her defiance. She tugged away from his touch, making the hair catch, hissing from the pain. Her eyes flared and grew urgent, her cheeks flushing with need. And through it all, she kept working him with her mouth.

"Violet..." *Crimson,* she was good. Hot, wet, tight. Just like... "Did you touch yourself?"

Again she ignored him as she continued to lick and savor. A sliver of warning coursed through him, coming deep from the same place between his ribs she already occupied. He reached for her, to give her pleasure, to make her feel as good as she made him feel. But she avoided him. She slid to the side and stroked him harder, squeezing him until he bucked and his eyes shuttered.

Fuck it.

She was holding out. She was...

He charmed his shadow snake awake. The shadow flickered and curled around his torso, winding downward, amplifying sensations until it slithered onto her arm. The link snapped into place, and he not only felt Violet's emotions, but the lust roaring through her body as though it were his own. She came off him, gasping and panting as she came to terms with her new bodily sensations—his, theirs. He eased her down against the bed, drinking in her desire, ready to give her more.

"What..." she panted. "What are you...?"

"You lied to me, sweetness."

"I didn't."

"As good as... you omitted the truth."

"And what is that?"

"That you're denying yourself, despite wanting it. Just like you did with the food, with the warmth from the fire."

She tensed, as though he'd ripped out her inner most thoughts and put them on display for the world to see.

He didn't know what else to do, so he kissed her neck, rolled his tongue around the hollow of her throat and sucked. When she arched and held his head to her flesh, he palmed her breast through the tunic, groaning as he found rock-hard nipples beading. She writhed, gasped, seemed to gather her resolve and then switched their positions with a rebellious grunt. She straddled him, her thighs hugging his hips, and looked down at him with a challenge in her eyes.

His gaze dipped to where her tunic rode up, to where her thighs met his, revealing everything he'd dreamed of. She made no move to hide herself. No underwear. Perfect, aroused, glistening sex nestled between a nest of dark hair. Her alluring scent intensified. Lust bolted through him. He reached, but she pressed her palms to his chest, urging him down. Palms that glowed and warmed deliciously. She wrapped her fingers around his shaft and continued to stroke, moaning deliciously as his own lust traveled down the shadow link, making her feel good whether she believed herself worthy or not.

Clever, fever-bright eyes lifted to his as she understood what he'd done, the mirror link within the shadow. Every bodily sensation he felt, she did too. She couldn't give him pleasure without taking it herself. A moment's hesitation, of stubborn refusal and self-indulgence, and then dark clouds shadowed her face. She slammed her fists onto his chest and reared back, frustrated.

They stared at each other. A silent, sexually charged standoff.

He knew she wanted him. The struggle played over her face, and down their bond—confusion, want, need, denial. Hurt. Guilt.

This was one of those moments, he realized. Her boundaries were failing her. She was suffering because she believed herself unworthy, but she was already everything to him. Couldn't she see how much he wanted her... needed her? Couldn't she see how much she was worth to him?

Slowly, cautiously, daringly, he squeezed his aching cock, showing her how she made him feel. Heat flared along his spine and he gave a low grunt. A gasp. She felt everything, resisted for too long, and then finally... finally started rocking against his thighs, chasing the same kind of release.

A crease formed between her brows. Already she was in her head too much. So he pumped from the base of his shaft to the tip. Then he did it again. And again. With each pass, he increased the tempo, the pressure, and watched her reaction. She tried not to succumb, but she felt his growing desire as much as he felt hers.

They were a Molotov cocktail about to explode.

"Touch yourself, Violet," he demanded. "Feel good."

Her plump bottom lip disappeared between her teeth. Sweat dappled her brow. He kept stroking himself, losing his breath, falling.

"Do it," he growled. *Come on, Violet.*

Her fingers dipped between her legs. Hesitated. Hovered. And then she touched herself, shuddering as she hit the right spot. Elation soared through him. Watching her take control of her desire was the hottest thing he'd ever seen. She threw back her head and submitted to the sensations she created, looking every bit the moon goddess. The more she worked herself, the more her skin glowed. She rocked against her fingers, and he pumped himself. Together they felt the buildup. Together they felt the tightening, the rush, the storm beneath their skin until he climaxed first... felt the wet warmth at his fist. Violet cried out. The glow in her skin burst, flashing brightly. He closed his eyes against the glare and fell back, at the mercy of the pure bliss pulsing through his body. She filled the room. She chased the shadows away. She stole his breath.

He could see why they called it the little death. He wasn't sure if he was alive or floating in the afterlife. Stunned, he laid there languidly, waiting for Violet's light to dim. When it did, she climbed off him and stormed to the fireplace, eyes luminous and furious.

"Violet?" He propped himself up on an elbow, frowning. "Are you okay?"

The shadow snake draped between them, a reminder of what he'd done. Of what he'd made her feel. He collapsed again on the bed and saw stars as the aftershocks of her light and their shared pleasure still skipped through him. But the satisfaction he felt was a long way from her reaction. Hurt, betrayal, confusion, guilt. It all bubbled down their bond. He took a deep breath and called the snake back to him. When it sighed and fell asleep, curled around his torso, he cleaned himself and pulled his pants back into order. Running his fingers through his hair, he sat on the edge of the bed, watching her.

Had he royally fucked up?

Still staring at the fire, she brought her finger to her swollen lip. Cold fear stabbed down their bond like shards of glass. She glared at him in accusation.

He held his palms up. "Violet. I'm not going to hurt you. Ever."

"I know," she murmured, more to herself than anything. "I *know* that. I feel it in my bones. I just... can't seem to... let go of the other feelings too. The guilt. The doubt. The..." She forced herself to exhale in a long, shaky breath. "I'm so sorry. I'm ruining everything. I always do."

He stood. "Never apologize, Violet. Never."

She shot him a wry look. "Or else I'm in your debt? I think we've crossed that line a long time ago."

"You don't owe me anything." He scoffed and tried to inject some humor into his tone. "In fact, after that performance, it's me who owes you."

She went silent.

"You weren't ready," he murmured apologetically.

She chewed her nails. "I don't know. Maybe."

"But it felt good, right?"

"Yes."

"So don't feel bad. Enjoy it."

"But—"

"You wanted it?"

"*Yes*," she said, more frustrated. "Of course I wanted it. You're..." She gestured up and down his body. "All that."

His lips curved. "Then no buts. Your life is going to be filled with pleasure, Violet. I'll make it my life's duty. So get used to it." He went to his jacket that had somehow been discarded—he didn't even remember removing it—and pulled out the small tinder box from the pocket.

"Here," he said, holding it out. "Forrest found this beneath your bed. It looked important, so I kept it."

"You brought it here? Even though it's metal?"

"Don't get me wrong, I'll destroy the box the moment you collect whatever is inside, but I thought you might want it."

She blinked. "You didn't even look?"

He shook his head. She took it carefully and opened the lid. Inside were two items. One was a dotted scrap of peach patterned cloth. The other was a lock of braided silver hair. Violet touched each item reverently.

"We exchanged a piece of ourselves before we split up," she revealed.

"Who?"

"The two other women who were... assaulted with me. We didn't have much else. And we didn't want to separate, but we knew if we were caught together, someone might discover that between the three of us, we could build another nuclear bomb." Tears glistened in her eyes. "So we split, but we gave each other these scraps so we knew it was real. That it wasn't some dream or nightmare. That we'd survived and we could master our own fate. I hope they're okay. I hope..."

"You sacrificed a friendship for the good of the world." He gathered her hands in his, holding both her and the box between them. "We'll find them," he promised. "We'll bring them in and we'll keep them safe. I vow it, just as I vow to keep you safe."

Violet pressed her tear-stained cheek to his chest and hugged tight. One of the strongest women he'd ever met fell to pieces in his arms. She cried. She sobbed. She cursed until she ran out of tears. Then he carried her to bed and laid down next to her, holding her close, stroking her hair and whispering about stupid things he'd done in his youth. Stupid adventures she seemed to enjoy hearing about as she trailed her fingers over the shape of the snake coiled around his torso, pushing his shirt up to get to more, and then leaving her hand wedged beneath the shirt, feeling his heartbeat.

When she was almost asleep, he started telling her about his parents. The first vampires in the history of Elphyne who'd mated for life, and how he was honored to be counted in the same group. To have her in his life.

"They had a hard time dealing with vampire society after they mated," he said quietly, tracing a circle pattern on her spine. "I remember a time when we were walking through the market. Florrie was young—"

"Florrie?" She mumbled.

"My sister, Florence. You'll like her." He loved how he felt her smile against his chest. "During this particular market trip, we were singled out by members of a well known colony. And well, heated words were exchanged. They called us unnatural. My mother insisted we take the high road and ignore them, but I went back after dusk the following night and used shadow to glamor a piece of warada shit I'd collected from the woods."

She snickered and shook her head.

"I returned every night for a month, placing a new pile of steaming shit in a different location, then used my shadow to hide it. It's probably why I'm so good at using shadow now. I've had a lot of practice."

She chuckled some more, but he could see her eyelids drooping. "Sounds like your parents had their hands full with you."

"They did." He paused, thinking of his recent encounter with them and how good it felt to see them. How shameful he felt to have let their feud go for so long. "You should have seen their faces when they found out I was mated." He smiled wistfully. "They're over the moon. They want to meet you, too."

When he looked down, she was fast asleep. She'd drifted off hearing how valued she was, how wanted, and that made him smile.

CHAPTER TWENTY-EIGHT

Sometime after midday, Violet awoke wrapped in the arms and wings of a vampire, knowing she'd just had the best sleep of her life. It had been solid. Not once did she wake afraid of being fed on. She also didn't wake early, a habit ingrained in her since her childhood competitive need to always beat her brothers. They would get up to train for whatever sport held their fancy at that time, and she took great joy in beating them to the breakfast table.

Resting against the soft cotton on Indigo's chest, this went against everything she stood for. Had stood for. But she couldn't muster the effort to care. All she cared about was this moment. The warmth beneath her cheek, his beating heart, his wings cocooning them, the orange sunset glimmering through the membrane. She pushed up his shirt and traced patterns on his skin, marveling at how the sunlight disappeared into the shadow snake like a black hole.

The snake's shadowy head was at his neck, out of his shirt collar, and the eyes seemed to watch her warily, letting her know that in some deep, hidden place, Indigo was worthy of protection too. That it would fight to keep him safe. A stupid thought, considering it wasn't alive, just a manifestation of his power. She shook the idea away, but the feeling stayed. She wasn't alone. Not anymore.

The blue from her arm markings added to the prism of color in her little bubble world, creating a wash that reminded her of balmy sunsets on a Hawaiian beach. That island might not exist anymore, but others had been born. She was on one of them. For the first time since forever, she started wondering what her future might look like. There was no doubt that Indigo would be in it. He continued to surprise her and melt her resistance every minute of the day.

Maybe her shame and guilt had a purpose. Maybe it meant that she'd actually cared, that Indigo had been right at the springs when he said she was the perfect person to understand how precious life was. Moments like these were worth fighting for.

She traced a larger vein in his wing from top to bottom. When she hit the large boney edge of his wing, she dipped along the skeletal limb before following smaller capillaries. This was definitely real, not part of the nightmare she'd been living. With the next light scrape of her touch, Indigo shuddered awake. He captured her wrist with a low growl and halted her movement.

"Those bits are sensitive," he warned, voice scratchy and oh so sexy. "Only touch them if you mean business, Vi."

Her cheek moved against his chest as she smiled. "I like that nickname best."

"I'll call you Vi if you call me Indi."

She rolled inward and kissed him over the fabric, reveling in his responding rumble of pure, masculine appreciation. His wings loosened, a silent plea, perhaps, for her to climb on top. She slid her arm over his stomach, and—

The door flung open, banging against the wall. Indigo pushed her behind him and moved to the floor, standing between the bed and the intruder. Dark shadows filled the room, both from his wings and his gift, blocking her view. Protecting her.

"Put that on."

Violet immediately recognized Shade's deep drawl. Indigo grasped something against his chest but kept his wings out. From where she sat, he was a magnificent sight. Defined back muscles rolled, dark wings flared majestically, and the snake slithered, a shadow beneath the white shirt, ready to bite.

"You look like shit. What happened?" Indigo asked. The snake slowed its movement, calming down.

"Best you come down for that. The others are in the living room."

The sound of the door clicking closed was the trigger for Indigo's wings to shimmer, and shift back into his body. Violet marveled at how the mass simply transferred, disappearing through slits in his shirt.

There would be a scientific explanation for the shift, she was sure of it. Someone, somewhere would someday discover how it worked, and she hoped she was still around to witness it. For a moment, her mind went sideways as she realized mana was more than a form of energy. It could be ingested and used. It was probably filled with ions, protons and electrons like everything else in life. Infusing ions into a solid object had the power to change its makeup... maybe that's what happened when someone ingested mana. They de-aged, but with the risk of madness, or so she'd been warned once.

She never got to finish her train of thought because her mate rounded on her, a stern look on his scruff covered face. She knew that look. Knew the feelings of anxiety coming at her from down their bond. Before he could tell her otherwise, she shot out of bed and found the clothes she'd worn the previous day.

"I'm coming with you," she insisted.

He stared. Blinked. Took one look at her determined strides to clothe herself and sighed. "Okay. But... I'm going to need you sitting on my lap."

"What?" She expected him to smirk, a joke, but he was deadly serious.

Slotting his arms into his jacket, he explained. "It's the

mating hormones. I want you for myself, Vi. I need you in my bed where I can spend days making you smell like me."

Her brows lifted. "Days."

"Days."

She shivered with the realization she might not be completely averse to that idea. "Will it be better after? I mean, your... urges?"

He shrugged. "I guess. Maybe. My parents were the first vampires to mate in centuries, perhaps since the dawn of our race. There have only been a few handfuls after. This is still new territory."

"Okay, then," she said, thinking as she slipped on her pants. "What exactly happened with your parents?"

What was she in for?

Guilt flashed on his face. "They locked themselves in a room to mate for days. My father almost bit the heads off anyone who approached. My mother said she almost didn't survive. They fed on each other. I..." He cupped the back of his neck. "I don't want you to go back to hating me."

She took his hand. "We'll figure it out. Just... don't shut me out."

Everyone waited in the small living room.

River and a crow shifter she'd not met perched on one of the two sofas. The Guardian next to them, Violet recognized as a patrol guard from the keep. This one was tall, broad shouldered and had antlers branching out from his blond head. Unlike the crows and Shade, he was squeaky clean. No dirt on him. No dust, no swollen skin, no blood of their enemy. With a stein in his hand, he watched Violet and Indigo enter with curious eyes.

Shade was on the second sofa next to another nameless Guardian. This one Violet failed to recognize, and there was no way she'd have missed his enormous frame. Muscles stretched his jacket to the point of bursting the seams. Long muskoxen tusks draped down from his forehead to his cheeks, flaring out in a deadly sweep. He glared at the two crows opposite and also held a stein in his hand. He must be a traveler.

Dirt and blood dusted the crows' faces and hair. Their wings had shifted away so they could fit on the sofa. Their weapons were gone, and their messy uniforms looked shoved on. Perhaps they'd been in Aconite City in crow form and had only hastily dressed to come to this meeting.

Shade, also dirty and in disarray, sat on the edge of the second couch, raking his fingers through his normally slick hair. But it seemed crusted in something—probably blood.

So they'd been in a battle.

No one seemed to have the energy to acknowledge their entrance. Indigo sat next to the big Guardian and squished into the corner as far from him as he could. True to his word, he tugged Violet onto his lap and locked her in with his arms. No one commented. The big Guardian glanced at her warily, at the marks on their hands, and then tried to inch closer to Shade.

Violet almost made a snarky comment about it looking like a funeral parlor in there but held her tongue. It very well might be the truth. Someone might have died.

No one spoke for long minutes.

She started to wonder what the holdup was when Cloud stalked in, just as dirty and disheveled as his fellow crows. When he got to the sofa, he flipped the stein out of the stag-shifter's hand. Just like that. No preamble, no warning. Just knocked it out of his hands.

Violet's brows shot sky high. Indigo clenched at her front, but that was the only sign of anyone caring. Through the fall of his loose curls, Cloud stared down the stag until he got up, collected his fallen stein with a huff and went to stand by the wall. Then the tattooed fae collapsed onto the sofa and made a disgusted sound, as if it was beneath him to sit in the same position a lowly non-cadre Guardian had sat in.

"Right. Now we're all here," Shade said, coming to a stand so he could see everyone at once. Even covered in dirt and blood as he was, Shade carried his deportment impeccably. "We have a situation."

Indigo cursed softly, his breath tickling Violet's nape.

"We were unable to lay eyes on Haze," Shade confirmed. "But we tracked his scent all over the queen's palace and grounds. We attempted to get in, but you've seen the evidence. All we've accomplished is arousing Maebh's wrath. She denies it, but we're certain Haze has been taken prisoner."

"How can you be sure if you never saw him?" Indigo asked.

"We spoke directly with someone who had," River answered. He focused on smoke weaving between his fingers, curling in a way that reminded Violet of Indigo's snake.

"You can't trust anyone in that court," the big Guardian grunted.

River scowled at him. "She wasn't a member of the court. This informant was a prisoner too."

"Still..." Indigo shifted beneath Violet, his voice tight. "What do we know about her?"

Shade turned to the crow shifter Violet didn't know. "Ash?"

Ash tugged the cord from around his head and raked his fingers through his dark hair. Wind seemed to be attracted to him, sifting stray hair like static. All the others turned to him, waiting for his response. He took his time tying the cord back around his hair before answering.

"She'd been tortured and mutilated. A pixie with her wings pulled off. The tips of her ears were cut to make them round. She was a tiny, thin, timid thing. Orange hair—"

A knot formed in Violet's stomach.

"Orange?" she blurted. Maybe he had meant peach. Was it a coincidence?

"Who the fuck cares?" Cloud snapped. "It was colored. She was a damned pix. Moving on."

Violet leaned back against Indigo, who'd stilled. It was

like sitting on a rock. She placed her palm over his to calm the anger bubbling down their bond. If she wasn't sitting on him, he'd have attacked Cloud by now.

She held her tongue, but only because she needed to think. They continued to talk, to reveal how this damaged pixie had described a large vampire of Haze's description brought in. She'd heard his screams from down in the dungeon. Apparently this pixie had been a prisoner for a while, and her leash had been loosened enough for her to wander about the grounds for daily exercise.

Too much of what they said only confirmed Violet's suspicions. Only a prisoner of value would be allowed to keep in physical shape. *It must be her.* Having peach colored hair was too much of a coincidence. Especially considering Peaches was tiny in frame *and* timid. Under five foot, if Violet remembered correctly.

Violet had pretended to be an elf, but Peaches could have scarred her back to make it look like wings had been removed. She could even have filed her teeth to look like a piranha's, or seen a body modification specialist. Violet had seen plenty of vendors who'd practiced the art of tattooing, piercing, and implants. The art hadn't disappeared in thousands of years. She may even had paid someone to glamor her... or done it herself if she'd learned she had a gift.

"I don't know," Indigo said. "This is all hinging on the word of a prisoner. An Unseelie prisoner."

"What did she look like?" Violet asked, interrupting.

"Like a pixie," River said, getting irritated.

"Don't be a floater," Indigo growled. "Just answer the question."

Violet squeezed his hand. "I meant, her facial features. Were they the same as mine, or slightly different?"

Peaches was Korean. Violet was Caucasian. Pixies had a certain look about them—high cheekbones, pointed chin, round eyes, heart-shaped face.

"Come to think of it, she did look a little different to other pixies I've seen." Ash rubbed his jaw.

"It has to be her!" Violet twisted to look at Indigo. "Peaches. It has to be her. It's too coincidental. The hair, the mutilation—it's the same sort of things I did to hide my identity."

Shade pointed at her, thinking. "Prisoners usually don't come out alive from those dungeons. The fact that her leash was given some slack could mean she's important to them, as in, she's Well-blessed too."

"Maybe the pix is lying," Cloud countered.

"Which is it?" Violet snapped at Cloud. "She's either fae, or she's lying. You can't have both."

The big-tusked fae beside Violet rumbled, "I think the human could be right."

"My name is Violet."

"Caraway," he mumbled, cheeks turning pink.

She gave a curt nod.

"So what does this mean?" Cloud said, studying each of them with astute eyes. "Does it change anything? She could still be a liar. Or bait."

Violet straightened her spine. "I don't care what she is. We need to rescue her."

"Agreed," Indigo said. "We'll have to go back. Together."

"No," Shade said. "We already made things worse with our attempt to get in. The queen has now shut her borders. Just because she can't lie, doesn't mean Haze isn't there. She might not have him directly, but someone else could. She might even consider herself beneath the day-to-day runnings of her dungeons. We need more intel."

"She can't just fucking take us prisoner. We're the Order," River snarled, leaning forward menacingly. He'd drawn an obsidian coin from somewhere and twirled it around his knuckles. "We're the ones who make the rules. They answer to us."

Multiple voices raised in agreement.

Shade lifted his hand, quietening them. "She's done it. She's taken Haze. So in my opinion, this is an act of war. Cloud?" he asked. "You're the only other council member here. What do you think?"

Cloud's eyes narrowed. "I think she's fucked with the wrong fae."

"Shit," Indigo murmured against Violet's back. She felt his forehead land between her shoulder blades. "This is bad."

"So we fight," the stag said. "We make a show of force and storm the castle."

"Nah," Ash drawled, his dark eyes too knowing, too calculating. Unseen wind ruffled his hair, and if Violet didn't know any better, she'd have thought someone stood behind him and blew him a kiss. When Ash cocked his head as though listening to that wind, Violet started. He probably was. There was a forest somewhere south where the winds whispered sweet nothings in your ear... sweet until they coaxed you off a cliff, or into the lair of a nasty fae. Ash's eyes slid Violet's way, as though he knew she'd unlocked one of his secrets. "We can't attack yet," he said. "The High Queen is up to something. Something important enough she's risking war against the Order."

Everyone deferred to his intel, which only confirmed Violet's suspicions. Ash was someone who *knew* things. But it wasn't enough. Violet needed action, not sitting around and listening to whispers.

"She's got Peaches," Violet said through a dry throat. "And if she was after Silver and me years ago, then she's probably wanting the same thing she did then."

Bleak eyes landed on her.

"She wants to be the first fae to build a nuclear warhead."

"Crimson save us," Caraway grumbled, shaking his head. "I need to get back to my post at Crescent Hollow, but you just let me know if I can be of assistance."

Shade nodded. "We need to get word to the Prime and the rest of the council."

"Fuck waiting on them," River said. "They'll talk about it for days, meanwhile, Maebh's got one of ours."

"But he's okay for the moment," Shade said, frowning to himself as though he didn't like his answer either.

"Peaches said he was beaten and shackled. He's alive, because Maebh knows if she kills him, she can't return from that. Perhaps she's holding him hostage, waiting for the opportunity to ask us for something."

His eyes slid to Violet. Indigo's hold tightened around her.

Cloud also glanced at Violet, then back to Shade. "We don't negotiate with madness. We won't be bullied into giving her anything. Or anyone. But if we want a chance at infiltrating the Winter Palace, we need to get through the Sluagh."

Ominous silence roared into the room. Cloud was right. The Sluagh were nigh on invincible. The demon-like creatures could detach their spirit from their bodies. They could invade minds and shatter them to pieces. They could steal souls and eat them, or worse, hold them prisoner, forever tasked as incorporeal soldiers in their soul stealing Wild Hunt. When they sent their wraith forms ahead of their bodies, decimation was unstoppable. How could you fight something you couldn't see?

"Then we need help in learning how to defeat them," Shade said.

"What do you suggest?" Indigo asked.

"Two things. One, we ask the Six."

Violet turned to Indigo with questioning eyes. He whispered, "They're the Sluagh Guardians. But they do what they want, when they want. We hardly see them."

"Dibs not doing that." River held up his hand.

"Fuck it," Cloud ground out. "I'll do it."

"Ask Laurel," Caraway said from the doorway. "I heard one of them had a thing for her."

"A *thing* for her?" Cloud's dark brows disappeared beneath his mop of hair. "Do they even have dicks?"

Caraway waved his hand. "Anise said something about it. I'll ask her when I get back." His eyes skipped to Violet and he explained. "Anise is my mate."

"Oh." She smiled gratefully. It was hard keeping up sometimes.

"So," Shade said. "You crows head to the Order, check in with the Six and rally the council. Indi and I will head to Helianthus City and ask for help. Jasper is the only fae I've ever heard of who has bested a Sluagh in battle."

"*King* Jasper," Cloud said wryly. "And it was only one Sluagh. Singular. If they call on the Wild Hunt, we're all screwed."

"Precisely why we need to leave tonight."

They all stood. Caraway left. The crows started to follow, but the antlered Guardian put up his hand, halting everyone. "What about me?"

The crows gave him a dismissive glance and then continued to walk out.

Shade turned to the Guardian and said, "You need to stay here and make sure any arrivals are extra careful in Aconite City. We'll keep you apprised."

Shade tipped his chin at Indigo. "It's too far to fly tonight. We'll use a portal stone."

"I can help you with that," the stag said.

Shade nodded and left with him.

"I'm going with you," Violet blurted before Indigo could say otherwise.

He frowned and nodded, surprising her. "I was just thinking it's probably just as safe for you in the court of the queen's enemy as it is at the Order. Maybe even more so considering Maebh has publicly denied representatives of the Order access into her castle. Plus, Ada will be there. She's from your time. You could learn from her."

"I meant, I'm coming with you to rescue Peaches."

"No," he clipped. "Absolutely not."

"It's not a question. I'm going and that's all there is to it."

"Violet, don't be daft. Gastnor is after you. The queen is after you. They want what's in your head. You said the three of you shouldn't be in the same place together, and Maebh already has Peaches. What will happen if she has you too?"

"Peaches needs me. She's been a prisoner for God knows how long. I can't leave her there."

"No."

"You don't understand. When I first met her, she was deeply traumatized from living in that cage. That was only a week or two!" She clenched her fists. "Silver couldn't save them. It was me who fought back. I'm the one who can do this. If you try to stop me, I'll just find a way, even if that means I have to fight my way through."

Dark eyes alight with emotion glared at her. Then he cocked his head, considering. "I tell you what. If you can best me in a duel, a fight, then you can go."

Violet glared at him as the familiar rise of indignation bathed her body. She hated it when men thought they were better than her. Her father, her brothers, her colleagues. She never stood for it then and wouldn't now.

"Deal." He had no idea how much she'd trained before she met him. Sure, it had been with metal weapons and she'd relied on that advantage, but she was a quick study. She would learn what she could from Queen Ada and use it to beat him. She just hoped Ada was a fighter.

"And furthermore," he added. "You will continue to feed. None of this half-finished plate business."

"You can talk," she snapped. "Or did my ears deceive me when Shade complained about your lack of nutrition."

His expression shut down. "That's different."

"Why? Because you drink blood?"

A pause. A heartbeat.

"Because I only want to drink *your* blood. Everything else tastes like shit."

"Oh." She blinked. "Well. I didn't know that. I thought you could take it from anyone."

He stepped closer and lowered his voice to a deep rumble. "Do you *want* me feeding from just anyone?"

Heat flooded her cheeks as she thought about that sinful tongue lapping at someone else's skin. A shiver ran down her spine. She didn't know. Maybe not. Definitely not.

"We're not talking about blood," she said. "We're talking about me kicking your ass in a fight. After we visit the Seelie King and Queen, you and I will have a sparring match. If I can't best you, then I'll concede and stay wherever you need me to stay."

"So a bargain," he agreed, lips curving, somehow finding something he liked shining in Violet's eyes. "A binding one."

"I wouldn't have it any other way." She stuck out her hand for a shake. He ignored it and instead cupped her cheek. Staring into each other's eyes, they forged a deal fortified with their mana. The bargain clicked into place like an unseen snap of elastic. She felt its metaphysical boundaries ripple outward from their connection. Whatever happened, whoever won, would have no choice but to follow their agreement.

CHAPTER TWENTY-NINE

Having portaled just outside the boundary near the ocean, Indigo guided Violet to the Helianthus citadel walls, wincing at the setting sun. Rising like a tsunami, the fortified glass walls swarmed with trapped manabeeze. During the day they were hard to see because the sun was so bright in the summer city. But tonight, they would twinkle like stars and illuminate the perimeter, guiding guards patrolling the battlement. Beyond the rolling glass walls was the city, and further inside, the Summer Palace—a castle made from glass and stone.

They could have flown over the wall but risked being spotted by guards on their descent—guards remarkably more vigilant now with Jasper as king. Since Jasper was an ex-Guardian, they thought it more prudent to walk up to the glass gates and simply ask for an audience. The red-coated guards took one look at them and allowed entry.

Shade gave Indigo a grunt of surprise and then flared his wings wide to take the rest of the journey by air. Like Indigo, he'd be keen to get out of the sun. Also, the locals weren't too receptive to Guardians, and Indigo didn't want Violet to suffer the wrath meant for him. He hoped with an ex-Guardian as king, this attitude would eventually shift to something more amicable.

Indigo smiled at his mate and held out his hand. She came into his arms; he gathered her up, and they followed Shade, flying over the estuary and canals making up the citadel maze. The smell of fish and salty brine wafted over the townhouses and high into the air. Even though it was late in the day, city folk walked the streets and paddled in their boats. Fishermen set their nets for the coming night. The city canals fed the palace moat and kept it populated with fish, and Crimson only knew what kind of water fae. More than once Indigo had to dodge a seagull trying to steal food.

Violet squeaked when he made the fast maneuver, and he couldn't help playing into it. With a grin frozen on his face, he dove, weaved, and soared through the city.

When they arrived at the palace gates, Violet's face was flush with excitement. It reminded him of wicked things he shouldn't be thinking about. *Later*, he promised himself.

The gates were made of the same mana-strengthened glass as the citadel walls. It would take the might of ten thousand orcs to batter that down.

"This is incredible," Violet gaped, peering closely at the walls. "It's like they've caught and tamed the stars."

"It's even more remarkable at night. And you should see the sky under the hill at Cornucopia," he said. "There are so many manabeeze there, collectively, they make a false sky bursting with sunlight."

Her eyes widened. "You're talking about the prison beneath the Ring?"

He nodded.

"No, thanks. I don't ever want to visit there."

"Fair enough," he chuckled.

Shade walked up to the guards and squinted. "We're here to see Jasper."

"Hmm. I see. High King Jasper Darkfoot doesn't just see any riff-raff," the first guard answered. A ram-horned fae with dark skin. Yellow epaulettes on his shoulders, dangling tassels, glinted in the light. New uniform. It had only been two months since Jasper seized power, but changes were already visible. The pompous guard looked down at them. "Do you have an appointment?"

Shade's expression flattened. Indigo snorted.

"We don't," Violet confirmed. "But I believe if you let him know two Guardians and one Well-blessed human are here to see him, he'll allow us entry."

The guard narrowed his eyes. "I don't care who you are, you need—"

"Ah, come now, Pippin." A shaggy-haired wolf shifter arrived. He couldn't be more than fifteen. There was something familiar about him. Unlike the red-coated guards, he was dressed in a casual suede jacket fringed under the sleeves. "Jasper won't mind. Trust me."

Pippin harrumphed. "Sir Lake, I believe you may be overstepping your station."

"Pippin," Lake pouted dramatically. "Jasper brought me here from the *Darkfoot* pack because he couldn't trust a single one of you after Mithras's reign. So pipe down. Let the Guardians enter."

Pippin's cheeks mottled a bright red. But he said nothing. Did nothing.

Lake saw it as a sign. He grinned at the Guardians and then let his open curiosity rake over Violet. Swiftly, and with a vengeance, Indigo's wrath rose to burst out as a snarl of warning. Lake blinked at him. His ears flattened, and then he lifted his palms in surrender.

"Don't worry. I have zero intention of standing in the way of a Well-blessed mating."

Lake hastily waved them in. Once safely out of earshot, Indigo said through gritted teeth, "I thought the Darkfoot Village had been slaughtered."

Lake's lopsided smile was full of melancholy. "Some of us escaped." A pause. "Too few. The truth is, Queen Ada saved my life once. I'm here to pledge myself as her personal guard." He puffed his chest out, then deflated a little. "Jasper's just making me work for it."

Indigo gave the youth a once over. In a few years his frame would fill out. The wolf shifter would be strong. It was smart of Jasper to train him until then.

They were led inside the palace and to a long dining hall. As they approached, a server rushed out, eyes brimming with tears, her tray dangling at her side. She almost crashed into them, apologized with a fist to the heart, and then ran off.

Shade and Indigo shared a surprised look. They all stopped outside the dining hall. Lake gave them an awkward look but made no move to announce them. He held his palm up for them to wait.

Okay.

A male voice boomed from inside. “I didn’t mean to frighten her! It’s this damn crown. It’s ridiculous.”

The low hum of a calm, female voice came next, followed by a second, more sarcastic female voice. Indigo didn’t quite catch their words, but they sounded like a reprimand.

“Why do I even have to wear it inside? Can’t I just.... Grr.”

“You need to wear it because you have guests in the castle,” said a female—the calm one. “It reminds your subjects that you have power.”

“You’re the guest, Laurel. You,” the king snarled. “I hate it. I hate this branding thing you talk about. I hate stuffing myself up like a frill-neck dragon. And—”

“What would you have the crown made of then, manaweed?”

“Now that’s an idea.”

Someone laughed. Probably the queen.

“Well, you asked me here to help you with your brand, so I’m here. Do as you’re told King Sourpuss.”

A low, acquiescing grumble. A pause. “I’m only putting up with this for you, my love.”

The queen laughed. “Um. You’re putting up with this because she’s right. The city can only handle so many changes at once. Just do it. You won’t die.”

Lake knocked on the door and entered. He opened his mouth to announce them, but when Jasper saw Indigo walk in, he stood from his spot at the head of the long jarrah table and snarled—wolfish fangs dripping with warning. It looked rather comical with the heavy glass crown weighted on his head, making his fur-tipped and pointed ears stick out.

The rest of his outfit was equally humorous. A frilly top, a red jacket embroidered with yellow wolves, and his usually scruffy brown hair neatly brushed. Indigo tried to hide his smile, but failed.

“I told you to never get within five feet of my mate,” Jasper growled.

“Relax,” Ada said. “He’s not here for my blood. That was a onetime deal only.”

Indigo didn’t dare look at the queen but could see her blond hair in his periphery. Next to her was Laurel’s darker haired figure. A single glance could have the king hurtling toward him, claws out, questions later. He dropped his smile and met Jasper’s stare.

“I’m not here for her blood, trust me.”

“Is this true?” Jasper asked Shade.

“Show him,” Shade said to Indigo.

He lifted his blue marked arm and bid Violet to do the same. Overdressed in a long sleeve tunic and pants, Violet must be warm. Sweat peppered her upper lip. She swallowed, pushed up her sleeve and showed the king.

Jasper narrowed his golden eyed glare but then sat before glancing at Violet and grumbling, "You have my condolences."

"Why?" Violet asked.

"Your mate is a cheeky twat."

The tension released from Indigo's shoulders and he smirked at Violet, who only raised her brows back at him.

Jasper gestured at the Guardians. "Shouldn't you two curtsy or something?"

They laughed. Lake released his breath and made his exit, but not before casting an awestruck look at the queen.

Jasper frowned at Laurel. "I'm serious. Do they need to curtsy? You know I never thought I'd be king. I have no idea."

But Laurel was staring at Violet. As was Ada.

"You're like us." Laurel swiftly stood, knocking the table in her enthusiasm. "You're one of the women Clarke's been searching for."

Unused dinner plates and cutlery clattered. Glasses filled with wine and water sloshed. Violet took a step closer to Indigo, fidgeting at her sides.

Ada joined Laurel in standing. The petite, freckle-nosed woman had long flowing locks dangling down her regal gown. When she placed her hand over her flat stomach, Indigo remembered she was pregnant. She'd be coming up to the end of her first trimester, if he remembered correctly.

Laurel dressed in form fitting knit clothes—some kind of revealing camisole he knew Thorne wouldn't like her wearing, but these women from the old world were strong willed and independent. They didn't like being told what to do or what to wear. He smiled and softened his gaze on his own mate, having a surreal moment realizing that he was in this group now. Mated to a beautiful, strong woman.

"We came here for your help," Shade said as he strode to the table edge. "Queen Maebh has taken Haze and denies it. And"—he swallowed, a nervous glance to Laurel—"Bones is alive."

"What?" Laurel snapped, her eyes flaring. "Since when? Damn it, I knew I should have killed him when I had the chance."

Thorne hadn't told her yet? Indigo's eyes widened. There would be harsh words between them when Thorne finally caught up to Laurel.

"And Peaches," Violet stuttered. "Don't forget Peaches."

All eyes turned to her, confused.

"Peaches is one of the women who woke at the same time as Violet," Indigo explained. "She's been held captive for—" He looked to Shade.

"Possibly years. Maybe months. I'm not sure, but we know it's long enough for her security to have been relaxed."

Ada made a pitiful sound. "Oh, that poor dear. I only spent a few days locked in that place, but at least we were treated fairly. We weren't prisoners."

Jasper took off his crown and placed it on the table. The blue twinkling teardrop beneath his eye sparkled. "What can I do?" he asked, then remembered his manners. "Please sit. All of you. Join us for dinner."

Ada called in the server who'd fled in tears and ordered more table settings for the meal. Indigo made sure to place Violet next to Laurel and Ada, while he, Jasper and Shade sat on the other side. He still couldn't shake the feeling to keep males away from her. The feeling was becoming a hindrance. He glanced at Violet, who already looked at him. He would have to consummate their union, completely, before going after Haze and Peaches. There's no way he'd be able to fight clear-headed without the security of completing their mating.

"We need to know how you defeated the Sluagh," Shade asked.

"Firstly," Jasper said. "I didn't specifically defeat him; I outwitted the queen whilst distracting the Sluagh."

Indigo deflated. "So it's impossible?"

"I didn't say that." Jasper's lips stretched into a devious smile. "There is a way. It's just impossible without me."

CHAPTER THIRTY

Violet fidgeted beneath the table. Why was she nervous? She'd given keynote speeches at physics seminars around the world, an industry heavily dominated by men. She'd lived with bossy sportsmen for brothers with toxic masculinity coming out of their ears. Two women shouldn't make the back of her neck itch like crazy, but she scratched under the weight of their attention.

Laurel opened her mouth. Violet whipped her hand out, halting her.

"Before you say anything," Violet said. "There's something you should know about me."

Laurel's lips clamped shut.

Ada leaned forward.

Violet studied their expressions. In neither did she find animosity, hate, or prejudice. But all of that could change when she confessed. She plucked at the embroidered tablecloth.

"I'm a nuclear physicist. Was, rather. I haven't practiced since I woke." She looked down at her hands and gave a deprecating shake of her head. That was a stupid thing to add.

"Well, it's a bit hard, I imagine without all the lab equipment," Ada remarked.

"What I mean is, that I worked in the engineering field. Building weapons."

The women stared. Then Laurel blurted, "Were we not supposed to know that? Am I missing something?"

"A brain," Ada drawled, chuckling.

"Oh shut it. You can talk, Miss Queen of Half the Land who doesn't know jack about queening." Laurel punched her friend on the upper arm and then fanned herself in a mock display of ego. "I, on the other hand, am a queen in everything I do."

Ada snorted, shot Violet a wry smile, and then rolled her eyes at her friend. And they *were* friends, Violet realized. To have that easy, teasing rapport, they must have known each other for a long time. It made Violet feel even more like a fish out of water.

"I'm just setting the expectations," she clipped in a tone ruder than she'd intended. "In case you thought I was someone I wasn't."

Ada's eyes softened with some kind of understanding. She reached across Laurel and took Violet's fidgeting hand. Warmth rushed into Violet. It was like someone had injected her with some kind of morphine. Her limbs loosened. Her lips parted.

"What did you do?" she whispered, feeling like a bowl of Jell-O.

"It's my gift," Ada replied. "I make people feel better."

"Oh. It's... nice."

"We've all done bad things," Ada said softly. "You shouldn't get so hung up on something out of your control. Believe me"—she shared a look with Laurel—"we all know exactly how that goes."

Laurel smiled tightly and showed Violet her fingernails. They were gnarled and twisted, but she'd painted them proudly with bright colors.

"Bones tortured me," she confessed. "Because Clarke is like a sister to me, and the Void knew it. So when he found out Clarke was psychic, he decided to send Bones to hurt me, knowing it would force Clarke into giving up the codes for the nuclear warheads."

"The ones I designed."

Laurel nodded. "I guess that's true. Funny how we're all starting to pop up here in this time, with these gifts."

Ada let go of Violet and sat back in her chair, a palm resting on her stomach.

"And we're finding each other," she said. "We're becoming a force to be reckoned with. You included."

Violet swallowed. She wanted to say more, to point out what was wrong with herself to these women, but they didn't really care. By the sounds of it, they all had similar stories. Similar regrets. Choices made that couldn't be erased. Choices that urged them to become better women.

"Queens." Laurel nodded. "All of us, in our own way."

"I like that," Violet murmured. "Queens."

"Oh, don't give Laurel a big head." Ada smirked. "She used to run Queen Fitness and now she thinks everything is her domain."

"I had a membership," Violet blurted, surprised. "There was that hiking machine in the corner no one wanted to use, but I loved it. What was it called again?"

She clicked her fingers, trying to remember.

"The Punisher." Laurel laughed, then her eyes flashed with respect. "Damn. You have balls, lady."

Violet shrugged, a blush heating her cheeks.

They all laughed. And with each breath, she felt the ground shifting again, taking her another way, forcing the view to change into something worth fighting for, something that pulled her head out of the sand and gave her the confidence to reach further.

"So how long have you two been awake in this time?" Violet asked.

"Nowhere near as long as you," Laurel replied. "Less than a year for us two. Clarke has maybe three or four. What did you do for six years?"

Thankfully, before Violet could reply, the server arrived with more behind her, each carrying trays laden with delicious smelling, steaming food. Her mouth watered.

"I forgot to ask if you have any dietary requirements." Ada scrunched up her face. "I'm shit at this job."

Laurel placed a palm on her hand. "That's why you pay someone to do it. Like a steward."

"Good point. Let's get one of those. I think Jasper fired half the staff."

"It's okay," Violet smiled. "I'll eat anything."

She didn't miss the sparkle in Indigo's eyes as he caught her words from across the table. It took all of her resolve to hold back her middle finger from flipping up in his general direction. Instead, she gave him a tight smile full of mystery. He leaned back as the server filled his goblet with blood. A flicker of disgust crossed his expression, but he quickly covered it with a smile and the hand-sign for gratitude. Violet felt his apprehension down their bond.

He really needed to feed properly from a vein. From her vein. He'd been so patient and considerate with her anxieties, but it was time for her to give back.

No longer did she feel the spike of adrenaline when thinking about his fangs sinking into her neck... well, not in the bad way. The thought of Indigo's mouth on her brought heat to her cheeks and a rush of warmth between her legs. She pressed her thighs together and glanced at him.

His brows knitted together.

He'd probably sensed a rush of affection for him down their bond. Thank God the shadow snake wasn't connected, or he'd be squirming in his seat just as she was, thinking of excuses to leave the dinner table early.

Violet hastily accepted her wine and took a guzzling

sip, grateful for the distracting burn down her throat. She turned to the two women.

"It sounds like you two have stories to tell. I'd like to hear them one day, if that's okay."

"Of course!" Ada said. "And we'd love to hear yours. But for now, tell us about your friend, Peaches. How can we help?"

Another wry smile of Violet's slid toward Indigo, just briefly, before she lowered her voice. Not that it made a difference. Shifters had excellent hearing. Vampires the best among them.

"I would like you to train me in using my gift for battle," Violet said.

Laurel grinned and fist pumped. "Oh yeah."

"Don't have an orgasm, Laurel," Ada intoned. "She doesn't even know you've had MMA training."

"You do?" Violet gaped. Mixed martial arts! All she had was a defunct scientific doctorate.

Laurel shrugged. "A bit. But Thorne—my mate—has continued to train me. We've had a few weird run-ins with one of the Sluagh in the Six. So he likes to know I can handle myself when he's not around. And, you know what? I'm not so bad if I say so myself. Even had a bout in the Ring."

Jasper cleared his throat loudly. Laurel waved him down. "You were under the influence of a curse. I hold nothing against you."

He rolled his eyes and then went back to his quiet conversation with the vampires.

"Thorne did most of the killing," Laurel went on. "Okay, all of it. But I held my own."

She looked to Ada for support.

Ada smiled reluctantly. "Yeah, she's okay. Nothing to write home about."

Laurel punched her again.

"Hey," Ada groused. "Pregnant lady here."

"Whatever."

Their friendship made Violet a little envious. Peaches' and Silver's faces sprang to mind along with a stab of guilt. Leaving them, separating… it was a mistake. One she was going to correct. She'd correct them all.

"So can you help?" she asked bluntly and then winced at her tone. "I sound bossy. I'm not. I'm just—"

"Grumpy," Indigo shot from over the table. And if it wasn't for his infectious, incorrigible smile, she would have found a way to kick him across the expanse. "I can help with that."

"Yes," Laurel said to Violet, after sending Indigo a derisive look.

"We'd love to help you," Ada added. "I'm more of a healer myself, but I can help you control your gift."

Violet touched her fingers to her lips and pushed them down and out.

"You've certainly got the hang of the 'fae never say thank you' thing quicker than me," Laurel picked up her fork and started eating.

"Six years," Violet reminded them.

Laurel paused.

Ada frowned. "It must have been awful, not to know anyone. To have no help."

"It hasn't been fun... and... I may have strayed down the wrong path for a while."

"What does that mean?" Ada asked, taking a sip of water from her crystal glass.

Across the table, Violet's eyes met with Indigo's. He smiled gently, and she had the courage to tell her shame.

"I killed vampires."

Ada spat water. "You what?"

Violet laughed nervously. "It's probably not a conversation for the table."

"But one we'd like to hear." Laurel dabbed down the mess Ada made with a napkin.

"Okay, Buffy," Ada drawled. "Color me intrigued. I'll take you up on that conversation at a later date."

"Well," Laurel said, with more gusto in her tone. "I suggest we get a good sleep tonight. Tomorrow we can start on your training while that lot work on their plan. We can all swap stories then." She checked her wrist, then chided herself, "I still look for my watch. Silly."

"It's not," Violet said with a small smile. "I still dream about cheeseburgers."

"Ooh and thick shakes," Ada added.

"Electricity!" Laurel blurted.

They all settled into a wistful silence while the males continued to talk amongst themselves.

Laurel twisted the napkin in her hands. "I think Thorne is due soon, too. He'll help. We'll all help." She looked to the three Guardians. "I mean, Jasper might not be able to, with his responsibilities, but—"

"Oh, I'm going all right," Jasper announced and then pointed at the Guardians. "Don't think you can infiltrate Maebh's palace without me."

Ada put her arm on his forearm. "Do you think that's wise considering the Spring Court is still not falling in line? Or that the Autumn Court is just waiting for us to fail?"

"I admit," he replied. "Taking over Mithras's reign has been harder than we anticipated. But the Autumn Court are spineless wonders, and the Spring Court will either bend the knee or I'll do it for them. Love, I *have* to go with the Guardians. No one will know I'm gone. It will be quick."

"Then I'll go too," Ada insisted. "A healer is—"

"Bloody not likely," Jasper snapped. "You and our unborn child will stay here."

Ada raised a brow. The tiny movement was all it took to redden Jasper's cheeks.

"You'll need me," she said, voice slow and deliberate. "Because you'll need to tap into my mana stores. I don't have to be in the fight but nearby."

Jasper's scruff-covered jaw tensed. The tendons at the side popped. He lifted a glass of red wine to his lips.

"We'll finish talking about this later," he said and took a big guzzle. When he put the empty glass down, he looked thoughtful.

Ada did too. She tapped him on the arm. "You should tell them."

Shade and Indigo straightened, their leather creaking.

Jasper lifted his head. "There have been... many surprises since I've come here. The spies, the traitors, the amount of coin in the coffers... or lack thereof."

"The human slaves," Ada added.

"Yes, the slaves. But chiefly among the surprises has been the mana I inherited."

"Mana?" Violet asked.

"Mithras and Maebh have been keeping secrets," he continued. "It seems the royals in this land also have an extra something. I guess you can call it a tithe I get from the Well for being custodian of half of Elphyne. My capacity to hold mana has grown and it's linked to the warm climate. We think it's an incentive the Well gives its leaders to encourage them to look after it."

"None of us knew that," Shade said. "I don't even think the Prime knows."

Indigo scoffed. "She probably gets it too. Why do you think she's so strong?"

A dark shadow crossed Shade's face, and he sat back, scowling.

"I know," Jasper said. "It's unusual. But Ada is getting it too. I dare say the two of us have the strongest capacity in all of Elphyne, even including Queen Maebh as she's operating without a co-ruler."

"You'll be a target," Indigo pointed out.

"Maebh's not answering my requests for a meeting to discuss the disbandment of the Ring," he said. "Even though we made a bargain to at least talk about it."

"It seems to me she's been occupied experimenting in warped ways with mana." Shade ran his finger around his goblet.

"Is she trying to create something like the Sluagh?" Jasper narrowed his eyes. "It wouldn't surprise me considering I only taught her mere months ago that they're not invincible, as she'd like everyone to believe."

Shade's finger stopped rimming the goblet. "That's a good point."

"And there's another thing. Knowing about the tithe the Well gives its rulers, knowing Maebh once ruled all of Elphyne, how is it possible she simply handed half of it to Mithras after the Great War against the humans?"

His words penetrated all of them, twisting and settling like indigestion. Violet pushed away her plate and forced her voice not to tremble when she spoke.

"Peaches is a geologist," she said. "And I helped design nuclear warheads. There's a third woman who woke at the same time as me. A welder. When we first met, we realized that our combined skills made it possible to build another bomb." She lifted her gaze and stared at each set of eyes. "If the queen wants a nuke, it's for only one reason. Power. She wants to rule the world."

CHAPTER THIRTY-ONE

The following morning, Violet left Indigo sleeping in their guest chambers and made her way down to the king's private gardens.

Now that she had a goal, achieving it was all she could think about. To become a master at it. The males would focus on Haze, and Violet would ensure Peaches was rescued.

She also needed to prove Indigo wrong.

The thought of him sleeping, still in their bed without her, caused something to tweak inside her chest. She'd retired to their room much earlier than he did. Even though she'd known he was nocturnal, a part of her expected—hoped—that he would return with her.

But he hadn't.

And unless Violet shifted her circadian rhythm to matching Indigo's nocturnal one, they'd forever be missing each other, like ships in the moonlight. But Violet wasn't ready to give up the sun, and she never needed much sleep. There was too much to do, learn and see. They would find time together.

But first. Training.

The king's gardens were to the side of the palace, between the outer glass wall and the main palace building. It was a little pocket of lush, high greenery, blooming flowers and fountains. When Violet arrived, a guard let her in.

"Call that a sit up?" Ada snarked. She sat on a stone bench while Laurel completed some sort of sprint-circuit workout. "You look like you're having a fit, not trying to exercise."

"At least I'm exercising," Laurel huffed, a smile on her lips.

"I resent that comment," Ada returned, but she didn't look resentful. She wiggled her rear on the seat and settled in, quite content to supervise. "Keeping you motivated *is* exercise. Now give me ten more."

Violet smiled. Trash talk. She liked these women. While she would never had been friends with them in the old world, it would have been Violet's fault, and nothing more. Violet had been too busy with her work, too busy trying to impress people she shouldn't have.

Upon seeing Violet, Laurel stopped her workout and waved her over.

"You're certainly up early," Violet remarked.

Laurel winced, doubled over, panting. She wore some sort of tight, knit yoga attire. Even though Violet had never seen the likes in this time, Laurel must have commissioned a dressmaker to create clothing suitable for her needs. She caught Violet looking at them and gestured to a neatly stacked pile of clothing on the stone bench next to Ada.

"I brought you something to wear," she said. "If you're serious about training with me, then you'll need to keep up."

A little burst of fear skipped through Violet at the expectations, but she exhaled in a huff and psyched herself up.

Peaches.

Silver.

For them she would become a weapon sharper than a sword and brighter than the moon.

"That's the plan," she confirmed.

"I'm just going to supervise." Ada held up her hand and tugged on her long, golden braid. Her dress was made of something more flexible than what she'd worn last night. A pair of pruners lay next to her with more gardening tools and a basket, half filled with weeds.

"This is your garden," Violet stated, looking around.

A blush hit Ada's freckled cheeks. "It *was* Mithras's. When we arrived, we found it overrun with neglect, full of weeds and brambles. I think Mithras was madder than we all knew. It even has a creepy coffin back there, covered in thorns and carved with antlers. Gross. Jasper wanted to tear the garden down, but I convinced him to let me revive it." She smiled and glanced around. "There's just a magical quality to it. It's not the garden's fault its master was a cock-head."

Laurel laughed. "You got that right."

"Well it's stunning," Violet remarked. "And I guess I should call it the queen's garden. Not the king's."

Ada pointed her pruners at Violet with a joyful expression. "Now that, I'm all here for."

Violet picked up the clothes, went to change in a vestibule just off the garden door. The pants were stretchy and molded to her legs. The black singlet was tight, even on her slim frame. Since the weather was warmer here, she had no need for the jacket she'd worn down from her room, so left it in the vestibule with everything else. Her only personal item was her boots. As she tied her long hair back with a leather cord, she caught sight of her reflection in a dark window and paused. The scars were visible, and they were everywhere. But instead of making her self-conscious, they fired her up. Her blood started to simmer with pent up rage.

When she'd gone to college, she'd acquired the nickname *The Machine* because when she set her mind to studying for an exam, she didn't stop. She compartmentalized and approached the task with single minded ferocity. Nothing filtered into her mindset except scoring top marks. She forwent dating. Apart from using her family to drive her motivation, she ignored them. She only had eyes for the textbooks.

Giving herself one last look, she returned to the garden.

"Will it be just us?" Violet asked.

"For now," Laurel confirmed. "But Thorne is here. And unlike the others, he wasn't up all night chin-wagging, so he said he might come down at some point and help."

Their gazes flicked to the scars on Violet's arms and throat. Violet drew in a breath. She may as well mention the obvious so they could get past it.

"Vampires," she said. "Unseelie soldiers. A mob of them attacked me not long after I woke. They'd kept Peaches and Silver in a cage for weeks, passing them around, letting all the vampires feed from them."

"That sounds so horrible." Ada frowned, then a flicker of confusion crossed her expression. "Our blood makes them drunk. Were they really intoxicated the entire time?"

"They didn't seem to care. They became junkies for our blood." Violet frowned as a memory bubbled to the surface. "There was this vampire a few years ago, right at the start of my... being on my own, I guess you could say. He got the better of me once, and I moved out of town. It took him over a month to track me down and when he did, he confessed my blood had sustained him the entire time."

"You're saying he only needed to feed from you once, and then he didn't feed again for over a month?"

Violet nodded.

Ada's eyes narrowed. "Indigo never told me that."

Laurel pointed out, "He didn't really have a chance, what with Jasper growling every second he got near."

"Still," Ada mumbled. "I think it's something we should have known."

Violet remembered how Indigo had hesitated revealing his needs to her. When he'd confessed he only wanted her blood, and no one else's, he'd blushed. He was probably embarrassed to admit this weakness.

"I'm sorry you had to go through that," Laurel said, her hand fluttering to her throat.

Violet's brow lifted. "You're okay saying sorry?"

Laurel shrugged. "That's a fae rule. Between us girls, we can thank as much as we want, and we can apologize. We make our own rules."

Violet's lip twitched upward. "I like the sound of that."

"I can see why you... how did you say it... went down the wrong path?" Laurel scowled. "I might have done the same."

"You know," Ada said, concerned eyes tracing Violet's arms. "I can heal your scars. If you want."

Taken aback, Violet blinked. Heal them? As in erase them?

Unease prickled through her.

The scars had been a driving force in her survival. She'd never looked at them and thought herself ugly or wanted them gone for vain purposes.

"I don't know..." She bit her lip. "That sounds stupid, I know, but... the scars have become my identity. And... I'm just not sure."

"I get it." Laurel flashed her gnarled nails. "These are my battle scars."

She smiled flatly. "Is it okay if I think about it?"

"Sure." Ada picked up her weeding basket and stood.

"I'm here if you need me. I would love to be setting up a public clinic in the citadel somewhere, but we're not ready for that yet."

"As your brand manager, there's a process," Laurel pointed out. "Steps we need to take. But believe me, Pretty, it's on the cards. Any goodwill we can inspire in these people, the better."

"Pretty?" Violet asked.

Ada scowled and clicked her pruners. "Don't you start too. It's a ridiculous nickname her and Clarke came up with. Just call me Ada."

Laurel patted Violet on the back. "First things first, we're going to head to the training courtyard at the center of the palace. And then we'll run laps."

"We're not going to get straight to it?"

A drill sergeant type smile split Laurel's face. "One thing I've learned about besting my mate in battle is endurance. Those testosterone-filled buffoons rely too much on strength. So first, we run track."

An hour later, Violet was dying quietly on the inside. On the outside, she ran martial arts drills with Laurel on the dirt courtyard surrounded by hedges and the occasional curious side-eye from palace staff. The large rectangle of space looked mainly to be for walking horses and kuturi, the griffin-like creatures. The stables were nearby, and the hands stuck mainly to one side, allowing them space to do what they wanted. An armory or the barracks must have been nearby because, occasionally,

Violet saw red-coated guards sparring with their bone or rock weapons. But they never stayed long.

After running themselves ragged, the women stopped for lunch, ate burgers and green smoothies—at Laurel's insistence—and then returned to the courtyard for some magic training drills where Ada and Laurel both taught Violet the process of how they access their personal mana stores, and how they shut it off. Each had a different process and Violet would need to find her own.

For the next week, that's how it went.

Get up early, train her body to the point of collapse, eat lunch, and then train her magic until she was mentally exhausted. Occasionally the males turned up and tried to snoop, but were sent away by Ada or Laurel. Violet realized it was not only for privacy but also because if Indigo smelled another male on her, he became frantic, irritated and dominant. Somewhere deep inside, Violet knew she was avoiding him, but when she became The Machine, there was no room for anything else. He would distract her. Him, and that incorrigible trickster smile. And then she'd forget her own name.

So she trained.

Slept at opposite times to Indigo.

And trained.

And ran her new friends ragged with her demands for perfection. A few times, Ada tapped out and rested, but Laurel was as driven as Violet. A kinship developed. Perhaps it was because both of them carried a similar weight from their guilt, or maybe it was simply their personalities. But when Laurel told Violet to jump, she did. When Violet demanded they extend their training an hour longer, Laurel agreed without complaint.

CHAPTER
THIRTY-TWO

In the late afternoon of the seventh day, Indigo and Shade came down with Jasper and Thorne. All were in their battle leathers. Up until now, they'd kept their own training efforts to the evenings. But for some reason, this late afternoon, they took up residence on the other side of the courtyard—where the guards had sparred —and resumed their training, despite Ada's insistence they find somewhere else to peacock shirtless.

Ada stuck her tongue out at Jasper, who then turned back to her, scowling, a teasing gleam in his eyes.

"Always so snoopy," Ada said.

"Ignore them," Violet replied and gestured for Ada to return to her demonstration.

"They're only here because they're jealous." Laurel chopped her hand through the air, planted her thighs in a warrior's pose, and then repeated her action. "This kind of movement needs to become second nature. We're building muscle memory. Do you understand?"

Violet nodded. "It looks like a block."

"That's right. Kind of Mr. Miyagi style."

Ada sighed wistfully. "I remember that movie."

Laurel added her sigh to the mix. "I remember movies, period."

While Violet practiced the blocking drills, Laurel made a showy display of conjuring a fireball in each hand and juggling. When water suddenly doused her, raining down to plaster her short dark bob to her face, Laurel spluttered. A flair of her power filled the air, tingling the tip of Violet's tongue and itching her inner ears.

Damn, Laurel was powerful.

Glaring at the males across the courtyard, Laurel kept her temper in check. She smiled flatly and projected her voice across the yard. "Who had the giant cajones to do that?"

All fingers pointed to Jasper, who barked at his so-called comrades something about sending them to his dungeon for treason. They only laughed. It wasn't a reaction of disrespect, but of long held camaraderie. Violet's chest swelled at the sight. She was glad to see Indigo had that, despite claiming to her they weren't his friends. When Jasper met Laurel's eyes, his pointed ears flattened like a wolf in trouble.

Laurel glared at Ada. "I'm going to throat-punch your mate."

"Good. He's getting cocky."

The males still laughed. Including Indigo. The one who'd said he would never hurt her.

It grated on Violet that the males were making fun of the women.

"They don't think I can do it," Violet mumbled, her face going cold as the realization hit.

They all believed their decades of warrior training would be enough to rescue Haze and Peaches—without her help. Did they believe they were that good? That invincible?

Was Violet that impotent?

"No—" Laurel wiped her face with a towel. "They think you *will*."

Violet met her firm gaze. "What makes you say that?"

"Think about it," Laurel said. "I mean, really think about it. Focus on your bond, on what Indi is feeling."

"He's nervous," Violet confirmed, her brows puckering. He stood to the side under the shadows of eves and had the kind of forced posture that was probably meant to look intimidating. But Violet saw through it. She saw the shadow snake slither and coil with restless energy. "This is killing him," she added quietly.

"To them, having a mate is like splitting their soul. It's a stronger bond than marriage," Ada explained. "It's both physical and metaphysical. The idea of losing us, even for a second, terrifies them. Jasper wakes up in cold sweats thinking about it."

"Thorne too," Laurel mused, smiling gently at her mate. "They're little puppy dogs, if you think about it.

Stubbornly possessive, and sometimes a little dominant, but adorable as hell and push overs when they realize how stupid they're being."

"Then shouldn't they be helping us learn?" Violet asked.

"They will," Ada said confidently. "Probably in their roundabout way. But they can be pig-headed for a while first. I blame it on their animal blended DNA. It makes them possessive, slaves to their testosterone, and aggressive. Primal. They're not human, Violet. Never mistake them for it. But like Laurel said, they can be little puppies inside all that bravado. Well, at least when they realize they're not going to get any rumpy-pumpy tonight unless they start to cool down."

Someone barked out a laugh across the courtyard, another's voice raised in protest, and a third shot out an affronted grunt of protest. They'd been listening to every word the women had said. Spying. Snooping. Low grade murderous intent started to bubble under her skin.

Ada gestured at Violet's hands. "So, let's see what you've learned. Show me."

Wrenching her attention back, Violet summoned her light, allowed a ball of it to diffuse from her hand and gather like a tiny moon in her palm. Then she snuffed it out with a clench of her fist. It was so tiny. Self-doubt washed through her.

"Honestly, maybe it's me being stupid. Not them," Violet confessed. "How is a ball of light going to help in a battle?"

"Not just a ball," Ada reminded her. "You can make your entire body glow so much it can be blinding."

"But is that all I've got?"

Laurel smirked. "We haven't even gotten to the good stuff."

"Oh?"

"Well, it's like this. Every fae, or mana-filled human like us, has a certain affinity with different elements. You said Skye tested you for yours. We've all had ours isolated. Now that we've perfected your control, and increased your endurance, I think it's time we start working on what spells you can conjure."

"I'm listening."

"You know how the vampires use shadow to conceal? Well, a cloaking spell is kind of the same thing."

Indigo had once told Violet that her gift was a mirror image of his. There might be more things she could do that he could, but in reverse. Better. For a moment, regret squeezed her heart and she wished Indigo was the one teaching her to use her gift, but maybe it was better this way. He wanted to keep her from joining the fight.

"Essentially," Laurel explained. "It's about making the air around your body reflect what's behind you. It's a bending of the light mixed with a dash of spirit for the mind, and a cloaking of your energy in case someone senses your power nearby."

"Light refraction," Violet mumbled, mind turning inward, dredging up old physics equations and theories. "And if you can do that just as you are, then with my gift, and the ability to control photons outside my body, I might be able to do more than cloak myself."

"Now you're being all sciencey on us." Ada's face lit up. "What do you mean?"

"Indigo and Shade can direct their shadows into forming shapes. The shadow particles exist—you know, considering Skye mentioned they were all chaos element, I wonder if it's got something to do with dark matter—" At their blank faces, she realized she'd digressed too far. "Sorry. Where was I?" She scratched her head. "Oh yeah, it seems that pushing the mana into these shadow particles, somehow changing their ionic makeup, they're creating something new." She looked across the courtyard and leaned in close to the girls to whisper, "Indigo's snake is almost a living thing he commands. It starts out small but can be manipulated into something larger to hide his entire body if he wills it. What if, with my light, I can power more than a snake? What if I can create mirages? What if I can make people think they're seeing things that aren't there?"

Ada and Laurel blinked at her.

"Then not only can you slip behind enemy lines unnoticed but create mass confusion in your wake."

"You're a genius," Ada drawled. "Dead-set. You're a genius."

"Well, I was a—" She bit her lip, about to talk about her old vocation, but held it back. That woman no longer existed. For good reason. "Never mind."

Guessing where Violet's mind was headed, Ada piped

up. "You didn't do it, Vi. Stop torturing yourself. It's time to give up the ghost."

"It doesn't matter if I pulled the trigger. There was only one possible outcome of what I built. I knew that when I designed it."

"You never expected it to be used. People make mistakes."

"Yeah. Except my mistake cost the world." Violet pushed extra power into her next summoning. Light burst from her hand and she fashioned it into a ray, shooting straight up, aiming for the sky as though it could pierce the setting sun.

"If it wasn't you, it would have been someone else," Laurel said. "And if you ask me, I think you're being a little self-involved."

Violet raised her brows. *Self-involved?*

CHAPTER THIRTY-THREE

For a moment, Laurel and Violet stared at each other, and since Ada made no effort to comment, Violet took it as her feeling the same way. Breathing through her defensive reaction, she forced her shoulders to relax and actually process Laurel's words. Self-involved... She may very well be right. Since Violet had awoken in this time, all she'd thought about was how everything had affected *her*. But she wasn't the only one in the world. These women all had a similar story to Violet. Every single one of them had been attacked, displaced in time, and somehow used by enemy forces. Violet wasn't special in that regard. With each breath, some of the anger and self loathing melted away.

"You're right," Violet said, meeting Laurel's steady gaze. "I have been, and for that I apologize. Letting go of the past has never been my strong suit. I have to do better this time. What's important is that we protect the future."

Laurel grinned. "Yes, queen!"

"Whatcha doing?" Indigo strolled up. Considering she was annoyed at him, Violet didn't want to notice the way his leather breeches fit snugly at the thigh, or the way the hard and sweaty muscles on his naked torso flexed and rolled with each step, or how he'd arrived just after Laurel had said something potentially inflammatory as though he'd protect her from the words.

His wings trailed behind him, and his hair caught the wind. Damn that dying sun, giving him a twinkle in his eye. The stupid shadow snake had taken to winking at her like they were old friends—almost as if it adopted the friendly ribbing Laurel and Ada had with each other. She glared back.

"Just practicing," Violet said sweetly, a tone that sounded foreign on her tongue. As if he didn't know. As if he wasn't listening from his side of the courtyard with his twitching vampire ears. "We could ask the same of all you."

He scratched the back of his neck and gave her suspicious eyes. "We're waiting on word from Rush. He's at the Order with the rest of the council."

Oh.

"Have you heard from your brother?" she asked.

He shook his head grimly. "He's still not answering my calls, but reports coming in from the Winter Palace say that he's there, alive and kicking."

They shared a worried stare as Laurel and Ada slipped away and joined their mates and Shade. This was the first of Indigo Violet had seen in two days. Apart from sharing the same bed, which he had kept extremely G-rated, all he did was cover her with his scent—like an animal—so no other male would approach her. If it wasn't for that, she might wonder if he'd had second thoughts about their union. He never had a choice either.

Damn it. Now she doubted herself. And him. And... she made a frustrated sound and turned away.

They'd been like separate souls. The males' training hadn't progressed well, from what she'd gathered. Laurel and Ada had filled her in after drilling their mates for information at night.

On one of those rare moments Violet had crossed paths with Indigo, he'd let it slip that Shade was the only one who could walk through the shadows, and for Jasper's method of defeating a Sluagh, it wasn't nearly enough to separate the wraith from its physical body. They were going to rely heavily on Jasper, a king who was under extreme public pressure, to do all their dirty work. If Queen Maebh found out, his actions could start a war.

Jasper had a backup theory—he could portal himself inside a Sluagh with metal in his hands, a feat only a Guardian could manage. He'd surmised that, if the metal didn't do the job of doing the Sluagh in, then both Jasper and the Sluagh's cells might not be able to co-exist in the same place and one, or both of them might die.

Violet agreed. One of the main laws of physics states that energy can't be created nor destroyed, but only transferred. This meant that the energy Jasper used to move inside the Sluagh had to go somewhere, either transferred into the Sluagh—possibly creating an explosion, or back into himself. He might not absorb it. He might explode too.

There was a reason metals and plastics were forbidden. They made mana unpredictable and unstable, if it worked at all. Having Jasper resort to this sort of tactic left them all unsettled.

He was a king, a mate, and he had a child on the way.

If Violet was going to be happy with this approach, she'd need time studying the effects of portaling. She considered letting Indigo know about her mirage theory, but knew she needed any advantage to outwit him in their looming sparring match. If anything, the past week had solidified the need to prove herself a worthy warrior.

They needed her.

Over the past week, Indigo had been tense and clearly didn't want to further their sexual relationship until after their bargain outcome was revealed. At first, she'd thought it was because drinking her blood might very well involve the act of making love. The act of feeding could be an aphrodisiac for both parties. And if he fed from her, his mind might be addled for more than a day afterward, therefore giving him a handicap going into their sparring match.

He'd kept his hours nocturnal and the opposite of Violet's daytime training schedule. He'd avoided speaking much, and he'd grumbled and muttered under his breath if he even caught the slightest whiff of another male on her. She almost felt sorry for him.

Puppies. Baby bats were called pups too. Violet smiled at that thought.

Maybe to beat him in a sparring match, she only had to hug another male first.

But she couldn't do that. To him, or herself. She needed to best him fair and square.

"Are you okay?" she asked. His nerves fizzed through their connection. "Haze has been gone for over a week now."

He squinted at the setting sun, sinking over the horizon of the glass palace roof. "It's your friend in there as well. And... never mind."

She stepped closer to him. "What is it?"

The moment she entered his orbit, his nostrils flared and his eyes turned smokey. "You smell good," he admitted. "Like..."

He growled low and pulled her closer so he could bury his nose in her neck, holding her cautiously as though he might break her.

"You didn't answer my question," she prompted.

She pulled back. He'd already shuttered his expression and desires. Fine lines were etched at the corners of his eyes—worry marks that hadn't been there before. He suddenly grinned and raised his brows.

"You have some meat on you." He squeezed her upper arms. "I'm going to enjoy beating you. At least now you won't be a push over."

"You won't beat me, and you know it," she accused, firing up. "Or you wouldn't feel the need to spy on me."

He caught a strand of hair from her ponytail and curled it around his finger, as if he hadn't just said the most demoralizing thing to her. He studied her brown tresses in the sunset. She was ready to begin their match right now. The urge to fight him was that strong, but she needed to train. To work on this spell she'd theorized. It could very well be the difference between winning or losing.

Peaches.

Silver.

A commotion at the gate drew their attention. The male Guardians had moved from their side of the courtyard to huddle around a newcomer. No, two newcomers in Guardian battle gear. One had long blond hair and golden skin—an elf. The other was Forrest.

Indigo took Violet's hand and walked them over.

"I'm going to have to start charging the Order rent," Jasper joked. "Leaf. Forrest. What brings you here?"

Leaf's battle leathers looked a little different from the others. More blue in the piping and on the pauldrons. Some kind of star motto crested over his breast pocket. He might be their superior. Her spine went bolt straight with intuition. If the leader was here, something had happened.

Leaf ignored Jasper's snark, and the fact he was a king. No bow. No curtsy. But from Leaf's stiff posture and impeccable grooming, she didn't think he deferred to many people at all. Not even kings and queens. He caught sight of Violet and pushed through the group of males to get to her.

Indigo stepped in front of Violet.

"Leaf," he greeted, his voice low and tight.

"D'arn Indigo," Leaf replied. "You were due to report to the Prime over a week ago. She is displeased."

"Something came up."

"Hmm." Leaf's arrogant lips flattened. Ocean blue eyes flicked to Violet. "It seems something always comes up when these Well-blessed humans are discovered."

Violet raised her brows, the hairs on the back of her neck rising.

Leaf shifted his gaze back to Indigo. "What's your reason for disobeying orders?"

"You know exactly what it is."

"Haze missing is no excuse. She was expected at the Order last week."

Violet stepped around Indigo. Seriously, these Guardians needed a lesson in respect. "*She* has a name. And *she* is standing right here."

Leaf folded his arms and looked down his nose at Violet. There was something about his skin—smooth and ageless. Almost timeless. Beautiful and masculine at the same time. Power radiated from him. So much that she started to wonder about his age. Until Violet, and the other Well-blessed humans arrived, usually power equated with age or being initiated at the ceremonial lake.

Plus the arrogance. It dripped from his every pore.

Shade asked, none too welcoming, "Why did you come, Leaf?"

A look passed between Shade and Leaf no one would call friendly.

"I've come to let you know the Six will be of no help."

Shade's eyes narrowed. "Why do I feel there's something you're not telling us."

"Cloud asked. They shut the door on his face. That's it. We're lucky he walked off their porch with his soul intact."

"Why the fuck are the Sluagh in the Order if they do nothing but hide away in their house all day and night?" Shade grumbled.

"Maybe you should ask them," Leaf dared.

Shade's lips flattened.

"It is not for us to question the ways of the Well," Leaf ground out, his eyes skating to Violet and silently assessing. "The Sluagh are of no help."

"Rush could have communicated that to Thorne." Shade cocked his head, studying Leaf. "You didn't need to come all the way out here to let us know that."

Again, Leaf focused on Violet. This time, Indigo did more than step before her. He hissed and bared his fangs, his wings slowly arched out. The shadow snake slithered out of his collar, coiling around his neck, slithering down his arm, ready to strike.

"If you're here for Violet, you can think again," he warned.

"Indigo," Leaf said, as though speaking with a child. "The Prime needs to meet with her. If she wants our protection... and our help, she also needs to be tested and to swear fealty to the Well."

"*She* has a name," Violet repeated. "One you just heard."

Leaf's attention never wavered. It made her more determined to finish her training, and to show all of them what she could do. Then again, maybe he already knew. Maybe that's why he was here. To monitor her progress, and to ensure the knowledge in her mind—or her burgeoning skills—remained the property of the Order.

"You know about me, don't you?" Violet asked. "My old history. The new history. The killing."

Tension crackled in the air as the unseen power of multiple males competed for dominance. Violet half expected a brawl, but a sudden blue twinkle to their left caught their attention. One of the feature fountains gave off an ambient blue halo.

"Someone is trying to contact one of us," Leaf said, dismissing them with a hand.

"It's for me," Indigo noted, flexing out his fist as though it tingled. "It must be Demeter. Finally."

CHAPTER THIRTY-FOUR

Conflicted between leaving Violet unattended in a courtyard full of males, and answering the call he'd been waiting for, Indigo froze. In the end, his mating instincts won over. He'd suppressed them for the past week, and they'd had enough of playing second fiddle to his logic.

He pulled Violet to the side, ignoring Leaf's furrowed brow.

"I need you to go to our room," he said.

Violet gave him a look that said he tried her patience, but he couldn't focus with her here. Watching her run around in tight-fitting clothes, getting sweaty, and—even better—putting weight and curves onto her skinny frame had been torturous. He was about ready to crawl out of his skin any time they were close. She invaded his dreams, waking and asleep.

It had been better for both of them that they woke at

different hours, to stay separate, because if he was present during her training, he'd find a way to meddle, and then he'd find a way to dominate, and then he'd be all over her whenever another male entered her orbit. The look she cut him said she was at the end of her rope. He wasn't sure how long he could keep this distance between them.

Violet narrowed clever eyes at him, suspecting everything, but not knowing enough. She ground her teeth.

"I need to practice, anyway," she said, and left.

Breathing a sigh of relief, Indigo went to the fountain. But before he moved his head in line with the water, he looked for Jasper and Shade. They were right behind him. Shade gave Indigo a nod.

They were listening. And they would stay out of range.

Indigo walked up to the fountain and looked down at a reflection almost identical to his. Dark eyes, vampire ears, scruffy black hair. Demeter.

"Brother," Indigo greeted. "I've been trying to contact you."

"I heard," Demeter replied dryly. His voice sounded warbled through the water, as though he truly were beneath the surface.

Indigo tried to see beyond Demeter, to anything behind him, but there was only a stone wall. He could be anywhere. Demeter appeared unharmed. Healthy, even. So definitely not coerced or forced.

Demeter looked beyond Indigo's shoulders, probably trying to ascertain if he was alone just the same as Indigo had done for him.

"You know why I've been trying to contact you," Indigo said. "Is it true? Did you betray us? Did you take Haze?"

"What?" Demeter gaped, then quickly covered his surprise by scowling. He leaned closer to the connection and hissed. "My only loyalty is to my queen. So how can I betray you?"

He'd been surprised, Indigo realized. But he'd also declared family meant nothing to him. The queen must be listening.

"You have Haze in the queen's dungeons, admit it," Indigo said.

Demeter straightened. His jaw clenched. "I have no such fae in the queen's dungeons. Your Guardian colleague failed to show at our meeting. Your accusation is not taken lightly and has caused offense."

If the queen was there, Demeter had all but admitted to a meeting of subterfuge with a Guardian. There was no way he'd put himself at risk so easily. Not for Indigo.

He didn't believe his brother for a second. And the nerve of him to speak like that. Florence had been right. Demeter had changed. Indigo thought back to the way he used to be, remembering the pranks and roughhousing. Maybe this was always Demeter. Maybe it was Indigo who'd changed and finally saw Demeter's behavior for what it truly was. Cruelty.

"Release him," Indigo demanded, pressing on.

"Like I said, I don't have him."

"Then why are you contacting me?"

Demeter looked to his right. His ears twitched, and he nodded to whoever spoke before returning to Indigo.

"My queen would like to extend a formal invitation to the Seelie High King."

Indigo stiffened. "Why are you telling me?"

"Indi," Demeter breathed impatiently. "Don't be obtuse. We know you're in Helianthus City. We know you're at the palace."

A low, guttural growl reverberated from somewhere behind Indigo—Jasper, as he registered the threat.

"An invitation to what?" Indigo asked, pretending it didn't concern him the queen had been tracking him. May as well see where this was headed.

"Darkfoot requested a parlay with the queen—"

"Months ago," Jasper muttered under his breath.

"—regarding the state of The Ring at Cornucopia. She is ready to hear his request and fulfill her end of the bargain between them over a special state dinner."

Indigo couldn't help his eyebrows winging up. That was a paper thin reason for inviting the new Seelie King and Queen to Unseelie lands. None of this felt right. Not the request. Not the timing. Not the knowledge Demeter had about them. There was no doubt in Indigo's head that this was a trap.

Shade stepped closer to Indigo, into view. Demeter glared at him.

"You say you have not taken Haze," Shade said calmly. When his voice hit that level of intonation, there was no calm.

It was flat because all of Shade's unseen effort went to restraining the darkness, itching to burst forth and smother everyone whole. "Yet when Guardians, I among them, came to confront your queen—who is listening—we were met with undue force and secrecy. What do you expect us to think?"

Again, Demeter turned to a voice to his side.

"Bring two Guardians, then," Demeter decreed. "The queen agrees to let them tour the dungeons and see for themselves that Haze is not here. They will be welcome at her table, along with the Seelie High King and Queen."

Demeter's hand hovered before his face, ready to dash through the water and cut their connection.

"You have forty-eight hours to respond," Demeter announced. "And then the window closes."

Demeter's reflection turned into Indigo's own scowling face, the connection lost.

"Fuck that," Jasper spat, prowling like a caged Well Hound. "It's all bullshit. If she thinks I'm going to put my mate and unborn child in jeopardy..."

"Calm down," Leaf drawled.

Shade paced. "It's clearly a trap."

"Agreed," Indigo said. "But at least Haze is alive."

"What makes you think that? He denied it."

"He also went to great pains to remain rigidly clear in his retort. He said *he* doesn't have Haze, and Haze isn't in the dungeons," Jasper pointed out.

"I'm not convinced you're right, but it's a way into the Winter Palace," Shade said. "Forty-eight hours. It's already been a week. She could be doing anything to Haze right now."

"And Peaches," Indigo reminded. If this human was important to Violet, then she was important to him.

Leaf looked around the courtyard suspiciously before settling on Jasper. "If Maebh knows who is in your home, you have spies in your midst. You'll need to clean house. Again."

Jasper jabbed a finger at Leaf. His upper lip curled, and his next words came out menacingly slow. "Don't tell me how to run my house. You don't lead me anymore."

The words were defiant, but a sliver of fear broke through his expression. Jasper had been trying for months to clear the rabble from his staff. Mithras sympathizers, human spies that had somehow infiltrated the palace before Jasper's reign, human slaves, Unseelie spies, Spring or Autumn Court sympathizers. He'd been telling them all about it over the past few nights. Indigo felt bad for the fae. At least with the Guardians, he knew who to trust. Some of them might not be friends, but one thing always remained constant—when it came to life or death situations, they had each other's backs.

"Fuck it," Jasper growled, his temper flaring, his newfound power stifling the room. The fountain bubbled as though boiled. Water vapor in the air popped and crackled. He scowled at them and then rounded on his heels, growling over his shoulder, "War room. Now."

The war room was a long, stone room triple warded for privacy. No glass ceiling. No windows. The Well would freeze over before anyone could spy on what happened in here.

Manabee filled lanterns glowed softly on hooks between tapestries depicting Seelie histories. A map of Elphyne covered a long quartz table stretching down the middle of the oblong room. Miniature wooden figurines of different colors represented different fae races and the humans in Crystal City in the western wasteland.

Indigo, Jasper, Shade, Thorne, Leaf and Forrest surrounded the table, all with dark scowls on their faces.

"This involves both of us," Jasper prefaced, gesturing between the Guardians and himself. "Meaning the Order, and the Seelie kingdom. Whatever decision I make about this should involve all of us."

"Then the Prime should be here," Leaf said. "Or at the very least listening via communication."

Shade shot Leaf a scowl that said he was being a goodie-two-shoes, but Leaf was probably right. If they wanted backup for any kind of offensive attack against Queen Maebh, it would have to be with the Prime's blessing. There would be consequences, and a trial by Council, if the Guardians went rogue. It was bad enough Indigo had stretched his mission to secure Violet and bring her back to the Order.

"She can listen in," Jasper agreed and collected a bowl from a side table with a pitcher of water and glasses. He put the bowl in the center of the table and filled it with water.

With a flick of his wrist, the water cascaded into the air, forming a tunnel that almost hit the ceiling. He looked to Thorne, who then used his dagger to prick his finger and flick blood into the waterspout. Within moments, a blue glow emanated and Rush's visage appeared in the water. His long silver hair was half tied to display furred shifter ears. A dark beard covered a face Indigo thought managed to somehow look more seasoned than the rest of them. Hard, golden eyes and flared nostrils, ready to hear what news they revealed. No matter what side of the table they were on, everyone could view him.

Rush, Thorne's father, had been stationed at the Order while he and Clarke raised their daughter Willow. Occasionally, they traveled around Elphyne following Clarke's psychic visions to hunt down the next human waking from the old world. But fortunately, today, they were at the Order. These kinds of communications only worked between blooded kin.

"What is it?" Rush asked gruffly. His long silver hair looked disheveled, and when a pale feminine hand swiped over it, tidying him up, Indigo smiled. Clarke was there.

"We have a situation the Prime needs to be aware of," Leaf said.

Rush mustn't have been able to see Leaf, because he frowned at Thorne and raised his brow for an explanation.

"We're in the war room at the Summer Palace," Thorne explained. "There are a few of us here."

"Right," Rush said. "I'll find her."

"Don't leave yet." Jasper folded his arms.

"We only have forty-eight hours to prepare a strike," Shade said. "We don't have time to keep the Prime in the loop."

The glare Leaf sent Shade could have stripped the tapestries off the walls, but it slid off the vampire like water. Indigo didn't think anything ruffled Shade's wings.

"You're not the leader of the Twelve, Shade. I am," Leaf reminded him.

"But I'm also on the Council with you."

"If the Prime's not involved, then I'll make those decisions on behalf of the Order."

The shadows suddenly grew inexplicably darker. Shade's gaze grew cold, and he paced along the length of the table, flexing his fists.

Jasper clipped, "Let's focus on the facts at hand. We must be certain there's a reason for a strike, first. You've damning evidence Haze is there, correct?"

"We have the word of a mana-filled human from the old world," Thorne replied, frowning.

Silence stretched. Most of them wanted to believe the human was telling the truth, and every experience they'd had with an awoken Well-blessed human had been fortuitous. Indigo certainly wasn't complaining about his mate. She was the one for him, and she'd never lied beyond the odd denial to take care of herself. He trusted her.

"But there is no actual proof?" Jasper frowned, saying

what they were all mostly thinking. "We're going on the word of someone we don't know."

"Violet knows her. She vouches for her." As the words came out of Indigo, he knew them to be as paper thin as they sounded. In terms of fae lifespan, Indigo barely knew Violet herself, yet he was asking them to trust a woman Violet had only met briefly six years ago. It could all be lies, just as Cloud had said. But they had to trust their instincts. "Clarke has *Seen* these women, has she not?"

A female voice came through the connection, somewhere to Rush's side. "Yes, I did. In all of my visions, all three of them play an important role, depending on who gets them on their side."

Jasper nodded. "So if we accept the invitation, we get inside the Winter Palace. Surely she knows we can see through her ploy."

"You're a king now, Jasper," Leaf reminded him. "These are the games royals play with each other."

"But what does Maebh want?" Jasper threw his hands in the air.

No one had an answer.

A cold stone settled in Indigo's gut as he pointed out the facts. "They knew I was here. They have Haze. They've probably learned why we were in Obscendia, especially since Gastnor has been hunting Violet."

The mention of Gastnor sparked something within Shade. He stopped pacing and spoke to the fountain. "Rush, Shade here. Were the mana-warped bodies retrieved from Redvein Forest?"

"Yes," Rush confirmed. "They're here. Barrow is conducting autopsies as we speak. So far all he's come up with is that these poor souls have been mutated, limbs growing out of them that shouldn't be there."

"I might know what Maebh's end game is, but not how she will achieve it."

"Go on." Leaf's leather creaked as he crossed his arms and parted his feet. He dropped his jaw, darkness flitting over his expression. The elf was likely the oldest among them—they didn't even know his true age—and he had power. Enough to generate his own portals without needing a portal stone. Finding out that Shade had knowledge before him was not going down well.

The power struggle between the two had begun the moment Shade was promoted to cadre level, long before Indigo had joined the Order. Then when Shade became a council member, the tension increased. The two had been verbally sparring, trading jibes, and competing ever since. It was no secret Shade wanted Leaf's job as cadre leader.

Shade said, "Since Jasper took over Mithras's reign, he's learned that being king also comes with certain perks—chiefly a growing capacity for storing mana and withdrawing power from the Well. I think it's safe to say that the queen also has this, and that for some unknown reason, Mithras had conned her out of ruling half of Elphyne."

Rush nodded. "With Mithras gone, she wants it back."

CHAPTER THIRTY-FIVE

Violet walked into their chambers the following evening. Indigo rolled out of the large four-poster bed and scrubbed his hair. “We’ll spar tomorrow evening,” he said.

Having just come from a training session with Laurel and Ada, Violet felt depleted, but in good spirits. Her theories had proved correct. She’d spent most of the day working on pulsing light outside her body and then shifting it to create mini mirages. Mini, being the operative word, because the size of her deception was nothing but the size of the palm of her hand. But it was a win, all the same.

She’d hoped that, despite their bargain, Indigo would have let this need to keep her cloistered go by now. She’d hoped he’d trust her as much as she trusted him. It irritated her enough that she made sure she was already awake and out when he'd returned to the room, exhausted from talking with the Order. Talks she'd not been invited to.

Fortunately for her, today Ada and Laurel had revealed plenty. They'd received an ultimatum from the queen regarding an invitation to visit. The king, his queen, and two Guardians were on the guest list. It was obvious to Violet that Indigo intended to be among the two Guardians, and Violet was not going at all.

Over her dead body.

"I would like to be alone," she said to him. "Until the match."

His chin snapped up. "You're kicking me out?"

"Yes."

"Vi..." He stood. The blanket fell from his waist, revealing full frontal nudity, and for once Violet was too angry to care. She stared directly at his eyes, holding her own against the arrogance and ego and... considerable length hanging between his thighs. She didn't back down.

He lowered his brows in defeat. "Fine. I'll get my things and tomorrow evening, we'll satisfy this bargain."

She kept her back to him until he dressed and went to the door. With his hand on the knob, he paused. Out of the corner of her eye she could see his mouth open, as if he had something to say, but then must have thought better of it. He left.

Alone, she collapsed on the bed, sitting with her head in her hands. Her weary body wanted to do what she'd been doing most nights, bathing and then falling asleep, dead to the world until morning. But she had to perfect her mirage spell. And then there were the martial arts drills she wanted to do, one last time. And the dagger—the one he'd given her—she wanted to make sure the special runes worked to keep it clean and sharp.

She had to be ready, because tomorrow she was going to beat Indigo and ruin any kind of relationship they'd built. He would either hate her for proving him wrong, or she would hate him for holding her back. There would be no consummation of their union. They were too different. And this had all happened too fast.

A rebellious surge of denial stung her eyes. When she wiped them, her fingers came away wet. Was she... crying? Over Indigo? Her throat clogged. Yes, she was. She didn't want to separate from him. She didn't want to be on opposite sides. Sleeping together, even if that's all it had been for the past week, had made her feel more at home than ever. More secure. More loved.

It was as though, despite their tension and competition during their waking hours, their bodies and hearts knew the truth—that they belonged together.

Her feelings didn't change the fact he was trying to suppress her or keep her from helping her friend. And she wouldn't be influenced by a male like she had with her father and brothers. Her mother's voice echoed in her mind. *Don't let the bastards win.*

Violet ran her hand over the empty sheets. She had to fly free, without the need to impress, or she would end up in the same position as before—using her power for the wrong reasons.

WITHOUT INDIGO EMBRACING HER, Violet fell into a fitful, restless delirium—dreaming of irritating things. She woke around midnight, realizing that she'd allowed herself to rely on a vampire for comfort and, on some level, protection. Why else would she sleep so deeply when he was there?

Annoyance swept the last cobwebs of sleep from her mind.

When she had been living on her own, traveling around the Unseelie realm slaying vampires, she would wake frequently during the night. It was safer that way. Catnapping was more her style of sleep, and she'd managed fine. Now her body protested at the rude awakening.

How things had changed.

With a growl, she threw off her coverlet and stepped out of bed, ignoring the ache in her muscles from training. A few minutes of activity would loosen her up.

Why not start practicing for the sparring match now? And what better way to ensure a cloaking spell worked, than to walk around the palace using it. If anyone spotted her, she would know she failed immediately. But if she could complete a lap of the common rooms without being seen, she would know she succeeded.

She shoved on soft knit pants and a loose linen tunic she tied with her belt—purely to holster her dagger. She liked to carry it to get used to the weight. When she finally beat Indigo, and proved to herself she had value, she wanted a weapon she was familiar with.

It was a pity she couldn't carry metal, but now she recognized the benefit of her new gift. She wouldn't give it up. Not for the world.

Once or twice Violet had considered taking a dip in the ceremonial lake to see if she would be judged worthy enough to hold the forbidden substance, but fear and doubt won over. The Well may have brought her from her time, but asking it twice to trust Violet was a little too much. Especially since she'd been going about her retribution the wrong way. She knew that now. Killing was wrong. She wasn't God. Punishment wasn't her right to dole out, whether to herself or others.

Except maybe where Gastnor was concerned. Vengeance was hard to forget. Even as the thought formed in her head, she felt a stab in her chest. Would she really kill him, given the chance? Is that what Laurel or Ada would do? It was certainly what Indigo would do. And the other males. But why would she want to be like them? This whole bargain thing was to prove she was good enough as she was.

Before stepping outside of the room, Violet summoned her mana and fashioned it into a cloaking spell. Looking down at her hands, she found them missing. Her body was gone too. A rush of endorphins washed through her. Pride.

That's what she felt. She'd worked her butt off to get this far in the allotted time. She had callouses on her hands and aches in her bones. Mental exhaustion meant she'd slept almost ten hours a night. And... a growl in her stomach reminded her that she'd been eating more too. The extra physical exertion required it.

Indigo had been right, she needed to look after herself. It was the path to strength and healing.

It used to pain her to admit any male was more right than her. If her father or brothers had claimed something to be right, she would have proven them wrong. If they had said to eat a diet full of protein, she would have researched a hundred scientific research papers to find out why it was wrong, or which protein was better. If they'd told her the Nets were the best basketball team, she'd have looked up the stats of all time and calculated her own best team. Now that she looked back at her old self, she knew it had never been about the desire to be right. It had been about wanting their respect.

With a last look at her empty bed, Violet left the safety of her bed chambers. Her stomach decided to head to the kitchen. She weaved her way through the palace halls, sticking to the sides, avoiding any late night staff going about their duties. Not a single one of them noticed her.

When she found a housekeeper dusting the skirting boards of a hallway, she couldn't help herself and conjured the mirage of a tiny mouse scampering across the floor. The poor house brownie squealed in terror and then chased after the mirage with her broom. Unable to hold her grin, Violet continued to the kitchen feeling as though she was walking on air.

She was really getting the hang of this.

Just outside the kitchen doorway, she stopped at familiar voices.

Guardians.

"Now," Shade mumbled. "I know Jasper said he asked the chef to procure some. It must be here somewhere."

Cupboards banged and clanged.

"Try the meat locker," Indigo suggested.

Violet froze at the sound of her mate's voice. *Don't sense me. Please don't sense me.*

"That makes sense," added Forrest, crunching on something.

Heart thumping in her chest, Violet stretched her hearing to see if others were in there. Then she realized she didn't need to stretch, she could simply walk in and see for herself. Indigo had failed to notice her with his senses... yet, so this could be an opportunity. If she was brave enough. If there was any test she needed to pass, it was this. Two vampires with a strong sense of smell—one of them her mate—and an elf proficient in magic.

I'm not here.

She held her breath, checked her cloaking spell, and then entered the kitchen. Long rows of tables and counters lined the walls. Another long counter was at the center of the room. Racks of utensils and pots and pans—all wooden, ceramic or stone—were plunged into any nook or cranny. The industrial sized ovens and hearths were at the back and cold. Dried garlands and bouquets of various herbs hung from ropes over the fireplace and dangled at corners of racks.

The three Guardians gathered on stools at the central counter. None of the vampires had their wings out. They just looked like three regular men—well muscled men—having a midnight snack.

No one noticed her. Not even Indigo. She exhaled in relief.

Forrest ate some kind of homemade burger he'd slapped together. Shade poured from a pitcher of blood into two stone cups. Then he warmed the contents with his mana and slid one to Indigo. Shade took a tentative sip of his and scrunched up his nose.

"I'm going to find one of those waitresses." He put the cup down and flicked his gaze to Indigo. "You coming?"

Indigo had been staring morosely at his cup and pushed it away. Violet's heart skipped a beat. He was going to feed on someone else? Her hand fluttered to her throat. Did she have a right to be upset?

The vampire had to feed.

"No," Indigo answered. "I'm good."

Shade's impeccable brows lowered and concern flickered in his eyes. "You haven't fed from her yet, have you? You haven't fed at all."

Violet's gaze roved over Indigo. Dressed in a simple soft tunic and pants, she noticed more of his frame. The battle leathers had hidden too much, and come to think of it, when she'd been studiously avoiding seeing him naked, he'd seemed thinner too. Muscle and tendon on his frame was more defined, as though he was dehydrated. Compared to Shade, whose bulk was healthy, Indigo looked tired. Withdrawn.

Forrest chewed, darted his green gaze to Indigo, then raised his brows and nodded in agreement with Shade.

"She's not ready," Indigo said defensively. "You wouldn't understand."

Another heartbeat skipped.

"She isn't ready, or you aren't?" Shade tipped the unused blood down the drain of a nearby sink.

Indigo's fingers speared through his hair.

"I smell her everywhere I go," he admitted, shaking his head incredulously. Violet wanted to smile, to know that she messed with his mind, but the tortured look in his eyes gave her pause. "Even now I can smell her. I sense her. I can't stop thinking about her. What do you think's going to happen when I finally sink my fangs into her?"

Forrest studied his burger.

"That was a long time ago," Shade pointed out. "You weren't a Guardian. You hadn't met me. You were different."

"If she finds out I killed someone because I couldn't stop—because the blood tasted too good, because—" He cut himself off, frustrated. "No. It's better this way. She needs to focus on training, and I need to do the same. Why do you think I've kept our waking moments separate? I can't concentrate when I'm around her."

He'd kept their waking hours separate. Violet had

thought she'd done that. Did he mean to say he'd been manipulating her just as she'd been avoiding him? She started to back out of the kitchen, but Shade's next words stopped her in her tracks.

"Has she worked it out yet?"

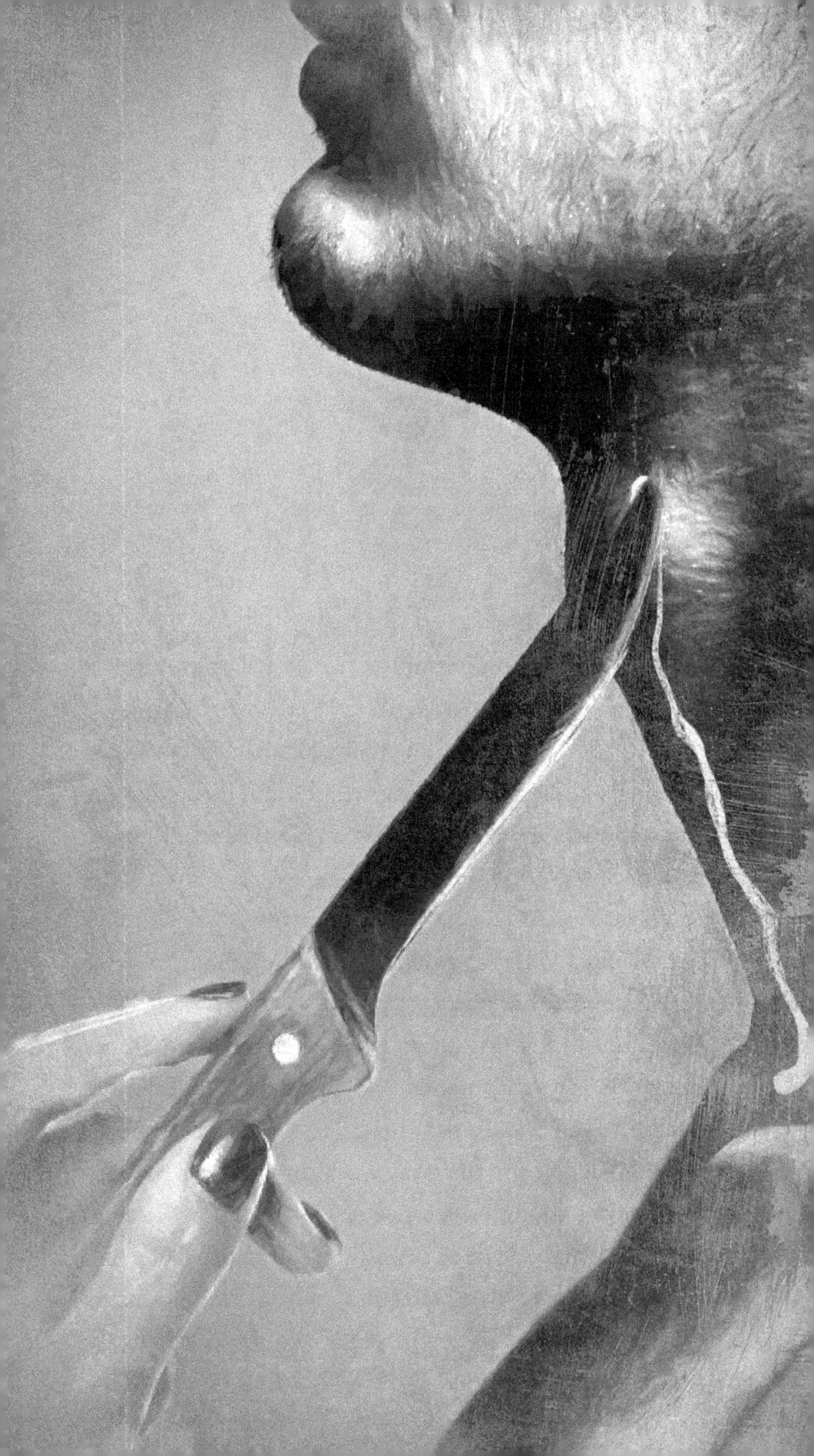

CHAPTER THIRTY-SIX

"Worked what out?" Forrest asked through a full mouth of food.

Indigo stared at him. Was that elf ever not eating? He'd left disgusting crumbs and food supplies all over the counter. Tomatoes. Bread. Some sort of goopy substance. Sliced animal flesh.

Shade answered Forrest with a knowing smirk. "Indigo only challenged Violet to a duel because he's manipulating her into accepting her gift."

A flash of something sharp pierced Indigo through his bond marks. He straightened and inspected the kitchen, frowning. *Nothing*. She's not there. It only feels like she is, the same as it felt for the past week no matter where he went. It was as though the sense of Violet had invaded his reason. He scratched the markings on his arm. Maybe she was having a dream. He should probably lay down next to her like he'd done every night while she slept, especially when he'd noticed her emotions waver during the day. She might not admit it yet, but she needed him as much as he needed her.

She had no idea how much he thought of her, or how much his body needed her. Even now he was semi-hard just from imagining her scent. Floral, soapy, and delectably feminine.

He'd pretended the only reason he'd slept next to her was to plaster his scent all over her, but it was to store up that intoxicating feminine smell in his mind bank. He wasn't sorry. Every time he'd returned at night while she slept, she would sigh and roll into him as though she missed him. She would reach around his waist, tug him close, and burrow in deep. Sometimes she sleep-talked and asked for his wings. He gave them, without hesitation, knowing she liked the feel of them wrapped tightly around her.

"Manipulation?" Forrest gaped, then wiped his mouth.

"Well..." Indigo shook his head. "When you two put it like that..."

"Hey," Forrest said, holding his palms up. "I'm not judging."

Shade scoffed at Forrest. "You wouldn't, would you?"

"Shut up." Forrest threw a slice of onion at Shade. It landed on his shoulder and he flicked it off with a grimace. "You can talk with your relationship antics. I don't need judgement for mine."

"You know my thoughts," Shade said wryly to Indigo. "We need her A-game. Personally, I would have handled it with a timely spank in the bedroom—like we discussed."

A sound burst through the room, something like a gasp. This time they all heard it.

"Someone's here." Forrest slowly lowered his half-eaten burger, eyes hardening.

They tensed and scanned the kitchen. Indigo opened his senses and smelled—

Floral, soapy, feminine. He jolted.

"You bastard!" Out of thin air, Violet appeared, the bodily incarnation of fury.

Dark hair cascaded down her shoulders, whipping about with the aftereffects of her cloaking spell. Her tunic gaped at the middle, as though she'd only spared an afterthought to dress. The bone dagger he'd gifted her glittered at her belt.

She unsheathed it and then launched at him. Indigo caught her wrist before the point pierced his face, but he had the sense she was holding back. She countered with a solid punch to his gut. The wind knocked out of him, along with his pride, and he stumbled. His stool clattered to the ground. She was... good. Better than before. He smiled. Violet had done exactly what he'd hoped. She'd used that competitive drive to become a weapon. She'd accepted her gift.

Forrest watched them, chewing his burger.

Shade's brow lifted, amused, and he settled back to watch the show.

"Vi—" Indigo started.

A harpy's scream tore from her lips and she twisted, elbowing him in the solar plexus. He grunted, wheezed, but grappled her wrists and held tight. Facing him with eyes full of lightning, anger, and life, she slammed her forehead into his.

Pain. Eye watering pain.

And something else. Excitement. The thrill of the challenge. He sensed it, but couldn't tell if it was his or hers... maybe both.

Here she was—his warrior mate. Nothing would hold her down, never again. The light shimmered around her and Indigo's snake peeked out of his collar, curious, but she disappeared. Completely. Every hair on Indigo's body stood to attention as the power in the room ramped up, tingling his tongue. He bared his fangs at the Guardians.

"Leave," he snarled. Violet wasn't going to give up. And this was between the two of them. Their sparring match started now.

Ribbons of shadow enveloped Shade until he was covered in darkness, and then he winked out of existence, shadow walking somewhere else. Forrest swiftly stood and turned to leave, but hesitated and reached back for his burger, spilling the sauce and lettuce head he'd left lying out. With a hasty fist circled over his heart, he retreated through the galley exit.

Indigo turned back to where he'd last seen Violet and used his senses to feel her out. He now realized why her scent had been so strong earlier. She'd been spying on them, and it hadn't even crossed his mind that she could.

Manipulation. His stomach dropped. She'd heard. She'd heard it all out of context. Panic gripped him, squeezing until he couldn't breathe.

Let me explain. "Vi—"

A hit to the jaw sent him careening into the center counter, knocking utensils and food. Tomatoes rolled and squashed on the floor. He stopped a head of lettuce from falling off, but then picked it up with a grin, an idea forming.

"You want to play?" He tossed the lettuce in the air before catching it. Let's see exactly how good she'd become.

But before he had a chance to throw the lettuce, objects flew toward him. Wooden spoons. Pots. Stone cookware. Potatoes. He dodged and blocked everything and took the hit on his shoulder for what he couldn't. Something squishy hit him in the head and he fell backward, skidding across the dirty floor, unable to contain his laughter.

She let loose the growl of a tigress and appeared again... as did two other versions of her. Carbon copies on either side. Or perhaps... which one was her?

Oh shit.

He scrambled to his feet and sent his snake lashing out, but it missed—it went straight through the mirage of one Violet, and then sprung back to him, hissing and spitting in fury. Violet circled him, or rather, the Violets did. Indigo backed up until he hit a rack of cooking supplies. He fumbled behind and found a sack of something. Flour. Perfect. He threw it everywhere. White powder exploded, covering everything. Especially the one, true Violet. She sputtered, and then she was after him. No holding back this time. The dagger struck. It stabbed. It barely missed his neck and nicked his shoulder, slicing right through the simple tunic. Before giving the blade to Violet, he'd asked Forrest to carve runes into it that kept it forever sharp. He was happy to see it worked.

On the back foot, he tried to take hold of her again, but missed. *Fast.*

Good. She could keep up.

Suddenly Indigo found himself thrown backward. He landed on the floor with a spine jarring crack. When his vision cleared, he felt the tip of a dagger prick his throat. Something warm trickled down his neck. Blood.

"Enough, Vi," he demanded.

"Yield."

They stared at each other, chests heaving. She, with her harpy's rage. He, with his need to devour her. To celebrate her. He found something squishy on the floor, grasped, and splatted it on the side of her head. Red juice spilled down her cheekbone.

"Argh!" she shouted. "You're infuriating."

"You're gorgeous." He rolled their positions until he flattened her with his weight, smiling gleefully at her moxie.

Light burst from her pores. He winced away, momentarily blinded. She throat punched him. He coughed. She rolled them again, straddled his hips, and then pressed her forearm against his windpipe. The other hand balanced the dagger over her forearm, aimed at his face in an impressive maneuver that would have taken time to learn. Now she had the strength of two arms and her body on that lethal point. One push and she'd crush his larynx and simultaneously stab into the vulnerable flesh beneath his jaw. A kill shot for many lesser fae.

"You manipulated me," she accused. "After everything. After saying you would never hurt me, *ever*. Well, guess what? It looks like fae *can* lie!"

"I never intended to," he claimed. It was true.

"Why, Indi?" she snarled. "Why?"

"You weren't eating!" He craned his neck forward, his fangs aching at the sight of her pulse throbbing in her neck. *So close.* His body sang for sustenance, he didn't even care that he pressed into the dagger and felt the wetness increase. He bared his teeth at the agony of denying himself. "You weren't sleeping. You weren't accepting your gift."

"So that makes it okay to manipulate me?" She laughed cruelly. "Look at you. You're not even taking care of yourself."

He clamped his lips shut. Dropped his head back and stared at the ceiling. His heart thudded once, twice, against her chest as she lay atop of him. All humor died. This was not fun anymore. This was... he snarled as the truth welled up inside him.

"I hate the taste of normal blood now," he confessed. "It makes my skin crawl to drink. Yours is the only blood I want, so I deny myself anything less than you." He was a hypocrite. "Are you happy now?"

"So why didn't you ask?" The dagger eased, just a little.

"Because you needed to get strong first." His eyes hurt from looking at her scars, a visual reminder that a sensuous act had been torture for her. "I hate seeing these," he whispered, touching a scar at her neck. "I can't stand to see how you've suffered. If I fed from you, you might have hated me... or I might have weakened you." Worse... he might have killed her if he lost control.

"What's the point if I'm weak or strong? You were so convinced you'd beat me anyway and I'd be left behind."

All the fight, all the anger and defiance melted away from him. His gaze softened on her face, her beautiful face that haunted his dreams. He narrowed in on her rejection down their bond, her sadness.

"Vi," he murmured. Pleaded. "I had to make sure you were strong."

She rallied her hold on him and lifted her chin. "Why, if you were just going to leave me here?"

"Because I had to make sure you could protect yourself. Not just from what's coming, but... *from me*." His shameful words echoed in the kitchen. "Violet, I was always going to let you come with us. I was never going to leave you."

She eased off, confused.

"Peaches is your friend," he continued. "I know what she means to you."

"But..."

"But I can't hold myself back anymore." His fangs ached. His cock ached. His entire body hurt for her touch. He knew that one day he wouldn't be able to hold himself back, and when that day came, he had to know she could fight him off. One day, she might be the only thing standing between him and a dark place. "I'm in love with you, Vi. If I hurt you, the way these others had, I wouldn't be able to live with myself. Making you think I was like your family, like you couldn't live up to my standards, it was the only way I could inspire you to train hard, to hold your own against me. I thought"—he licked his lips—"I thought if I gave you something to focus that rage on, you'd let your warrior out again. Just like you did when we first met."

Her face paled, almost to the color of the flour dusting her hair and skin. She eased back. The dagger clattered to the ground.

"That's why you slept during the day," she murmured. "That's why you stayed away from me just as much as I stayed away from you. You were afraid you'd hurt me."

He looked away, closed his eyes and squeezed the burn. Even now his mouth watered for her. His cells were in a frenzy. Without opening his eyes, he snarled. The sound was deep, guttural and unlike himself. "You need to leave. Now. If you value your life."

"I'm not afraid of you, Indi. I never have been."

"Vi—"

Her lips landed on his, swallowing his protest. He inhaled her taste, taking her in, sucking her deep into his lungs. Fire ignited in his blood. Desire, hunger, need... it all burned through him. Raged. He grabbed her hair and held her lips to his, mashing together hard, not caring if they hurt, if they bled, if they fell. There was nowhere else to go. They were here, at the bottom.

"Vi—" he gasped.

She fisted his tunic and shoved. "You're an asshole."

"I know." He chased her lips, needing more.

Again, she shoved him. And he took it. Needed it. Needed her fire. Because it meant she would handle anything. Even him at his worst.

"You don't get to decide what's good for me."

Guilt stabbed him. "I know. I'm sorry."

His apology froze time. Her eyes widened. It felt as though the world hung in the balance. As though they were back underwater in the springs, floating. She brought her dagger back to his tunic and dragged the tip down the center, ripping it open, exposing him. Flour fell from her hair to dust his chest. It tickled. She swiped it away, bent down and licked. She scraped her teeth against his skin. Bit him. Nipped him. Tortured him.

He hissed and bucked his hips.

Violet continued her assault down his torso, tasting and teasing, using that clever tongue in a way that had him feel like he was sinking... falling... drowning. In her. The dagger scraped alongside her mouth, cutting a sharp sting. Going lower. Lower.

"Violet," he growled, panicked, sucking in his stomach. *She wouldn't.*

She laughed and kissed her way back up, circling her

tongue around his nipple, coming higher to the underside of his jaw, his lips. "You don't deserve to feed. You've been a very naughty vampire."

She rocked her hips into his, reminding him who was in control.

He groaned, "Tell me what you need, Violet."

She made patterns on his skin with the dagger. Not enough to cut, but enough to scrape, demonstrating her control of her weapon. The balance, the uncertainty, it sent his senses soaring to new heights. He thrust upward, his hips clashing with hers, trying to relieve the heavy throb in his erection.

She moaned. Melted. A brief white flag. Only for a second. It was all he needed. He sat up and gripped her waist hard, holding her down on his lap. He licked along her fault line—the vein in her neck that would rock his world. Her blood called to him. *Drink me, take me. Mine.* But when his tongue slid over the scar of another's bite, he growled.

"I'm going to kill them," he promised. "Every single one of them."

"There's only one left alive..."

"He's a dead fae walking."

He kissed her lips. Suckled on her ear. Tasted flour and didn't give a flying fuck. Then his fang pierced the lobe. A drop. A lick. His restraint unraveled with an animalistic snarl. He became a beast of need and obsession, tasting her all over. Touching her. From her back, to her front, under her shirt—breast, nipple. *Sweet goddess.*

She shoved him away, panting with a wicked gleam. *Come and get me,* her eyes said. He hesitated… in case he was reading things wrong, but she kissed the air in his direction and then fled. He chased her, dragged her back down to the powdered floor where they rolled and left shapes. There was no sense anymore. He crawled on top of her. She tried to scramble backward, kicked him in the chest, but he kept tugging her back to him. No fear came down their bond. Only excitement. Anticipation. Churning desire.

"You want me to chase you," he breathed, chuckling deeply. "How are you so perfect for me?"

She grinned. Suddenly the dagger was at his throat. He paused, only then realizing he was inches from her neck, his fangs already dripping with the histamines that would make her drowsy.

"If we do this now, Vi," he warned. "There's no going back. I might keep you locked in our room for days. Are you ready?"

CHAPTER
THIRTY-SEVEN

Are you ready?

Indigo's words echoed in Violet's mind as she stared down her ripped tunic to where he held her ankles, looking up at her with a smoldering, almost pained expression. He'd waited so long for her. Yes, she was ready. Damned ready. But she wanted to make him pay, just a little longer. While his methods had infuriated her... they had worked. She'd trained. She'd gotten stronger.

This would be the first and only time she'd ever let him believe he had the right to manipulate her. With the dagger pointed his way, she slowly got to her feet, never letting go of the predator's gaze.

She took one step away.

One.

And then she turned, losing sight of him. He was on her, pinning her to the table. She slammed forward, her palms slapping, the dagger skidding away. He pressed in behind her, caging her in with his arms. Hot breath at her ear sent shivers dancing down her spine.

"Vi—" he begged, burying his face into her hair.

Desire threaded into every inch of her body. All she wanted, all she needed was him. She moaned and pressed her rear back in invitation. He wrapped fingers around her throat and pulled her back, until the full length of her was pinned flush against his hard body, the extra hard pressure digging into her bottom. Feeling his strength, his raw masculine power, it flooded her with needy heat.

He kept the hand at her neck gentle yet firm. The other scraped down from her chest. Down. Until he hit her belt and snarled. Talons ripped out, shredded, and then retreated behind his fingertips so he could burrow into her pants, searching.

"I'm going to feed on you like this," he said, voice low. "One hand down here"—a finger swiped straight through her slick center—"And one on your neck."

She moaned as he swiped his finger again, dipping through her desire. He licked beneath her ear. His teeth grazed along her shoulder, cursed at the tunic collar in the way, and ripped it with his razor sharp fangs until the fabric shredded. He pulled her head to the side, stretching her neck tendons, and then plunged his fingers inside her aching core, snarling softly as though he felt the same sweet lick of heaven she did.

"Last chance, Vi—last chance to back out."

He let go of her neck briefly and then pressed her

dagger into her palm. A burst of emotion exploded in her chest and she almost cried. He wanted her to feel safe. Her throat clogged as she placed the blade against his neck, and he placed his fangs on her vein. Breathing hard, feeling too many sensations at once, she wasn't sure if she could focus long enough to keep him honest. To endanger him as he did her. To love him as he loved her...

Her fingers gripped tight around the hilt and she nodded. "I'm ready."

Pain pierced her shoulder as his fingers dove deep inside her, lifting her up, pushing her against his mouth where he licked and laved.

Gasping, she threw her head back until she rested against him, but no more pain came. He'd done something... rubbed his own blood into the bite wound—tingling fire entered her veins, burning a path to her extremities.

"Indi..." she cried out helplessly. This was too much. It felt too good.

Her vision blurred and her mind became less thought, more instinct, more sensation. Licking on her neck. Grip around her neck, holding her still. Fingers between her legs, circling, sliding, driving. Through the haze, she realized she rode his fingers, not the other way around. *More.* She pressed into him. They careened backward and hit something. A wall, a table, a shelf. Something rattled. But he held her neck steady as he toyed between her legs. It was too much and not enough. She was at the wrong angle. Pinned to him. She needed more from his fingers. His mouth. Faster. Harder. *More, more, more.*

"Vi—" he groaned against her. "My greedy Violet."

Floating in a cloud of euphoria, her entire body wanted to rise. The only points grounded were the parts connected to him—his hand around her neck, his fingers working her sex, and his tongue lapping at her shoulder.

This was... this was... bliss. Heaven. Why the fuck didn't they do this sooner?

As if reading her mind, a hungry, guttural sound shot out of him and quivered down her spine. His laps turned urgent. His fingers went faster. He gripped her neck, holding her steady. And he rocked, his hips thrusting against her rear, teasing her with his steel length. It sent her over the edge, spiraling.

She cried out his name. Her knees buckled. The dagger clattered to the ground. He kept working her, fueled by every little whimper out of her mouth. Every little plea and prayer for more. She was almost there, almost there. And then... and then...

Light exploded behind her eyelids as she climaxed, releasing a long drawn-out moan.

He reared off her neck, his chest heaving against her spine.

"Did it taste good?" she breathed.

He lifted his hand out of her pants and brought his glistening fingers to his lips with a deep satisfied sound from the base of his throat. "Now it does."

Her lashes fluttered, and she raised her hands to rest

against his sweaty neck. This. Always. Again. Forever. How he made her feel. It was incomprehensible. And he still suckled on his fingers, the ones that had been inside her.

"That good, huh?"

He made another sound, and then she heard his slow inhale through his nose, and long exhale ending in a deep masculine growl. He pushed her forward, over the table, and tugged her pants down. Cool air hit her bare bottom, her wetness. A brief rasping of his belt ties, and then she felt him—that hard steel searching between her legs, finding her still pulsing center.

With a wicked smile stretching her lips, she collected the dagger, this time promising herself she wouldn't let go. She twisted out of his grip until she faced him.

Brown pleasure-soaked eyes dragged over her. His brows met in the middle as she pointed the dagger at him, then lowered it to the proud erection jutting out.

"Slowly," she ordered.

Something like panic flittered over his flushed expression, but he nodded, and her smile widened. He lifted her by the waist onto the counter top, and then he dragged her pants off completely. She kept her dagger steady and widened her knees, exposing herself to him.

In one slick move, he entered her.

A gasp shot out. Of her... him... Her palm hit on the surface of the table, barely registering the mess—theirs from the fight. Left overs from Forrest's meal. She didn't care. She swiped it all out of the way so nothing impeded them. He filled her completely. Wholly. It was all she could think about. Tight, stretching her to the limits.

"Slow..." His voice tightened, his words a little slurred. "Vi—I need... I need..."

Eyes full of doubt clashed with hers. In them, she saw his fear, felt it hurtling down their bond. The first time he'd fed, he only worried about his hunger and her desire. Now he had his own desire thrown in the mix to tease his restraint. And he was falling under the influence of her blood. His lip curled, his fangs started dripping, ready for more.

She maintained her claim earlier. She wasn't afraid of him. The dagger was more for him, a visual safety net so he could let go and enjoy himself too.

"It's okay," she panted, eyes darting to her weapon still aimed steadily at him. "We're ready for this."

Strong hands gripped her hips and he slid himself out. She whimpered at the loss, begged for him to return. He eased back in, stretching her again. They both watched as they came together. The sheer erotic sight of his length covered in her slick juices made them both shudder.

"Faster," she murmured, squirming on the counter.

Each stroke, each pump inside her, he increased the tempo. The male was a study in discipline. Every line of his body, every muscle and tendon was stretched tight and focused. His tongue darted out to lick his fangs, but he resisted the urge to bite. Instead, he kissed her. He ravaged her mouth and plundered her body.

The entire long counter jolted. Utensils went flying. Things rolled.

"Fuck," he swore.

"More," she growled.

Without hesitation, without mercy, he gave her what she wanted. He thrust into her, groaning with pleasure every time he buried to the hilt. Rolling around, savoring. He took her, and he claimed her. Hard, fast, fierce. Indigo was hostile in his lovemaking. Insatiable. She writhed as the pressure built again. There was nowhere to go. God, if anyone walked in...

He took her hard, sending bolts of lightning searing through her. Heat, everywhere. Growing. Intensifying. Bright light burst from her pores, bathing the room in pure white light.

Indigo slammed in and held. A strangled, shuddering moan escaped him and he collapsed against her, hands moving into her hair, kissing along her exposed neck, whispering how much he loved her. Needed her. Would die for her.

With him still filling her, as hard as he was at the beginning, she blinked and wrangled her power in. Her light was everywhere, filling every corner, chasing all the shadows away. She'd thought with all her training she could control it... but she wasn't even sure if she knew her name.

"Holy heaven on earth," she mumbled. "I'm so sorry. I hope you're not blind."

He found her neck wound and laved a few times,

ensuring his saliva coated the bite—ensuring he healed her, something the others had never bothered to do. A languid sleepiness slaked every limb.

"Never dim your light for me, Violet. Ever."

Tears stung her eyes, and she nodded.

"Bed chambers," he ground out huskily. "Now."

"Now?"

"*Now.*" He pressed the dagger into her palm, a gleam in his eyes. "Don't forget this."

THEY'D LEFT the kitchen in disarray.

Jasper would be pissed. But Violet couldn't bring herself to care. The moment they burst through the door of their chambers, and Indigo slammed it shut, they only had eyes for the bed. He annihilated her clothes. She wasn't even sure what happened to them. Some kind of shadow trickery, or incendiary effect, because when she fell back on the bed, and he was on top of her—he dove straight between her legs and continued his feast. She'd thought her blood would slow him, but it made him ravenous. At least for now. He licked and probed, slid and plunged until she tried to wriggle back from the onslaught.

He held her pelvis, pinning her down. His tongue rolled and nipped her most sensitive flesh until she begged—begged for him to finish, to not be cruel and give her what she needed. It was this last plea, the yanking on his hair, the knife to his throat, that forced him to submit. He brought her to completion with his tongue, and then while the stars were still churning in her eyes, he fit himself between her legs.

This time, the lovemaking was tamer... slower... unhurried. Lazy. Indulgent.

With every stroke, he fought the drugging properties of her blood. A smokiness settled. A dreamlike state. But he wanted more from her. She watched him drink in her body with his hands, his cock, his eyes, and she did the same to him—reveling in every flex of his taut muscles, the way the shadow snake curled around him, molding to his shape. The way a sheen of sweat made him seem like a fantasy.

She felt like the only person in his world.

"You were right," he said, fingers tracing her inner thighs, watching where he moved inside her. "We should have done this sooner."

"I don't remember saying that." *Out loud.*

A slow curve of his lips. "Your blood told me." He reached for her neck, where a few drops had spilled, and wiped them clean before licking his finger. Dark eyes met hers and became oh, so darker. More wicked. More knowing.

She'd never seen him this... vibrant. Color had returned to his cheeks. He was flush with health, with virility, that she finally understood how undernourished he'd been. For her. All to protect her. To give her time. To please her. To make her strong.

She brought his lips to hers. Their kiss was sweet and heady, like wine. She tasted herself on his tongue. Not just there—her taste, her scent—it was everywhere on him, just as he was all over her. There was no going back. They were joined, irrevocably. Permanently.

To them, having a mate is like splitting their soul. It's stronger than marriage.

Violet the Violent and her vampire lover. Her mate.

CHAPTER
THIRTY-EIGHT

The following afternoon, they were still in their chambers. Violet's blood had completely sated Indigo, but she was ravenous. Already bathed and dressed, she stopped at the black glass mirror to check her reflection. She fluffed her long hair around her shoulders, hoping to cover any bite marks not quite healed. Stupid, really. Everyone knew they were together. No one cared.

Especially not Indigo as he reclined, naked and tangled in the sheets, one leg bent up, the other flat, hands resting behind his head... smugly watching her with unbridled lust and curiosity. It made her arch a little more seductively when she straightened her shirt, run her fingers more slowly over her curves, and glance coyly at him over her shoulder. He tensed. His eyes widened. Caught.

She gave him a self-satisfied smile. Having him worship every inch of her body had done things to her psyche. She felt like a goddess this morning... afternoon. Whatever time it was. "You're not going to come with me?" she asked.

"Order in," he urged. "Get your food delivered and then come back to bed."

"I'm not sure they'll be so accommodating after the mess we left in the kitchen."

"Blame it on Forrest. He left the food out."

"And the flour?"

He had the decency to look guilty. "That's my bad."

"Forrest might not even be here."

Indigo jackknifed up. "Shit."

"What is it?" She walked back to the bed and sat down next to him.

"What day is it?"

"Sunsday, I think."

He threw the covers off and found some pants, jumping into them. "Tonight is the night Demeter wants an answer to Maebh's ultimatum."

Violet pulled the drapes closed beside the bed. The sun was still up, but descending over the palace gardens and the sparkling city beyond. "We have an hour or two, don't—"

Indigo took her from behind and pressed his hips—his arousal—into her rear with a hungry growl. "When you bend over like that..."

She rotated in his arms and slid her hands around his neck. He looked down between them and nudged her, his bottom lip between his teeth.

"It was more of a lean than a bend over," she laughed.

"Same thing."

"This isn't going to be a problem, is it?" she asked. "I thought you were feeling... good. Satisfied. Not all psycho mate."

"Where you are concerned, I will always be your psycho."

"I'm serious." She swatted him playfully. "Do I need to bring the dagger out?"

It had become almost a joke, but with an underlying seriousness. She knew she'd use it if she had to, and he loved that she would.

He stepped back and scrubbed his face. "I'm okay."

"And out there? Is it safe for us to go together?"

He shot her a wry smile. "I can control myself around other males, if that's what you're asking. I think your blood has relaxed me. Can you control yourself?"

"Ha ha." She blushed at his jibe, trying not to think about how she'd worshipped him as much as he had her. "I don't think my body could take anymore, so yes."

A door rattling knock thundered through the room. Before Violet could call out, Indigo's wings shifted out of his back and he stood between her and the door, shielding in case someone walked in.

"I thought you said this wasn't going to be an issue," she joked.

He cleared his throat and shifted his wings away with a rustle. "It won't... it's just going to take some getting used to."

She kissed him between his shoulder blades. “You’ll be fine.”

The pounding came again. This time more insistent.

Indigo glanced down at his crotch—at the hardness tenting his pants—and swore. “You get it.”

Then he went back to the bed to sit down.

Violet opened the door to find the king.

“Oh,” she said and curtsied, or bowed... or something in between.

“Enough,” Jasper grunted.

She thought he meant the bow so straightened, but Jasper was staring into the room where Indigo sat on the bed.

“Enough with the mating,” he snapped. “We can hear you throughout the palace.”

Indigo snorted. “Good.”

Violet’s cheeks burned so hot she thought flames would come out of them. “You can all hear?”

“He failed to set a privacy ward. Every fae with preternatural hearing caught every last whimper and sound,” Jasper replied, noticed her mortification, and then frowned. “I actually came here because we have visitors. The Prime and one of the Six are here. Be down in the war room an hour after sundown.”

He looked slightly apologetic, and then he was gone, his boots thudding on the carpet.

Violet shut the door and glared at Indigo. “You knew?”

Her little trickster grinned. “Now everyone knows you’re mine.”

An hour after sundown, Violet walked into the Seelie King's war room holding Indigo's hand—he'd insisted. She'd fed, another embarrassing feat considering she had to go straight to the kitchen and ask the staff to make something outside of normal serving hours. But she'd survived.

She wasn't sure she'd survive this.

The knowing smirks and looks as they walked into the room. God, she'd kill Indigo tonight. But he strutted next to her like a tiger on parade, wearing his leather battle gear, not a care in the world. When he glanced down at her, pride shone in his eyes, and every irritation melted away. He truly cared for her. Loved her.

There were so many leather clad bodies in the cramped room, it smelled like a tannery. They all gathered around a long central table covered in a map of Elphyne that had a bowl of water sitting in the middle. A glass-crowned Jasper stood at the head. His coroneted queen perched on a stool next to him, fiddling with her long braid. Shade, Leaf, and Forrest stood to one side next to Laurel and Thorne. Cloud and Ash were on the opposite side with more newcomers next to them. One was an imperious female with dark skin and bouncing silver ringlets. White feathered wings flowed from her shoulders and covered a vibrant blue dress. She was majestic. Stunning. And a little imposing. But nothing compared to what stood next to her. A Sluagh.

The name echoed through her mind. *Sluagh Sluagh. Danger danger.*

Masculine and beautiful at the same time. Long, lithe, and imposing. Beneath a widow's peak and black silken hair tied at the nape, his face was a work of art. A blue teardrop twinkled on skin so pale it was almost translucent, like carved crystal. Broad shoulders fit snugly into the Guardian uniform. On him, the battle worn leathers appeared almost suave. Seductive. But it was his wings that terrified her. Long, leathery and taloned, they spilled from his shoulders like a cape. Similar to the vampires, yet somehow more decadent. More lethal. They vibrated when she looked at them, as though purring under her attention. A feeling brushed against her mind—a whisper—a breath on the back of her neck.

Shivers skipped down her spine and every hair on her body lifted. She did something stupid. She met its eyes. Dark, large, and intense. It took everything she had to tear her gaze away, and yet, she still felt trapped.

Indigo squeezed her hand, and they went to stand at the head of the table, opposite the king and queen down the other end. Violet tried not to look, tried to study the towns and pieces on the map, but her instincts screamed for her to turn her head, to be caught in the seductive snare of the Sluagh. *Behold the danger. Look at the ecstasy. See what will devour you.* A pretty nightmare. Unbidden, her instincts kicked into protective mode and she started to glow. Hot. Bright.

The Sluagh hissed and flinched.

"Shit," she mumbled. "My bad."

Indigo let go of her hand and traced patterns on her back, comforting her. Then he tugged her closer with a warning glare sent the Sluagh's way, which made Violet even more nervous. If the Sluagh decided, it could shred Indigo's mind in an instant. Nothing could stop it. With a few deep, calming breaths, she reined in her gift and silenced her glow. When it was done, the white-winged female met Violet's eyes.

"You must be Violet," she said, her voice somehow ancient and fresh at the same time. "I'm Aleksandra. The Prime of the Order of the Well. It is nice to finally meet you."

Her undertone of displeasure was not lost. Violet felt a prickle of Indigo's defiance down the bond. She wanted to squeeze his hand, but he kept his firm against the small of her back.

"That's my fault," Violet said, raising her hand gingerly. "I wasn't ready to visit you. To be honest, I wasn't ready to be in the same room as Indigo at first. Now..."

"Now you're one of us," the Prime smiled tightly.

Violet jolted. She supposed she was. She glanced around the table. Especially at the other humans. Ada and Laurel both smiled nervously at her. The Sluagh made everyone anxious. Violet tentatively returned their smile. It felt odd to have so many people on her side. After everything, she still felt like she didn't deserve it. There would probably always be a part of her that believed it.

"Yes," she said. "I guess I am."

"Good," the Prime snapped. "Now let's get to the order of business."

Violet blinked, unsure what had just happened. Every set of eyes landed on her, the Guardians' filled with respect. Had she just declared her loyalty to the Order? Had the Prime just accepted it?

Jasper cleared his throat and raised his brows at the Prime. She widened her eyes and inclined her head with a fist circled over her heart. "Ah. King Darkfoot. I have begun when it is your dominion. I am still coming to terms with your new role. You must be patient with me."

He cut her a glare which said she knew exactly what she was doing, and then he surveyed his guests slowly and deliberately. Like a king.

"After much consideration, I have decided—"

Ada cleared her throat and raised indignant brows. Her hand drifted to her belly and idly stroked. This time, it was Jasper who inclined his head to his mate in a way that connected with Violet. A warmth rushed through her and she glanced up at Indigo. He noticed. His long-lashed gaze flicked down at her and crinkled around the edges.

"What I meant to say," Jasper said, tugging on his regal, embroidered tunic. No shirt frills this time. He must have won that battle with Laurel. "Was that *we* have decided *we* will accept High Queen Maebh's invitation."

Ada snorted at his exaggeration. Many grunts and nods of assent passed around the table. Including the Prime's and the Sluagh's. Violet wondered if it had a name. Not it, she reminded herself. He... If *he* had a name. She'd heard rumors that they weren't real males in the sense Indigo was, but the Sluagh looked male to Violet. Everyone kept calling the Sluagh an *it*. He should have a name. Maybe she would ask him one day—if she had the nerve.

Not only was a name a sign of respect, but giving him a name would demystify the danger. It would help her master her fear. He was here to help. He deserved respect.

I am Legion.

The words hit Violet's mind so suddenly and smoothly that it was as if she'd thought them herself.

And I am male.

This time it was a whisper. A deep, masculine sigh iced with humor. Her eyes shot to the Sluagh's face, to *Legion's* face, and found him staring right at her. Into her. Indigo noticed at the same time. His fingers flexed against her back and a low hissing sound came out of his throat. Everyone at the table turned their way, eyes wide and uncertain of the exchange. So jumpy.

Violet placed her palm on Indigo's thigh.

"It's fine," she whispered. "He was just telling me his name."

The hissing stopped. Indigo's face deadpanned. Everyone gaped and then tried to hide their surprise by coughing or shifting. Indigo's hand tightened on her hip.

She forced a smile and met the Sluagh's piercing gaze.

Nice to meet you, Legion, she said with her mind, having no idea if he heard her or not.

But the corner of his sensuous lips curved up a notch, and he turned back to look at the king.

"So we need to pick two Guardians to come with us," Jasper said, glancing around the room before settling on the Prime. Even though the Order wasn't a dictatorship, without the full Council's presence, she would have a final say. Maybe that's why she brought Legion with her.

"The problem is that we don't know exactly where Haze is being held," Shade said before Leaf could open his mouth. "We know what Violet's acquaintance—"

"Peaches," Violet said. "Her name is Peaches."

How many times did she have to say it?

Shade pressed his lips together. "All right. Peaches. We don't know if she's telling the truth about Haze being in the queen's dungeons. Maebh claimed she wasn't holding him, as did Demeter."

"What were their words, exactly?" Leaf asked, his eyes shrewd.

Shade looked to Indigo.

"Demeter said 'I have no such fae in the queen's dungeons.' He also said Haze never showed for their meeting."

"And he said that the queen said to invite the Guardians to tour the dungeon and see for themselves Haze isn't there."

Leaf looked at Shade and Cloud. "And this Peaches woman. What did she say?"

Shade answered. "She said she saw Haze. She shared a cell with him. I asked her to keep an eye on him and she agreed. Clearly, since it's Haze, I think Indigo and myself should go. We can travel unseen in the shadows. I've been training with Jasper to—" He looked at the Sluagh and clicked his jaw shut.

"To kill my kind," Legion finished with an amused glint in his eye. But then he locked eyes with Violet and said, "I have a better plan."

CHAPTER THIRTY-NINE

Indigo's blood went cold. The Sluagh watched Violet as though he wanted to take her for himself. Every primitive, possessive instinct of Indigo's snarled.

A better plan? Indigo had a better plan—*Stop staring at my mate or I gut you. How's that for a plan?*

The shadow snake started coiling, slithering, coming out of hibernation. Over Indigo's dead body would he ever allow that soul-stealing monster to have anything to do with Violet. He would die to protect her. And if the Sluagh captured Indigo's soul to fight in his Wild Hunt, Indigo would terrorize him from within. Perhaps Legion read Indigo's mind, or perhaps he simply picked up the vibe, but he slid his gaze Indigo's way and surprised him.

No retort. No threat. But a nod of regard.

Blue glow emitted from the center bowl. Demeter.

Jasper put his finger to his lips and looked at everyone, then gestured for them all to step back. If they could avoid the queen knowing how many of them worked against her, the better.

"Demeter," Indigo greeted.

His brother got straight to the point. "Your king's answer?"

"Firstly," Indigo replied. "He's not my king. The Order answer to no one. Secondly—"

Jasper stepped forward. "We graciously accept your queen's invitation, including the additional Guardians and tour of the dungeons."

"Good," Demeter clipped. "We expect to see you at the Obsidian Palace in five days' time."

The connection cut.

"Five days?" Shade roared, the shadows hugging him burst out as though startled. "She's toying with us."

"Haze and Peaches could be in pain," Indigo added. His snake hissed and bared its fangs. "This is not acceptable."

"Five days," the Prime said, "means we have time to prepare."

"For what?" Shade growled, flinging his hand at the Sluagh. "We don't even know what its plan is or if it will work."

"Legion," Violet clipped, "is a *he*, not an *it*."

Indigo blinked at his mate. Had something passed between Violet and the Sluagh—Legion—privately? Indigo's fists flexed as his temper raged. Unlike Indigo, Shade had the good sense to look contrite.

"Legion," the Prime said, "has kindly offered his help. Don't spit on his goodwill."

"Why *are* you helping?" Cloud asked Legion. "Why now?"

The Sluagh's eyes widened. A flicker of electricity burned the tip of Indigo's tongue, and they all caught a glimpse of the skull beneath that haunting face. Then it was gone. Was that... fear... nerves? Did the Sluagh stay behind closed doors too much that they now feared social interaction? Or was it something else... were they as depraved as the world made them out to be?

The Prime smoothed her dress and answered Cloud. "Every Seer at the Order, including Clarke, Dawn, and one of the Six, has caught a glimpse of Queen Maebh's future world." Ice leached into the Prime's tone. "We all know of the battle coming against the Void for custody of this earth, but there will also be a second battle against the queen... one for our very souls."

Legion's wings vibrated, buzzing like a bee, pushing the space around him into a state of flux.

"She is creating," he warned. "Something more dangerous than the Sluagh."

The Prime swiped her hand across the table. The bowl of water turned murky. "And if she succeeds in her plans, the Well will survive, but it will turn dark."

INDIGO LEVELED his stare on the Sluagh—Legion. Interesting name. It meant *many*, but he was only one. He wondered... were the Sluagh some sort of hive mind? Were they interconnected? Clearly they heard everything going on in anyone's head, perhaps even each other's. He simply didn't know enough about them. It was why they were in this position.

Something flickered in Legion's dark eyes.

"So what now?" Shade snapped. "We're just going to leave Haze and Peaches to the mercy of this mad female?"

"D'arn Shade," the Prime snapped, her wings rustling behind her. "If you held your tongue a moment, we were getting to that."

The darkness in Shade flared. Indigo felt it in his marrow—like calling to like, shadow to shadow. His brother in arms was on the verge of snapping, of doing exactly what he'd said and storming the palace whether he had their support or not.

"Fine," he ground out. "What is the plan?"

"Queen Maebh has fortified her security since you went in without permission. So we have to play this game of hers, but we can change the rules as we go. Indigo and Shade will attend the dinner with Jasper and Ada," the Prime confirmed. Violet bristled beside Indigo, but before she could protest, the Prime looked at her and said, "And you, Violet. You will be going as well. You are our surprise move."

Leaf straightened. "I can create portals. If part of the tactic to defeat the queen's Sluagh is to separate their physical bodies from their wraith forms, then I can help."

"That could kill them," Legion said. "And there is a way to disarm them. Us."

"We're listening," Jasper said.

Legion looked at Indigo and Violet. "It has to be the vampires because they can draw my blood. And it must be the moonlit one because she can chase the shadows away."

Violet blinked. Indigo felt her surprise.

"My light," she said. "You flinched when I lost control."

Legion inclined his head.

Indigo understood. "The Six never come out during the day. I always thought it was simply a lifestyle habit, like us vampires, but it's not. Is it? The sunlight affects you."

"The moon gets its power from the sun," Violet mumbled. "It reflects the sun."

Another incline of the head.

"What will your blood do?" Shade asked, frowning.

"That, D'arn Shade," the Prime said. "Is an answer for only you and Indigo."

"That's hardly fair," Cloud grumbled. "Don't we all deserve the knowledge?"

Legion made no move, no recognition of Cloud's accusation, but the Prime, she straightened her shoulders and said, "Unless you've taken to drinking blood, D'arn Cloud. There is nothing you can do."

"That doesn't answer my question."

"Blood holds secrets," Indigo said. "Blood also holds power. When I drank from Ada, and from Violet, it came with something extra."

All eyes locked on him, and every muscle in his body went taut. Jasper gave him a warning glare, but Indigo had to tell them. It was wrong to keep secrets when they were working to the same goal.

"I suspect it is why Gastnor wants Violet and the others so badly. Not just because their blood makes them feel good, but because it goes beyond that." He looked at Shade. "You saw how I was before I fed from Violet."

Shade nodded. "You were too thin."

"That's because after tasting Ada's blood, everything was foul. Nothing fulfilled me in the same way."

Violet's gaze softened on him, and her regret hit him squarely in the chest. "I didn't know."

He whispered, "It was my choice to keep it hidden."

"So what are you saying?" Thorne said, slinging his arm protectively around Laurel. "That any human from the old world is some kind of—"

"I don't know exactly," Indigo said quickly. "Only that I feel amazing now. I feel restored. I feel strong. Powerful. Like I could go out and take down a manticore with my bare hands. Like I don't need a source of power to replenish my inner Well. But that could be because we're mated."

"Peaches," Violet muttered, her eyes watering. "She's been there for months."

"And she will survive a few more days," the Prime said. "From what we've seen, the rescue must happen during the dinner. Not before, not after."

The Sluagh waited for Indigo under the cover of night in the king's gardens. For this, Legion had requested to be outside. Privacy and nature. Moonlight. As Indigo walked through the gardens, he followed the sense of stillness, of silence, to where Legion sat perched on the stone coffin overgrown with vines.

When he saw Indigo approach, Legion's long slender fingers began undoing the bone studs of his Guardian jacket until he could open and expose his neck. This was madness.

Indigo was going to taste his blood. Drink his secrets. Or something. He wasn't even hungry. But what made him more nervous was the vulnerable state he would be in during the feed, and the fact that the Sluagh could take some part of him in return.

I ask for one thing, Legion's voice slid into Indigo's mind.

"What?"

For a memory. Of my choosing.

"Okay." He narrowed his eyes.

And once I've tasted it, you will forget.

"No," Indigo snapped. "You can't have her."

The moment the words came out, he knew them to be true. The Sluagh wanted a piece of Violet. He shook his head and walked away, only to stop upon seeing Violet at the palace door, watching with a grim expression on her shadowed face, a plea in her eyes.

"You already asked her, didn't you?" Indigo asked.

Yes.

Indigo's heart cleaved in two. Violet would give up some part of their history? To save her friend from suffering, she would. Violet would give up everything. She was no longer focusing on her own pain, but that of others. That aching feeling turned to strength. And he would give Violet anything. She already had his heart. Losing a memory wouldn't change that.

"What did she say when you asked her?" Indigo asked, holding his breath.

She said if I hurt you, she would find a way to kill me. A pause. *I believe her.*

Laughter barked out of him. So it seemed Violet was willing to defend him as much as he was her. Holding Violet's stare, he made a fist and circled his heart, for he was sorry for the part of her he'd lose. He would do this for her, for Peaches, for Haze. Tears glistened in her eyes. Then she nodded and entered the palace.

"So you will choose which memory to take?" Indigo asked, still staring at the space Violet had vacated, wondering if that was how it would feel... an emptiness, knowledge that something important had once been there.

Yes.

Fuck. "Remind me why I'm doing this."

Because by taking my blood, you will take a piece of me. Of us. We will scent you as our own. We will not be able to take your mind. And we will not be able to take your soul.

"I'll become immune."

From the Sluagh, yes.

He would be able to infiltrate the Winter Palace. Any

Sluagh there will not be able to raid his mind, pilfer his soul, or even detect him. One memory. He frowned at what the Prime had said about Maebh's plans. *For the integrity of the Well. For Haze and Peaches.*

"Let's do this."

Call him crazy, but he could have sworn the Sluagh's eyes flashed with excitement. It only made Indigo more nervous, but he strolled over as if he'd not a care in the world. Think of it as a grand adventure. New territory. To boldly go where no fae has gone—drinking the blood of the most feared fae in the history of Elphyne.

As he neared, the Sluagh widened his knees, allowing Indigo to get intimately close. Then he tilted his neck and pulled down his collar, exposing the strong pulsing vein beneath the moonlit skin. Something glittered there. It sparkled like power. Electricity. Life. And beneath it, something darker swam that reminded Indigo of slithering Well Worms.

Indigo wrapped his fingers around Legion's neck and marked the thickness compared to Violet. It felt wrong. Doubt prickled in. He hesitated.

She will not forgive you if her friend dies, Legion's voice crooned in Indigo's mind. *She will put you back in the same box as the ones who violated her.*

No. Indigo shook his head. She wouldn't do that. They were beyond that now.

Take my blood. Or she will find you weak. Useless.

Warning bells went off.

She already beat you in a duel. She doesn't need you.

Indigo lowered his face and trailed his nose along the skin, hunting for the vein, the right place. The wrong place. When he found the heat, he bared his fangs and paused.

Do it, vampire. Before she sees the weakness in you.

A snarl of defiance ripped out of Indigo. His fangs clamped onto the Sluagh, causing him to gasp at the pain. Flesh gave way easily. Blood welled like oil, but it tasted like the dark, the night, the stars and a thousand screams locked in a cage. Indigo choked as it flowed fast. He swallowed and spluttered against Legion's lifeforce, gulping it down. Pressure on the back of his head—Legion's hand as he forced Indigo onto him.

Drink me in.

⚖

SCREAMS. Everywhere. The tortured, pained, and soulful cries never stopped. Indigo's ears hurt. Wetness oozed from them. Blood. They were the souls of the damned, the caught, the trapped. They were the Wild Hunt, living inside the Sluagh, and now inside Indigo. He felt their power rip into him, gushing, perversely invading, taking every part of Indigo's identity, ripping him apart and forging him anew.

Desperately, he tried to hold on to something—the moonlight. His goddess. Violet.

But Legion took her too.

Indigo shouted into the abyss. "Bring her back. She's mine."

Now she's mine. Just for a little. And I will savor her, just as you have. For this gift, for the moon, I give you all that I am.

Indigo roared. No. This wasn't what he agreed to. This wasn't it. One memory. One memory for the power to... to... become like the Sluagh. At least, become so similar that the others couldn't tell the difference. Now he didn't know what he was. His mind was a blank slate and full at the same time.

The world shifted. The earth moved, and Indigo hurtled through the abyss. Not an abyss, but the viscous weight of water moving against his skin, caressing in waves.

He was beneath it. In the Well—the ceremonial lake, looking up into the reflection of himself, at Legion. Despair. Sadness, death, anguish. Never ending. Indigo couldn't tell where the Sluagh's agony ended, and the souls of the Wild Hunt began. The screams. He blocked his ears and bellowed until a whisper floated up from the bottom of the lake. A conversation from another time.

"What is the point?"

It is not for us to decide. We are what she made us.

"Why do it when it hurt us so?"

Because it is our purpose.

"Why steal souls and keep them?"

It is our food. Our sustenance. We... are nothing alone... but together... we are many.

"But it hurts. We don't want it. We don't want any of it."

We just want life.

Indigo couldn't tell who was speaking. Him. Perhaps a memory of Legion, perhaps all of them. Legion's warbled reflection looked so forlorn. So full of agony that even Indigo felt pity.

We want life.

We want... something other than the abyss.

Legion lowered his fingers, Indigo reached up. As one, they connected.

He woke, air bursting into his lungs in one great gulp.

Where was he?

Dark. Soft. Floral. Heady. Female.

Violet.

They were in their bedchambers. On the bed. Violet curled into Indigo's side. They weren't alone. There were more... the distant feeling of more. The many. The souls of the damned crammed into Indigo's mind. He clutched his head, wincing, his ears hurting.

"Indi?" Violet jackknifed up, her eyes full of concern. "You're awake?"

He squeezed his ears.

"I'm so sorry," she sobbed. "I had no idea this would happen. I just thought, I just thought you would lose a small memory, like of me pointing a sword at you or something."

And I would give anything to save Peaches. You would give anything to save Haze.

Indigo frowned at her. Did she speak?

Oh God, he remembers me, right? Why is he looking at me

like that? Legion didn't take all of it? He didn't shatter his mind, did he?

Violet's hand clamped over her mouth, her eyes wide and glistening.

"Of course I remember you," he said, pulling her hand to his chest. "He can't take what exists in here."

She burst out crying and launched onto him, sending them both flinging back onto the bed. Her mouth was all over him, kissing him on every piece of skin she could find. Torching his skin. Setting it on fire. She ripped at his tunic—*tunic?* He frowned. When had that changed? How long had he been asleep?

There was no time to ponder when Violet took his face and pulled him close for a kiss that stole his breath. Her taste cleared his head of all else but the insatiable need for his mate. He remembered being with her—in the kitchen, in the bedchambers. He remembered meeting her at his family home. He remembered fighting her in the woods. He remembered *her*. Whatever the Sluagh had taken, it hadn't dimmed his love. Not one bit.

With a grumble of need, he rolled them and flattened her with his body so he could see her, soak her in. "You're mine, Violet, and no one can take that away."

Yes... we want life.

CHAPTER FORTY

Indigo had changed on a fundamental level. Violet could see it in his eyes. They were distant, as though he listened to someone else, or some*thing* else. But they were also full of savage need—the same consuming passion she'd always seen. He was still the same fae she'd fallen in love with. And after him being in a coma for five days, she needed him more than ever.

She slipped her hands inside his tunic, grasping for that heat she loved so much—the hard, smooth skin. The flat stomach. The ridges. The life.

He blinked at her and pulled back, shaking his head as though to clear some fog.

"What did you say?" he mumbled.

"Nothing. Are you okay?" she asked, pausing.

"I'm... I'm fine." Another shake of his head. "How's Shade?"

"He's still asleep. Probably waking up soon, like you. You sure you're okay?"

Darkness swam over his expression as he looked at her, studied her, devoured her. Everywhere his eyes went, it felt like a brand scorching her skin. He flicked his fingers and talons shot out, clawed and lethal. Holding her gaze, daring her to stop him, he used a single talon to cleave her shirt from top to bottom, exposing her nakedness. The cool air kissed her nipples and they hardened instantly.

"You owe me new clothes," she said wryly.

"You've been taking care of yourself." His voice was low, throaty, needy. His talons retracted, and he placed a calloused palm on her, taking care to move slowly and savor the weight of her breast. "These feel fuller. Is that possible?"

His thumb grazed over her nipple, arcing lightning through her body. She arched into him. "Tease."

"And here." He felt her stomach—more taut, more muscular. While he'd slept, while Legion had promised Indigo and Shade would rise in time to leave for Aconite City, she'd continued to train every waking hour. Indigo gave a grunt of consent, a sweep of appreciation. Honey-brown eyes snapped to hers, and every feminine wall in her body quivered at the sight. "You kept yourself strong."

"Yes," she gasped as he traced along her waistband, and then dipped inside.

"For the fight. For Peaches."

She sat up, scowling in his face. "For *you*, asshole."

"Me." He blinked.

"Yes. It's been five days." She swallowed the lump in her throat. "Legion told me you'd be okay, but you were so still, so cold for so long. I wasn't sure if we made the wrong choice. I... I had to stay strong in case you needed to feed from me."

He gripped her face, intense eyes locked with hers. "For me," he repeated.

She nodded.

He kissed her thoroughly, as though she were the air he breathed. Clashing, breaking for air, crashing again. Like waves meeting the shore, they came back to each other time and again. Bruised lips. Teeth knocking. Hands grasping, rubbing, stroking. No more talking. She needed him now. Finding his pants, she tugged at the ties while he removed hers. Naked in moments, they met again like a storm, lightning and thunder, trying to consume each other, rolling around on the bed until finally he stopped them, with him on top.

He cupped her mound and dug the heel of his palm into her sensitive spot and then rubbed in a circular motion. Every mewl she made, every time she arched her hips, he watched with fascination, reveling in the responses he elicited from her. When she whimpered impatiently, he tested her slick folds and found her ready. His lashes fluttered.

She opened her thighs wide, and he seated himself deep with a long, drawn-out, shuddering groan that rattled her heart.

That was the only respite they had, that singular

moment when they looked into each other's eyes, coming to terms with their sensations. And then it was the crashing, the storm, and the greed. It filled them up, chewed them up. With every bone tingling thrust he made, Violet wondered if it was always going to be like this between them. Always this need, this fire, this urgency.

She hoped so.

She'd only spent a few days without him, and the emptiness inside her soul had almost ended her. Never again, she realized. Because they were each other's strength. He made her feel wanted, needed, treasured. And she—

She took his sweat dappled face and pulled him down to her neck. "Feed."

He dipped lower to lick at her collar bone, his hair tickling her skin.

"Indi, feed," she insisted. "You need to be at full strength for what happens next."

All he did was thrust inside her, driving her insane. This would... this would take her over the edge. It would burst that bubble, tightening her skin. He licked and laved with his perfectly pointed tongue. He teased his way over her breasts, suckling her nipples, relishing every inch. She whimpered when he nipped her.

"Please," she begged, arching into him.

"Where?" A guttural grunt. "Here?"

Her nipple. She tensed. "Wherever you want." *I trust you.*

Fangs bared, he looked up at her through his lashes,

made sure she watched, and then pierced his tongue on a fang until a single drop of blood bubbled. Then he lowered himself, took her breast into his warm mouth, around her nipple, and pierced the sensitive flesh. She cried out. The sting lasted a second and then his blood melded with hers, destroying all sense.

Napalm in her veins, scorching all that she was, bringing bliss to every cell in her body.

Time blended into a euphoric haze. All she knew was him. All she wanted was him. And that was a dangerous thought, because when he'd sated himself, and when they'd finally climaxed, she still saw the otherness in his eyes as he sighed and lay beside her.

He watched his finger trace circles around her tingling and healing bite mark. His tongue slid out to lick a drop of blood from the corner of his lips, and he smiled wistfully, satisfied.

And it didn't seem like Indigo. It should. It was him. It looked like him. It moved like him. But it wasn't.

"What did he do to you?" she blurted. "Legion. What did he do?"

He sighed. "I don't know. Something. Nothing. Everything."

"Do you feel like a memory is missing? Do you remember meeting me... when we were together for the first time... anything else?"

He shook his head. "I don't feel like anything is gone. It feels like... I don't know. Like he left a part of himself."

He traced idly over her torso.

She rolled to face him and rested her head on her hand. A flicker of approval danced over his features as he stroked the curve of her hip.

"I feel… like… this is life. You, us. This is what we're fighting for. And I feel because we know that, we'll save our friends."

Violet just hoped it wasn't at a cost they'd regret.

Maebh checked over her shoulder and then entered the locked room two doors down from her sleeping chambers. Shutting the door, facing it, she tensed and steeled herself for what lay inside.

Cobwebs stretched from ceiling to furniture to floor. Undisturbed for almost a century, the nursery suffocated under a blanket of dust. The bassinet—once regally made from antlers and thorns, just like her crown, a symbol of everything Maebh had sacrificed to build this kingdom. But now, it was a symbol of everything she'd lost.

A glimmer at the window caught her eye, and she walked closer to the stained glass, the train of her dress rustling behind her, stirring the dust. With a flick of her wrist, the window opened. Fresh air gushed in on the wings of a crow. Dark glossy feathers glinted in the gray light. Maebh held her wrist out of the window for the bird to rest. It cawed at her, its mind whispering lies and secrets, truths and fables.

They were coming. The Seelie King and his mate were bringing what she needed. The science woman. The human with her terribly violent mind. The crow cawed and Maebh smiled, her cold eyes tracking over the frozen sea outside the palace. She saw the shadow of the land beyond, the snowcapped mountains, and felt the empty pull of the Seelie Kingdom—the land that was once hers. And beyond that... Crystal City, where nothingness yawned.

Maebh would take it all back. She would fill the gaping hole in her heart and stuff it with new life. Mithras had taken everything from her, and if she couldn't make him suffer in his death, then she would take it out on his descendants... and anyone who stood in her way.

A knock came at the door. Maebh's fingers twitched on the crow, snapping its neck, snuffing the light from its eyes. With a sneer, she dropped the carcass and watched it fall the five stories to dash on the rocks below. Then she turned and left the broken nursery.

"What?" she snapped to Gastnor, who stood in the hallway with his head bowed, waiting for her permission. Another curl of her lip pulled at the sight of the failure. Once he had been bright and full of masculinity, strength, virility, and power. Then he'd succumbed to his cravings and lost it all. Now he groveled at her feet. It was the only reason she kept him around, she knew he was desperate to please her.

"I..." He licked his lips, uncertain. "I know you have plans for her, but I would ask your permission to have her after you."

Maebh's brow arched cruelly. "The science woman."

"Yes." He bowed lower, prostrating himself on the floor.

Disgusting. But Maebh supposed after she got what she wanted from the human, she had no need of her.

"You may do whatever you want with her after I am finished, but not before then."

Maebh closed the nursery door, locking it up tight.

CHAPTER FORTY-TWO

Hiding her appearance and scent, Violet followed closely behind Indigo as they walked into a large courtyard inside the Winter Palace—Queen Maebh's domain. Leaf had created a portal in Helianthus so they could easily walk through and all arrive at once. He was still upset that he hadn't been one of the chosen Guardians, but respected the Prime's decision. He, with the others, waited at their rendezvous point somewhere on the frozen shore on the other side of the Aconite Sea.

Shade, Indigo, Jasper, Ada and Violet. They were the first line of attack.

It had been five days and three hours since they'd agreed to come to the Queen's dinner. It had been over two weeks since Haze had gone missing. It had been years since Peaches had been caught, probably used as a blood slave for any vampire within the queen's employ.

And Violet was ready. She didn't know many spells, but what she knew, she knew well. She had weapons strapped to her body from the daggers strapped to her ankles, to the new bone sword between her shoulder blades, and the long thin garrote woven through the belt loops on her pants. The five days Indigo and Shade had been in a coma were put to use by creating custom battle armor for her protection, commissioned by the Prime. Similar to the Guardian outfit, it was made of black leather with petite segmented pauldrons at the shoulder, and blue piping along the seams. She wasn't a Guardian, but something else. Something yet to be defined beyond her recent pledge to the Well.

You're one of us.

The Prime had said nothing upon handing it to her, but the assumption was clear. When this was all done, she wanted Violet as one of them. Officially. To expand on this *something else* she was becoming.

Attached to Violet's belt was the thin scrap of Peaches' old blouse. She wore Haze's ivory ring on a leather cord around her neck. The Prime had used the items to scry for their location, but when nothing came up, she switched the spell to a homing beacon embedded in the items. If Violet got close enough, and if forbidden substances weren't blocking the spell, the fabric and ring should softly glow.

Shade and Indigo were relieved of their weapons at the gate. Jasper and Ada didn't bring anything. They didn't need it. Their strength lay in their Well-blessed bond and the mana they shared. Before they'd come, Indigo had discussed with Violet how he may need to borrow her mana and vice versa.

She didn't care. She just wanted to save her friend. The plan was to follow the team into the dining hall and to wait to see if Gastnor turned up. If he did, and he left, Violet was to follow him—hopefully to where the prisoners were kept, which was most likely not the dungeon. Violet had also studied a map of the Winter Palace, and where the dungeons were. They probably weren't completely accurate, but hopefully it would all be enough. It had to be a start.

Hopefully.

At the center of the courtyard was a long dining table set on dark flagstones. The open sky glittered with a million stars and the crescent moon. No snow. No rain. Violet wondered if Maebh had the power to affect the weather or if she'd simply taken advantage of the clear night sky.

High obsidian walls covered in blood red vines surrounded the courtyard. Pearlescent Hellenistic type statues stood intermittently throughout the rose garden, each holding a tray brimming with either food and wine, or manabee lamps. When a statue blinked, Violet had to hold her gasp.

They weren't sculptures, but people—humans. Slaves.

Violet's heart beat harder. It hurt not to reach out for Indigo, to feel the solid comfort of his grip. She swallowed and continued along behind him. None of their party had flinched or acknowledged the statues, but when they arrived at the dining table, and noted what held up the large obsidian table slab, even Jasper gasped.

More pearlescent painted bodies kneeled on the flagstones, bent over, carrying the load on their backs. More humans. More slaves.

Don't look at them, Indigo said to her, mind to mind.

Indigo? She gaped. Was he speaking in her mind... like Legion had?

Yes, he said. *It's a side effect of drinking the Sluagh. I guess he gave me more of himself than I realized. Don't look at the humans.*

It's disgusting. Horrific.

Stay focused, he reminded her. *And remember, if you're in trouble, I'll know. I'll find you through our bond.*

At the head of the table, the queen's purple lips curved. Resplendently sinister in a ruby dress, she leaned back casually on the bone chair—no. People. More naked people. Vomit rose in Violet's throat. It was impossible not to look. The queen had somehow twisted and molded a collection of bodies—still alive—into a throne. The back of three heads were the headrest. On the queen's long afro hair, a crown of thorns and antlers balanced. Inset within, rubies twinkled like spilled blood.

This crown set the aesthetic for the entire scene. Antlers were the center pieces on the table, thorns and brambles entwined over the length and wound down the people holding the table aloft. They never twitched, they didn't breathe, but they blinked and their eyes followed the newcomers as they arrived.

Behind the queen stood Gastnor and Demeter, Indigo's brother. Violet knew it was him because he looked almost identical to Indigo, but that trickster twinkle was not there. Instead, Demeter's gaze looked flat. Hard. Perhaps even cruel.

Perched on the high walls and scattered throughout the garden were crows. Everywhere. Whether they were shifters, or simply birds, Violet couldn't tell. She didn't want to know. As long as she stayed invisible to all of them, it shouldn't matter. It was just creepy.

"The Darkfoots," the queen crooned in a deep, smooth voice. "Welcome to my home."

Jasper and Ada inclined their heads but did not bow. Neither did the queen. They stared at each other as though they knew this entire event was a sham. Maebh gestured to the Guardians with long, black stained fingers and nails. That was her acknowledgement. If Shade and Indigo were meant to bow, they didn't.

"A bit overdramatic, don't you think, Maebh?" Jasper drawled, gesturing to the human furniture.

"Well," she said, amusement in her dark eyes. "What can I say... raiding my land has consequences. What do you do with your human invaders? Oh. Of course, silly question. You make them royalty."

"Maebh." He bared teeth in what Violet supposed was a smile. "Are you jealous?"

She snorted, but a small smile tickled her lips. With a sweep of her hand, she invited them to take a seat. Maebh's eyes tracked the Guardians as they sat and then narrowed. Maybe she recognized the Sluagh in them, as temporary as it was. But she watched them for too long before indicating for some of the statues to come over and serve them. Like puppets jerking on their master's string, the humans walked over. Violet had to sidestep one, almost colliding with a wall. The closer the human got, the more their eyes screamed. Indigo and Shade both tensed measurably.

They could hear thoughts, Violet realized. Maybe even the human's silent screams.

Can you hear the queen's thoughts? she asked Indigo, hoping he would hear her. But he made no response. She thought for a moment it hadn't worked, but then he responded.

The queen seems to be immune. Possibly because she created the Sluagh. She'd never give them the power to defeat her.

That made sense. Jasper started talking about Cornucopia, the neutral city between the two realms and how he wanted the Ring disbanded.

I can hear Gastnor's thoughts. Indigo's voice snarled into Violet's head. *Promise me you'll be careful around him.*

Believe me, I want nothing to do with him. Except maybe to kill him.

Violet, Indigo warned.

Fine. I'll stay away from him.

Indigo went silent as a server neglected to pour him wine and instead offered her neck. This time, it was Violet who growled, but Indigo held up his palm and declined. When the server left, he spoke again into Violet's mind.

Demeter is thinking of Haze. And Bones. He's... nervous and flitters between the— Indigo paused for a few seconds and then continued to relay his brother's thoughts. *They've done something to Haze. Or to Bones, I can't tell. Some kind of unfinished experiment. Perhaps torture.*

Peaches?

Nothing yet. Another pause. *Legion's gift... it feels weaker. Perhaps it's running out of power.*

Demeter and Gastnor could be here all night. We're running out of time. I'm going to use the location spell on the items.

Before Indigo could respond, Violet started toward the exit in the direction she remembered the dungeons had been on the map. Safely out of the courtyard, she heard Indigo reaching toward her with his mind, but it sounded more like a whisper.

It might not be the Sluagh's gift wearing off... but something the queen...

Indigo's voice went quiet. She considered heading back, but the sense of him down their bond remained steady. So she had to move forward. Pulling out the cloth and the ring, she held them before her and walked.

CHAPTER
FORTY-THREE

The Winter Palace only remained a palace for so long. Eventually Violet followed the hallways to where the building was cut into the mountainside. She knew, because the windows disappeared, and the cold intensified, and the smell became stale. More soldiers replaced the servers in the corridors lit by softly glowing lanterns. The manabeeze inside buzzed about and cast moving shadows on the walls.

The corridors became narrower, rockier, and soon had a strange substance leaking down. She had no idea what it was, but it smelled putrid. The way became twisted and bent, sometimes going up and sometimes further down. It was a maze, she realized, and intended to confuse. She had no idea where she'd been. Would she even be able to find her way out?

She would have to.

Eventually, the screaming of prisoners filled her ears and the items in her hands started to glow. No... just the ring. The cloth remained dormant. She almost whimpered at the sight. Just get to Haze, hopefully he would know where Peaches was. They would figure out the rest later. A door opened as she passed, and Violet flattened herself against the rocky wall to avoid being hit. Holding her breath, hand clutching the cloth, she tried not to think or move, despite her cloaking spell still in full force.

The fae who exited the door was a senior soldier—he wore a similar black embroidered jacket as Gastnor. And right behind him was... Violet's heart leaped into her throat. It was a Sluagh. Oh, Holy Hell.

The Sluagh moved as though he skipped frames in a film. One second there, the next two steps ahead. He stopped in the middle of the doorway, blocking the soldier from exiting.

"Hurry up," grunted the soldier behind him.

Through the door, strange glass jars filled with all manner of things sat on tables. Herbs and flowers were pinned to the wall. Apothecary tinctures, or perhaps it was something different. Violet desperately wanted to crane her neck for a better look, but when moaning came from inside, she froze.

The Sluagh stared right at Violet. He was different from Legion. This one was more decrepit, more sallow. His dark eyes glittered with insanity. She swallowed. If it tried to reach into her mind, she would have to use her light and giveaway her position. She hadn't even found Peaches.

"Go," the soldier insisted.

The Sluagh moved, skip-walking down the corridor in the opposite direction to Violet. She still had no idea if it had heard her mind, or sensed her soul, or if her cloaking and insulation spells had done their job. *Better make this quick.*

She increased her pace, taking twists and turns, avoiding sporadic soldiers until the light glowed brightly before a large, heavy steel door. Violet gasped. Metal. So much of it. She surveyed the walls beside the door. They were still rock, and perhaps the only reason the location spell had worked at all. There was a hatch. She opened it and peered inside, surprised when a waft of heat burst out. It took her a moment to gather her wits, and then she looked again.

It was some kind of pit. She sniffed and recognized the smell—molten rock, just like the obsidian mine. Shouts and cries and moans came from within. Soldiers barking for the prisoners to work. Prisoners lashing out. Prisoners suffering the consequences. Hunched and undernourished shadows moved around, some carrying pickaxes, some with wheelbarrows. Definitely a mine. But what were they mining?

Haze was in there. Was Peaches too?

Violet had thought Shade had asked Peaches to look after Haze. He'd also said she was allowed to walk about outside for fresh air. Violet had no idea it was because Peaches needed a reprieve from *this*. Fuck. She stood back and forced her mind to calm. Instinctively, she checked on her bond—Indigo was fine. Still there. Still strong. No worrisome emotions filtering back to her.

You can do this, Violet. Think. How to get through the metal door? She glanced up. The peeky-boo hatch could open all the way. And the rocky walls meant her location spell had gotten through. Maybe it came down to Haze being a Guardian, and certain rules about the flow of mana didn't apply to him. An idea formed in her head, and she pocketed the special items and withdrew her dagger and held it at the ready. Then she looked through the hatch and found a nearby guard.

This is it, Violet. The moment of reckoning.

She summoned her gift and willed photons out of her body and to mold into a shape her mind created—the senior soldier she'd seen with the Sluagh. She made him stand on the other side of the door, gesturing. The guard immediately came over, but as he arrived, Violet realized she couldn't make her mirage talk. So had to create another one on her side, something to cover her face. *Shit.* Panicking, her mind flew to Gastnor. At least she knew what he looked like intimately.

"The door is stuck," she growled low in her best male voice, then winced and stepped out of the view of the hatch, holding her breath and the mirage on the other side, hoping to dear God the guard wasn't smart. "Hurry up," she snapped. "I have my hands full here."

She heard the sound of keys rattling just before the lock clicked open. At the last moment, she decided to put away the dagger and slid the garrote from her belt loops. She wrapped the ends around her hands and waited, pulling the garrote taut, waiting. The door opened... and she dragged the guard into the empty hallway. As he stumbled, she looped the thin cord around his neck and choked. The guard was stronger than she'd planned for. Dumb, but strong. Some kind of green-skinned orc. He took her to the ground, but her cloaking spell helped her. The guard had no idea how to defend himself, especially when the imposing mirage of an angry Gastnor looked down at him. His big meaty fingers grappled at his throat, trying to pull the garrote. He found her arms and tapped heavily, punching, slapping. Violet's hold on her magic flickered. Her cloaking spell dropped, but she had to feed all her attention into the chokehold.

They rolled together on the ground, but she didn't let up. Eventually the garrote did its job, and the guard went lax in her arms. Panting heavily, she pushed the dead weight off her and got to her feet. At least he wasn't bleeding everywhere. Now she could cover him with a cloaking spell and know the blood wouldn't run out of its radius, exposing what she'd done, as it might have done if she'd stabbed him.

Once satisfied the guard was hidden and to the side, Violet quickly shoved the garrote into her pocket and stepped into the prison, being careful not to close the door all the way.

A blow to her head sent her careening across the rocky

floor. Her vision swirled. Nausea rose in her stomach and she almost fainted. A shadow loomed over her, and all she could do was hold up her hand. Stupid. She'd forgotten to put the cloaking spell back on herself.

"Stop, Haze!"

The looming shadow paused, the rock in his fist hovering in the air.

"I know her."

That voice...

"Peaches?" Violet muttered, her hand testing the wound at her head. She hissed at the pain, at the swelling.

"Violet?"

Violet blinked rapidly until her vision cleared. A petite, peach-haired woman kneeled down beside her, tears in her eyes. "It's you," Peaches said.

"I heard you were here."

Haze stood beside Peaches, a big protective hand almost swallowed her shoulder. He glared down at Violet's hand, at the blue glowing Well-blessed marks. Intense eyes met Violet's but gave nothing else away. He knew what the marks meant, but he wanted to hear it from her.

Good Lord, he was huge. He towered over Violet and Peaches. If he'd worn a Guardian uniform when he'd been captured, he wasn't now. Vampire ears. Wingless. Scruff covered jaw. The past few weeks had turned his shaved head into half an inch of hair. The fae stood naked from the waist up, his olive skin covered in old scars and new. Tattoos swirled over his muscled torso, glinting wetly like the iridescence in an oil slick. Violet had seen the same sort of power enhancing tattoos on Cloud and River.

With a quick glance over his shoulder to see if they'd been noticed, Haze let go of Peaches and limped closer. That's when Violet saw his shackles—not only metal, but pierced through his ankles. That's why the location spell on his ring had flickered in and out of effectiveness.

"I'm Violet," she said. "Indigo, Shade, Jasper and Ada are upstairs dining with Maebh. Others are waiting for us on the Aconite Sea shore, across from the palace. We need to leave now."

Haze's hand snapped around Violet's wrist and he wrenched her to her feet but didn't let go. He gave her a look that withered her insides and for a split second, Violet feared he'd snap her wrist. Haze said nothing, just lifted her blue marked arm and waited for an explanation.

"Indigo," she burst out. "He's my mate."

A gush of air expelled from Haze's mouth, and his broad shoulders relaxed. Violet could have sworn she saw a glimmer of emotion in his eyes, a softening of the stone, and then he straightened his spine and grunted, "Let's go."

Peaches and Violet shared a look she could only explain as—everything. Everything they felt burst through their eyes, and they silently promised each other they'd say it all. Later.

Violet handed her dagger to Peaches and then withdrew her bone sword from between her shoulder blades. She summoned her gift and recast the cloaking spell, but it skittered right over him. She felt the magic try to grasp

Peaches, but something got in the way. The spell flickered and sputtered until it gave up.

"It won't work on you two," Violet gasped.

He nodded. "Don't worry about us."

"No cloaking spell."

"No spell," Haze confirmed.

"Shit. Do I even know how to get out?"

"I know the way," Peaches offered. "I've been out that many times, and I always have to come back on my own. They don't think I'm strong enough to..."

When the ghost of pain flashed in Peaches' eyes, Violet knew much worse had happened to her since those horrible few weeks as a blood slave in a cage. She wanted to reach out to her, to apologize for leaving. Instead, she pulled the small cloth from her pocket and handed it back to Peaches.

"I kept it," Violet said.

"You kept it," Peaches breathed.

"Hurry," Haze growled with a glance over his shoulder. Peaches handed him the cloth, and he pocketed it for her. "Now. They're coming."

Other prisoners had started to notice. Some of them looked like they deserved to be there. But what if they didn't?

"Should we leave the door open?" Violet asked.

"No, we fucking shouldn't," Haze snapped. "None of these floaters deserve to come out."

Peaches opened her cupid's bow mouth. "But what about—"

"None, Sweetness. *None.*" Haze's brows knitted, darkening his face.

Sweetness? Violet glanced between the two of them, but Haze was already limping for the door, dragging Peaches behind him. Violet rushed to catch up. The keys had fallen inside next to the door. Haze took them and locked the door from the outside, just as something enormous hit the heavy metal door, shuddering it.

Haze dropped the keys. "Let's go."

Peaches led them in the opposite direction from which Violet had come. It must be another exit. Despite it looking excruciating, despite him limping and oozing blood, Haze never complained about the manacles. He held Peaches' hand and followed her through the dim tunnels. It was like the lamb leading the lion. Violet took up the rear, keeping an eye and ear focused behind for anyone following them.

They walked for long minutes, never coming across anyone.

"Shouldn't you remove the manacles?" Violet whispered.

Haze grunted, "Can't."

"But if you shift, you'll heal, right?"

He glowered at her from over his shoulder. "I have no mana left. If I remove them, I might bleed out."

That was the last word for another few minutes until Violet had the creeping sense they weren't alone in the tunnels. "Are these corridors deserted?" she asked.

Peaches looked over her shoulder, around Haze's hulking form filling much of the tunnel. "This used to be an old mine entrance, but now no one comes this way because a giant wyrm moved in. It still lives here somewhere."

Violet had heard about them. Big, ugly worm type things with gaping maws made of nothing but teeth.

"Don't worry," Peaches said. "It's sleeping."

"How do you know?" Violet asked. "Your gift?"

Had she manifested one after all?

Haze grumbled, "Let's talk about this when we get out."

They continued for a few more minutes before Peaches slowed and said to Violet, "I never got my gift. I'm immune to everything. How did you..."

Violet stopped and caught her breath, realizing that Haze also needed to rest. His legs were hurting, but he refused to admit it. Peaches knew, though. It was probably why she'd struck up a conversation with Violet. It saved face for the proud Guardian. He was stubborn. Kind of like another Guardian Violet knew, pretending he was fine when he wasn't.

Violet's eyes softened on the pixie-like woman. She really did look similar to Mitzie. Small, dainty, pretty. Indestructible.

"I always had it, Peaches," Violet said. "The gift. It was there waiting for me. But I also had metal in my hands. Almost always, anyway. There's just something blocking you, like it did with me."

Haze leaned heavily against the wall and bent down to inspect the manacles, wincing as he touched them.

Violet stepped up to him. "Ada is here somewhere. If we can get to the rendezvous point, then she can heal you as soon as you get those off."

Haze nodded and rubbed his ankles. Peaches looked at him, and her face said it all. She was in love with him. *My God.* He looked at her the same way. The big brute of a vampire and the timid pixie. Just what exactly had happened in the past two weeks down there?

"I've not held metal in... Since I don't know how long," Peaches said. "It's not like..."

Her voice trailed off and her eyes widened, snapping to Haze.

Haze frowned at her. "What is it?"

"I've had this implant since the old world." She rubbed her arm, pointing to a small lump beneath the skin.

"The contraception implant," Violet said. "That's copper, right?"

"This one is plastic. I figured it wasn't hurting me. It would have run out of effectiveness, anyway. But I'm such a wimp. I couldn't take it out."

"Plastic," Haze rumbled, "is also forbidden."

Sounds behind them.

All three whirled around. Violet raised her sword—

Indigo and Shade.

"It's you," Violet said, lowering her sword. But they looked odd, and when they jerked toward her, like puppets on a string, she screamed.

"Move," she shouted. "Get out. I'll hold them off."

Peaches tried to protest, but Haze grabbed her by the

collar and shoved her ahead of him. They ran, the clinking of Haze's manacles the only sound echoing in the tunnel. Violet held it in, waiting as long as she could, for the sounds of retreating footsteps, and then she summoned her gift.

Blinding light burst into the tunnel, bathing everything.

When she heard the sound of her lover cry out in pain, Violet hesitated. She recalled her light, horrified at what she'd done. Was he hurt? Had she made a mistake? All of her doubts about her choices came back to haunt her. Her choices had never been right. Maybe she'd imagined the otherness about them.

The light dimmed.

A snake rearing out of the glare came for her face. She threw her hands up stupidly, because the two ends of the snake whipped around her wrists, locking on tight. Night flooded the tunnel, drowning out any last drop of light. And then Shade was behind her, locking her hands at her back, whispering into her ear.

"Gotcha."

Violet struggled. "What the hell?"

But she knew in her heart Indigo was different. She'd had her doubts since he had taken Legion's blood. She just never expected this... betrayal. Legion seemed on their side. Violet shook her head just as Indigo stepped up, his handsome face a mask of nothing.

Violet's pulse spiked. Another face appeared in the darkness. Gastnor. Then Demeter. Queen Maebh.

"Oh, sweet little human girl," the queen crooned. "You didn't think I'd not recognize my own creations when they walked into my palace, did you?"

CHAPTER
FORTY-FOUR

Indigo threw Violet onto the floor of a cell. With her hands restrained, she skidded across the stone and hit something—a table leg. Glass tinkled and clattered. Something toppled off and crashed to the ground. It was one of those glass containers filled with manabeeze. Little balls of white light buzzed about, finally free, searching for freedom. She shuffled away, trying not to let one hit her. She didn't want another's memories or loss of sense that came with them. They swarmed frantically about the room. A few hit Indigo and Shade, and they did nothing. No reaction. Like robots, or rather puppets without their master.

Violet watched the manabeeze float to the ceiling and stay where they buzzed along the surface, trapped. She never knew where manabeeze went after releasing from a body. She'd always assumed they floated higher into the stratosphere, somehow changing enough to fall back down with the rain. Perhaps that's why water was so magical and revered to fae.

She searched around the room. Plants and herbs were pinned to the ceiling and shelves. Glass containers were filled with all sorts of tinctures. And those lumpy things on the tables. What were they?

Oh God. Violet rolled to the side and vomited—those lumps were hands, arms, wings, limbs. She'd seen body parts. Fae body parts. This was some kind of mad scientist's laboratory.

Somebody groaned alongside her. Behind and up. She craned her neck, and the vomit wanted out again. It was Bones—in chains, spread-eagle and naked on the wall. He was in bad shape, worse than when she'd seen him in Redvein Forest. She screwed up her nose as the smell amplified. Putrid, pus, excrement. It was like seeing it made the smell worse. And there was something going on with his back she couldn't see. Lumps stuck out of his shoulders and at the sides. Something growing and moving inside.

Violet turned her face away, disgusted, and came face to face with Indigo. He stood to the side of the doorway, and Shade was on the other. Maebh walked in, her dress rustling on the dirty floor. She rested her hip against an apothecary table and gave Violet a sweeping gaze. It felt like fingernails scraping against her mind.

"So this is the science woman," Maebh said. When no answer came, she clicked her fingers in Bones' direction.

He groaned. His reply may have sounded like, “I don’t know.”

“I’ve been hunting you for a long time.” Maebh pouted at Violet. “For who they say you are, I imagined someone taller. Someone... I don’t know... I suppose someone who looked more like me.”

Violet’s mouth twisted, wanting to say something she’d regret but instead fished for information. “Where are the Seelie Queen and King?”

“Where do you think?” Maebh laughed. “The moment I took control of my Sluagh”—she gestured at Indigo and Shade—“they disappeared like the cowards they are. You know, I expected at least a little push back.” She frowned. “But you’re either that stupid, or you haven’t played your wild card yet.”

Violet didn’t think so. Ada was pregnant. Jasper would have simply portaled her to safety. He would be back. And he would bring the might of the Order because this went beyond her blatant disregard for the law. This was outright insanity. Then Maebh’s claim hit.

“*Your* Sluagh?” Violet hissed, glancing at the empty expression on her mate’s face. “They’re not yours. He’s not yours.”

“Oh, darling.” Maebh inspected her black fingertips. “The Sluagh were created by me, using parts of me. And your vampires invited those parts into their bodies. Even your Well-blessed bond can’t compete with my will. I *am* creation. So yes, they now belong to me.”

If she was so mighty and powerful, then how come she needed Violet?

"And Legion?" Violet asked. "Did you get to him? Was this your plan all along?"

Maebh's brow puckered, and she cocked her head, studying Violet for a long time. Something in Violet's words had rattled the queen. She tried not to show it, but Maebh's silence revealed her doubt. Could it be possible she never even knew Legion's name? Or that she had no idea what he was doing, despite her claims all the Sluagh belonged to her. If that were so, then it was highly unlikely Legion was conspiring with her.

"It's not my fault if your idiotic Guardian friends fed from the wrong fae," Maebh finally said. "They all but fell into my lap." She flicked her fingers toward Gastnor, who watched creepily from the hallway. "I had other plans to nab you. He set a trap in the dungeon, but you didn't even go there. Somehow you went straight for the pit. Now I've had to send my new pet to go and clean up the mess you made." She tapped her chin, wondering about something. "Never mind. I have you here now and there are soldiers hunting your friends. We can start."

"Someone will come for us," Violet warned. "You won't get away with this for long."

"I don't need long," the queen said. "You committed murder in my territory. I own you."

Violet went cold.

"What about Gastnor? What about justice for all these scars on my body from him and his soldiers?"

"You're alive, aren't you? The vampires you killed are not."

"The Prime will punish you for what you've done to them." Violet looked at Indigo.

"That?" Maebh laughed. "That's going to wear off, eventually. They'll leave here unharmed, and it will be nothing but an Unseelie joke. A bad dream."

Relief crashed through Violet, but she managed to keep a poker face. Probably because she was out of excuses. Knowing that hurt. She tried to wrench her hands out of the shadow bond, but it was no use. Maebh smiled coldly, picked up a manabee jar and walked over to Bones, studying him.

The most shocking thing about this female wasn't that she was insane, but that half the time she seemed completely in control of her mind. That she was evil with intent.

"I'll never create another nuclear warhead," Violet said. "So if that's why you brought me here, you can just fuck off."

The queen blinked rapidly. Violet guessed no one had ever told her to fuck off before, but she lifted her chin because the words had felt so good. She could say no. Never again would she be pressured into being someone she wasn't. She had power over her choices. She was a smart woman. A goddamned smart, mother fucking woman. And she'd said *no*.

Maebh's plum lips stretched into a crazy-eyed smile. "My dear, if I wanted what was in your head, I would have simply taken it. And I concede, at first I thought I did want it. It sounded too good to be true—something that instilled fear across the world without even having to use it. But then something strange happened... the Well started to reward Darkfoot for stealing the land Mithras stole from me." Fury sparked in her eyes. "I was furious. Enraged. I realized if I made this bomb, then someone else could steal it just as my land had been ripped away from me. I needed a weapon I could control—like the Sluagh." She pursed her lips. "I need you to create something for me. Something new."

She said all this as though ideas were just popping into her head.

"No," Violet returned, liking the taste of that word better this time.

Maebh flattened her shoulders. "My efforts at creating a fae able to simultaneously use metal and their mana, have been, let's just say... ineffective." She stared at Violet with eyes that made her shiver. "I need you to use that clever little science mind and apply it to my problem. I want my own Guardians."

Violet jolted. So she didn't want a nuclear bomb? At all?

As if hearing her thoughts, the queen added, "Why would I want to destroy the world I live in? I want to control it. One thing I've learned from the humans, from this Bones creature, is that the Well can indeed be controlled if you know how. I want it all, and you're going to help me get it."

"I don't understand," Violet said. "I know nothing about creating new fae."

"Surely studying science can't be too different from studying mana."

Hadn't Violet once asked herself the same question?

Maebh scowled at Bones, her displeasure evident. "I thought you said she was clever? This is *not* clever." Bones mumbled something inaudible, and it infuriated the queen. She picked up a severed hand and shook it at Violet. "I want you to use this stuff. I want you to make me something that works like a Guardian."

She threw the hand at Violet. It bounced off her shoulder.

"Like I said before," Violet gritted out. "Fuck. Off."

The queen screamed. She swiped the table and more limbs fell, thudding wetly to the floor. "You will use your science, or I will break you like I broke Bones. I will have one of my Sluagh rip it from your mind."

One of her Sluagh? But not *her*? Interesting.

Violet reassessed the queen. Perhaps she wasn't as powerful as everyone thought. Maebh's ragged breathing slowed. She lifted her chin and looked down at Violet.

"When I return, I will have results. One chance. That's all you get, and then the Sluagh will pillage your mind. I will have your science one way or another."

She spun on her heels, her dress dragging through the blood-stained floor, and she barged through the door, knocking Gastnor out of the way. He glared at Violet and then followed his queen. She shouted at him in the corridor.

Violet used the chance to try to reach Indigo.

Indigo, she shouted with her mind. *It's me. Violet.*

But he stared blankly ahead. Down their bond she could hardly feel him, only that he was there.

Maebh returned and stood in the doorway, inspecting Shade and Indigo. Probably wondering whether to leave them and torture Violet, or take them and use them for herself. She even trailed a stained finger along Shade's jawline.

"Always a pity," she mumbled to him, "to lose a fae like you to the Order. Perhaps... perhaps you can return to my bed. Perhaps you can show your queen what you've learned since you left me, and what you still use that I taught you."

Gastnor made a sound and Maebh snatched her hand back from Shade. She gave Gastnor a dark look. "You know what I need you to do. Don't fail me again, Gastnor. You're out of second chances."

She glanced at Indigo and Shade in a way that made Violet's skin crawl, and then she left.

When she was gone, Violet couldn't hold it in anymore. She laughed. She laughed so hard it hurt. She clutched her stomach and rolled to the side, away from her vomit, and couldn't stop.

"Science," she spluttered. "She wants to use my science!" As though it was as intangible as magic!

They knew nothing. These fae, they were so far from

understanding that they didn't even use the word properly in a sentence. So, to the queen, this had simply been a case of, get to Violet before her enemies. And now that she had her, she wanted to make the most of her.

"Too deep, too deep," Bones croaked like a madman, the whites of his eyes showing, his mouth frothing. He squirmed as though to get the things out of his back, but with his hands locked, he couldn't reach. "Went too deep."

Violet tried to wipe her tears with her shoulder, but couldn't reach with her hands tied behind her back. Eventually, all the laughter died. She was left with bone cold exhaustion and the creeping sensation of being watched. By Indigo. By Shade. By Gastnor. By Bones.

She swallowed.

"Are you finished with the hysterics?" Gastnor drawled, eyes like hot pokers.

"You fucking touch me, and I swear to God..."

Her hands might be tied, but she could still use her light. She could still create mirages. It might be enough to startle them all so she could slip out.

Gastnor's laugh was short and sharp. "No one is going to save you. Not you, not your new friends at the Order, and certainly not your mate."

He went to Indigo and stroked along his jaw, just as the queen had done with Shade. Indigo didn't even twitch under Gastnor's leer.

"I could do anything to you," Gastnor said to her, excitement dripping from his expression. "And all your mate can do is watch. He's probably screaming somewhere, locked in his mind right now." Gastnor knocked on Indigo's head. "You can hear me, can't you? The Sluagh always seemed like they remembered when she made them do things."

"The queen needs me," Violet said, throwing up her only defense. Maebh may have threatened to have her mind raided, but she'd already admitted that she'd rather have Violet use her mind herself. "So if you hurt me, she'll be angry."

Gastnor was before her in a flash, baring fangs dripping with histamines, his ugly scar puckered. "The queen gave you to me. As soon as she's through with you, you're mine."

Violet spat in his face. His pointed tongue darted out and licked it off.

"You're repulsive," Violet muttered.

His greedy eyes dipped to her mouth, then back up, and she tasted bile again.

"Use your science, human," he growled.

"Go to hell."

He backhanded her on the cheek. Light exploded in her eyes—in other places, too. Her power had burst. But the moment the floodgates opened, agonizing pain exploded in her side. Violet's light shut off like a switch being flipped. Blinking, she saw why. He'd stabbed her. A metal dagger in his fist, the pointy end in her side, cutting off her flow of magic.

"You don't need to access the Well for what we need," he said, grinning as her blood welled over his fingers. "You never had the Well back in your time, and you could use your science, anyway."

"You idiot," she cried. "Science needs me to think, and you've just—"

Her vision went sideways, and she landed hard on her side, panting hard through the pain. It was unlike anything she'd felt. It was more than pain. An absence of the light she'd become accustomed to—completely cut off from the Well. She'd never noticed it before. Before when she'd barely touched it. But now... after weeks of sharing her body with the magic that fueled the world, she felt empty. Alone. Hopeless. Tears brimmed.

Gastnor let go and stood back with a gasp as his own connection to the Well no doubt came rushing back into him. His eyes widened a fraction, perhaps seeing that he'd made things worse. The queen wanted results, and if she was in pain, she couldn't think. Not like they wanted her to. Physics demanded a clear head. Mostly. There were times she'd had a few drinks and spouted theories with co-workers, but this... results oriented work...

She groaned into the floor, wanting to cover her wound but unable. She looked at Indigo, silently begging for his help. From the corner of her eyes, she saw Gastnor stare at his bloodied hand, his eyes flickering red, full of lust for her blood.

"You fucked up," Violet said, seeing his mental struggle all over his face. The queen must have told him to keep his desires in check, to lay off her blood until the job was done, and he couldn't resist. All she needed to do was push him a little further. "This might be your only chance to taste my blood because I can't work for you now, even if I wanted to. My mind is too clouded with pain." She winced, moaning for effect.

Gastnor looked at her. Then at his bloody hand. He licked his lips.

Stupid old fae.

She moaned again and tried not to smile when he laved his hand in one long stroke, eyes fluttering with the taste of her blood. And that was it. He went at his hand with ferocity, sucking his fingers, moaning in pleasure, licking every last drop.

It made her sick to watch. She rested her head on the cold, dirty floor and wished she hadn't been right. The pain *was* clouding her mind. More than that, it blocked her gift. She had to get the dagger out. But then what would she do? Burst her light and blind them? Run? How far would she get with the Sluagh stalking these halls?

At least Peaches and Haze had got out. She hoped.

"Science," Bones hissed from his position, then laughed, gurgling and convulsing.

He probably just got the joke.

Science.

As Gastnor started to lose control of his limbs, and lowered to the floor, the word bounced around in her head. *Science, science, science.*

It was stupid to boil down what she'd spent her life learning to that one, misrepresented word. What Violet had learned was more than that. It was chemicals. Electrons. Ions. Photons.

Photons.

She jolted. Blinked. Violet knew photons. She *knew* them. And now she had the power of them burning through her body... at least she did without the dagger in her side. Violet knew exactly what happened when you heated light particles up. They became gamma rays. They irradiated like a nuclear bomb. And photons... when they clashed... they created matter.

All these thoughts and more swirled around her head as she tried to pick out which parts were useful, and which were noise.

Violet glanced at Indigo. He was being controlled because of the Sluagh blood in him. Legion had been frightened of her light. When Indigo had first accosted them in the corridors leading from the pit, he'd cried out in pain when her light had hit him. He'd never done that before. He'd winced, but he'd taken the temporary blindness without complaint. That's why she'd hesitated.

Never dim your light for me, Violet. Ever.

Perhaps if Violet could amplify her light, if she pushed more mana into her photons, turning them into something that irradiated, she might be able to burn the Sluagh out of Indigo. She could save him.

It could also give him radiation poisoning.

But Ada was somewhere about. She was a healer like no one had ever seen before. If she could erase scars, surely she could heal radiation poisoning.

With a solid plan forming, Violet gathered her resolve. She had to try something. Even if it didn't work. She licked her lips and steeled herself for what she had to do next. She looked at Gastnor. He'd crawled over to her, eyelids half lowered, staring at her wound and the blood still oozing from it. Because she'd seen it before, because she knew how he'd react, she crooned softly, "You'll get more blood if you take the dagger out."

Gastnor leaped onto her. He dragged her by the legs into the center of the floor, and then he hesitated.

"I'm not going to help her," Violet rasped. "You may as well feed from me while you can. She'll kill you and then she'll kill me."

He yanked the dagger out and latched onto the wound, tearing an agonizing scream from her lungs. His tongue speared into her as he lapped greedily, and mana soared back into her body, filling her with power. It had been there all the time, just blocked. Just waiting for her.

It had always been there.

Tears of joy ran down her cheeks. Again the Well had chosen her, trusted her. She rolled her head and looked at her lover. He blinked impassively. But he'd blinked.

"Close your eyes," she whispered, and then became master of her fate once more. She unleashed.

CHAPTER FORTY-FIVE

Light burst from Violet with such intensity that she *felt* it release from her body. She became the sun. The moon. The stars. Yet she kept pumping power —*mana*—from deep within her body, amping it up by drawing from her surroundings, wherever she could find it. She used it to power the light, to feed it, to become its master. She twisted it, molded it to her will. Her light became more than photons. And she became more than Violet. She beamed inside the bodies of anyone nearby. She chased the shadows, chased whatever made up the Sluagh... chased it all away until there was nothing.

Violet awoke to the sound of battle. Snarling. Ripping. Shredding wet flesh.

Blinking, she tried to sit up. *Must have passed out.*

Red blood had sprayed everywhere. The shadow snake no longer bound her wrists. Violet scrambled to her feet, staunching her wound, wincing. What the hell? Was that hers? Blood coated her... the floor, the ceiling, Bones hanging limply on the wall. And Indigo. He stood with his back to her, his enormous wings out, filling the room. His back lifted and fell with ragged breath.

Fear choked her.

It hadn't worked. A sob burst out. Her light hadn't worked.

Indigo whirled, his eyes the only white on his red, angry face. She flinched and stepped back. The fury from his expression dropped, and he held his hand out.

"It's okay," he said. "It's me. It's me."

"Indi?"

He nodded grimly, then winced. "Whatever you did hurt... but it worked."

Then he turned to the side and fell to his knees, vomiting. His wings almost hit her. The room was too small. She dropped to the floor with him and put her hand on his forehead. It was hot. Feverish. There were lesions on his skin from the radiation.

They had to get to Ada.

"Where's Shade?" she asked.

Indigo gulped air.

"Gastnor?"

He shook his head and retched. The body parts—the severed limbs. She picked out half a scarred face and a vampire's pointed ear on the floor. Indigo's fingers were torn. He'd ripped Gastnor apart. This was the power he'd feared in himself, the part of him he needed her to be strong for.

"Holy shit, Indi. What did you do to him?"

"What he deserved," he croaked.

Violet searched the room and saw something outside the hall. Legs. Boots. *Shade.* With a last check on Indigo, she held her wound and scrambled to the door. What if he wasn't...

She cautiously approached. "Shade?"

"I'm here," he panted and threw his hand into the doorway so she could see. He also had lesions on him. But he was Shade, not something the queen controlled.

"Are you okay? Are you... you?"

He nodded. "It was better out here than in there... Indi..."

"He went a little..."

"I know," he said, then looked like he was going to vomit too.

"It's the radiation," she said. "We need to get both you and Indi to Ada."

Shade nodded and forced himself to his feet. "I can help with that."

"How?" They both went back to Indigo and crouched beside him. Violet thought his sickness was worse. Maybe it was also because of how Gastnor ended up.

"I've been working on my shadow walking. I can take us short distances. Possibly out to the rendezvous point."

Shade held his hand out to Violet and put the other on Indigo's shoulder. "You ready?"

She took his hand and placed her trust in a vampire. She nodded. Darkness peeled away from Shade until it filled the room, and then the ground moved. The walls shook. The ceiling crumbled. She lost hold of Shade's hand and tried to balance herself.

"What was that?" she gasped, as the shadows snapped back into Shade. They all looked at each other, still in the laboratory. Crumbs and debris continued to fall from the ceiling. The earth shook again. *Earthquake*.

"It could all come down on us," Indigo burst out.

"The Sluagh?" she asked. Panic lit their faces.

"I don't know. Hurry," Shade growled. He took her hand again. This time, when his shadows came, they swarmed. They weren't gentle. They ripped Violet from the room.

STILL WITH BLOODLUST and sickness riding his system, Indigo broke away from Shade and Violet with one thought—*traitor.* Whatever had happened in there was Legion's fault. He searched the crowd of Guardians on the shore until he found the face he wanted. All others were a blur as Indigo attacked, his fist connecting with the smug bastard's smooth face, but then the ground shifted. Indigo fell to the floor, retching. Whatever Violet had done to them...

"Ada!" Violet shouted from somewhere. "We need healers."

Cool hands landed on Indigo's hot forehead and eased him down to the even colder sandy shore. But it felt so good. The stars and the moon came into focus and he realized he was staring at the night sky. Voices everywhere. Shouting. Barking.

"Shade, you too." Violet sounded... afraid. "Oh God. I think he's worse. Shade... get down so Ada can heal you." A scuffle. A drop. Someone else retching.

Indigo tried to reach for Violet—his mate—but his limbs were too heavy. All he wanted was her.

"What happened?" Ada asked, running her hands over Indigo's body, feeling with her gift where the sickness was.

"Radiation poisoning," Violet said. "I had to. They were being controlled by the queen. It was the only way to force the Sluagh blood out of their bodies, to destroy the cells."

Someone cursed. A cool sensation started flowing through his body. His mind blurred. Everything blended. Sight, vision, sound. He could hardly stay conscious. He closed his eyes and listened to the words.

"Jasper?" Ada's voice was small. Tight. "Did he find you?"

"No... I never saw him. Is he still in there?" Violet's voice was tight.

Silence.

"Call him back." Violet urged.

"How? I'm not—"

"Use your bond. Make yourself afraid. He'll sense it and come."

More coolness flowed into Indigo, and it was better than dipping into a lake.

"Haze," someone rasped... Shade.

"They were on their way out, escaping through the tunnels. Someone needs to search for them."

"On it." A male voice.

"Shade's not responding to my healing," Ada said, voice strained. "But Indigo is."

"It might be my blood," Violet suggested. "I'm not sick. I was exposed to the same radiation."

"Then you should feed him."

"No..." Shade moaned.

"Shade, open your mouth," Violet growled. "Don't make me force it down your throat."

"No."

Indigo tried to stay awake, to tell Shade it was okay, but then the night came for him.

CHAPTER FORTY-SIX

Peaches tried to hold Haze, but he was too big. Too heavy. And he was doing his damndest to move with those cursed metal manacles.

"We're almost there, baby," she gasped, her shoulders straining.

He dropped to a knee, taking her with him.

"Sweetness," he sighed.

She'd always loved that soft word coming out of such a hard, strong man. She'd always loved that he'd said it to her, for her. But the next words he muttered, she wanted none of it.

"I'm sorry," he rumbled. "I'm so sorry."

"Stop it," she cried and cupped his face. "Stop it right now. I don't accept your apology. I won't. We're almost there. Just a little more. Look—" She pointed to the light at the end of the tunnel. An old mine shaft exit where she used to slip out for exercise. The yard was fenced in, but she knew places to hide. She knew where the fence was weakest and the Guardians might find them.

"I should have been stronger," Haze groaned. "I can't..."

The manacles were killing him. Bolts pierced through his ankles, put there by the Unseelie Queen bitch herself.

"Now you listen to me, you big brute," she snapped at him, her voice trembling. "If I can survive what they did to me, you can survive this. You're stronger than me."

She hit a thick slab of pectoral, but he didn't even flinch. Nothing. Until he nodded and clenched his jaw. He gripped the chain dangling between the manacles. He took a deep breath and held it.

Peaches' blood ran cold. "What are you doing?"

"You were right," he gritted out. "I'm stronger than this."

His muscles bulged. His neck tendons popped. Veins wreathed in his arms like hissing snakes. And then he broke the chain.

"Don't..." Peaches shouted. "No more. It's not worth the pain."

"If I get them off, then I'll replenish from the Well. It might take some time before I have enough to shift, but a couple of flesh wounds won't kill me."

Flesh wounds? He was talking about ripping bolts out of his ankles. What if he hit an artery?

Two solemn eyes met hers. His broad chest expanded as he sucked in another breath, held it, and then grasped the bolts on either side of his ankles. Tears spilled from Peaches' eyes. There was nothing she could do but watch as he roared in agony and pulled the bolts clean out of his flesh, including the broken chain they were attached to. When the last wall-shaking note of his roar died, his lashes fluttered closed, and he hunched over, spent.

She used Violet's dagger to rip a strip off the bottom of her shirt and then wound it around his left ankle. That was *not* his blood gushing from the wounds. That was just a dribble. *Just a dribble.*

After she'd secured the first leg, she wrapped the second.

"Go without me," he rasped, sweat covering his face. "I'll catch up."

She stood back and shoved fingers into her long, messy hair. She wouldn't leave him. Not when they'd been through too much together. Not when she—her heart clenched.

If only she had magic like Violet had. Who knows, maybe she could signal for help. Maybe she'd end up with healing magic. If only she could... she looked at the dagger, and then to the stupid implant she'd been too weak to dig out.

But now... after years of torture and torment, pain was her friend.

If he could wrench bolts from his ankles, then she could be brave too.

She pointed the dagger at her skin and dragged it through the flesh, deep. That familiar feeling, that sharp sting and bite of a razor, filled her with adrenaline. She'd been wrong to wait so long. She'd thought she feared pain, but it had become her friend. She dropped the dagger and dug her fingers into her wound until she found the stupid little piece of plastic and held it bloody and impotent before her face.

"You." She glared at it. "You've caused me the most pain of all."

Then she flicked it, watched it flip and rotate in the air until it bounced off the ground. She rushed back to Haze, put her hands on his knees, and looked into a face carved from grief. It wasn't from the pain in his ankles. He thought he'd failed her.

"We made it, baby," Peaches said. "We're here. You did it, Haze. You kept me safe. These past few weeks have been —" She choked up. So much emotion. Liquid brown eyes met hers. They were the softest part of him. They were the first part she'd seen. They'd shown her his secrets. His heart. They were the reason she'd fallen in love with him. A tear leaked from her eye and dribbled down her face.

"Sweetness," he sighed again. His giant hand consumed her cheek as he rubbed the tear away. "You—"

She held her wounded arm out.

"Drink," she demanded. "My blood will dull your pain. It will make you stronger."

Cold, hard determination flickered in his expression. His pointed pink tongue darted out, and he held it to his fang, deliberately showing her that he drew blood. He would make her feel good, just as she would for him. Always. Then he latched onto her arm and covered her wound with his mouth. The single drop of his potent vampire blood zinged into her system, liquefying her limbs. The thick column of his throat worked as he swallowed, and it was all she could do to hold on to him.

Through the pleasurable haze of his feeding, a blue light flashed. The ground shook. The walls crumbled. Electricity swarmed through Peaches' body, jolting and convulsing. She seized. She lost her breath, and then finally, she gasped and broke away from Haze with a stumble.

Well-blessed marks swirled and twined over her entire arm—over *his* arm—glancing off the walls.

"Violet was right," she mumbled. The Well had been blocked from both of them... and now it flowed unhindered. Now it connected them completely. "She was right. Look at us."

Her tears turned to joy and she laughed. She took Haze's face, as stunned as her own, and she kissed him hard on the lips. Those strong lips. Hot. Hers. Forever.

The earth rumbled some more, showering more dust on them. They broke apart and something had returned to Haze's eyes. The will to survive. To fight.

"I was right first," he insisted. "Not Violet. What did I tell you?"

She bit her lip, holding back a smile. "That I'm yours."

A growl of approval rattled through him, and he levered himself up. "Let's go."

Together they hobbled to the exit, to the light. Finally. Free.

She should have known freedom came in shades of

gray. Ten feet out, Peaches doubled over as a jolt of new power rippled through her. The world spun. Haze tried to hold her up, but he stumbled himself. Her palm hit the wall, and it shook with such ferocity that Peaches felt like it came from within her. She felt it *vibrate* through her. It *was* her.

Holy hell, she *was* the earthquake. This was her gift.

Wooden beams creaked above, cracking under stress. The earthquake worsened. More rumbling. More cracking walls and dust falling.

"Haze?" She met his bleak gaze, her voice helpless and pitched high. "What do we do?"

He'd always known what to do. Any time they were stuck, in danger, or... alone together, he knew what to do. He was her rock.

A loud crack sounded above them. Haze shoved Peaches toward the exit just before a wooden beam crashed down. He caught it on his shoulder and staggered to the ground, holding the beam, preventing the tunnel from completely caving in. Dust piled on top of his head and collected at his twitching ears.

"Hurry," he roared at her. "Run, Sweetness. Get out of here before it all comes down."

"No!" she cried, startling herself. But the rumbling wouldn't stop. More parts fell. Rocks. Bigger ones. One hit her shoulder.

"Run, Peaches," he snarled, bending under the immense weight. "If you ever meant any of those things you said to me, run. Survive like you promised." She shook her head, but his eyes said everything. They said goodbye. "You promised."

Her heart ripped apart. How dare he use that promise against her now. She'd been close to death then, not the other way around.

"Go!" His roar rattled the air. "I'll catch up."

His brows lifted in the middle like she betrayed him. Not that. Not that look, she'd take any but that.

So she did what she always did. She took the coward's way out. She turned. And she ran. And the walls came tumbling down after.

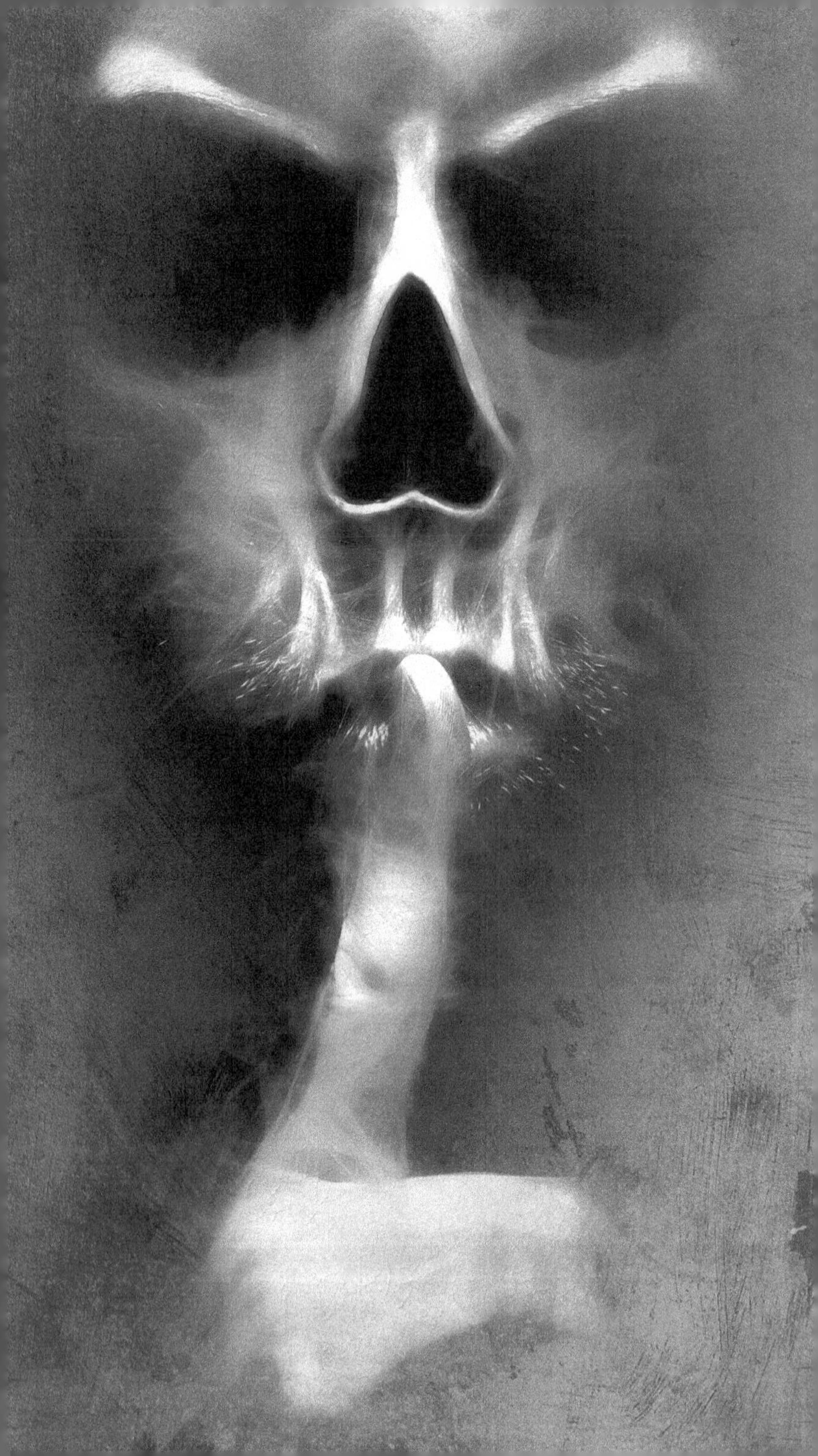

CHAPTER
FORTY-SEVEN

After they'd all returned to the Order campus via one of Leaf's portals, and Ada had done everything she could to heal Indigo, Violet went to find Legion. Both Indigo and Shade were sleeping, and there wasn't much to do about it. Their bodies had to recover. She still waited for news of Peaches and Haze, and needed something to occupy her time.

Finding out what the hell had gone through Legion's mind sounded like just the thing. She made her way down the stairs of the two story cadre house and paused at the landing. She didn't know where to find the Six. She'd never been to this campus. This was all new.

I'm waiting on the front lawn, Legion's voice slid into her mind on a whisper.

Her instincts fired up, ready for battle, but then she forced herself to relax. She didn't need to fear Legion, or the Sluagh. She might be the only person alive apart from Maebh who could claim that advantage. So she lifted her chin and walked out the front door and into the night.

He waited exactly where he said he would be. The front lawn of the Twelve's house was a long rectangle that stretched toward the Guardian barracks in the distance. The cool wind lifted Legion's long hair and rustled his wings, but he stood stoically, waiting for her.

And there was a second Sluagh, another from the Six. This one was male, as far as she could tell. Similar in every way to Legion except his hair. It was cut short at the back and sides, and long on the top. Dressed all in black, he would have fit in nicely with the Goths and Death Metal enthusiasts.

"You know why I'm here," she said, glancing between the two of them.

Legion's sensuous lips twitched. *You want to know if we betrayed you.*

She put her hands on her hips. "And?"

As if he'd actually tell her, anyway. Unless Violet was a mind reader herself, there was no way of knowing if he spoke the truth.

We would never betray you after Indigo's gift. This came from the second one's mind. His voice felt more like absinthe to Legion's whiskey. A sweet, addictive bitterness to Legion's smooth, warm burn.

For a moment, she saw in his eyes the same hunger she'd seen in Gastnor's, and an icky feeling started to bloom in her chest. Indigo's gift? The memory?

Indigo had said he didn't feel like Legion had taken anything, rather that he'd left something behind.

"Did you even take a memory?" she asked Legion.

His lips twitched and his eyes crinkled in what Violet thought might have been a smile.

Yes, he replied. *Just one that was yet to happen.*

She gasped. That far off look in Indigo's eyes when they'd made love... had Legion... and this other Sluagh... maybe all of the Six. Had they all been there... watching? Both Sluagh studied Violet.

In you, we thought we wanted death, but you gave us life through Indigo's memory, said the newcomer. *And my name is Varen.*

"You said you'd take a memory," Violet accused. "You tricked us."

We did take a memory. A future one.

"You say that like you all experienced it."

They made no answer. A small glow pulsed in her fingers and she considered obliterating them with her light, but something Varen had said gave her pause. They were searching for death. They'd wanted... to die? Her heart ached. No one should feel that helpless, that alone. She let her light go.

"Are you telling me Indigo will have no recollection of that moment?" She scrunched up her nose. "And you're both gross. I can't believe you did that. It's an invasion of our privacy. Do it again, and I won't be so forgiving."

Legion's shoulder lifted half-heartedly, and a sadness flickered in his eyes.

"There's more you're not telling us," she accused. "It was more than that memory."

He inclined his head and looked to Varen. *Varen is our Seer. He had many visions. Ones that saw all the ways your infiltration of the Winter Palace played out. The only scenario where your mate could get down to that cell to save you, and for you to learn the true power of your gift, was one where the queen thought he was hers.*

"You could have warned us."

The Sluagh can read minds, Varen replied. *They would have found out.*

"And the only way to make someone immune to that was for the vampires to feed from you. It both put them at risk and saved them." She threw up her hands, frustrated, and paced alongside them on the grass. "I've had just about enough of manipulation," she said. "From Indigo, from you. Who's next?"

You are in Elphyne, Violet. You are fae.

"I'm human," she insisted.

Are you?

"And I suppose this is what fae do... trick, manipulate, bargain. It's stupid."

This is why we came to you to learn.

About life? She slid her gaze to Legion. He blinked at her innocently. "You knew I'd discover a way to kill the Sluagh," she said. "Yet you sent me into that fate, anyway. Why?"

A single, slow blink, and then Legion and Varen simply walked away.

"Hey!" she shouted at them. "Seriously, I know I threatened you, but you can't come inside Indigo's head again, can you? You can't watch us, can you?"

She could have sworn she heard Varen chuckle, but Legion's voice whispered back to her, *His mind is his own now. And you are there to protect him.*

⚖

WHEN VIOLET WALKED BACK to Indigo's room, she found Ada leaving Shade's next door.

"How is he?" she asked quietly.

"He's good," Ada replied. "He's responding well to your blood and my healing methods. He's awake, but he's grumpy, so I wouldn't go in there if I was you. At least not until the shock of what your blood has done to him wears off. He's still coming to terms with the fact he's going to want the blood of a Well-blessed human for a while, but he's alive and he has you to thank for that in more ways than one."

Violet let Ada's words sink in. It might be more than a while before Shade got control of his new cravings. Indigo had tasted Ada's blood months before he'd met Violet, and he'd said the entire time other blood had tasted like cardboard.

Ada squeezed Violet's shoulder. "You also gave me the knowledge to bring Jasper back. Your trick worked. I made myself feel frightened, and he came back to me. He's downstairs now with the others, so thank you."

Violet gave the petite blond a small smile. "It's me who should be thanking you."

"Don't mention it. I'm glad to be out of that palace and to be useful for once." She stared at Violet for a moment. "You've come a long way, Violet."

She was right. No longer did Violet feel so weak and helpless. No longer did she feel alone. Even in her darkest hour, she'd fought back. She'd survived.

Don't let the bastards win, her mother had said. Violet ran her fingers over the bumpy scars on her arms. Her mother had it wrong. By fighting against them, she'd been as bad as they were. The best way to heal would have been to forgive and move on with her life.

"Maybe there's one last thing you could do for me," she said to Ada. "Before you go."

CHAPTER
FORTY-EIGHT

Indigo woke in his room in the cadre's house at the Order. The curtains were drawn. He felt like shit. And Violet was sitting on a chair next to the bed.

"Hey," he croaked.

She lifted her head. Dark circles under her eyes suggested she'd probably not slept. He reached out, and she came over, lying down next to him. No words. No sounds. But he felt her relief, her angst, her love... all washing into him down their bond. He held her as she curled into his side and buried her face in the crook of his neck. He felt a wetness against his skin. Tears.

"Hey, hey... don't cry." He cupped the back of her head and stroked. Tangled hair. Messy. "I'm okay, Vi."

She shook her head and clutched him. A band constricted around his chest. Maybe someone else wasn't okay. He was almost too afraid to ask.

“Who?” he asked. “Who’s not here?”

“You’ve been asleep for hours.” Sniffing, she sat up so they could meet eyes. “I feel like so much has happened. They just found Peaches.”

“She’s okay?”

She nodded. “She’s in Haze’s room, but...”

He lifted to his elbows. “Haze?”

Her face screwed up, and she broke down, sobbing into her hands. A burn at the back of his eyes made him blink. “He’s dead?”

“I don’t know. Peaches was screaming his name, over and over. Ash found her and the tunnel had caved in. She was trying to dig her way into the mine with her hands, but Ash took her before... before the queen sent her army.” Steady eyes lifted to meet Indigo’s. “Peaches is Haze’s Well-blessed mate.”

He slid his palm along Violet’s smooth forearm, soothing her with a stroke. “Can she feel him through their bond? Check to see if he’s alive?”

Violet dashed tears away with a frown. “That’s a good question. I never thought to ask. I was too—and she was too distraught to even talk to me.”

“It’s okay.” Indigo sat all the way up and smoothed hair from her face. “We’ll go and see.”

She nodded, went to move, and then came back to him. From the way her shoulders set, he could tell there was more.

“Shade is awake,” she said. “He didn’t want to take my

blood, but I had to force it on him." Her eyes watered again. "He's going to hate me, but there was no other way."

"He's alive," Indigo reminded her. "He won't hate you. He'll hate—"

Anger fired in Indigo's veins as he remembered the true villain here... not just Maebh but Legion. He'd tricked them. He was the one who deserved their wrath. Clenching his jaw, Indigo swung his legs over the side of the bed and tugged on some pants. He was going to find a way to murder that bastard.

"Why do I feel some kind of murderous intent coming from you?" Violet asked.

"Legion," he gritted out.

Pants up, he strode to the door with one thought on his mind—vengeance. Violet stopped him with a palm to the chest.

"Don't," she said. "Believe me, I felt the same way when I got back and saw his face."

"Violet," he gaped incredulously. "Because of him, we almost all died. Haze is still there, with that insane queen."

"No," she said, lifting her chin. "Because of Legion, we lived."

"What?"

"While you were out, Legion told me everything. A while ago, the Seer in the Six—Varen—had a vision. In fact, more than one. He saw multiple ways that mission was going to end, and only in one did we survive. He knew the only way you and Shade would get down to that cell to save me was if the queen thought you were hers. If she was complacent enough to leave you alone with me."

A low growl emitted from Indigo's throat and he shook his head, too furious to let go. His fists clenched at his side. "He still knew. He could have warned us."

"He gave up the one thing that was protecting them," she said.

"What do you mean?"

Violet's hands smoothed up to his neck, then clasped behind. "I can kill them, Indigo."

"The Sluagh?"

She nodded, her eyes solemn. "All of them."

"How?"

"Maebh could control you through the Sluagh blood you drank. For me to destroy it, I had to push so much power into my light, that it entered your body. It worked. It will work on the queen's Sluagh too."

He clasped her hands at his neck. "I don't understand."

"To put it simply, I became the sun. The light I emitted was so full of ions and energy that it beamed right into your bodies and burned their cells away." She took a deep breath. "Theoretically, if we face the Sluagh again, I can do the same thing. I can destroy them. Legion knew this. He knew that he'd be giving me the key to annihilating them and yet he still helped."

"So *you* can go and kill him then. Kill Legion."

She laughed, and then for a moment she looked forlorn. "I think maybe that's what they wanted in the beginning."

"I'm serious," he growled.

She only patted him affectionately on the chest. He smoothed his hands up her arms and tried to let his anger go. That's when he noticed something odd. He glanced down.

"Your skin is smooth," he noted. "Where're the scars?"

Violet bit her lip. "I asked Ada to heal them. I hope that's not vain."

Indigo's throat closed up with emotion. "Vi," he rasped, grazing his knuckles against her jaw. "I only hated seeing them because I hated knowing you'd suffered."

"I know." She smiled. "I did this because I wanted to give you something that meant I was yours. That you have something no one else has seen. Something new. I hope you—"

He kissed her, swallowing her words. There was no need for more. He felt it all down their bond. She was his... always, and he couldn't wait to learn all the new spots on her body. For the next hour, he did exactly that. He rediscovered his mate, reveled in her body, and learned every contour. They made love, this time with privacy wards around their room. He didn't want to share this moment with anyone.

When they were done, sweaty and panting in the sheets of his bed, she sat up quietly and patted him on the chest.

"Let's go and see Peaches."

THEY'D SET Peaches up in Haze's room. It was just as dark as Indigo's but she refused to light candles. When Indigo walked in with Violet, the small woman with brightly colored hair laid on the bed, curled into a ball, her marked hand beneath her face and glowing softly. The devastation in her expression made Indigo's heart clench. This small pixie-like female was mated to Haze.

He glanced at Violet, suddenly so grateful for her gift, for her blood, for her everything. If she hadn't done what she did... it might be him on the bed with the devastated face.

Ada walked into the room, a gentle touch on his arm. "Good to see you up, Indigo. How are you feeling?"

"Fine." He hand signed his thanks. "You saved us."

"Don't mention it," she whispered. "But maybe... if you could... find Jasper soon. He's pretty upset he left you and Shade behind. Maybe if you could set his mind at ease?"

"Say no more," he replied. "I would have done the same thing. My mate comes first."

With a grateful smile, the healer went to speak quietly with Violet, who stood a few feet away from the bed watching Peaches, her hands fidgeting at her side. Indigo couldn't leave just yet. He needed to know for sure if Haze was alive or... so he stood back against the wall near the door, keeping to the shadows.

"She won't let me look at her," Ada said to Violet. "Her hands are cut. She's scarred all over. She needs care."

"I'll talk with her." Violet padded over to the bed and

sat down gently. She put a hand on Peaches' arm. "Peaches, Ada needs to check you over."

"I'm fine," she sniffed. "Go away."

Violet gave Indigo a grim look before steeling herself and asking the next question.

"Peaches... the bond. Can you feel Haze? Is he alive?"

"It's my fault," Peaches said, her voice small. "I made the earthquake."

"Don't think like that."

"But it *was* me. My gift. I took the implant out and straight away it happened."

Violet's shoulders slumped and Indigo's heart went out to them.

"Hey," Violet said. "I accidentally blinded Indigo the first time my light came out. I also just gave Indigo and Shade radiation poisoning. He's okay. He's forgiven me."

Indigo smiled. He loved that about their relationship. She already knew he would always forgive her, just as he knew she would do the same for him. She could have found a way to get out of that laboratory herself, but she'd done the risky thing. She took a chance and chose to rescue him. To rescue Shade. A few weeks ago, she would have left them to rot.

"You did what?" Peaches asked. "Radiation?"

"Long story. But I turned my light into something that harmed the Sluagh. It worked. We got out."

Peaches stared. "You became... ultraviolet?"

Violet huffed. "Don't ever call me that again."

They laughed. Just a little.

"Anyway," Violet mumbled. "It was more like a gamma ray than UV, but—okay, shut up, Violet. I'm doing it again." She touched Peaches' blue markings and then her own. "Listen. This bond, it connects us to our mate. And I know this is going to be difficult, but you need to try to sense him."

Peaches frowned at Violet. "What do you mean?"

"If you concentrate, you can feel your mate through your connected emotions," she said. "I can feel Indigo, even when he's not here with me."

Peaches sat up and wiped her nose. "I didn't know that."

"Try it. Close your eyes and focus on the bond."

Violet took Peaches' hands in her own and they sat together, eyes closed, silent. Peaches looked so small, timid, and undernourished. A little like Violet had been when Indigo had first met her. Now in comparison, her cheeks glowed, and she filled out her clothes. Despite the exhaustion on her face, Violet looked strong.

"What do you feel?" Violet asked.

"I don't know what I'm looking for."

"You're looking for the other half of your heart."

Indigo's throat closed. Violet's eyes darted to him, and he couldn't even summon a smile. Too much emotion hit him. He froze.

"I feel... I feel..." Peaches started crying and Indigo couldn't look. Indigo looked down at his feet, preparing himself for the worst, but her voice filtered back to him. "He's there, Violet. Oh my God. I can feel him."

Relief surged through Indigo. He slumped against the wall, resting his head in his hands. Ada's gaze softened. She smiled and touched Indigo's shoulder, then took a step toward the bed. Just one. Just something small to let them know she was there, ready to help.

"Good, that's good," Violet said. "If Haze is alive, we'll find him. We won't stop until he's back with us."

Peaches nodded, tears tracking down her dirty face. She also needed a bath, Indigo realized. The poor female had been a prisoner for so long.

"Peaches," Violet said gently, "you need to let Ada take a look at you. Haze would want you to look after yourself."

She nodded. "I promised."

"Good." Violet stood and waved Ada over. "I'm going to be just outside the door."

Indigo left first and waited in the hallway. When Violet came out of the room, he pulled her into his arms and didn't let go. He inhaled her scent, drawing her deep into his lungs with a profound sense of satisfaction. Haze was okay. Somewhere. Probably still in the queen's clutches, but alive.

"What happens now?" Violet asked quietly. "I mean... how do we get to him?"

"Well, Maebh has clearly been breaking the laws of the Well. So my guess is the Order will raid the Winter Palace and dungeons, but by then, she'll have found a way to hide her metal. The laboratory will be gone. If we see anything, it will have been planted."

"That's hardly fair."

"It is what it is."

"And Haze?"

"We'll get to him," he said, proudly sliding his fingers through her hair. "We have you, the greatest weapon the world has ever seen. Peaches can sense Haze. We'll figure out how to get to him. And we'll figure out how to stop Maebh. It might not be right away, but we will."

"How can she just get away with this?" Violet growled.

"Because she's the queen, she's old and powerful, and she likes to play games." Indigo frowned, thinking back to how he had ripped Gastnor apart with his teeth. There had been memories in the blood. Strange ones. He frowned.

A flicker of something entered his mind. *Cobwebs stretched from ceiling to furniture to floor. A nursery suffocating under a blanket of dust. A bassinet—once regally made from antlers and thorns, just like her crown...*

"I saw something in Gastnor's blood," he said. "A nursery covered in cobwebs, and the queen standing in the middle of it."

"Does she have children?"

"I never thought so, but maybe she did. Maybe she has an heir out there somewhere."

"Or maybe it's dead. Maybe she can't have children. Maybe someone stole it from her, who knows!"

"Anything could be possible."

Indigo sighed and gathered his mate into his arms

again. “Let’s not talk about the queen anymore. Not tonight. She’s taken so much of our time.”

They embraced in silence. He tried to ignore the conversation going on in the room, but something Ada said had his ears pricking up with alarm. Violet noticed the change in his posture.

“What is it?”

“I don’t know if it’s my place to say.”

“Indi,” she growled. “If she needs me, you tell me right now.”

He winced. “She’ll need you in a minute. She’ll need all the support she can get. Violet... Peaches is pregnant.”

She covered her mouth, her eyes questioning, and he nodded. It was Haze’s.

“You should go in there,” he murmured, but before she left, he pulled her back. “Wait.”

She came back to him, such fondness in her eyes when she looked at him.

“I heard what you said in there and I need you to know something. You’re not just the other half of my heart, Violet. You’re the reason it beats. You’re my moon.”

“Moon?”

He grinned. “If I was ever lost, I would look into the sky and see the moon. I’d see our goddess shining down on us and know I would be fine. Maybe I was just waiting for you.”

“Indigo,” she breathed, a tear in her eye. “If I’m the moon, then you give me a reason to shine.”

"You never needed me for that, Vi. You always had it in you."

"Evidently. But you're the one who showed it to me." She ran a finger over his lips. "I hope I can give you what you've given me."

He grinned at her with a wink. "You can give it to me later."

"Again?" She laughed, then dashed happy tears from her eyes. "I love you. You know that, right?"

His kiss told her exactly how much he knew, and how he would have held her in the shadows forever, but he pulled back. There was someone who needed her more than him right now. He glanced through the dark doorway.

"She needs your strength," he said. "For what's coming, she's going to need all of us."

Violet agreed, steely determination in her eyes. "Maebh better be shitting in her ruby red dress right now, because I'm not going to stop coming at her until we get Haze back." She took a deep breath. "It's taken me a long time to realize this, but power isn't what I thought it was. It's not the ability to tear apart." She glanced around the hallway, to the other rooms where the cadre members slept. "It's this, Indi. It's family, and I'm going to fight tooth and nail to protect all of them."

The End.

NEED TO TALK TO OTHER READERS?

Join Lana's Angels Facebook Group for fun chats, giveaways, and exclusive content. https://www.facebook.com/groups/lanasangels

Get exclusive short stories, character art, polls, reader community, nsfw content, and bonus material when you support Lana on Patreon.

NEED TO TALK TO OTHER READERS?

ALSO BY LANA PECHERCZYK

The Deadly Seven

(Paranormal/Sci-Fi Romance)

The Deadly Seven Box Set Books 1-3

Sinner

Envy

Greed

Wrath

Sloth

Gluttony

Lust

Pride

Despair

Fae Guardians

(Fantasy/Paranormal Romance)

Season of the Wolf Trilogy

The Longing of Lone Wolves

The Solace of Sharp Claws

Of Kisses & Wishes Novella (free for subscribers)

The Dreams of Broken Kings

Season of the Vampire Trilogy

The Secrets in Shadow and Blood

A Labyrinth of Fangs and Thorns

A Symphony of Savage Hearts

Game of Gods

(Romantic Urban Fantasy)

Soul Thing

The Devil Inside

Playing God

Game Over

Game of Gods Box Set

ACKNOWLEDGMENTS

Thank you to all the members of my ARC team, Lana's ARC Angels. Every book I release I thank my lucky stars to have you with me.

Thank you to my editor, Ann Harth, who always helps turn these books from black and white to full technicolor glory.

To the most awesome readers in the world... keep reading romance. It loves you too.

ABOUT THE AUTHOR

OMG! How do you say my name?

Lana (straight forward enough - Lah-nah) **Pecherczyk** (this is where it gets tricky - Pe-her-chick).

I've been called Lana Price-Check, Lana Pera-Chick-ywack, Lana Pressed-Chicken, Lana Pech...*that girl!* You name it, they said it. So if it's so hard to spell, why on earth would I use this name instead of an easy pen name?

To put it simply, it belonged to my mother. And she was my dream champion.

For most of my life, I've been good at one thing – art. The world around me saw my work, and said I should do more of it, so I did.

But, when at the age of eight, I said I wanted to write stories, and even though we were poor, my mother came home with a blank notebook and a pencil saying I should follow my dreams, no matter where they take me for they will make me happy. I wasn't very good at it, but it didn't matter because I had her support and I liked it.

She died when I was thirteen, and left her four daughters orphaned. Suddenly, I had lost my dream champion, I was split from my youngest two sisters and had no one to talk to about the challenge of life.

So, I wrote in secret. I poured my heart out daily to a diary and sometimes imagined that she would listen. At the end of the day, even if she couldn't hear, writing kept that dream alive.

Eventually, after having my own children (two firecrackers in the guise of little boys) and ignoring my inner voice for too long, I decided to lead by example. How could I teach my children to follow their dreams if I wasn't? I became my own dream champion and the rest is history, here I am.

When I'm not writing the next great action-packed romantic novel, or wrangling the rug rats, or rescuing GI Joe from the jaws of my Kelpie, I fight evil by moonlight, win love by daylight and never run from a real fight.

I live in Australia, but I'm up for a chat anytime online. Come and find me.

Subscribe & Follow

subscribe.lanapecherczyk.com

lp@lanapecherczyk.com

facebook.com/lanapecherczykauthor

twitter.com/lana_p_author

instagram.com/lana_p_author

amazon.com/-/e/B00V2TP0HG

bookbub.com/profile/lana-pecherczyk

tiktok.com/@lanapauthor

Printed in the USA
CPSIA information can be obtained
at www.ICGtesting.com
LVHW091302151023
761121LV00001BC/31

9 780645 088434